BEAST WITHIN 4:
GEARS & GROWLS

Edited by Jennifer Brozek

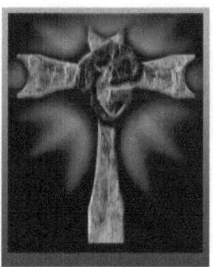

Graveside Tales

CREDITS

ACKNOWLEDGMENTS

No anthology happens in a vacuum. I want to thank Max Booth III for being an excellent editorial assistant. Jenna Fowler for perfect interior art. It was like you were in my head. Shane Tyree for providing exactly what I was looking for in the cover art. Dale Murphy of Graveside Tales for allowing me to play with this theme. Finally, my husband, Jeff, who always listens to my random brainstorms with a smile.

TABLE OF CONTENTS

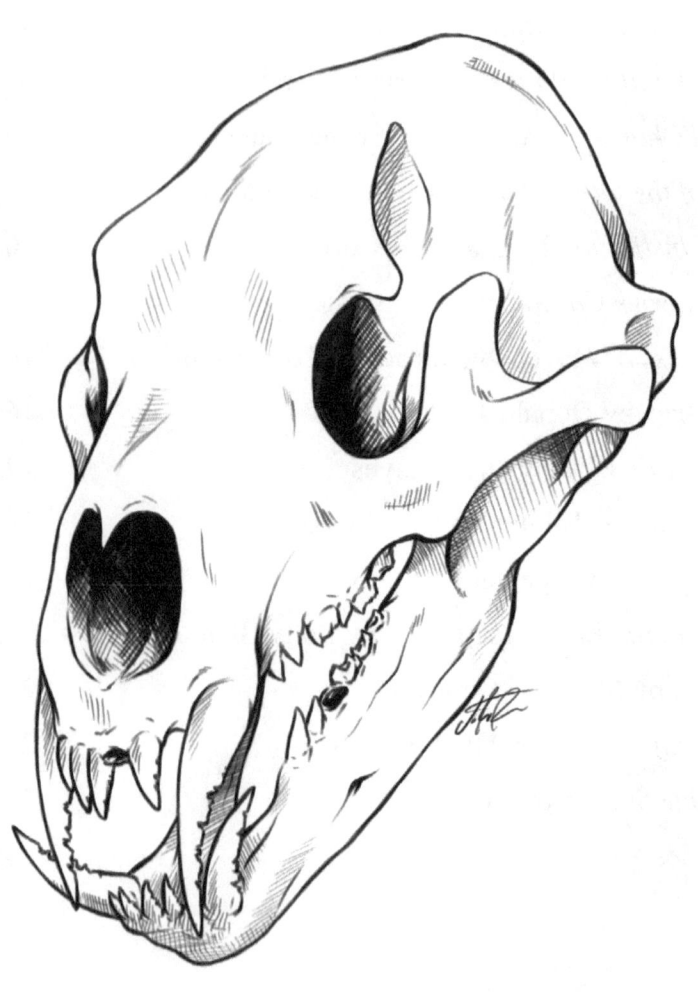

The Ussuri Bear
Ken Liu

February 11, 1907

By the time we arrived in the Manchu settlement of Tanbian, the Russian expedition had already left a day earlier.

For the last five days, we have been moving through deep snow and dense primeval forest in the Changbai Mountains, trying to catch up. The superiority of the mechanical horse is becoming clearer with each passing minute.

Look at these magnificent creatures. Observe each steel foot confidently stepping forward, gripping the snow with meter-wide lattice-work snowshoes. Be amazed at the smooth ride as they effortlessly carry five men and eight hundred kilograms of supplies. Marvel at the frictionless joints flexing and bending in complete silence, lubricated by whale oil. Hear the overlapping metal plates slide over each other as the horses leap over dangerous crevasses. Feel the rumbling warmth as you run your hand over the chrome skin, heated by the pumping engine within while feathery snow falls all around you.

I cannot imagine conducting the current expedition using dog sleds. Dogs require sustenance and rest, but mechanical horses do not. Taking turns to rest on horseback while our companions held the reins, we have been moving nonstop.

"Yirin," I call to our Manchu guide—barely sixteen, hardly more than a boy. "How much further to the spot you spoke of?"

"Maybe as long as it takes to drink a pot of tea, Dr. Nakamatsu," he replies, brushing his mop of unruly black hair out of his eyes. "Soon, very soon."

As Yirin knows no Japanese and I no Manchu, we are forced to converse in Chinese.

Hissssss. The horses open the exhaust valves located in their mouths, and white steam ascends into the frigid Manchurian winter air like smoke rising out of the crater on Mount Changbai.

The Imperial Army, which paid for this expedition, has supplied us with ten Type Ten mechanical horses, each costing as much as a small gunboat. These were designed for cold climate operation in anticipation of an inevitable second war with Russia in Manchuria in the future. Part of my mission is to field-test them.

So far, I think they are passing with flying colors.

"We're here," Yirin says. "This is where my father and I saw the bear last spring."

We emerge from the forest into a clearing, in the middle of which lies an enormous heap of bones.

~

I still remember that night, almost four decades earlier, as though it were yesterday.

I woke to the sound of a loud crash. As I sat up and opened my eyes, I did not understand what I was seeing. The eastern wall of our one-room house had disappeared: in its place, the howling wind made visible in the moonlight by swirling drifts of snow.

"Jokichi, run!" Father called to me.

He stood in front of me, trying to block me from a shadowy figure seen indistinctly through the snow. My mother lay before him, unmoving. As I watched, the shadow came closer, stood up like a man, and loomed over my father.

The shadow growled, a sound that made me shiver. I saw the great, black, furry head, the sharp white teeth—the front ones curiously notched, like a key, the outstretched paws promising a deadly embrace.

I screamed.

My father shouted and rushed forward, his spear aimed at the bear's heart. But the bear swiped at him with a speed and agility unbelievable in a creature of such size. The spear snapped like a toothpick. A moment later, my father flew through the air like a rag doll, his head already crushed by the bear's paw.

I forgot how to move. The bear shuffled closer, and the smell of rotting meat and animal sweat was overwhelming. I felt as if I sat at the bottom of a mountain, a mountain of flesh, fur, and death.

I closed my eyes, waiting to die, the bear's hot breath on my face.

A searing white flash of pain, then nothing.

Later, the rescuers told me twenty-six men, women, and children were killed by the bear that night. I lost a father, a mother, and my right arm.

Today, if you go to the place where the village once stood, tucked into a cove on the western coast of Hokkaido, you will find a stone monument with the names of the victims in the spot where our house used to be.

I have visited once every few years to say a prayer for my dead parents and to make a promise.

The bear was never found.

~

I pace from one end of the skeleton to the other, examining each bone.

The Ussuri bear—*Ursus arctos lasiotus*—of Northeast Asia is the ancestor of the American grizzly. A fierce and powerful predator, it has no equal in its domain—indeed, it regularly seizes prey from Siberian tigers and even occasionally kills the big cats. On Hokkaido, the native Ainu used to worship the Ussuri bear as a god.

The largest Ussuri bear I have ever laid my eyes on weighed six hundred fifty kilograms. Alive, the one before me would have weighed three times as much.

"It is too large to be an Ussuri," I say to Shiro Ito, our weapons master.

He nods, awed into silence.

Many cultures in Northeast Asia have legends of a race of gigantic bears. The Ainu speak of the god who possesses the mountains. The Manchus and Koreans tell stories of enormous bears that live near the peaks of the Changbai Mountains. The Chinese call the great bears *xiongjing*, or bear spirit.

In these stories, besides their enormous size, the bears are distinguished by their ferocity and the possession of near-magical abilities of healing and regeneration. Most fantastic of all, they are supposed to be highly intelligent and able to take on the form of a man when desired.

I do not put much credit in the superstitious elements of these tales. All bears occasionally stand on their hind legs, and it is easy to see how frightened peasants could mistake such a posture for a magical transformation.

But other aspects of the legends have the ring of truth. The Chinese put much stock in the medicinal qualities of bear gallbladder, and a fast-healing bear may well teach something of use to a man of science. The Army is certainly interested in such knowledge as well as the possibility of taming and training such intelligent bears for military use. Like the mechanical horses, bear-soldiers might prove to be the decisive factor for victory in the harsh conditions of remote Manchuria.

Such are the official goals of our expedition.

I run the fingers of my right hand, the one made of metal, over the large ribs gently. The prosthetic is outsized, thicker and longer than a real arm, dangling past my knees. The actuators hiss as the chrome fingers flex and bend, tapping against the bones like delicate hammers striking against the keys of an oversized xylophone. The sound is muffled, indicating that the skeleton is not very old, likely picked clean by scavengers.

The position of the skeleton is curious. The body has been arranged so that the bear lies on its back, face pointing up and the hind limbs kept straight, with the forelimbs folded across the chest, like a man having gone to sleep.

But it is the bear's teeth that are of most interest to me; the lone front tooth remaining in the jaw is curiously notched, like a key. I lean down and stare at it, trying to match it to a child's memory.

I take out a compass and verify that the bear's head is pointed directly south.

This is not how wild animals die.

"My father and I were tracking a herd of wapiti last spring when we followed a doe into this clearing," Yirin offers.

"Did you move the skeleton?"

"We took some finger bones and teeth as proof, but nothing else."

"No one in the village had ever seen it before?"

He shakes his head.

"You are certain that there are no villages closer to here than Tanbian?"

"I'm certain."

I dismiss him and continue to examine the skeleton. He probably is telling the truth. If other villagers had seen the bear, they would have taken more of the bones, which can be quite lucrative for bone carvings or as ingredients for traditional Chinese medicine. It would have been a hard secret to keep. Indeed, Yirin and his father had sold the teeth they took in Mukden, which was how we heard about the discovery in the first place.

I had seen one of those notched teeth and immediately pushed for the expedition.

So I can safely rule out human intervention as the cause of the skeleton's strange posture.

I gaze into the hollow eyes of the bear's empty skull, almost as large as my torso. I try to match it to the shadow in my memory.

Could the legends be true? Could this skull once have housed a deadly mind as intelligent as a man's?

I pick up one of the arm bones.

Even after all these years, I can still feel my phantom right arm, the arm that the bear took away from me on that night.

As I lift the phantom arm, the impulses in my severed nerves charge tiny capacitors, which amplify the signals via resonator circuits. The signals, in turn, drive electromagnets that are attached to governor gears, altering the power the steam engine sends to the intricate gear train until my piston-driven steel arm has assumed the posture of my phantom one.

I will my phantom fingers to squeeze, and my metal fingers follow suit. I will my phantom fingers to squeeze harder, and as hundreds of gears grind, the pistons of my hand are brought to their full power, and suddenly, the bone in my hand shatters into a thousand pieces.

The grin in my memory matches the grin in the skull, perfectly.

This is the bear that attacked my family decades ago.

I will not be able to keep my promise to my family after all. The bear is already dead.

"Dr. Nakamatsu," Yirin calls from the edge of the clearing. "You must come see this."

I walk over. Yirin is pointing to a dead man's hand sticking out of the snow.

~

"The Russians did beat us after all." Daiki Hayashi is our mechanic.

"Not that it matters," says Ginnosuke Abe, the medic, "by the look of things."

We dig through the snow. Altogether, we find the remains of six bodies.

One is remarkably complete, missing only a hand. The others are less intact. Of the last one, only a stump of a foot is left, the oozing blood frozen into tiny icicles.

Ginnosuke bends down and warms the frozen blood with his hand, sniffs.

"Less than two days old," he declares. He examines the bite marks and the way the bodies have been flattened. "The bear that did this isn't quite as large as the skeleton. But still, it must weigh nearly a thousand kilograms."

I bend down to examine the bite marks myself. The cold has preserved the wounds in remarkable detail. I can even see the lines made by the individual teeth: like scraping marks left by a key.

"It will be back tonight," Shiro says.

"Why?" asks Daiki.

"The bear is still hungry," I reply. "It's been using the snow as an icebox to keep the food fresh. Let's set up camp and perimeter defenses."

~

Daiki has arranged the ten mechanical horses in a circle around the campfire: their hindquarters facing us, their heads facing out.

In the flickering firelight, they stand still, without the fidgeting and snickering that real horses would have engaged in. Now that their boilers are set to low heat, their shells have cooled and the falling snow soon covers them, turning them into snow sculptures.

But wisps of white steam continue to escape from their chrome nostrils, melting the snow over their faces and rising into the crisp night air. Their eyes glow red with the heat deep inside.

I brush the snow off the horses and open each belly, taking out the rolls of paper covered with holes arranged in neat patterns and replacing them with new ones. The old rolls were for marching, the new ones for defense.

"What do the holes do?" Yirin asks.

"Have you ever seen a player piano?" I ask.

Yirin nods. "When I went to Mukden with my father to sell the bear teeth."

"It's the same principle. The holes are instructions like the scores for the pianos. It's called Lovelace code. If anything approaches from outside the camp, with a light tap, the man keeping watch can make the horses come to life without a rider. They will then move in accordance with the directions on the paper to fight the intruder."

Yirin touches the metal skin of the horse gingerly. I see he has gained a new respect for the horses. They are more than mere beasts of burden.

Shiro shoots a half dozen hares for our dinner. Ginnosuke sets them to roasting over the fire. We sit in a circle sipping from cups filled with tea made with melted snow water, waiting.

"They're ready," Shiro says.

I reach into the flames with my metal hand. pull out the meat, and pass the pieces around the fire.

"Dr. Nakamatsu," Yirin asks, as he accepts his portion. "Is it strange to have a metal hand?"

"I'm used to it."

He continues to stare at my hand, and I smile, indicating that he may touch it.

Watching him approach my hand and arm the way he approached the mechanical horses gives me an odd feeling, as though I am looking at myself through the eyes of a stranger.

~

The bear attack had occurred a few years after the Emperor took his power from the Shogun, the beginning of the Meiji Restoration.

My family was not from Hokkaido. Samurai loyal to the Shogun, including my father, had come to Hokkaido to set up a separate country.

"The Emperor wishes for us to use the foreigners' machines and to learn to think like them," my father said. "He wants to make Japan no longer Japan. We must chart a separate course."

I nodded, secure in my father's wisdom.

There was much that had to be done: chopping down trees to build houses and to clear out fields for the crops; burning charcoal for the weaponsmiths' forges to fashion the best samurai swords; hunting for bears and wolves to make the land secure so that we could sleep at night.

I still have fond memories from that time, following my father around with a toy sword, stabbing at imaginary bears.

But the Emperor did not leave my father and his companions alone. The Emperor's soldiers, masses of peasants armed with European guns, came to Hokkaido, surrounded the samurai, and slaughtered most of them in a battle with little honor. My father had been lucky to escape, hoping to hide with my mother and me in an obscure village.

But the bear had found him.

To show compassion to his former enemies, the Emperor's men took me, an orphan, back to Tokyo.

At first I did not wish to study the things my teachers wanted to teach me. I sat in silence and held onto my empty sleeve with my left hand.

"Japan must remain Japan," I said stubbornly, repeating the words of my father.

"Japan must change to remain Japan," my teachers said, "or else the foreigners with their gunboats will turn us into meat lying upon a butcher block."

A child could resist only so long. Eventually, I was given a proper and modern education and fitted with a series of new arms.

At first, my arm was carved out of wood, like the arms that had been given to cripples for hundreds of years. It could not do much save for filling out the right sleeves of my robes.

Then, as the country humbly learned the secret of steam and machinery from the Western powers, my arm also began to change.

When I was ten, I was given a clockwork arm, full of springs and gears and a key that I could wind with my left hand so that the iron fingers of my right hand could open and close. I studied mathematics and works of science translated from English and French while mills and workshops sprang up around me like mushrooms after rain.

When I was twenty, I was given an arm driven by steam. It was bulky and heavy and the boiler sometimes burned me. I had to keep it fed with water and coal, but it was also strong and hardy. I entertained my friends with feats of strength and helped them carry their heavy luggage as we went to the harbor to get on ships bound for Europe and America, where we were to study the latest knowledge of Western science. As I left for America, I waved to the new gunboats of the Imperial Navy in the harbor, modeled on British ships.

When I was thirty, I returned to Japan as a doctor of biology.

My arm was now much lighter and stronger, and it was powered by electricity stored in a battery. Just by pressing a few buttons I could make it flex and bend, and by twisting a few knobs I could make the fingers open and close and hold any position. And I remember waving it in the air as everyone in the city celebrated Japan's defeat of China and the conquest of Taiwan and Korea. We were on the rise, like a blast of steam from the exhaust at the top of a factory.

When I was forty, I finally received my present arm. It was the first arm that obeyed my will directly, its wires and components embedded into my nerves and flesh, its gears and levers driven by a steam turbine. As I and the others rejoiced in disbelief at our victory over Russia in Manchuria—the first victory by an Asian power over a European one for as long as people could remember—I felt an electrical surge from my joyfully pumping heart to the tips of my steel fingers.

Just as my country had transformed itself from a feudal backwater into a world power under the Bright Reign of the Meiji Emperor, finally, this foreign thing, this piece of machinery, had been transformed into a part of me under the light of science.

But through it all, I never forgot the bear.

In my years in America, I traveled widely, studying the habits of grizzlies and learning their lore. And after my return, I crisscrossed Hokkaido for many years without ever finding any signs of the bear that attacked my family. Yet, I did not believe it had died. I could feel it still out there in the world, mocking me.

And now it seems that the bear had left his home to wander the world just as I did, and the bear has multiplied.

~

"That's enough," I tell Yirin and pull my arm away from him. "It's late. Time for rest."

Shiro agrees to take the first watch while the rest of us sleep.

Exhaustion from the past five days finally catches up to me, and I welcome the oblivious embrace of sleep almost immediately.

~

I wake up to a nightmare.

For a moment, I do not understand what I am seeing. Under the moonlight, bits of torn paper are everywhere, swirling with drifts of snow in the howling wind.

Then I notice that nine of the mechanical horses have the flaps under their bellies hanging open, the space inside, where the scrolls of code should be, is empty.

A dark shadow is crouched next to the last horse.

I am frozen. I have forgotten how to move or speak.

The shadow rises from next to the horse. It is a bear standing on its hind legs: a big bear, as big as any Ussuri I have ever seen.

A figure lies unmoving next to the bear: Shiro. The bear must have killed him first as he was the watchman.

An electrical tingling in my mechanical arm rouses me from my stupor. "Daiki!" I call out. "Ginnosuke! Yirin!"

Daiki rises from next to me. He fumbles for his gun.

In a second the bear is next to me. He growls, and I shiver.

The bear swipes and Daiki is hurtling through the air, like a flying fish leaping out of the water, casting a graceful arc across the falling snow, through the cold Manchurian moonlight.

The bear continues to grab onto everything in camp and tosses it out of the way. Boxes and bundles—a few that might have been Ginnosuke and Yirin in sleeping bags—are flung afar like broken toys. The bear is like a typhoon, an unstoppable force of nature.

I roll away from the chaos and find myself next to the last horse, the one horse that still has its fighting instructions.

I reach up and tap the switch next to the horse's neck.

And then I am flying through the air too, and as I land in the soft snow, I feel a searing pain in my thighs. I try to stand up but can no longer make my legs obey.

The bear growls and lumbers through the snow towards me. I smell the rotten stench of its breath and sweat. The bear's eyes are inches from mine. There is nowhere for me to run, even if I could move.

The bear opens its mouth and growls again, lunging towards me. Without thinking, my right arm shoots out and my steel fist connects with the great snout. The bear backs off in pain, surprised by the power in my arm. But it shakes the blood from its nose and is back in an instant, and swipes at me.

We wrestle and I grab the bear's arm with my metal fingers. I

16

squeeze, trying to crush its bones. But the bear seems to feel nothing as it leans down, slowly pinning my mechanical arm to the ground with its weight.

I look towards my steel fingers and see that I am holding onto a thick branch. The bear has fooled me. It had swiped at me with a club like a false arm.

I close my eyes. I have been outwitted by a bear, a bear that does not behave as one. I will die as my father before me. The pressure on my chest is crushing and I cannot breathe.

Suddenly, the bear roars in pain and the weight on me is gone.

I open my eyes and see that the mechanical horse has finally come alive. It rears up its forelegs and stomps them on the hard-packed snow.

The bear limps a bit, and I can see a swelling lump on its back where it was kicked. It stands up warily to face this new menace, this mechanical foe.

Animal and machine rush at each other, clashing in the snow. The sound of claw scraping against metal grates at my ears, accompanied by the labored breath of the bear and the straining whine from the horse's boilers. The two pit their strengths against each other: one an ancient nightmare, the other a modern wonder.

Gradually, the horse appears to gain the upper hand: it pushes the bear ever so slowly backwards. The bear strains, tries to hold its position, but its legs tremble with the effort. It stumbles back a few steps and with a roar halts the retreat momentarily, but in a few seconds stumbles back again.

I smile. Muscle, after all, cannot match piston.

But my smile freezes as I realize that the bear is shifting direction, lurching backwards towards me. The wily beast, knowing that I am paralyzed, is pretending to lose. Since I cannot move, I will be crushed either by the bear's paws or the horse's hoofs as the pair step over me.

The horse pushes forward relentlessly, oblivious to the scheme. Animal intelligence has found a weakness in my programming.

A gunshot cracks.

I see that Daiki is sitting up in the snow, his gun cradled in his lap as he aims at the bear's head for a second shot.

The bear, realizing its weak position, roars and shoves the horse back, ducks and rolls out of the way, surprisingly agile. The horse

17

stumbles, loses balance, and crashes to the snow. The bear, now ten meters away, gets back up on its feet and begins to run.

Another gunshot, another miss.

The bear disappears into the swirling snow and dark night.

The mechanical horse regains its feet. Now that the threat is no longer nearby, it stops moving, though its red eyes continue to glow in the darkness, like night lanterns at a harbor.

Daiki and I stare at each other, unable to believe our luck.

Suddenly, the horse comes back to life and rears up on its hind legs.

"It's us! Don't shoot!" someone shouts.

Ginnosuke stumbles back into camp, his leg wounded. Behind him comes Yirin, who is also limping, a hand on his back. Their faces are white, the look of haunted survivors.

The bear had indeed thrown them out of the camp in its frenzy. They are lucky to be alive.

All four of us look towards the unmoving body of Shiro, not nearly as lucky.

~

"To stay here is madness," Ginnosuke says. "All of our horses, but one, have lost the ability to fight. Our best warrior is dead. Your legs are broken and the rest of us are injured. The only course is to admit defeat and retreat."

Ginnosuke speaks sense, but I cannot help being who I am. If I cannot have my vengeance against the bear, I must have it against the bear's children. I cannot forget that night so many decades ago. Our obsessions are a part of us, like our scars and phantom limbs.

"We cannot return empty-handed," I say. "The bear who attacked us last night was juvenile. We have not yet seen the adult who killed the Russian team. We must capture both."

Ginnosuke, Daike, and Yirin look at me as though I am mad. Perhaps I am, a little.

~

I sit in the middle of the camp. Snow has covered the shredded tents and our scattered boxes of supplies, turning them into misshapen mounds of snow. Now and again, I brush the snow off of myself.

Before they left, Ginnosuke and Daike took off a pair of legs from one of the horses to fashion splints for me. At least the pain is now bearable, even if I cannot move.

My companions have taken the other horses and left me behind. The giant bear skeleton alone keeps me company.

Slowly, oh so slowly, the light fades, and evening falls.

A roar fills the woods, and winter birds, roused from their sleep, burst into the sky in panic.

The second roar is much closer.

I pull my coat tighter around me. The electrical tingling shimmies through my arm again. I open my metal fingers and look at the tiny glass vial held inside, filled with a clear liquid that refuses to freeze in the sub-zero cold.

This is my secret weapon: there is enough neuropoison in that vial to paralyze a great whale. We brought it to tranquilize any bears we catch.

The bear roars again, and I look towards the edge of the clearing. The trees shake and tremble as though they are in the middle of a storm.

The ground shakes, and a large shadow steps into the clearing, a shadow that is a reflection of the one I have seen a thousand times in my dreams.

The great bear rears up on its hind legs and opens its mouth. I see the notches in its teeth glinting in the moonlight.

Then it plunges back to the ground and snow explodes around it like icebergs calving. Its demon eyes are bright in the moonlight.

"You're from Hokkaido," I say.

The bear cocks its ear, as though listening. Then it grins. It growls lightly in answer, like a chuckle.

"I have been looking for your father," I say.

It stares at me for a while, then nods and lumbers forward, slowly at first, and then gradually picking up speed.

I curl my hand and lay my arm down in the snow, an obvious target. After all these years of searching and plotting, my plan has come to this: I must allow it to take my arm into its mouth, where I can crush the vial and release the toxin. I am both the bait and the bear trap.

The bear stops a meter away from me, breathing hard. We stare into each other's eyes. *Who is the hunter and who is the prey?*

The bear looks down at my mechanical arm and shakes its head. I tense. Has it divined my plan?

Quicker than I can believe is possible, it pounces on my arm and the weight of its massive forepaws immobilizes my artificial limb. I am pulled to the ground and groan as my broken legs are jostled. The bear grins, contemptuous.

But my arm has tricks that the bear does not know. Unlike an arm of flesh, my prosthetic arm is capable of continuously turning in its socket in the same direction like a wheel. As I turn my arm one revolution after another, I move the bear's weight off of it like a slab rolling off of a log.

The bear, surprised, is too late to react as I grab onto its forepaw and squeezes with every bit of strength my gears and levers can muster. It howls, an inhuman sound. The pain immobilizes it. I continue to increase the pressure, a force that no flesh can compete with. I hear the bones in the bear's arm crack and shatter.

A momentary lull in the swirling snow allows the moonlight to glow brighter, and shadows stir behind the bear. Three mechanical horses emerge from the snow. Their riders hold guns aimed at the great bear.

I grin back at the bear and let up the pressure for a moment. "I have you now."

The bear bites down hard to stop the howling. It turns its head and sees the riders. Behind them, the rest of the horses appear, tied together with chains so that they form a moving wall of iron. Though the horses can no longer fight, they still have their riding instructions and will follow a rein. No matter how strong the bear is, it will not be able to break that wall.

The bear roars, a sound of surprise and despair.

The real trap has sprung. My companions have been hiding behind a nearby hill. They have cut off the bear's route of retreat. The bear will die today in this clearing, even if I die with it.

I see Daiki, Ginnosuke, and Yirin raise their guns. I begin to laugh. Finally, after all these years, my nightmare is about to end. I squeeze my mechanical hand even harder, wishing to literally rip the bear's arm off.

The smallest of the three riders—it must be Yirin—drops his aim, grabs his gun like a club and swings it at the heads of the other two men before him. Without any sound, the two of them fall from their horses. Yirin jumps off his horse and lets the reins dangle.

I do not understand what I am seeing.

Now bereft of guidance from their riders, all the horses stop moving.

Yirin alone approaches the bear and me. He points his gun at me. "Stop."

I let the bear's arm go.

"Father, please excuse my tardiness," Yirin says in perfect Japanese, and bows to the bear.

~

I watch, mesmerized, as Yirin transforms into the bear who broke my legs last night, and then back to Yirin again. I watch, wonder filling my heart, as the great bear transforms into an older version of Yirin, a tall and broad-shouldered giant of a man with a head of hair and a beard as bushy as a hedgehog. He cradles his bloody, broken arm as we talk.

"My name is Airin." His voice is deep and resonant, sorrowful but calm.

I look into the man's eyes. "Your father killed my family, almost forty years ago."

"As yours did mine."

I shake my head, not understanding.

"Since time immemorial, our clan of bear-men have lived in the snowy forests of Hokkaido, away from the presence of men.

"Then, gradually, more and more men from the southern islands came, and began to cut down the ancient trees of the forest, to burn down our home so that they could have flat fields on which to plant their crops.

"And they hunted us, killed us as we slumbered in winter."

I remember how my father's people had to make homes for themselves in the wilderness of Hokkaido, how they had to tame a land that was uncultivated, how they had to kill the bears to make the village safe. The bears had to make way for people.

"A blood debt demands payment in blood," Airin says. "My father went to your village to avenge the deaths of his brothers."

I feel my mechanical arm tingle, the phantom limb in pain.

"But more men soon followed those he killed, and eventually

21

we had to flee Hokkaido altogether and come to this new land, where the smell of men is faint. But blood always calls for more blood."

I look at Airin. *Who between us is the prey and who the hunter?*
"What do you want?" I ask.
"To change."

~

I watch as Daiki cuts my arm away from me. The pain is excruciating. Losing my arm a second time is even worse than the first.

Ginnosuke helps by separating the nerves and blood vessels that have grown into the spaces between the wires and gears with a scalpel. He cauterizes the wounds with a heated iron. I know that the cauterization process, though necessary to save my life, will make it impossible to receive a new arm.

"Drink," Ginnosuke says, and feeds me a burning liquor that will bring me sleep.

You have not left us alone. I hear the words of Airin through a haze. *Every year, men cut down more trees, burn more grass, open up more fields. You can do it so much more efficiently now with the aid of your machines, powered by belching mechanical engines.*

Our magic has always come from the earth, the raw soil of endless life. But men have torn open the earth to plunder the energy locked away in death, for coal and oil, and for lumber and stone with which to build. They have bound Manchuria in iron chains laid across her so that steam-powered monsters could huff and puff over the land and haul the goods to the sea.

Drowsy, I watch as Ginnosuke and Daike work together to attach my arm to Airin. An arm for an arm, the oldest law of the world. The amputation of his broken, useless arm is every bit as brutal as a scene from a butcher shop, with bone saws and gushing blood and gore-soaked tourniquets. But Airin endures it all without making any sound.

Yirin watches anxiously.

"Do not make a mistake," he says. He makes his voice menacing but it is hardly necessary. Ginnosuke and Daike remember well what he had done on the night he killed Shiro.

Daike has reinforced and thickened the mechanical arm with components from the horse legs to fit Airin's size. As Daike clamps the mechanical arm to Airin's stump, and Ginnosuke begins the process of suturing Airin's nerves and blood vessels to the wires, Airin hisses but does not otherwise make any sound. He bites down on his lower lip until blood oozes from his mouth.

We have run out of places to hide. We can feel our old magic seeping away as the land loses its life, its energy. It is the same as how it was in Hokkaido. There will be a time when we will want to do nothing but to sleep, even knowing that in slumber men will slaughter us.

If we cannot fight your machines, we must learn to adopt them: your iron horses, your iron arms. The machines have given you power, and perhaps they will give us power, too.

They used the teeth of their father to lure us here, I think. They've learned to exploit the energy locked away in death, too.

I watch as the bear-man and the mechanical arm become one. Even with his powers of healing, it will take some time before he learns how to wield this new arm, how to stop feeling the revolting alienness of metal laid over a phantom. But by then he will have felt the power, understood the beauty of cold, invincible steel.

Starting tomorrow, the bears want me to teach them the art of programming the mechanical horses, so that they can be taught to fight. They want Daiki to instruct them in the art of horse maintenance. They want to learn from Ginnosuke how to meld flesh and metal. When they have learned enough, they will let us go.

As I drift towards sleep, I imagine an army of bear-men augmented with mechanical limbs and mechanical horses making a stand against the ever-encroaching tide of men. I imagine a race losing an old magic as they learn to live with a new one. I do not know if I should feel pity or terror.

Airin's flesh and the metal of the arm will fuse into one, as tangled as blood debts, as beautiful and strange as the great metropolis of Tokyo, where ancient rice-paper lanterns now glow with the burning heat of tiny lightnings, voltaic arcs created by electricity leaping across leads.

I close my eyes and give in to sleep, though my phantom arm throbs with an old magic that refuses to die.

Indentured
Jay Wilburn

Molly Cog lay prone on her belly in the mud. The ground sloped down toward the waterfront and the blood had begun to rush to her head. She felt her heartbeat behind her eyes. The hemp wrap made her itch. The bane burned her nose and made her eyes feel dry.

No other plantation manager along the coast would ever do this. It was a job for servants or children. No men would work for her. Half her servants couldn't be trusted outside the grounds of the mill and the other half were made of metal and couldn't lay on their hollow bellies in the mud. Like most things in the business of Cog Mills, it was left to her.

She fought the urge to scratch.

The outline of an airship emerged from the tall clouds above the ocean. She could tell it was lighter than air, but she could not decipher the make or the corporate loyalty. It almost didn't matter. No other company or guild was friendly toward her family on her behalf. Assuming enemies on every side had served her well during her stewardship of the family mill. The sky and the water's surface were not safe passage for her product across the ocean. The land itself was becoming more hostile.

As the red piping came into view along one side of the zeppelin, she decided it was either from the Campton Carbon and Fiber Guilds or the Castile Mercantile Consortium. One was just slightly more of a bastard than the other.

Something pulled on the line. She hardly dared to move her eyes in their dry sockets. She did not dare to blink. It tugged again. She willed patience through her aching muscles and spring-tight joints. Enthusiasm was yet another of her enemies on this muddy shore. There was a third tug and then a fourth that was discouragingly weaker. Molly jerked the trip wire and snapped the canister closed. The silence that greeted her broke her heart.

You have given away your position.

There was a clicking inside the canister.

You are too harsh, Molly. You have too many enemies and two few allies to become your own antagonist.

She mucked out from under her torturous screen and shed her hemp wrap. The cool air accentuated the skin irritation she had been ignoring.

The canister threatened to roll out of its frame into the water. Making room for her prey to breathe meant there was room to drown. She snatched it up by the pail handle and felt the creature inside drop. It was heavier than she expected. She should have been watching instead of spying airships drifting inland through the clouds. She assumed she had what she needed, but a muskrat or a common badger would not do and something too large could not navigate the maze of the machinery as she needed.

Molly stroked her fingertips lightly over the lid and lock latch. The prey scampered from one side to the other shifting its disturbing weight.

You would be foolish to peek inside and unleash what you might have, foolish girl. Get back to your fences before you become the prey.

Molly worked her way up through the reeds into the hardwoods. The field would be quicker, but she could not afford to cross the low country in the open.

She smelled the stink over the normal swampy musk. She dropped to her knees and held onto the shaved bark on the trunk of the cypress. She listened to the buzz of the insects and hoped that was a good sign. Molly looked up through the branches. The Spanish moss and resurrection ferns blocked out most of the sky.

I can't crouch in the mud forever… especially now that I may be the prey.

The clearing was furrowed from claws and struggle. The blood on the ground was lost except for the metallic smell, but the splatter around foliage was stark. The human bones were striped clean of flesh. Molly could tell there were too many of certain bones for there to be just one, dead human. One ribcage was intact, but the individual ribs were spread apart by whatever had waylaid the band. Molly fought the temptation to feel the shreds of clothing and try to identify which of her competitors had fallen prey to the monsters. A drop of blood ran down a grove in one of the ribs and fell into the gory mud. Molly couldn't tell what species of monster had consumed the travelers. She did see human tracks leading off into the swamp.

A full belly tamed the beasts for a time. What breed of half-beast is stalking near my gates?

Molly skirted the clearing and bone yard to continue toward her property. The leaves seemed to rustle too much. The underbrush seemed to be cluttered with twigs and branches. The crackling and rustle continued behind her after she passed. She didn't dare to look back.

She left the woods a little farther down the fence line than she intended.

"Damn it… I barreled through and drifted off my path."

Molly followed the edge of the trees as far as she could, but she had to cross the field to reach the gate. The rustle behind her had continued, but was building into a crash.

"I'm not imagining it. Run, Molly… run. Run!"

The canister was bucking in her hand. Her feet broke loose from the fear that was holding them to the ground. The grass whipped around her calves and thighs. Dragonflies lifted up and circled above her head as she ran. She could not identify the animal based on the roar. It had left the woods and was charging through the grass behind her.

"Open the gate… open the gate. Let me through. Hurry!"

The chains began to crank. The gate was lifting, but slowly. The spikes lifted out of the catch pits with a wash of brackish water over the metal plates.

She was charging at an angle to the fence. The hard, wire links and support wires flashing by beside her made her dizzy. The inhuman growl bellowed out low to the ground in the grass close behind her.

I'm not going to make it.

The gate wasn't open enough. She yelled anyway. "Close it. Drop the gate. Close it. Close it. Close it!"

She lay down on the gravel and slid over the sharp edge of the metal plate. She heard the chains click loose. She did not look as the spikes fell toward her face. Her trousers tore as she skinned over the tough trail. The spike slammed into the grooves behind her and sent black water spitting into her hair. She hissed in pain as she collapsed on the ground at the end of her slide.

Molly startled when the monster slammed into the metal mesh of the gate behind her. Her foot struck the canister a few more rotations along the trail. The prey inside was silent. She smelled rotten flesh on the balmy breath that wafted over her through the gate.

She turned back and peered briefly into the misty blue eyes. The long snout whipped away on the outside of the gate so that she was looking along the massive side of the beast. The flesh under the scales rippled. The deadly tail struck the gate as the monster scrambled back into the grass. The entire fence vibrated down both sides. It moved much faster than she expected. The grass parted as the reptile raced down the slope of the field back toward the swampy forest. As it vanished the monster's growl echoed across the land.

"I wish you had taken the spikes clean through your weak, blue eyes, half beast. I would have left you naked in your human form as a warning to the others."

Alligator half-beasts now? What hellish enemies hate me for simply living?

Molly stood up with a sting from her scraped skin and ache from her battered joints. Sweat blistered across her forehead like a common, field hand. She heaved for air and fought the urge to cry in the jarring calm inside the gate. There was no one there to see her except for the gate men, but she fought the urge anyway.

Molly looked from one side to the other. The two, clockwork men held the gate down with their arms locked from the ten foot top. They faced out toward the field in silent calm as if a changeling gator had not just tried to skirt under after Molly's flesh. Their barrel chests were tarnished and faded from the coastal weather. The exposed gate men were the toughest to keep operational. She would have to service them again soon, but she did not know when she would find the time.

Molly felt a second urge to thank the metallics for saving her or for at least following orders. She fought that urge as well. Instead, she turned, lifted the canister, and carried it toward the estate.

"Are you still breathing, my heavy rodent?"

She passed tiered boxes growing the blue and purple blooms and shoots at various stages. Her metallics harvested the indigo for blue dye. Across the ocean, the dye was precious. If she could launch her product without being eaten, raped, or sunk, greedy men on two continents could turn a large profit with a small shipment.

"My life is crucified upon a cross of 'IF's,' I fear."

Molly left the grow boxes and approached the high, block wall of the Cog family Mill. The tin door screeched on the slots at the bottom. She set down the canister to push it open with both hands. When she reached down for the container again, she spotted the ship crossing the sky over land.

She could see now that the red piping along the skin of the zeppelin outlined blue patches and purple crests. It was the Campton Guilds. They were the slightly worse of the two possible bastards. They weren't exactly flying over her property. They weren't exactly avoiding it either.

"You use my indigo blue to paint you ship and then you turn your ship to threaten me in return."

Molly drew the coil dangling from the ceiling inside the mill's tin door toward her lips. She spoke into the speaker at the end of the coiled tube. "Proceed to the roof. Track, but hold."

She considered saying 'thank you,' but she closed her mouth and released the coil. She pulled her canister inside and drew the tin door closed with a crash. The humid air outside was replaced by the dry heat from boilers and friction inside.

Hopefully, fear of artillery will overpower manly pride, Comptons.

She stared at the ribbed tin before turning and walking back along the interior wall. The crushed petals were taxied along the conveyor to the next engine. Steam released from a pressure spout above her as she passed. The air was suddenly humid again. She shivered in the wet heat as she flashed briefly to her exhausted run from the bloody, bone yard from the half beast croc. She shook the thought from her head and kept walking.

She managed a smile as she passed the glass, vacuum tubes running from the compressor to the salinator. A dozen mills up the coast were trying to copy her process. They were also failing for a dozen or more reasons. She had designed some of the works herself. She was using minerals in the chemical extraction that no other mill had ever employed in any process. They would not even know how to introduce some of her steps into their existing machinery or her works if she surrendered them to her enemies.

She climbed the stairs and crossed the catwalk above the bath vats. The gears along the sides spun one tooth into the next in perfect precision oscillating the multiple fans inside the salts, water, and ink.

They can tell by the separation in the vials that your product is far less quality than mine. That must really cut at your manhood. It would help if you had any idea how to grow indigo. Don't hurt yourself thinking too hard.

Molly left the mill floor and crossed into the concourse with a line of cages along both walls. Each of the rodents backed into the corners of their cages. Molly ignored them. Light from the gas lamps glinted off the chips around the outside of their collars. The tiny gears inside whirled with the motion of their retreats. The process for creating these instruments was her secret too. Their tiny, blue eyes followed her progress down the line.

Molly set the canister on the end of the work table. The creature inside had still not moved since their tumble from the jaws of the half beast gator and the jaws of the falling gate. Her untreated scraps under the rips in her pants stung as she sat down on the bench. She dragged the empty cage across the oak planks of the table. Several of the animals scurried helplessly inside their own cages at the harsh noise. The canister remained still.

Molly picked up the blue gloves and looked over her rough hands as she held tight to the leather. She imagined the scratches were from the teeth or claws of the half beasts instead of the swiping thorns and branches in the swamp. She smiled thinking of her own eyes fading to the color of a wispy sky and her flesh rippling under scales or fur. Molly pulled on the gloves.

She pulled the goggles over her loose hair and down over the bridge of her nose.

Last, she looped the strap of the blue leather apron over her head. Before she tied the waist strings, she ran her fingers over the apron above her chest. The simple crest carved into the leather was a perfectly round gear accented by even, square teeth. In the center, was a capital "M."

In the years of her grandfather, milling cotton and cane for the cut wages of the Compton Guilds, it had stood for Melvin Cog. In the time of her father, when the Guilds had forbade the Cogs to mill cotton, it stood for Martin and her father had struggled to ship cane rum around the embargos and between the patrols. If her brother had not perished trying to free their father before his exile, it would have stood for Marvin for another generation. As her finger traced the imprint of the pressed letter one more time, she could not bring herself to believe that it stood for Molly.

Even with all the true human workers abandoning her, she still believed it stood for a man buried under the great oak behind the mill between her mother and brother. Or for a man sequestered on an island in a distant, southern sea. Molly tied off the waist strings and looked away from the emblem.

She turned the canister over and heard the weighty contents thump against the lid. She moved the pail handle to allow the lid to lock into the apparatus above the open cage. Molly began to turn the crank. The canister spun on the wheel as the lid unlocked and released like a trapdoor. The ball of fur dumped onto the floor of the cage unceremoniously. Molly pulled the lever closing the cage access and clearing the lid from the interior. She watched the rodent lying motionless. She reached her gloved fingers into the wire and latched the access panel. The canister popped loose from the apparatus.

The body began to shiver and Molly smiled. There was a tiny ripple over the back under the fur that could almost be confused as a natural action. Molly nodded.

"Creature... you do not want to change inside this cage. It will not break and you will not survive your transmutation. This I promise you."

She waited several minutes. At last, the rodent unfolded without changing form. The hairless, pink tail rolled out from under its feet. The rat's sharp nose lifted and sniffed the air. It shivered again. The rat turned its head slightly, but kept its back to Molly. She saw one beady, blue eye and knew all she needed to know.

Finally, something goes as planned today.

"I know your kind and deception does not serve you under my charge. You are entering into a contract of service with me today, half beast. This contract is binding."

The flesh on the rat's back rippled again. The hair bristled slightly. It lifted one foot and began licking between the toes.

"I know you understand me. I've done this many times, creature. Your cooperation is the difference between eating and starving. There are more half beast rats creeping along the water, if you choose to play dumb and whither in your stubbornness."

The rat stopped licking and stood motionless on its flat feet. The rodent took a deep breath and sighed out a long, quiet whistle. Molly nodded as she looked on the rat's back.

"Good, then. We understand each other and we can complete this business. Your contract of service to me will be seven years. You work to eat. You follow my instructions as servant to master. At the end of this term of service, I will give you the option to work for wages or to go free back into the wild. These terms are not negotiable."

Molly paused and licked her top lip. In the silence, the rodent's skin rippled twice. It lowered its head.

As good as a handshake…

"There will be a test for you soon, with food at the end of a maze, of sorts. Now, however, we are going to apply a special collar of my making."

Molly manipulated the controls in front of her at the work station. The mechanical arms extended into the cage through the wire with a high screech. The cages behind her raddled again. The rat ran to an opposing corner and wrapped up into its body hiding its head.

"Less fight will result in less pain. More fight will not equal any more success, creature."

She continued to crank and twirl the controls. The gears spun in the joints as the arms extended across the cage. The claws opened and spread above the rat's body. As the claws locked on and tightened, the rat tried to run. Its tiny claws clicked against the metal floor until its body was lifted into the air. The metal claws wrapped around the curves of the creature's body and locked together. The rat fought and twisted, but did not escape the clutches. Molly tightened to hold until the rat squeaked one time. She heard the human voice under the rodent sound.

Pain it is.

Molly held up an open collar adorned with metal chips around its outside surface. The rat's blue eyes stared at Molly's gloved hands as she turned the collar in the light of the gas lamps.

"This is going around your neck and it will stay there. Your resistance is meaningless. Your pain in this process is unnecessary."

Molly looped the collar into the grasp of a third, mechanical arm. She cranked it forward. The chips clicked along the wire one at a time as the hand slid into the cage. Once it was through, Molly began cranking faster. The gears whirled and the arm raced across the interior of the cage. The rat quaked, but did not twist or move its head. The metal fingers spread in front of the rodent's face. With three moves, Molly locked the collar around the thick neck of the rat.

As she lowered the rat back to the floor of the cage, the fine gears hidden inside the chips of the collar turned and adjusted. The collar conformed to the shape of the rat's neck. Molly cranked the arms back out of the cage. There were three pings as they left the interior and then the process was done.

The specks of blue stared up at Molly. She smiled back and the creature shivered in its corner.

"That collar is my own design and it will not release until I command it. It will not release even if you attempt to break it by expanding your neck from furry to fleshy. Trying to break the links will result in their contraction. This contract is binding as is your collar."

After a short pause, Molly opened her mouth again. There was a concussion that vibrated down through the stone walls of the mill. The light from the lamps flickered and winked out for an instant. Then, they blazed back on to full brightness. Molly stood up flipped the bench with the back of her knees. As it crashed against the floor, she stared at the ceiling. There was no other noise.

"I hate being interrupted."

Molly charged out of the concourse leaving the cage on the work table and leaving her monologue unfinished.

~

"We have begun a war I am ill prepared to fight."

Smoke belched from the area of the back fin. The flame spread up the skin from the back. Molly just stared as the airship listed toward the woods and lost altitude. She watched the sharp blue of her own dyes scorch to carbon black as the vessel died in the air.

With the goggles lifted up onto her sweaty forehead, Molly turned and looked up at the dumb calm of the clockwork man still holding the controls of the artillery. Its glassy eyes stared out at the damaged zeppelin. The barrel of the launcher tracked the vessel down and to the left as the nose of the airship fell toward the trees.

"Release the controls. Step away from the gun."

The crosshairs of the artillery dropped away from the dying zeppelin. The clockwork man stepped back and left his curved claws open. One claw quivered slightly and then more severely as the mechanical palsy spread up the metal arm.

Molly sighed. "How many wars were started for want of a steady hand upon the trigger?"

She started to turn away, but she heard the gears spinning inside the metallic's bucket head and barrel chest. She shook her head.

"Belay that request, metallic… proceed to the repair bay and disengage engine functions."

The gears whirled more slowly as the clockwork man turned and paced toward the stairs.

She turned as the airship twisted down into the tree line in the distance. The flames had spread across the ship's belly. Through the fiery glow, the dark skeleton was exposed in a grid.

They must not have been trying to drop into the grounds after all.

"They will retaliate soon enough, Molly. You're an army of one about to take on the full wrath of the Comptons that hate your existence. They'll not accept an apology or an excuse. You'll just have to arm up like you meant it."

Molly looked down beyond the fences into the edge of the woods beyond. She started to calculate how much rainfall this season might be protecting her estate from a possible forest fire. Her train of thought was derailed by the spread of blue eyes peering out of the shadows below her position on the roof. They winked out, but then appeared again somewhere else between the leaves.

"Now… do I put the metallics on the fence or on the artillery. I could split them between both and weaken both positions. I suppose a day of lost work is a given."

A low growl from the trees started to form syllables, but dropped out before she picked up on the words.

"Nothing more to say, friends?"

~

Molly followed along the catwalk staring down into the works of the engines. There was a flash of motion along a strut below the spinning gears. She peered down through her goggles into the clockwork guts, but did not see it again. She followed along the catwalk a few more yards and then turned to lean over the opposing rail. It was there again. The tiny feet danced dangerously over the turning gears. The long, pink tail barely missed being wound into the moving works.

Molly hissed and looked away from the scene. "I do not want to clean your foul innards out of my gears, creature. Dance in your cage… not here."

She moved farther along until she was almost beyond the engines to the doors of a repair bay. She stared at them for a moment thinking about the clockwork man disengaged on the other side.

For want of a little maintenance, I have found a way to bring deeper doom upon my waylaid family.

"I can't keep doing this alone."

Molly turned around to retrace her steps, but froze as she looked down on the blue-eyed rat staring up at her on the catwalk. It held a blue ribbon dangling from both sides of its jaws behind its long, front teeth.

Molly knelt as best she could in the long apron. She reached out with her gloved hand and took the dyed ribbon. The rat released it and waited. Molly reached down and picked up the furry half-beast without protest. She held it in the same hand with the ribbon and extended her other glove cupped with seeds.

"Well done, half beast. You might make a fine engineer."

A scream rose from the steam siren on the western fence. The rat continued to eat without interruption.

What now? I should have placed the metallics on the fences it seems.

Molly ran through the mill toward the husbandry concourse. The rat continued to eat as Molly ran.

~

Molly leaned hard on the shaft of the spear to keep it from tilting and falling through the mesh of the fence. The metallics leaned over the top of the fence and held tight, but the weight was still substantial against Molly's arms.

"Are you and the gators working together or do you operate as two separate tribes?"

There was no answer, but she wasn't expecting one. The survivors had fled back to the trees for now and vapor boiled off the skull at the end of her spear. As the body folded back on itself in death, the weight dissipated. She waited. The half beast, black bear didn't return completely human. At first she thought his man form was just hairy, but she realized his dead skin was patched with unretracted fur. One arm was still capped with a misshapen paw and claws. His speared face still stretched out into a naked snout around the head of the spear that was cooking the inside of the skull.

"The other estates coat their weapons in gilded silver. It is worth the investment in pure silver smithed entirely through the core, I say."

The clockwork men lost their grip on him as his body shrank away from their metal claws. They continued to lean over the fence reaching. Molly backed up grinding the shaft back through the link in the mesh. The sharp edge of the spearhead snicked along the wire. Molly gritted her teeth fearing she might slice through weakening her defenses. The half man's face pressed into the fence as the silver spearhead extracted bloody and blackened from his snout.

Molly stumbled back free. The dead creature crumpled to the ground at the base of the fence outside. Molly stared at the face frozen in a scorched scream. The blue eyes had gone dark and were sunken into the head. He lay naked, dead, and exposed. Molly realized that the only naked men she had ever seen were the dead, half beasts.

There is something truly damaged in that.

"Set for burn."

The metallics left the fence and walked slowly toward the shed to retrieve the poles and oil. They would move the body away from the fence before setting it ablaze. She did not look back toward the trees. She knew they were watching.

~

With no other repairs or tests needed, Molly walked down the line of cages dropping feed laced with bane into the dishes. The half rodents ate with fury from their hunger. Molly turned to drop a little more feed in the cage of the newcomer. She still needed to move it from the work table now that she had a moment without war.

The fine gears in the collar whirled and clicked with endless anger. She stood staring down at the broken collar and the open door latch. Molly dropped the feed into the floor and ran down the concourse. She noted that none of the other cages were open as the rodents ate.

There is no spirit of loyalty among monsters.

"That should be a comfort."

Molly burst through the double doors and prepared to call the metallics back from the fences to lockdown the mill. She spotted the body folded up against a far wall below the catwalks. The half human head was bent over the knees and was covered in dark, filthy hair.

Molly whispered. "Do you lie in wait, half rat monster?"

Molly made her way to a maintenance ladder and climbed down to the stone floor next to the body. The engines hummed behind her in the darkness. The naked body was a girl that was barely at childbearing age.

I've never seen a female, half beast. I suppose they had to exist.

"How did you break my collar?"

The girl's voice began as a squeak that hurt Molly's ears, but dropped into a more human tone. "My mother taught me how to do things before she forgot she was human."

Molly stared for a moment not understanding the meaning. "Why didn't you flee or remain a beast to stay hidden?"

"I have nowhere safe to go. I can't sleep good as a rat. The bane you put in my food makes me forget who I am. I don't like it."

So that's how it discourages their change.

"What do you want?"

"May I eat real food with you? I won't cross you. I'll serve both as human and... creature."

Molly felt thickness in the back of her throat and swallowed several times to clear it. "I'll... allow it. I need your name and... for you to take a bath before we share food."

The girl lifted her head. Molly was surprised by the vapid blue eyes. She had actually expected a normal human color and pupils.

"My mother... I only remember being called... girl."

"Then it is time to bathe, Girl."

~

They watched the clockwork man leave the gate and pull the wagon down through the field from their position at the screen on the roof.

"Why did your mother let you be turned, Girl?"

"Rats need less food and no one outside of the estates was safe any longer."

"Safe from whom?"

37

The first musket balls ripped through the metallic's belly. It continued pulling the wagon. The men in Compton leathers charged from the woods and cut down the clockwork legs like trees.

Girl pointed. "From them."

The men pulled back the canvas on the wagon to find cut grass instead of indigo dye. They began to advance on the fence.

Molly looked back at the metallics on the artillery. "Be ready, but hold."

She heard the screams and turned back around.

"And them," Girl added.

The men were being pulled down into the grass. Blood splattered on the side of the wagon. One gator's head lifted up into sight as it locked on and brought down a man trying to flee.

"I have to find another way to smuggle my dye the hundred yards to the water or we are done here."

Girl looked up at Molly. There was a growl below that drew her attention back. The black bears charged out of the woods and began locking on the bodies in the gators' mouths. They fought and rolled in the grass. One crashed into the wagon tipping it over on the head of the metallic.

At least my enemies are divided.

"Ms. Cog, why are they struggling, but not biting each other?"

Molly opened her mouth and stopped when there was an explosion on the eastern fence. They ran across the roof and looked over the side. Gunpowder smoke rose from the collapsed sections. Several bears and alligators were crossing the grounds toward the mill.

They are so fast for their size.

Molly began shouting commands and the clockwork men turned the artillery east. As the first rounds fired, Molly saw that the fighting, half beasts around the wagons had abandoned their food and were charging the gate together.

"Bastards."

One round exploded in the woods beyond the collapsed gate and toppled a tree. The others exploded on the grounds creating deep scars. One indigo box shattered. Furry and scaly bodies lifted into the air and fell to the ground broken. The rest continued to charge. She heard pounding against the tin doors below where she couldn't see.

Molly looked back and saw the half beasts had already reached the gate. The metallics were reaching over stabbing and clawing at them.

"It's too late to fire artillery at them. I need some explosive with silver... shrapnel. I should have made it earlier. There is no time now."

Girl grabbed Molly's arm and pulled. Molly opened her mouth to reassure her, but Girl locked her half human teeth on Molly's forearm. Molly meant to scream, but no sound came. She tried to pull away, but Girl dug in her nails and whipped her head from side to side. Blood welled up under her curled lips and stained her teeth red.

A ripple crawled over Girl's half human skin. Molly watched fur erupt over the girl's flesh. Girl's teeth and ears began to grow.

~

The rat slinked under the roots and walked between the rocks along the waterfront until it reached the canvas and cut branches. A ripple traveled under its fur. It began to fold out and transmute.

"Are you still mad at me about the bite, Ms. Cog?"

Molly stretched and felt her naked skin to be sure the fur was gone. She blinked against the light off the ocean.

I still say the colors are wrong through half beast eyes. I have to feel to know if the dye is the right shade of blue.

"If you had waited a moment longer, Girl, I would have told you it would be alright and as I recall it was. A little silver and fire cleaned up the mess nicely, did it not?"

"It did. I was afraid of losing you, too."

"I just hate being interrupted."

Girl nodded and handed a cloak to Molly to cover her nakedness. The women pulled back the canvas and uncovered the crates branded with an "M" inside a gear.

Molly pulled the cord making it lift dripping above the surface of the water a few feet. The copper skin of the submersible emerged from the water near the shore. The hatch opened and the metallic inside extended the gangplank to the rocky sand. The women loaded the crates one at a time.

The clockwork driver closed the hatch and the submersible pulled out to sea as it sank away from view. Molly and Girl removed their cloaks and hid them back under the empty canvas and branches.

"Is the other side of the ocean far away, Ms. Cog?"

"Far enough. Let's away to the mill before we are discovered by jealous business men or other hungry monsters."

The two rats skittered up the slope through the trees as distant, inhuman growls echoed around them.

A Cage Gilded
Matthew Marovich

The body was cold and stinking by the time he arrived, the back room in the East End tenement smelling like a butcher shop in high summer. Hawthorne paused in the door and swallowed the rush of saliva that filled his mouth, hoping that no one could hear the rumble of his stomach. His assistant Reynolds had interrupted his dinner just as he and Mary were about to sit at the table. The smell of the meat and blood was almost enough to drive him to distraction.

"Ah, Detective Inspector Hawthorne, thank you for joining us," Chief Inspector Barclay said from the opposite side of the room. Brilliant crimson, now drying to a dull brown, covered the walls in liberal streaks and splashes, the floor positively wet with blood and thicker things. Around the periphery of the room were Reynolds and two other London bobbies who were doing their best to look anywhere but at the body; they were failing. The furniture in the room had been destroyed, as had the room's single window, and in the center of it all, the hub in the wheel of gore, was the corpse.

"Thank you for the steam coach, sir, I came straight away." He stepped into the room with a crisp step, hands clasped behind his back because he didn't trust them.

"I trust that this call hasn't been too much of a disruption in your evening?"

"No, sir, at you service as always," Hawthorne chose to be politic as he stared at the body, his mind almost not making sense of what he saw.

"Good, we thought we might need someone with your particular... background," the older constable glanced at Hawthorne's left forearm, where the tattoo was hidden beneath his sleeve.

"Sir?" Hawthorne looked down at the body again and really saw it for what it was. "Ah."

An older man judging by the half a face that was left him, his flesh had been rent and torn. The sternum was gone, the ribs pulled outward like an opening flower. Something had been at his middle, digging through the soft meat there, and ropes of intestines lay scattered about like lengths of discarded sausage. The man had an expression of mortal terror and agony, forever frozen for a death mask. A few feet from his left hand was an old shattered musket.

Hawthorne knelt, holding himself up by the toes of his shoes and the tips of his fingers in order to lean in close to the body without getting blood on his clothes, and took a deep breath in through his nose, then another. Beneath the copper, beneath the dead meat and filth of torn innards, was a muskier smell, like fresh-turned earth and pine trees at night, a smell instantly recognizable.

"Unless London has a circus missing a bear that somehow found its way into a locked room in a tenement in the slums, then I would say we appear to have a rogue afflicted." Hawthorne straightened, looking at his blood-stained fingers. He carefully took a handkerchief from his pocket and wiped his hands in order to avoid the temptation to lick them clean.

"Too early for the full moon by a day." Barclay frowned as he considered the corpse.

"Not necessarily. The proximity to the full moon, plus some other stimuli like a disagreement or extreme passion, could bring about an early change," Hawthorne explained, striving to keep a note of annoyance out of his tone; this wasn't the first time he had to elucidate on the topic for his fellow officers. "And if the afflicted is from this neighborhood I'd be surprised if it had access to a cage."

"And how is *your* control, inspector?" Barclay's voice was as clipped, professional, carefully so.

Hawthorne looked at him. "In fine form, sir, never fear."

The other man nodded. "Continue."

"Considering the state of this room, and that the window is broken from the inside out, I would say the afflicted changed here, in this house."

"You three, out now." The chief inspector's command came smooth, expecting immediate compliance. When Reynolds and the bobbies were gone the chief inspector closed the door and turned to regard Hawthorne. "You have until the end of Sunday to find this creature and either capture or kill it, am I understood?"

Hawthorne stared for a moment, pole-axed. "Chief Inspector, *Sunday?* It's Friday night now. I have no clues and no leads, other than the true nature of the killer."

"The reason is fear, Hawthorne," the older man said. "If the public gets wind that an afflicted is on the loose, those like you will become suspect and hunted. We cannot afford to have panic in this city, especially with Queen Victoria so recently in mourning. We shall do nothing to worry her or her people."

Hawthorne ground his teeth but snapped his heels together as he shot to attention. "Sir, yes, sir."

"Good." Barclay turned around and opened the door, paused. "There was a witness, this man's wife."

Hawthorne frowned. "Where is she now?"

"Bethlehem Royal Hospital. I suspect you will want to go tomorrow, with your cage."

"Yes, sir."

"Good, now go home, I'm sure your wife will be worried about you." The chief inspector sounded weary as he left the room.

Hawthorne looked down at the corpse, at the expression of mortal fear, and left a heartbeat after.

Reynolds was waiting for him outside, hands thrust into his pockets, one of his hand-rolled cigarettes hanging out of his mouth, the cherry on the end casting his face in planes of shadows. He straightened when he saw Hawthorne coming.

"Go home and get some sleep, Reynolds, I'm going to need you early tomorrow."

"Guv, where should I met ye'?" Reynolds' Cockney accent seasoned his words heavily but it was easy for Hawthorne to understand after the years they'd worked together.

"Bedlam."

"Gor blimey. Struth?"

"I'm afraid so." Hawthorne ignored the invective that followed from his young assistant's mouth.

Reynolds shook his head. "Should I call ye a steam coach, guv?"

"I'll find a hackney, I'd rather not go home half deaf and smelling even sootier." Hawthorne tipped his hat to Reynolds. "Nine tomorrow morning, sharp."

"Roight, sah, cheers." Reynolds slouched down the street, huddled against the cold that Hawthorne didn't feel. That was one benefit of being afflicted, his increased body temperature meant the weather had to truly be abominable to make him need more than a moderate coat. Hawthorne started off the opposite direction from where Reynolds had gone, leaving for a more civilized part of London.

~

Mary was asleep by the time he made it home and Hawthorne wolfed down the plate of dinner she'd left for him in the still warm oven. Padding silently through their home, he lit a candle to see by and slipped into their room. Undressing in the near dark, he regarded himself in the mirror.

Tall, broad-shouldered and barrel-chested, his was a handsome if rugged face with a square, beard-covered jaw, cleft chin, and what he thought were warm eyes although he could just see in them the hint of gold beginning to peek through; by this time tomorrow evening they would shine in low light. His brown hair was worn a bit long, a touch shaggy. On his left forearm was a tattoo of a crescent moon, the mark that all afflicted were given to show their status. He only paid the ink a moment of attention.

Set into his chest were three golden plugs shaped like rounded triangles, arranged in a triangular formation around his heart. Each plug was notched along the edges and had a slit in the center. The gold wouldn't rot in his skin, nor cause infection. It had been expensive to acquire — Mary had used all of her inheritance to get them and his cage that went with them. He knew it was necessary; the alternatives were so much worse.

From the closet he took down a wooden case. Lying in the center of the case on a pillow of velvet was his cage. Its steel, copper, and brass gears were cleaned to the point that they gleamed in the candle light, the three bladed prongs of silver shining. Hawthorne hated the cage. He hated looking at it and he hated touching it. He hated it nearly as much as he hated the beast inside him. Like so many other things in an imperfect world, the cage was the only solution that allowed him to pretend he was human during the nights of the full moon. His other choice was to go to one of the lock-ups where the less fortunate afflicted had to go, to be chained to a wall behind lock and key, left to rage and madness in the dark.

Pressing one of the knobs on the surface of the cage caused tiny silver barbs to pop out along the inside edges of the prongs; these barbs would extend toward his heart, using the instincts of the wolf inside him to keep his heartbeat steady and calm. The wolf would do nothing to jeopardize its existence and so his heart would remain quiescent enough that change was nigh impossible, the rise in blood pressure necessary to shift unavailable. If he did start to change, the barbs would tear his heart open, killing him. The cage effected sanity through suffering, the silver of the barbs burning him constantly for almost four days, any errant, rapid heartbeat causing the barbs to just prick his heart. Pressing the button again he retracted the barbs. Hawthorne grabbed the handle in the center of the cage's surface and twisted hard to the right six times until it would not turn anymore, priming the cage's clockwork innards.

Mary snorted in her sleep, rolled over, and opened one drowsy eye.

"Oh, Reginald," she said sleepily, mournfully, as she always did.

Shame, discomfort washed into him like a bucket at a pump, filling him up until it overflowed. His voice was strained when he spoke, the feelings inside spilling out. "Go back to sleep, dear."

She didn't. Instead, she got out of bed, her thin nightgown covering her as she made her way to him. She wrapped her arms around his waist, pressing her cheek against his back. "Now," she whispered.

Hawthorne lined up the bladed ends of the prongs, each sharpened enough to rival a surgeon's scalpel, with the slits in the plugs in his chest. He took hold of the rounded, flat surface of the cage with his left hand, made his right into a fist and bit down on it.

With a muffled scream he slammed the cage home, the prongs sliding into his chest through the slits in the plugs, their bladed ends slicing through meat and muscle. The cage clicked into place, locking to the notches on the edges of the plugs. He could feel the prongs inside him, his heart brushing against them with every beat. The pain of the wounds came, sharp enough to make him gag, followed by the burning sensation as his body reacted to the silver he'd just pushed into his chest.

In his reflection, the cage sat nestled against his skin like a copper and brass tick; the clockwork innards paused, ready. Biting down harder on his hand he pressed the handle in, felt a click from within the infernal device, and nearly screamed as the barbs slid outward, reaching toward his heart. His vision swam, darkened. He would've fallen before it cleared if Mary hadn't held him upright, her strength always surprising him. A thin trickle of blood oozed out from under the edge of the cage, the pressure of the device keeping most of it inside him.

Wound tight, the cage would keep the barbs in place for four days until after the full moon waned into gibbous and he was safe from involuntarily changing. Four days of never ending pin-pricks inside his chest, and of the constant fire of the silver as it poisoned him.

"Come to bed, love." Mary led him to the bedside before helping him sit on the edge. He moaned as he rolled to his back, his body shaking as he tried to acclimate to the pain and burning. She walked back to her side, climbed in behind him and put her arm around his middle, pressing her chest against his back.

"Thank you," she whispered. "I love you."

"I love you too." His voice barely trembled at all. "Go to sleep, love."

In a short time she was breathing deep and regular, her body still and her arm heavy. For Hawthorne, he could feel the ticking of his cage, the soft *tick-tick-tick* sounding thunderous, over-riding the sound of Mary's breathing. Sleep, for Hawthorne, was a long time coming.

~

The next morning Hawthorne met Reynolds outside of Bethlehem Royal Hospital. It loomed over them, the tall, soot-stained pillars like fangs in a maw or bars of a cage, the round windows of the cupola like the eyes of an insect, staring unblinking down at them. It wasn't Hawthorne's first visit to Bedlam, he had reason to go there on occasion for his work, but that didn't mean that he *liked* going there. Glancing over at Reynolds, he could tell by the young man's slouched stance and sour expression that Reynolds wanted to be there even less than he did. Inside him, the wolf cringed with a whimpering sensation like a dog stretching to the end of its leash to get away from something unpleasant.

They were eventually led in by a nurse who took them to see Dr. Brody, the head of the hospital. An older gentleman, Dr. Brody was as thin as a reed, the top of his head bald and surrounded by a ring of white hair that made his pate look like an egg in a nest of down. After they explained why they were there Dr. Brody took them to the secure wing, accompanied by an orderly who was as big as an aurochs.

The secure wing was for those patients of Bethlehem Royal Hospital that were too dangerous for the rest of the facility, let alone society—the murderers, psychopaths and other seriously insane—and it always doubly affected Hawthorne. The sight of people like him, so far lost to their mania, left him uncomfortable, a stark reminder of where he could potentially come to his end. The wolf inside of him curled up deep within his spirit, fearful of their madness and unpredictability. It was an odd sensation for something that would've been the pure embodiment of rage, hunger, and death if it were ever set free.

Finally they finished walking through the moldy halls with their faded and peeling paint, past the wood and metal doors and those they held inside. Dr. Brody consulted a slip of paper tacked beside a door, took a ring of keys from his pocket and released the lock before opening the door for them. Sitting inside the room was a woman, stout in figure with broad, cracked hands resting over her knees, her gown ill-fitting. Her curly brown hair was limp and dirty, clinging to pale skin. Thick bags hung under eyes that stared at nothing. She might've been called handsome if a person was feeling generous. But here in Bedlam, her expression was the very definition of lost. They stepped inside and Dr. Brody shut the door behind him, cutting off the screams and howls of the patients beyond.

"Her name is Mrs. Abigail Reedy and, as you know, she was brought here last night." Dr. Brody read from his notes, taken from his pocket, in a dull tone. "She was in deep shock when she arrived and as unresponsive as you see her now."

"Then why is she in the secure wing?" Reynolds asked.

"Because she had a moment of mania and it took two orderlies to restrain her," the doctor explained. "And not before she darkened one orderly's eye and broke the nose of the other."

"Seems 'armless enough," Reynolds remarked, leaning against the wall.

"Says the man across the room from her." James the orderly glared at Reynolds, narrowing his one blackened eye.

Hawthorne moved forward and knelt until he was at her level. "Mrs. Reedy?" He tried to make his voice as gentle as possible and spoke again when she didn't respond. "Mrs. Reedy, I'm Detective Inspector Reginald Hawthorne and I'm here with my assistant, Constable Reynolds. We would like to ask you some questions about last night."

No response, she didn't even bat an eye. Hawthorne frowned.

"Mrs. Reedy?" He asked again. "Mrs. Reedy, please."

49

Hawthorne was quiet and the silence dragged on. After a moment he became aware of a sound, the *tick-tick* of his cage, and he looked down at his chest and back up at Dr. Brody self-consciously.

Mrs. Reedy noticed it too, her eyes blinking into focus. Her hand lashed out with the quickness of a striking viper, slapping a wide palm against his chest right over his cage. Her fingers curled around its edges, searching it out, and in a flash she was bowling him over, moving more quickly than he'd expect from a woman of her size, to land astride his chest, her hands gripping his coat lapels.

"You!" Hissing, her eyes were wide and wild. "You did this, you did!"

"No!" Hawthorne threw a hand out toward James the orderly who'd stepped up behind her, billy club poised to strike. With a look of almost disappointment he lowered it and Hawthorne turned back to her. "What did I do?"

"You, people like you!" she spat. "Rich, moneyed, *afflicted*. We could never be like you, could never give our John what you 'ave, you and your precious cages."

Her accent was as thick as Reynolds but Hawthorne understood it, automatically putting in the missing h's at the beginning of words, the g's at the ends "Mrs. Reedy, who is John?"

"My son. The one you're after. You wouldn't be 'ere for anythin' else."

Hawthorne kept his hands wide, doing nothing to rattle her. "Ma'am, it is important that I find him."

"What, so you can shoot 'im like a dog in the street!" she sprayed spittle over his face. The hackles on the wolf inside him raised, cage or no, Bedlam or no, and he struggled to keep his heart calm; inside him the pain grew.

"Mrs. Reedy, your son has killed one already," Hawthorne pleaded, looking up at her. "We need to stop him before he does it again."

She shook Hawthorne before she let go and moved back to the bed, glaring at them all.

"What good would it do, what good would any of it do?" Her voice grew softer as she looked down at her hands. "It's not as if it would bring back 'is da."

"It may save lives." Hawthorne sat up with a wince. When she didn't respond he said, "I need you to tell me about John. What caused him to shift? Why did he kill his father?"

"It was the lock-ups." Mrs. Reedy's voice nearly too soft to hear. "'E'd been goin' to them ever since 'e was a wee boy, you see. Every month we'd take 'im to the lock-up, leave 'im there. It used to be 'e pleaded, begged us weepin' to not make 'im go, to take 'im 'ome. After awhile the tears stopped and 'e'd just go…dead. Flat. Away. That was worse."

"How'd he become afflicted?"

"Dr. 'Orvisham's experiments." The bitterness dripped from her words. Hawthorne hissed in a breath; Dr. Horvisham was well-known, a fraud of a doctor who believed that if children were exposed to lycanthromophosia at a young enough age they would acclimate and fight off the disease. All he did was cause over a hundred children to have to be locked up every month. When parents found out what he'd done, mostly without their knowledge, he'd been dragged out into the street and murdered, beaten to death, hung, and set ablaze from a lamp post,

"I'm so very sorry."

"Sorry? Everyone's sorry!" Mrs. Reedy raged, coming to her feet in a rush. "Everyone was sorry, sorry this, sorry that, sorry your son turns into a monster three nights out of thirty. At least at first. Then the neighbors stop talkin' t'you. 'Don't associate with them or play with that John boy, 'e could be catchin'.'"

She sat back down on the bed and Hawthorne took a deep breath. "What happened last night?"

"John didn't want t'go t'the lock-up today, was fightin' 'is da about it." Mrs. Reedy's body sagged with each word like air pouring out of a balloon. "'E kept goin' on about 'ow it wasn't right that 'e 'ad to be treated that way just because of a disease. That the only reason why 'e was treated poorly was because there were so few afflicted, that if there were more like 'im then they might get some respect."

"Was it the fight that did it?" Hawthorne stood up, brushing his hands down the fronts and backs of his trousers. "Did he lose control?"

Mrs. Reedy lifted her head and her expression made him take a step back.

"No," she said, her voice harsh. "'E was calm. Calmer than I'd ever seen 'im the night before the full moon.

"I watched 'im change, I'd never seen it before," she continued. "All of 'is attention was on 'is da, who'd been shoutin' at 'im. 'Is father

51

backed away, slowly at first, then scramblin', fleein', shoutin' and screamin' for John t'stay away from 'im. John followed after 'im, 'is new body fillin' the 'ouse, the stink of 'im I'll never forget. 'E followed 'is da to the backroom; 'e 'ad an old musket Michael did, from 'is days in the army, liked t'show it off when'ere 'e could. 'E must've kept it primed because I 'eard 'im warn John that 'e'd shoot if 'e got any closer."

"What happened next?"

"John spoke." Mrs. Reedy bit her bottom lip, tears springing to her eyes. "Lord God in 'eaven, I'd rather be struck down. 'Ell than ever hear a voice like that again. John growled at 'is da, said for 'im t'join John, t'be like 'im, father like son. 'E must've gotten too close t'Michael because 'e fired. John 'owled and that's when the screamin' began. Eventually, the back window broke and it was quiet. I went back and saw...and saw..."

"It's..." Hawthorne meant to say "all right" but that would be a lie, another lie to the long list of lies people had been giving her for years; he would not add another to the list. "Over," he finished. "It's done now. No one should have to see that."

"Done is done," she said, so lost, and looked down at her hands again. "What else do you want t'know?"

"We need to know where John may have gone, what he might plan."

"'E'll have gone 'ome, back t'the alleys and streets 'e knows," she said. "When 'e was old enough t'leave the lock-up on 'is own we'd always find 'im there, walkin' around like 'e'd been dazed. As to what 'e's plannin'..."

She was quiet for a few moments before she began again. "I think 'e's going to make 'imself normal by makin' more like 'im. The offer 'e made 'is da."

Hawthorne rocked back on his heels and Reynolds sucked in a breath.

"Reynolds, come, we must leave now." Hawthorne stood in a rush. As Dr. Brody turned to unlock the door Mrs. Reedy called to Reynolds.

"Detective, my son..."

"Mrs. Reedy, I cannot assure you of his safety, what is happening-"

"Detective, you misunderstand," she said, her voice flat and as lifeless as her affect had been when they arrived. "There's a picture of 'im from last year in the 'allway back 'ome. Take it and find 'im. Kill 'im, detective. Kill 'im before 'e curses other parents t'the 'Ell we lived. Kill 'im for their children."

No screams, no sight in Bedlam he'd seen that day or before, nor crime he'd ever laid witness to chilled Hawthorne the way her words did then, cowing even his wolf to stillness. Swallowing against a suddenly dry throat, he could only nod and duck out of the room as soon as the doctor opened the door, fleeing for fresh air and the freedom of sunlight.

~

It was the screaming that let Hawthorne know they'd found what they were looking for as he, Reynolds, and two other constables ran down the street. They'd been unsuccessful in their searches for John Reedy, sifting through the narrow streets and alleys of the East End, the buildings crowding around and above them. Hawthorne turned over what Mrs. Reedy had said, over and over again; John Reedy, voluntarily changing, remaining calm, *speaking*, these things were unheard of but the possibilities refused to leave his mind alone.

With each hour that fell behind them their desperation mounted; Hawthorne had been honest with the searchers regarding who, and what, they were looking for and their faces grew more grim as the day progressed. With a sense of despair they watched the sun fall behind the tenements, the shadows growing to fill the streets like water rushing into a ditch. That had been an hour ago, and now the screams had begun.

They came round the corner and skidded to a halt, people in dirty, well-used clothing streaming past them, terrified. Standing as if he'd just come out of a ramshackle building, framed by the dark expanse of an open door behind him, was John Reedy in the midst of changing.

Topless, his form roiled, the muscles shifting and slithering, stretching, growing like worms beneath his skin. Despite the distance, Hawthorne could hear Reedy's bones breaking, grating as they moved inside him, his body jerking back and forth as it reshaped itself, causing him to double over with a howl of pain. He grew in height and mass, splitting the thin trousers first before his skin burst like an overripe fruit, sloughing away to reveal the thick, black pelt beneath.

The street was empty now, silent aside from the pained breathing of Reedy on the porch, the frightened panting of the constables. Slowly he straightened, uncurling to his full height, a good two heads over Hawthorne, his face a bestial mask of hatred and restrained fury. The sight of the afflicted made the wolf inside him strain, wanting to howl out a challenge and fight. Hawthorne's heart began to beat hard, straining.

"Mother Mary and Joseph," one of the constables swore, his eyes wide.

"John Reedy!" Hawthorne shouted, the steam rifle held tight in his sweating hands, the wool overcoat he wore to protect his back from the rifle's boiler stifling. Inside his heart struck a fierce beat, the pricks against his heart almost continuous, the threat of his cage ever-present. "You are under arrest for the murder of your father, for inciting panic, and for disregarding the Afflicted Public Safety Act by refusing to go to a hold."

Reedy laughed, a deep, growling noise pouring from him as his shoulders shook. All but Hawthorne took a step back.

"Under arrest?" Reedy's voice was a deep bass, the words made rough as they came from a mouth not fully human, and the sound of it sent ice crackling down Hawthorne's spine. "And 'ow do think t'take me in?"

Hawthorne took a step forward. "By order of the Afflicted Public Safety Act if you do not come with us we will open fire."

Reedy laughed again, flexing hands that ended in sharp, black talons into fists. His nostrils flared and for a moment his lips pulled back over crooked, yellowed fangs.

"So *you* were the one in my 'ome," he said. "I didn't know they 'ad a *dog* on a leash."

"John, come with us." Hawthorne pleaded. "We spoke with your mother, she told us what you've planned."

Yellow, blazing eyes narrowed. "Did she?"

"Yes, it won't work, John," Hawthorne said. "There are more of *them*, John, so many more. You can't change them all."

"It'll be a start."

"I'll stop you, anyway that I have to."

"You?" Reedy snarled, spraying spittle. "*You* should be 'elpin' me. Do you think that *thing* in your chest makes you like them? You're just pretendin', forcin' yourself t'do somethin' you don't want to, not really."

"And what's that?"

"Be 'uman.'" Reedy grinned, yellow fangs showing in the dusk light. "I know you can feel it inside you, your wolf. It wants out, don't it? It wants nothin' more than t'owl and come at me."

Hawthorne couldn't deny it. If not for the cage he'd be lost, gone to the beast. Even with the threat of the device he could feel the pace of his breathing increasing, his heartbeat coming faster. "And that's what you want to let out? You want to get attacked, possibly killed?"

"I want you t'be free." Reedy snapped. "I want you t'be who you really are, free of worryin' about these." He said the last with a contemptuous wave at the other constables. "Free t'do as you wish.

"I don't want any more like me t'go t'the lock-ups," Reedy growled. "You've a cage, you 'ave no idea. Imagine it, copper, imagine bein' chained t' a wall for days, unable t'sit because the chain's too short. Fed moldy bread, given bad water when they remember, 'aving t'stand in your own piss and shit because they won't unchain you for anythin', even in the daytime. The lock-ups are 'orrible and the people who run them are 'orrible too. I would rather die than t'go back t'them. You should be fightin' t'do away with them."

"Reforms are working on—"

"'Reforms,'" the afflicted spat, mocking. "Nothing more than 'ot wind out your lungs t'make the normals feel good about themselves, like they really care."

Hawthorne shook his head. "Last chance, John. Will you come with me?"

"Why don't you come with me?" Reedy offered. "I could teach you, show you 'ow t'come t'terms with the wolf. Think about it, cop; no more fearin', no more 'idin' from yourself. Think about not 'avin' to 'old back for once in your life."

Hawthorne considered it. What would it be like to be at peace, to not have to fight the wolf every month? For a moment he entertained the fantasy, being able to run wild in the woods beyond the city, taking in the night with all new senses, in control and not a threat to anyone. An unexpected pang coursed through him, equal parts longing for the freedom, and revulsion at giving up what was him. He thought of Mary and the possibility of leaving her to go with Reedy, giving up everything they had.

Hawthorne shook his head to clear it; there were some things neither Hawthorne, nor his even his wolf, would consider."Nothing but poppycock and distractions."

Reedy's response was to charge them. His speed was shocking, and Hawthorne barely had time to lift the steam rifle before Reedy was among them. A backhanded sweep of the arm sent Reynolds and Hawthorne bowling over, the detective inspector crashing down hard on the boiler on his back. He looked up in time to see Reedy swipe his claws across the face of one of the constables, tearing it open; the other managed to throw himself backwards, lifting his revolver and firing. The bullet struck Reedy in shoulder, jerking him back as blood sprayed from the wound. Hawthorne knew that the bullet wouldn't have penetrated very deeply, afflicted muscle mass was so dense it took powerful firearms to bring them down, but the pain was enough to cause Reedy to take a step backward, his face twisted in shock, before turning and running down the street on all fours.

"Sah!" Reynolds cried as they both climbed to their knees.

"I know," Hawthorne growled. He lifted the rifle to his shoulder, eyes flickering to the gauge to make sure he still had pressure, sighted, and fired at the retreating form.

There was an explosive hiss, steam shooting from the barrel of the rifle. Down the block Reedy was knocked from his feet with a howl, the silver slug striking him in the lower back above the right buttock. He looked over his shoulder at Hawthorne and the detective thought he saw fear on Reedy's face as the afflicted climbed awkwardly to his feet and limped into an alley.

"After him!" Hawthorne shouted. Reynolds grabbed the fallen bobby's pistol and took off down the street, a gun in each hand as Hawthorne and the unhurt officer went to their injured compatriot's side. The wounds were deep and severe, Hawthorne could see the man's teeth through one of the tears, but he was awake and doing his best to hold his face together.

"I've got this, sir, go on after young Reynolds." The other bobby took his whistle from his belt and blew it, two short blasts and a long one for officer in trouble. Immediately other whistles could be heard from the distance, and Hawthorne had the sudden urge to howl, his wolf's pack coming to them. The bobby handed him his lit lantern. "Go, good luck, sir."

Hawthorne nodded and stood, running down the street after Reynolds as he pumped the bellows on the boiler to build up pressure for another shot. The trail was easy to find, Reedy was bleeding profusely; while afflicted did heal faster than normal humans the presence of silver in the wound would keep it fresh and open until the metal was removed. Ahead of him came first the rapport of one handgun, then another, followed by the sound of a howl and shattering wood. Hawthorne ran, his heart stinging.

He came upon Reynolds standing to the side of a doorway, the remnants of the door still hanging in the frame, peering around the edge.

"Marcus?" Reynolds asked as Hawthorne approached, referring to the injured officer.

"He'll live if infection doesn't set in. You shot him?"

"Twice, fat good these do." Reynolds looked down at the pistols in his hands.

Hawthorne lifted the lantern and brought it into the doorway. In the dim light beyond he could see stacks of crates but no Reedy. "Going in there is a bad idea. Too many places to hide, too many ways he can attack."

"But 'e's 'urt, sah," Reynolds said.

"I know he's hurt, and we're going to go in there, I just don't want to." Hawthorne sighed. He winced and clutched at his chest with his free hand. Reynolds gave him a sympathetic look.

"Your cage?"

"Yes, damnable thing."

"Are you sure you should be doin' this, sah?" Reynolds asked. "If it kills you…"

"Let's go." Hawthorne ignored the sentiment and led the way, lantern raised. The light didn't push the shadows back far enough for Hawthorne's comfort.

"Sah, did ye think about what 'e said?"

"Reedy?" Hawthorne kept his voice low.

"Yeah, 'bout 'im teachin' you 'bout bein' like 'im."

"Impossible." Hawthorne shook his head. "I'd have to give up control to do that and as the beast how could I learn? It's just… rage and hunger, no thought but instinct. All he's offering are lies."

Reynolds smiled. "That's good, s—"

A crate from out of the darkness crashed into him, hitting him in

57

the upper chest and face and sending him sprawling limp to the floor, guns clattering from his hands.

"Reynolds!" Hawthorne spun to face where the box had come from, holding the lantern high, his rifle down at his hip. A gasp of pain was pulled from him as he felt the barbs inside his chest scratch at his heart. "Monster!"

"Who's the bigger monster, me for actin' my nature or you for actin' outside it?" Reedy asked. "You didn't even consider my offer."

"I did consider it, Reedy, but it isn't possible." Hawthorne turned in place slowly, eyeing the black all around him. "To not have to worry about the wolf, to not fight... what a dream. But I do not trust myself, John, nor you; you're a murderer and an animal and only a fool puts his trust in a wild beast. Your offer is nothing but a pipe dream." Hawthorne narrowed his eyes and thought he saw a shape in the dark trying to move around him, but the lantern's light, for as much as it revealed, blinded him to what lay beyond.

A growling laugh from behind him. He spun and a shadow darted away, yellow eyes flashing for just a moment. All was quiet outside but inside Hawthorne's heart raged, his wolf at the end of its tether, snarling and snapping. The pain in his chest was growing by the moment as his heart began to swell, the precursor to the change.

"I know you're still here, John," Hawthorne said, gritting his teeth against the pain. "I can smell you."

"Maybe I just need t'stay in the dark, 'arass you until that thing in your chest kills you," Reedy growled from nearby. "Wouldn't that serve you well, eh? Killed by the tool of the people who keep you chained."

"You won't though," Hawthorne said. "You can't do that. It's not in your *nature*, is it, John? And if there's one thing you've made clear, it's that you're beholden to your nature. So what about it, John, why don't we just finish this."

A pause for a painful heartbeat, then another, and then, "Yes, let's."

The words came from Hawthorne's right and he had a moment to turn, lifting the lantern with one hand as he caught sight of yellow eyes not unlike his own shining in the dark before Reedy leapt at him, mouth and arms wide. Hawthorne fired from the hip and the slug caught Reedy in the belly, his snarl of fury giving way to a look of shock and pain before he crashed into Hawthorne, carrying them both to the ground.

Hawthorne's back screamed with pain as he was bent over the boiler, the steam rifle held crosswise against Reedy's throat to keep his jaws away. A slash of his claws drew lines of fire against Hawthorne's belly and severed the line that connected the rifle to the boiler, sending the hose whipping back and forth as steam poured from it, causing them both to howl in pain as it burned them. Reedy was mad with agony, his wounds and the fire from the silver driving him beyond sanity and he snapped and slavered at Hawthorne's face. Given enough time the wounds he'd suffered would be fatal, causing him to bleed to death, but that wouldn't be enough to save Hawthorne; already the pain in his chest was mounting, it was becoming more and more difficult to breathe against the weight of the afflicted on his chest.

Reedy drew back, pulling off of the rifle's stock and lunged forward, fangs bared. Hawthorne slammed the stock between his jaws, crying out as he struggled to keep the beast away from him. Moment by moment Reedy drew closer and it was a race between the afflicted and his cage as to which would kill him first. Hawthorne knew despair then, realizing there wasn't a way out of this, that he was a dead man either way. Mary would be so sad.

"Sah!" Reynolds cried out from the side. Hawthorne saw him grab one of the pistols. "'Ere!"

The pistol came sliding toward him just as Reedy's jaws convulsed, shattering the rifle's stock. He lunged again and Hawthorne stopped him the only way he could, by thrusting his forearm into Reedy's mouth. Cruel fangs tore through the wool overcoat and into Hawthorne's flesh, drawing a scream from him, and Reedy shook his head like a dog might shake a rat, nearly hard enough to pull the detective's arm out of its socket. With a cry of determination, Hawthorne grabbed the pistol with his right hand and slammed the barrel into Reedy's left eye. A sliver of awareness came back to Reedy, the frenzy leaving him for just a moment, and then Hawthorne pulled the trigger.

The silver round tore through the monster's eye and punched through the thin bone behind it, into his brain. The shot snapped Reedy's head back, arching his spine and sending him to the ground, his arms and legs flailing. Hawthorne threw himself forward and across Reedy's chest, pinning him to the floor, and fired shot after shot through his eye and into his brain until his gun clicked empty.

Hawthorne slid to the ground beside the corpse, pulling at the straps that held the boiler on. The pain was incredible, the barbs slashing at his heart. He had to calm down.

"Sah! Sah!" Reynolds shouted as he crawled across the floor.

Hawthorne closed his eyes and focused, concentrating his breathing. He held his savaged arm against his stomach, biting down on his right hand against the pain. When one heartbeat didn't kill him, and he lived through the next, Hawthorne felt a surge of hope flash through him.

"I'm alive, I'm alive," he panted in amazement, looking up at Reynolds. With an almost crazed laugh he said again, "I'm alive!"

~

They were found minutes later by the other constables who'd followed Reedy's blood trail to the warehouse. They bandaged Hawthorne's arm as best they were able but none of them wanted to get close to the body; it was leaking so much blood they were afraid to touch it, that they might catch the disease and become afflicted themselves. Eventually they sent for a large stretcher used by a local knacker to carry away animal corpses and used long poles to roll John Reedy's body onto it.

A crowd had gathered on the street outside of the warehouse, the local residents of the East End. They began to shout and cheer when Reedy's corpse made its appearance, and there was more than one cry of "Monster!" and "Foul beast!" They spat on Reedy's body, threw clods of dirt at it in place of their hate. Hawthorne watched it all from the shadows, silent, passive.

"They'd thank you, sah, if they knew," Reynolds offered.

"You have more faith in them than I do," Hawthorne's voice was weighed down with sadness and fatigue as he gave his assistant a tired smile.

"I do, and I still think they would, sah."

"Maybe so," Hawthorne said, shaking his head. "Get me home, Reynolds. I'm done."

~

Hawthorne stood naked in the near dark, the candle's flame

wavering before the vanity mirror. It was late when he finally made it home, his arm bandaged where Reedy had savaged it. He'd slipped through the house as quietly as possible to their room, his way guided by a candle. Now, he stared down at the cage in his chest, feeling and hearing its tick through his whole body. Slowly his hand lifted to it, grasping it. With a twist he could break the clockwork inside him, rip it from his chest with a surge of strength, be free, for once, of the pain, the humiliation, the responsibility. Just once…

Mary rolled over and opened her eyes, smiling when she saw him.

"Welcome home," she said, her voice heavy with sleep, just before her eyes drifted shut once more.

Hawthorne's hand dropped away and he climbed, shaking, into bed, pushing away dark thoughts with the warmth of his wife's body. She curled up behind him, wrapping an arm around him, her hand resting just below his cage, and he relaxed. Sleep, for Hawthorne, came quickly.

Wings of Feather, Wings of Brass
Sarah Hans

I noticed the crows on the first day of spring, as I bent over the hard earth, hoeing in preparation of seeds. The crows perched on the fence, watching me with glittering black eyes. They cocked their heads this way and that, calling to one another in high, raucous voices.

"Mirabeth, why ya stop?" Piotre demanded, smacking my backside with his shovel.

"I apologize," I said automatically. "My language protocols were trying to translate…"

He hit me again, this time hard enough to topple me over into the dirt. "I don't give a shit what you were doin', or thinkin'. You keep talkin' to me like you think I'm gonna *care*. Now get back to work, rust-ass."

I labored to pull myself up and returned to my work without another word. I was suddenly aware, for the first time in all the months I'd worked for Piotre, that my talents were wasted on the rocky ground and the scraggly seedlings that grew from it. I continued to work, but I knew, with a sinking feeling of dread, that I'd awoken at last.

When the sun started to set, Piotre bade me finish my work and come inside the ramshackle house we shared. I cooked him a meager dinner and then stepped obediently into the cabinet where I spent my nights. "See you in the morning, rust-ass," he growled, slamming the door and locking it.

I stood in my cabinet and remembered Miss Darla: her delicate curls, her pink cheeks, her cheerful laughter as she hid in my closet while we played hide-and-seek, the little song she used to sing me as she kissed my fingers and closed the door to my closet each night.

> *Good night Mirabeth, my sweet friend*
> *I hope that your dreams are happy*
> *Tomorrow we'll play without end*
> *And we'll be very happy*

It was a simple song, a child's song, without much meter or rhythm and no need for a proper rhyming scheme. But I loved it, because it was Miss Darla's gift to me, as sure a sign that I was loved by my mistress as any automaton companion could hope for. I sang it to myself, softly, there in my cabinet, remembering how I used to stand among rustling silks instead of filthy gardening implements.

I remembered how my closet was never, ever locked.

Piotre banged on the cabinet door. "Are you singing? Stop that, or I'll sell ya to the next junkman what passes through, ya hear?"

I closed my mouth and eyes and tried to dream.

The crows returned the following day, alighting on the fence. They were the same crows; I knew it by analyzing the pitch and cadence of their unique calls. Kneeling over the furrows in the earth, I planted seed after seed and listened to the crows chatter. My language protocols were slow, at first, having been long unused, but over the course of the day I found all the subroutines necessary to begin a rudimentary translation.

All night I stood in my cabinet, mulling over the language of the crows, processing and analyzing.

The third day, I stood in the garden, delivering a whisper of water to each planted seed, ripping out the tenacious weeds that sprouted up at even the promise of sustenance. The crows arrived in a flurry of wings.

"I think she's a man-made creature," the largest crow said, choosing the prime spot on the fence and making the others settle around him.

"I'll give you five beetles if she *is* man-made," one of the smaller males offered.

"I'll take that bet," the largest crow replied.

"If she is man-made her maker did good work. Her face is so expressive. And she's sweating!" One of the females chimed in. "So realistic!"

"Her owner takes poor care of her though," another observed. The crows nodded their shining heads and clicked their beaks in mournful agreement.

I glanced around for Piotre. He was on the far end of the field, hacking at the stump of a long-dead tree with an axe, trying to eke out whatever firewood remained. He liked cutting and hacking at things.

"It's true, Piotre is much crueler than my maker was," I confessed to the crows, doing my best approximation of their language. I wasn't sure they understood me at first, as they just stared, not a feather rustling. For a long moment of silence, we considered each other.

With a squawk, the largest crow spread his wings. Taking his cue, the entire murder rose from the fence and flew away toward the misty mountains sixty seven point three kilometers in the distance, leaving me standing there holding my watering can.

I supposed that I was a great fool to think I could make friends with crows.

"Back to work ya lazy tin can!" Piotre bellowed. He'd snuck up behind me while I was distracted. He smacked me hard with the flat of the axe.

~

A ragman arrived on the fourth day, an old model Stallix 3000 pulling his cart. "Have you any rags for trade?" he called, stopping before the gate. His glittering black eyes took in the stone path, the little house, and the automaton—me—in the garden.

"No rags," Piotre called back. "But I've a few potatoes to spare."

The ragman nodded and climbed down from his cart. Piotre ordered me to fetch the potatoes. I found a burlap sack with a few shriveled spuds in the larder and brought them to the ragman.

He pulled a single potato from the bag and held it up, examining it. He glared at Piotre, frowning, and then took a big bite of the raw tuber. He stood there crunching for several seconds, then nodded and walked to his cart, gesturing for us to follow. He threw the potatoes in the back and then dug around for suitable trade.

"Rice? Apples? I've a few stalks of celery still good," he offered.

Piotre shook his head. His eyes were wide as he pointed at a bottle of murky brown liquid. "Wazzat?"

The ragman smirked, then winked at me while Piotre wasn't looking. "Bourbon. I'll need more than just potatoes for bourbon, my friend."

Piotre licked his lips, his eyes fixed on the bottle. "Mirabeth, get the oil."

"This isn't a good idea. We need the oil," I protested.

The ragman chortled. "Robotic woman's not much better'n a real one, is she?"

Piotre nodded and turned to me. "Shut yer mouth and do as I say. And make it snappy!"

Cowed, I shuffled to the house and fetched a bucket of oil. The crows had arrived and watched me from the fence, beady eyes intent, their usual chatter quiet.

Oil was traded for bourbon. The ragman's one condition was that he share the drink with Piotre. My master didn't like it, but he was desperate enough to agree. And so Piotre and the ragman drank what might have been the last bottle of bourbon in the world, beside the fire, swapping stories.

Eventually, his speech slurred by drink, Piotre ordered me into my cabinet. He neglected to lock the door. The ragman told one last story, his deep, gravelly voice carrying to me even through the cabinet door. The story was about a clever crow who fetched a ball of daylight from a place in the south called the Summerlands for a tribe of people in the north. His gift enabled them to live half their lives in sunlight and half in darkness. I wished I could repeat the tale to Miss Darla; she would have liked it.

When the story was finished, I could hear Piotre's snores over the crackle of the fire.

The cabinet door opened. The ragman stood there, smiling at me. "Greetings, man-made woman," he said in the crow language, which sounded very strange from a human mouth.

"My name is Mirabeth," I told him, not knowing what else to say.

He snorted and reached for me. "My name is Sky Father. Come with me."

I followed Sky Father to his cart. When he gestured for me to climb aboard, I looked back at the house. "What about Piotre?"

"If you were a crow woman, you would have left him long ago."

"I'm neither a crow nor a woman."

"But perhaps you could be." His black eyes watched my face.

I climbed into the back of the cart. Pressed in among bags of rice and bottles of rancid milk, I watched as the house grew smaller and smaller, eventually disappearing over the horizon. The sun rose—my first sunrise. I'd always been shut away in a closet or cabinet or cart for all the sunrises prior. The sky turned first the color of sapphires, then the color of a robin's egg, and then the pink and yellow of a little girl's ribbons, warming the earth as it went.

In the mountains the cart ground to a halt and Sky Father hopped down from his seat. "We go on foot and wing from here," he told me, helping me climb down.

"What about the cart, and the Stallix 3000?" I asked.

"Concerned for the well-being of the horse? How touching." As we walked past the cart Sky Father patted the automaton's head. "It's nothing more than a collection of wires and brass."

"Then so am I."

He shook his head. "Oh no, no, no. You are much more than that and you know it." He pressed the Stallix's ear, deactivating it. "The ragman will be back for the cart soon anyway."

"You're not the ragman?"

Sky Father gave a short bark of laughter. "Of course not. Now you'd better get moving, you've got a long walk ahead of you."

"Where am I going?"

He pointed up the mountainside. "You'll know when you get there."

"Aren't you coming with me?"

Sky Father smirked and turned into a huge crow, his clothes falling away around him. I stood staring at his tail feathers for many long moments as he flew higher and higher up the mountainside.

And then I began to climb.

The crows watched me as I made my way up the mountain, perching in the trees and moving as I ascended to keep pace with me. Some called encouragement; others heckled. They'd taken bets on whether I would make it to the place they called the City of Pines.

The climb was easy enough at first, but gradually the ground became rockier and steeper, with fewer handholds. I slipped and fell three times. The third time I tumbled so far I lay there on my back for many long moments, discouraged, wondering whether I would ever finish the climb.

A small crow landed beside me and pecked at me with her beak. I pulled myself to my feet and stared up at the daunting, near-vertical mountain face.

"Don't give up," she said, turning into a human woman. She was very beautiful, with nut-brown skin and deep-set black eyes. She reminded me of Sky Father. "Are you tired?"

"I don't become tired. And I don't give up," I told her.

She smiled, transformed back into a crow, and glided away.

A few hours later I pulled myself over the lip of a cliff to a landing. Trees grew on the flat ground, and interspersed between them were thatched houses. Thirty-six naked people and too many crows to count stood waiting for me. They cheered as I heaved myself over the rim and staggered to my feet.

Sky Father approached me in human form, extending one hand. "Well done, man-made woman. You have proved your mettle and earned a place among us. Now we will choose a name for you."

I took his hand and smiled in return. His grip was warm and firm. "I have always been called Mirabeth."

"No more. Now you will be called Mountain Tamer. No mere human or crow could have made that climb without wings." The crow-people set up another cheer and rushed me to shake my hand and pat my back and head.

Some of their touches lingered a little long.

"Usually we celebrate with feasting," a woman said. She was the beautiful one who had encouraged me after my fall. "What do you eat, Mountain Tamer?"

"I do not eat. I use oil to power my functions and lubricate my joints."

"Fetch the bucket of oil from the cart," Sky Father commanded. Without hesitating, three young men threw themselves over the cliff, transforming into crows mid-fall, and soared away.

"This is my daughter, Headwind," Sky Father said.

"Headwind?" I repeated.

"Because I'm stubborn and intractable," Headwind offered, shrugging. "You can stay in my house, with me, until you build your own. Come."

"It's very kind of you to offer me a place," I said as I followed her. "I don't understand why you would be so generous to someone you've never met."

Headwind threw me a smile over her shoulder. "I'm curious about you. And I called first rights."

"First rights?"

SARAH HANS

"We corax are a greedy sort. When we spot something we like, we call first rights, and I called first rights on you when I spotted you there in that man's garden."

"The rest of the tribe will respect that?"

"They must. It's law."

Headwind's house was nestled far back in the City of Pines, sheltered from wind and sun by tall evergreens. The house itself was merely one room with a fire pit in the center. The walls sparkled with trinkets and baubles dangling from the thatch: a yellow fishing lure, a red velvet ribbon, an old dented compass, a single pearl earring, and countless other items.

"You have quite the collection," I observed, trying to be polite.

"All corax do," Headwind explained. "Mine is nothing special."

"You have no door to lock. How do you keep the others from taking what is yours?"

"I don't. Sometimes they wander in and take something."

I blinked at her, alarmed. "How do you get it back?"

"I don't. I let them enjoy it for a time and then I go to their house and take something I like. It would be silly to collect things and then not share the joy of having them."

"Of course," I said. "This is not the custom where I come from, but I think it's very nice."

Headwind pulled a calico dress off a hook on the wall and drew it over her head. The dress's baby pink fabric was so faded the pattern was lost, and it looked too small for her—the arms and hem were too short. Here and there the cotton had worn through and I got a glimpse of skin, but I imagined this was no cause for alarm among a people who regularly walked about naked. And somehow, in that dingy threadbare too-small dress, she was still breathtaking.

"It's time to feast," she announced, taking my hand.

Headwind led me to a massive fire pit. The entire population of the City of Pines was gathered, in either human or crow form. I counted one hundred twenty six individuals. Approximately three point seven-six meters from the fire a long table made of branches had been lashed between two trees. Birds and men alike brought food and piled it on the table, for everyone to share.

Sky Father brought me the bucket of oil. "So that you can share in the feast with us!"

"Thank you." I couldn't help but feel that we'd stolen the oil from the ragman, as it was his bourbon that had purchased it. It was clear, however, that I would have to push such ethical questions out of my mind if I were to live among the corax. Their concept of belonging was very different from the one Master Duncan had programmed in me.

The corax piled dead branches and moldy logs into the pit and used an old flint firestarter to strike a blaze. As the sun set, the bonfire reached for the sky, spitting sparks and roaring into the night. Drums appeared, and once the feasting was done the corax drummed and danced. Men and women and children alike twirled and stomped around the fire. Their bare feet pounded the earth, churning up clouds of dust, while their crow brothers and sisters called encouragement in piercing, cacophonous voices.

Eventually Headwind reached for me and brought me into the circle of dancers. I did my best to imitate their movements. Spinning around and around the fire was disorienting but in an exhilarating way. I couldn't help but think that Master Duncan would have found this all so inappropriate, so savage, so heathen. Miss Darla would have loved it.

When the dancing was done, we collapsed around the fire and the elders told stories about trickster crows doing clever things. The younger corax would often chime in during parts of the stories, indicating that these were tales they had heard many times before. Finally, Sky Father gestured to me.

"Mountain Tamer, weave us a yarn from your past."

I knew of only one tale I could tell.

"There was once an inventor who lived in a house on a hill in the noble city of Athgate. He was responsible for all the automatons the world had come to know and love and depend upon. He was a genius, but also generous and kind, and he had a little daughter named Miss Darla. Wanting to make Miss Darla happy after the death of her mother, he built for her an automaton like none the world had ever seen. An automaton that looked like a woman, and talked like a woman, but who was infinitely more clever and completely devoted to Miss Darla. She was the perfect companion.

"Miss Darla named the automaton Mirabeth." A soft sigh of recognition swept through the crowd as they realized that this was my tale. Their attention gave me a strange sensation in the pit of my brass belly—my first case of nerves—but I soldiered on. "Miss Darla and Mirabeth were inseparable, and very, very happy for almost two years."

"One day the inventor trusted Mirabeth to take Miss Darla to the fair. The automaton had been among his family for so long that he did not think there would be any danger. But he was wrong. The Great Drought was in its third year, and the jobless poor were desperate. Hungry. Angry.

"Though she was beautiful and the most cleverly constructed automaton in the world, Mirabeth was still obviously robotic." I looked down at one of my own hands. Though smeared with dirt and ash, my polymer skin still retained its unnatural luster. Miss Darla had once called me sparkly, as if I were made of stars. "She was made of wires and brass. And the people at the fair knew. She was a shining example of opulence in the face of their poverty, a reminder that while they went without, others had too much. "

I hesitated, not sure how best to share this part of the tale. I felt something on my cheek and reached up to brush it away. A single oily tear wet my finger. I had not known until that moment that I was even capable of crying tears. Master Duncan's design was even more genius than I knew.

Sky Father touched my shoulder. "What happened at the fair?"

"The mob attacked Mirabeth and Miss Darla. They ran home, and the mob followed. When the inventor opened the door for his daughter, the mob rushed in. They bludgeoned him to death and set his house ablaze, dragging Mirabeth screaming into the street.

"Mirabeth never again saw Miss Darla, and to this day does not know whether she survived the fire. A man on the street took Mirabeth home with him and tried to make her do his bidding. When she refused to obey him, he sold the recalcitrant automaton to a farmer named Piotre for four bags of potatoes, thinking he got the better end of the bargain. Piotre beat Mirabeth until she was compelled to obey. Then he brought her to the plains to be his slave, which she was for many long, grueling months.

"But one day, while she was digging furrows for planting, crows landed on the fence. She heard them talking and translated their speech. Learning the crow language brought her out of her stupor. She awakened."

The corax nodded and grinned.

71

"It's rare for an automaton to awaken, especially one as damaged and mistreated as Mirabeth. But she did. I did." I smiled though another tear etched a path down my cheek. "You know the rest."

A moment of respectful silence followed my tale, and then the corax, led by Sky Father, patted their legs and clicked their beaks in solemn appreciation. Many pairs of their upturned eyes brimmed with tears of their own.

~

The weeks that followed were blissful indeed. My programming made it difficult for me to be content without being useful, so I kept myself busy patching clothes and planting a garden. The corax brought me whatever items I needed, whether it was a spade or a needle. I elected not to worry about where they obtained these items.

I noticed that some of the adult corax didn't take to me right away, regarding me with slitted eyes and pursed lips. The corax children, on the other hand, were openly curious and friendly. I taught them how to dig furrows and plant seeds, how to sew, and how to sing the songs Miss Darla had once taught me. With the children acting as goodwill ambassadors, the adults warmed to my presence as well, and I became an accepted member of the clan.

Headwind and I slept on either side of the fire pit in her house. One morning I activated my processes to find that the temperature had dropped twenty eight full degrees overnight. Headwind lay curled against me, sheltering from the cold. I felt a strange sensation, something close to the love I felt for Miss Darla, but also altogether different. I couldn't resist the urge to touch her, and gently ran my hand over her glossy black hair.

Headwind shivered against me, so I rose to feed the fire. She sat up, stretching her brown limbs and scratching at her tangled hair. "Why did you get up?"

"You're cold, so I'm feeding the fire."

She rubbed at her eyes. "Thank you."

I brought her a tunic I'd recently sewn from an old dress. "You should put on clothes, you will be warmer."

"Must be first frost. That means we'll leave for the Summerlands soon."

Sky Father often told stories about the Summerlands. "I assumed the Summerlands were mythical."

"What does that mean?" She pulled the tunic down over her shoulders. I experienced a pang of regret as she covered herself.

"Not real, made up."

"Oh no, they're very real," Headwind replied, smiling a wistful, dreamy smile. She rose and searched the walls for a comb. "The Summerlands are magical. We shelter there in the Winter and return to the City of Pines in the Spring."

"Why do you return to the City of Pines at all, if the Summerlands are so nice?"

She found an old tortoiseshell comb with half the teeth missing and pulled it through her hair. "It's too hot during the summer. Besides, the City of Pines is our home, too."

"Do you fly to the Summerlands?" I asked, anxious to hear the answer.

"Of course. Flying is the fastest way to... oh." Her eyes grew wide and her mouth made a perfect little O shape. I wanted to kiss her. I'd never wanted to kiss anyone before.

I marshaled myself. "How can I accompany you?" The prospect of being far from Headwind was physically painful, just as the prospect of being away from Miss Darla had once made me ache.

"I don't know. But... we'll find a way. I'll speak to Sky Father this very day."

Sky Father frowned when Headwind breached the topic to him. "Sometimes we carry the sick or the elderly. Could we carry Mountain Tamer?" she asked, her voice hopeful.

He shook his head. "I'm sorry, Mountain Tamer, but you will have to stay behind. You're simply too heavy for crows to carry, and we can't teach you the magic to change your flesh to feathers, as you have no flesh."

"Can I travel overland?" I asked.

Another somber shake of his head. "It would take months of travel."

"How do you fly there so quickly?"

"Air currents." Headwind spread her arms and demonstrated. "They will hold us aloft for hours without a need to flap our wings, and they push us along very fast."

"Can you... deactivate for the time we're gone?" Sky Father didn't like being reminded that I was an automaton, and I could see from the way he frowned and stared at his feet that asking this question was difficult for him.

"Yes! Then you could sleep for the winter and never even know we were gone," Headwind agreed.

"I can deactivate. But there's always a danger that after such a long time without maintenance my circuits will fuse or rust and I won't be able to reactivate myself."

Headwind gasped and touched my arm. I did not have a heart, but something inside me clenched tight at the contact anyway.

Sky Father's gaze rested on Headwind's hand on my arm and his frown grew deeper. "We will build you a house," he declared. "It will be very nice, and comfortable for the long winter. I'm sorry, that's the best I can offer. I love you as if you were my kin, but..." Now he met my eyes with his, and there was a sadness in them I had not seen before. He sighed and mumbled, "Wires and brass."

Disheartened, I went to harvest the meager crops my garden had produced before the frost could kill them. The corax children noticed my somber mood. "Whaz wrong, Muntin Tamer?" asked one of the littlest boys.

"Soon your people will go to the Summerlands, and I am not to come with you."

"But you have to come!" His voice was shrill.

"I can't sprout wings and take to the air like you. I am not truly a corax."

"You are, you are," the boy insisted, throwing down the handful of turnips he'd pulled from the earth and throwing himself dramatically onto the ground to wail. I let him throw his tantrum and paid him no mind, as I was programmed to do. Eventually his mother heard his shrieking and came to collect him.

"You shouldn't upset the children so," she scolded me.

"I didn't intend to upset him. I simply told him the truth," I informed her. "Despite Sky Father's promises, I will never truly be a corax."

She glared at me. "You are a creation of surpassing beauty and brilliance who will probably outlive us all... and you're complaining? You don't feel the pangs of hunger, or the cold of winter. Your back never grows exhausted from carrying too many burdens. But you want to be a corax." She scoffed. "Well then why don't you stop complaining and build yourself some wings?"

I blinked at her, surprised. "Thank you."

~

That very day I began sending corax out to collect materials. I had only a matter of weeks before the cold became so unbearable that the corax would move on to the Summerlands, with or without me. I cleared a space near Headwind's house and began conducting experiments and constructing prototypes. I sketched formulas and designs on the back of discarded paper. I launched projectiles and charted their movement.

Sky Father came to view my progress after a week. "This is a strange house you're building."

"It's not a house."

His brow furrowed. "What…"

"Wings. I'm building wings, so that I can accompany you to the Summerlands."

"You should be building a house, so that you can be comfortable for the winter. This is foolishness."

"Would the clever crow in your stories have been content with staying behind?"

"This is a waste, Mountain Tamer. Or perhaps I should rename you Foolish Brass Woman."

"Call me whatever you like, but I'm coming with you to the Summerlands."

"Sky Father, leave her be." Headwind appeared, leading the band of young corax who had helped me gather supplies and perform experiments. "This is her time, and it's her choice."

"You've been helping her? Of course you've been helping her." Sky Father's demeanor was decidedly changed. "I forbid it. I forbid any of you to help her. Anyone who does will be… punished."

"And how will you punish us? Are we not free corax? Is not our freedom our greatest treasure?" Headwind demanded, squaring her shoulders and raising her chin to stare down her father.

"Silly girl. I'm doing this for your own good. Now come away and let's build Mountain Tamer a house. She'll need it when all this fails." He gestured to the collected supplies.

Headwind pressed her lips into a thin, determined line. Then she turned from her father and marched to me, dropping the basket of tools she'd collected at my feet.

"I see how it is. You're choosing a thing made of wires and brass over your own father." Sky Father growled at me, "I should never have brought you to the City of Pines."

"You thought I was a novelty," I replied. "Something to entertain you. But as it turns out, I have free will. I told you, I've awoken. I'm not just an automaton anymore."

Headwind took my hand in hers. Sky Father stalked away, grumbling curses. The young corax trailed after him, their eyes downcast.

"Where are you going?" Headwind called.

"They're afraid," I told her. I squeezed her hand. "It's alright; we can do it, just the two of us."

She smiled, though there was a shadow of sadness behind her eyes. "I know."

~

After that, I worked both day and night. Headwind joined my efforts during the day. Though we worked alone, a few of the young corax snuck us supplies without Sky Father's knowledge. A week later, we had completed our third glider prototype, the previous two having been scrapped. The chill in the air deepened enough that Headwind spent most of her time in crow form, which she insisted was warmer. I missed her pretty human face, but I enjoyed her constant companionship. I would often idly pet the crow that slept beside me while I worked through the night.

One dawn, Sky Father appeared in his crow form. He settled near my work and croaked, "We leave for the Summerlands today. We have waited long enough."

"Today?" Headwind cawed, rousing from her slumber. "But the glider isn't ready. We need more time!"

"He's right," I told her as I fitted a brass hinge into a wing joint. "He can't endanger everyone for me."

"We can't go without you!"

"And you won't." I stood and slid my arms into the straps, settling the wings on my shoulders. They were made of wooden pipes, brass fittings, and patched canvas. They were ugly in a way that would have made an engineer cringe.

"Those look ridiculous," Sky Father scolded.

"You haven't tested them!" Headwind cried.

"We tested the last two pairs, and I made my calculations. If I did it correctly, then this pair should work. I should be able to fly." I turned to Sky Father. "They look like this because I weigh ninety one kilograms. I need a wingspan of over three meters to bear my weight."

They both continued to caw at me as I made my way through the City of Pines, past the throngs of black crows, and to the cliff's edge. I ignored them. All I could hear was an omnipresent rushing sound, as if my entire existence were converging on this one point. The point at which I would live, and truly become a corax, or plummet to my destruction on the plains below.

I knew Headwind was right: I hadn't tested these wings. I had to put my faith in Master Duncan, the man who created me, the man who made me into the most brilliant automaton the world has ever seen. And if there was one person in whom I had total faith, it was Master Duncan.

I hesitated at the edge of the cliff and spread my wings. The sun had just finished its rise, casting its orange glow across the tortured landscape. Headwind appeared beside me.

"I think you should know that I love you," I said.

She stared, speechless, beautiful even as a crow, her feathers sleek and dark as shadows at noon.

I stepped over the edge and spread my wings.

Good night Mirabeth, my sweet friend
I hope that your dreams are happy
Tomorrow we'll play without end
And we'll be very happy

The Wild Charge They Made
Steven Saus

The valley lay before us, dry grasses softly shifting with the autumn breeze. Beyond the rough stalks moved the Russian infantry, constructing rough defensive positions. Both echoes from cannon fire and the cries of wounded men drifted on the wind, bringing the scents of gunpowder and blood. I closed my eyes and thought of England, Queen Victoria, and the sweet face of my Elizabeth. I wondered if I would see any of them again.

The hoof beats of two riders approaching interrupted my reverie. I could identify them by the way they rode, quickly confirmed by the glint of their insignia. I turned to my commander. He stood beside his horse, bushy mustache quivering as he surveyed this part of the battlefield.

"Lord Cardigan. I see that Captain Nolan and the General approach, sir."

"Of course, Sergeant Worthing," he replied, brushing an invisible bit of dirt from his uniform. "Perhaps we shall finally see some action before the morning leaves us."

I managed to control my look of surprise, but the word, "*Finally?*" escaped my lips.

"Yes, finally," he said. The eyebrow over his left eye rose, a white furry caterpillar of a thing. "Did you think we would continue to waltz through the Crimea without engaging the enemy?" He turned away without waiting for my answer.

Despite being late October, the sun beat down on us and our mounts as we waited for the two men to close the distance to us. A bit of sweat rolled down my back, insulated by the specialized gear our brigade now carried. *Elizabeth, I wish you were...* I paused. *I wish I wasn't here.* My right hand strayed to the small pocket watch on its chain, the one with her portrait inside.

General Lucan brought his horse to a halt near us as we saluted, barely acknowledging our existence with a nod. Captain Nolan stopped behind him, fixing me with a scowl. He had made his feelings about Lord Cardigan's appointment of a mere sergeant as a personal aide quite public in a tavern a few weeks ago. I let a twitch of a smile tick up the left side of my mouth, noticing that Captain Nolan's bruise had nearly healed. When he caught me looking, I pretended to studiously examine our scout balloons floating behind him. They floated peacefully, the only activity the glint of spyglasses and flapping of semaphore flags from their gondolas.

Lord Cardigan dropped his salute. "General Lucan. Captain Nolan. Do you have orders for us?"

General Lucan's face became very still as he looked down at us. "Of course." He shifted on his horse, inhaling deeply. "We wouldn't want you to have to act under your own initiative, would we?"

Lord Cardigan flushed, fingers curling around the horse's bride. "Sir, your orders clearly stated to stand our ground—"

Nolan spluttered. "The Russians were five hundred yards away—*retreating* just five hundred yards from you, man!"

General Lucan's raised his eyes to the sky and flexed his neck, but he did not turn toward his aide. "That is enough, *Captain*." He refocused on his brother-in-law. "*General* Cardigan, I bring word that Lord Raglan wishes for you to advance rapidly to the front, follow the enemy, and try to prevent them from moving their large guns."

Lord Cardigan raised one bushy eyebrow. "Which guns would those be, General?"

"There, my Lord," Nolan interrupted again. "Perhaps this morning demonstrates the failure of your eyesight." His voice lowered, as he muttered "Or perhaps your wits." Nolan gestured toward the east, down the long valley where the Russians had fortified themselves. From the valley floor, lousy with Russian infantry, the land rose on three sides. To the north and south, the hard metal rods of Russian cannon jutted from the shifting grass. "There is the enemy! There are your guns!"

But it still took me a moment to see what Nolan meant. "General Cardigan, look there." I pointed to the redoubt at the far end of the valley. I had thought the sound distant cannon fire at first. As they drew closer, we could not just hear them. We could feel the gargantuan footfalls as Russian steamwalkers rose to the top of the ridge. Though the details were obscured at this distance—perhaps half a league—we could see nearly a score of walkers taking positions on the far hill. Puffs of grey coal smoke came from their top smokestacks, nearly twenty feet above the men below them.

Lord Cardigan looked at the steamwalkers, then back to Lucan. His mustache twitched again before he spoke. "General, please allow me to note that there is a battery of guns in front, a battery at each flank, and the valley is covered with Russian riflemen."

Now General Lucan's mouth raised in a half-smile. "I know it, my dear brother-in-law, but Lord Raglan has *expressly* ordered it. Quite clearly." He wheeled his horse back toward his command. "As you said, you have no choice but to obey your orders." Without a further word, he rode off, Nolan trailing behind like an obedient dog.

I pulled the pocketwatch from my shirt, and closed my eyes again as I held its metal, warmed by the heat of my body, in my hand. *Goodbye, Elizabeth*, I thought.

~

I told Elizabeth about the Programme after I volunteered as we sat in the parlor of her parents' summer home. As with every time I saw Elizabeth, afterward I could not remember a single detail of her dress, or what scent she wore. My gaze was drawn to her face. I had heard poets speak of losing oneself in another's eyes, but until I met Elizabeth, I had never experienced it myself.

My confession had made those eyes fill with tears.

"John..." She looked away for a moment, gaze focused on her hands, fingers twisting anxiously in her lap. "We are betrothed. What will others think about this? About you?"

I reached out, daring to grasp her hands in mine. "My love, perhaps at the beginning of this century, they might have thought ill of me. But not now. Not after the Magyar rebellion against Austrian rule. And not now. The Empire is at war. They will simply think I am a soldier, serving my Queen and country."

She turned my hands over, examining them until she found the healing wound on my forearm. She looked up at me, and I nodded. She looked down at it again, ran her finger along the edge. "Did it hurt?"

"Not much."

Her hands slid my sleeve up more to expose my wrist. Her hands brushed along the soft hairs of my arm. "They aren't any different."

I took her hands in mine again. "*I'm* not any different, Elizabeth. I'm the same man."

She met my gaze again. "Promise me, John. Promise me that you'll come back just as you are now.

"I promise," I said, my soul falling into the depths of her eyes.

~

I opened my eyes again at the touch of Lord Cardigan's hand upon my shoulder. "Don't look so downcast, Sergeant." He considered me and the pocket watch for a moment before speaking again. "You've not seen battle before."

I lowered my chin toward my chest. "No, sir. I was promoted as part of the Programme."

He harrumphed. "I thought not." He paused for a moment. "A soldier, no matter his rank, must be aware of the tactical situation, even though we are simply asked to do or die. So, what hour is it, Sergeant?"

I opened the watch and looked at the clock face, trying to not see the image of Elizabeth lest my heart sink further into my stomach. "Eleven of the clock, my Lord."

Lord Cardigan smiled. "A trifle early, perhaps," he said, swinging up onto his mount, "but we shall make do." He drew his saber and raised it over his head so that it flashed in the sunlight. His grin reminded me of a wolf. "Do better than my grudging brother-in-law and consult your almanac, Sergeant. Take heart! There is a reason we did not engage the Russians this morning!"

As he rode to gather the brigade, I withdrew the small book from my saddlebag. It had been issued by the Programme, its charts and tables calibrated for this campaign. It took a moment to find the right page, then another to run my finger down until I found the entry Lord Cardigan had meant. I looked up into the blue sky.

"She is coming," I whispered, and began to believe that perhaps I would live to see Elizabeth again after all.

~

Elizabeth's father read in his study as I lay on their reclining couch in the parlor. She had insisted that she see the effects of the Programme for herself, and despite our shared misgivings, both her father and I were loathe to deny her.

Her hand rested, soft as down, upon my own. "Are you certain we do not need to restrain you?"

I laughed. "For the tenth time, no. That is a slander propagated by the Russians and Germans against the Magyar. Even in the rawest form of the so-called "curse", it is not always true, and our scientists have improved upon the natural state of things. They've altered it so much, brought the whole supposedly occult process under scientific control. We don't even need a full moon!"

Her eyes danced back and forth in an anxiety-fueled dance. "And shall you have to leave England?

"Well, yes." I laughed again. "How else would I fight the Russians? I have no intention of letting any enemy of the Empire close enough to see your face."

She squeezed my hand affectionately at my poor joke, then her expression soured. "No, afterward. Would you have to reside in Hungary? Now that their independence is won, they've made it safe for ani—" Her voice grew quiet. "People."

Now it was my turn to squeeze her hand. "No, my dear. Queen Victoria herself assured us of that. We will be heroes, and welcome in any of her lands."

And then the light of the crescent moon shone through the window onto my skin, and I could speak no longer.

~

As the brigade formed, I used my own spyglass to look upon the Russian forces. The steamwalkers looked no less intimidating through the glass. Each stood upon two rudely articulated legs painted a sickly yellow-orange. The metal had been shaped, along with the backward knees and yellow-orange paint, so that they resembled the legs of gigantic chickens. Atop the steel pelvis rested the central platform. The engine and control room had been fashioned to resemble a hut, with the engine's smoke billowing out a central smokestack. The platform was ringed by a solid metal fence, behind which the walker's crew manned their guns. The Russians had aided the Austrians during their war. These walkers had been used in the pogroms against the Magyar; skulls of changeling dead hung from the edges of the platform.

"Sergeant," Lord Cardigan said. "Do you see anything of use to us?"

I lowered the spyglass. "The walkers are much as they had been described to us, my Lord. They have not lowered to the ground, so I suspect the Lord General is correct. The conventional guns are preparing to move, and the steamwalkers are intended to provide an artificial defilade against our own guns."

Lord Cardigan nodded. "Very well. We shall have to move before we are fully ready, but a handful of minutes…"

"My Lord," I said, "perhaps I was not clear. These walkers were used against the Magyar." I handed him the spyglass. "Note the decorations, sir. Though I have not seen direct evidence of them, they almost certainly have silvered weapons."

The general pursed his lips. "The witches' hut," he murmured. "Interesting, sergeant. Despite their technology, they turn to one legend to protect them from another." He returned my spyglass, and motioned me onto my own horse. "But remember, Sergeant, the Magyar are wolves. And we, well, we are *Britons*."

We mounted our horses. Before I could think of anything more to say, Lord Cardigan raised his saber another time, paused a long, still moment, then slashed downward.

Our horses surged forward over the whipping grasses. A cry of defiance ripped out from our throats. Details blurred as my heart pounded, fast, faster, faster than the hoof beats below and beside me. My horse's muscles pulsed and surged beneath me as we entered the valley.

As we rode, I spotted movement in the air at the south side of the valley. Half a dozen powered Russian airships, each carrying a gondola resembling more a sailing ship than our scouts' baskets, came into view. Each dwarfed the scout balloons we used. Their engines made them far more mobile, and their cannon, undoubtedly filled with grapeshot, made them far more deadly. Their engines labored to turn them broadside, bringing their guns in position to rain enfilading fire down upon us.

There was no time to change our course. Lord Cardigan, in the lead, plunged into the first ranks of the Russian infantry, and a fevered heartbeat later I did as well. Across the line, sabers and lances flashed, the metal shining red with Russian blood. We did not, could not slow. Our horses pounded through the rude defensive position of the Cossacks. With each movement of my arm came a juddering thunk as my blade parted flesh, a clanging ring when it struck either helm or rifle. We did not look back, did not survey the damage we caused. We forged onward, our imprecise butchery simply a necessary task to get to the far side of the infantrymen.

The Russian guns on either side remained silent, waiting for us to get clear of their own comrades. Sunlight gleamed from the weapons of the Russian airships, from the steamwalkers, from the guns on either side. All waited for us to be repulsed or break free from their own men. All waiting to slaughter us on clear ground.

And we were still minutes early. Not a hint of the moon could be seen. We were still as vulnerable as any man.

The Russian infantry began to recover from the shock of our charge. British curses and the cries of horses intermingled with Russian screams as their defense began in earnest. My own horse shrieked and lurched to the left as a bayonet scored its flank. My blade sliced through the Russian's shoulder a moment later.

Then explosions shook the air like summer thunder. Perhaps a commander had panicked, or judged the lives of their men a worthwhile cost. The airship guns fired a second volley, though we were still in the thick of the infantry. Grapeshot seared through man and horse, felling them like a scythe on the battlefield. The shrapnel had no affinity for a particular country. The blood of Russian and Briton alike ran into the soil. We still fought forward; there was no point in retreat. Unlike the guns on the ground, the airships could continue to fire upon us, even if we maintained a full gallop.

The shriek of a hawk pierced the chaos. For a moment, all stopped. All eyes turned to the southwest rise. Captain Nolan, alone on his steed, rode onto the hill mere yards from the Russians. His head was that of the heathen Egyptian god Osiris, his hawk's beak parted in another haunting hunting scream. The Russians on the hill took aim, but even as they fired he leapt from the back of his horse, taking to the air on massive hawk wings. He banked as he rose, talons the size of butcher's knifes cleaving the faces of several Russians as he took fully to the air.

I heard his cries echoed behind us, but they were neither reflections of sound nor the cries of a Greek nymph. With a quick glance backward, I spied British aeronauts leaping from the gondolas of the scout balloons. Wings sprouted from them mid-leap. I realized with a laugh that from their height, the moon must have already risen above the redoubt. They angled southward toward the airships, giant seven-stone hawks rising high before diving toward the airbags of the Russian airships. Russian airships whose cannon were all pointed *downward*. In moments, the airships were sinking, some even burning, as the aeronaut's giant talons sliced through canvas and flesh.

Lord Cardigan struck down a Russian beside me, laughing as he rallied the men into another charge. "Only used to *wolves*," I muttered, then jockeyed my horse beside him. Within moments, the infantrymen broke ranks, dashing toward the reinforcements on either side of the valley. We had a brief moment of respite as we broke clear of the Russian men.

The land-based guns began to fire. The sound battered our ears and guts, the flashes horizontal lightning along the ridgeline. Men and horses fell in clattering jumbles of bodies and pain.

I thought again of Elizabeth, of her waiting for my return. Shards of metal sliced through the man to my right, his horse screaming as its intestines spilled from its flesh. I would never hold Elizabeth's soft hand again. Upon the steamwalkers, gunners began to fire the diskthrowers they had used against the Maygar. One of the spinning blades, tipped with silver, sliced through two men and a horse before me. My own mount lurched to the left to avoid the tangle of their dying limbs. Never again would I hold Elizabeth in my arms. Never again would I smell the sweet traces of her perfume as we danced. My horse screamed as it stumbled, its front foreleg severed at the knee by another steamwalker-fired disk. I flew through the air for a moment before thudding shoulder-first onto the body of a dead Russian. The taste of blood filled my mouth from where I had bitten my tongue. I spit it out, trying to remember the taste of Elizabeth's kisses. Never again would I see her face.

Then Lord Cardigan let out a cry of triumph. I looked up, and behind the steamwalkers I saw the glorious silver of the moon. As our bodies began to shift, uniforms splitting under new muscle and fur, Lord Cardigan shouted once more, his voice twisting with the change. "They're only used to wolves!" he cried as his snout elongated, the twin white stripes of fur decorating his face like war paint.

My uniform shredded with the force of the change, releasing the extra gear I had carried: twin specially-fitted gauntlets for my changed form. I slid my paws into them, where they latched with a satisfying click. I looked at the remains of my uniform, suddenly realizing my stupidity. My watch, my portrait of Elizabeth, lay in the rent cloth.

A buzzing annoyance struck my left shoulder. I turned my massive, furred head. A wounded Russian soldier, eyes wide and arms shaking, fired another round toward me. The conventional lead ball felt no worse than a mosquito bite. I raised my right paw, my digging claws sheathed in sharpened metal, and removed his head with a quick blow. Around me, the rest of my company, all badgers nearly twelve feet in length, began to dive into the soft ground with preternatural speed.

The earth vibrated around us. We joined tunnels just above the hard clay layer, lower than either the shrapnel or slicing blades of the steamwalkers could penetrate. The sheaths upon our claws allowed us to burrow nearly as fast as a horse could gallop. We spelled each other as the lead digger while we covered nearly three quarters of a mile underground. The steamwalker's footsteps shuddered through the earth as we drew near. Their vibrations provided excellent guidance, and when they grew strongest, I routed my squad's tunnel upward toward the surface.

I broke free of the dirt directly underneath a steamwalker, its ground support troops scattering before my claws. I roared, and struck, my jaws spilling the contents of a Russian's abdomen upon the ground.

On my right, another steamwalker stumbled, one of its legs buckling as it stepped onto earth weakened by one of our tunnels. Giant musteline forms scrambled onto the tipped steamwalker, powerful teeth and enhanced claws rending the flesh of unfortunate troops cast onto the ground. A cloud of steam and burning coals from its furnace billowed across the battlefield.

The Russians on the ground fell before us in moments. The steamwalkers stood too close to each other to bring their weapons to bear on us at first. But their giant legs already moved with massive hissing hydraulics. Their commanders shouted to each other as the walkers started to move away from each other so they could bring their weapons to bear.

Lord Cardigan appeared to be wrong; the superstitious design of the walker's legs was protecting them. The Russian troops on the ground fell easy prey to our badger forms, but the platforms were simply out of reach. In seconds, the hulking steam engines would shift them far enough apart that they could fire upon us without hitting another walker. Nearby anti-changling troops were closing on us from the north, the silvered tips of their sabers flashing in the light. Overhead, I heard the hunting screams of Captain Nolan's men as they harried the walkers. Unlike the airships, the walkers could to pivot their guns upward. A shrieking hawk fell nearby, left wing severed, stump smoking, and I knew the hawks alone would be unable to carry the day.

A store of gunpowder exploded in the downed walker. My body hunkered instinctively against the ground, lips bared back from teeth red with Russian blood. British soldiers too near to the blast were hurt, but were already healing from the unsilvered shrapnel. The steamwalker was mortally wounded. No longer merely downed, its right hip had shattered, destroying part of the central platform as well.

It took a precious few moments to realize what I had seen. The exploded walker was not just metal, but metal and *wood*. The chicken-leg appearance was not cast from solid metal, but a sheath of thick wood over the metal and gears. The platform was the inverse - thick wood clad in a thin covering of metal. Enough to protect against rifles, but not designed to withstand cannon fire. And perhaps not strong enough to withstand claws. I remembered one badger back home who kept raiding Elizabeth's bird feeder in their old elm tree, and grinned. *Used to wolves*, I thought again.

I rushed toward the nearest steamwalker, my long body scrambling low over the ground and Russian corpses. The walker had slowed to turn. I took the opportunity to gather my strength and reach up with my enhanced claws. They sliced into the left leg of the walker and held in the wood. I compressed my body, shoved my rear claws into the wood sheath, and reached upward again. In but a few moments, I was directly underneath the machine's hip. The metal and wood platform dipped and rolled with each footstep. Above, I heard the increasing whine of charging discthrowers preparing another volley of sawblades. With two quick, hard slashes of my claws, I opened a hole through the wood and metal and pulled myself through.

The first two Russians died by my claws before they realized I was on board, their lifeblood staining the deck. The soldier manning the leftmost discthrower stayed focused on his aim until my jaws closed on his thigh. I ripped his leg off with a hard shake of my powerful neck. Two more soldiers brandished conventional weapons, unable to turn the diskthrowers far enough to aim them at me. I leaned back on my powerful haunches and hissed. Their comrade's blood matted my fur, staining the white stripes across my forehead. They leapt over the side, taking their chances with the fall and my fellows below. I bashed in the door to the central "hut."

By the time I finished, the inside was painted with Russian blood.

I turned at the thump of boots behind me. A British—human—aeronaut stood on the deck. One of Nolan's hawks had already reversed course, pulling his balloon back across the battlefield. As I looked about, I saw that others had followed my lead. British badgers held all the steamwalkers, and British aeronauts were rappelling down from their balloons to man the giant siege engines. The Russians were in disarray across the battlefield.

"Well done!" the aeronaut called to me, and I snarled, heart pounding, a primal *need* unsatisfied. The aeronaut blanched, stumbling back against the were-skulls mounted on the deck railing. I scrambled back down through the hole in the deck, down the walker's leg, and gave chase to the fleeing Russian prey.

As I chased the *meat*.

~

The moon set as the day's battle drew to a close. Lord Cardigan, I, and the remainder of the brigade donned the spare utility uniforms awaiting us. I ran my fingers through my hair, trying to dislodge the dried blood. I stopped when I realized that my fingers were equally smeared with dried viscera. In the middle distance, one of the captured steamwalkers thumped along the ridge where Nolan had earlier launched himself from his horse. Nolan's body, cloven by a silver-tipped sawblade, had been found not an hour prior. I looked at the blood caked across my hands. I smelt it smeared across my face, from where it wafted from the corpses—both Briton and Russian—littering the valley.

Lord Cardigan stepped up to me, his face streaked with gunpowder and blood. "Sergeant, I shall be on my yacht, taking dinner. I am not to be disturbed."

Some small part of me was surprised. But a far larger part understood. "Yes, my Lord." With that, Lord Cardigan strode to a waiting horse, and galloped away.

I looked back across the valley, the weight of my gauntlets heavy on my belt. It had been a near thing; I imagined what would have happened without the "curse" our Magyar allies had provided. Six hundred men and horses, surrounded by artillery and enemy troops. It had been like riding into the mouth of Hell as it was. I could not imagine what it would have been like otherwise. I felt a fierce joy that I had survived this day. A fierce joy at how well we had done.

The memory of Elizabeth's voice came unbidden. "Promise me, John. Promise me that you'll come back just as you are now."

Somewhere in that mass of carnage lay the wreckage of my original uniform. Lay my watch with her picture. When I closed my eyes, I saw only images of violence and death.

"I'm sorry, my love," I said to the air, and began gathering the men to wash the blood away from our skin.

A Taste of the Other Side
Chadwick Ginther

I pried my eye away from the war wagon's back port. The wagon's engine was burning full steam and it was hotter inside than midsummer in Hell. But being inside beat being topside. Out where *they* could reach you. Especially when one bite, one scratch, was all it took for them to claim you. Behind the wolves, I caught a glimpse of the moon. Its glowing crescent hung there like a scythe, waiting to swing.

They ran on—pacing us, despite our speed—in an unending tide. They ran on all fours, no longer wholly men, but not quite true beasts, clad only in fur and fang.

There was barely enough room in the wagon for a soldier to breathe, let alone move. Our brass and copper limbs gathered and held the heat. Their green patina told tale that we weren't their first bearers. Gods willing, we'd be the last.

My tight-laced leather jerkin made it feel even hotter, but without it I'd burn my chest until it looked even less appealing. From the rear drive and past the metal pipes and gauges that made up most of the wagon I could just make out Seamus sitting at the front drive. Only room for two of us in here, and I'd be taking us home while he had the wolf watch. He was wearing the same leather cap and night lenses that I had strapped to my own head. If he was feeling anything like me, he had sweat running from under that leather and seeping past the seals, stinging his eyes and pooling, fogging up the glass.

I rubbed the fog from my lenses and put eyes back out the port. Claws flashed bright and I could see the shining of their eyes, glowing like malevolent fireflies.

"They're gaining on us!"

"One more corner and it's a straight shot to Beachhead," Seamus wheezed back. "We'll lose 'em."

I wasn't so sure. I'd rarely seen them out in such numbers. They were crafty devils, with more cunning than either wolf or man had alone. They had a plan.

Outside I could hear the synchronized firing of the topsiders. They were good and followed protocol. Lead bullets were no use for killing the wolves but they didn't run so all-fired fast while they were healing.

A cluster of shots. A wolf stumbled and fell in a rolling tumble. It had hardly stopped before it was back on its feet and running pell-mell.

Silver may make terrible bullets but the wolves would've been done for years ago if we'd made the metal we were hauling into weapons. The metal's touch seared their flesh like fire, one of the only things that seemed able to kill the beasts. Hell, fill a scattergun with silver shot and it'll put down a wolf fast enough. But we weren't allowed. Instead we sent it across the ocean to prop up the Empire's coffers. Men and women are a renewable resource to Her Majesty.

You would think that the wolves would be well rid of all the silver filling the mountains and caves of their homeland. Instead, this very vulnerability made the metal holy to them. It belonged to the moon or some such rot.

Each soldier riding the wagons *was* issued a short silver punch dagger. I'm sure Her Majesty would've been happier had I lied on my back and birthed her a new generation of soldiers than taking up blade and bullets myself. But the wolves'd taken enough from me, and with the scars they'd left behind, who'd have me?

One wolf out of the pack caught my eye, then. He ran on four metal limbs and was shouldering his way through the tide of fur, gaining on us. And I knew him.

"Well, look see who's joined us," I called out over the steady chug of the engine. "Bert. The moony bastard."

Bert had always been a little… off. But I'd known the man as an able field mechanic and surgeon. Was a shame he'd got himself scratched, a shame he'd hidden it, and an even bigger shame he'd clawed up three soldiers so bad even Doc couldn't cut enough of them off to save them. Shame he'd done for me too.

It happened though. I knew that well enough. Staring up every night, shuddering at every howl in the dark. Knowing what awaited you if their jaws bit down… if a single claw drew the thinnest line of blood…. Waiting for them to come pouring over the walls. They seemed… endless.

The pistons in Bert's metal legs pounded holes in the road deep enough to rest a pile in, before long, he was beside us. Shooters fired, but by the time I got to the side port to see, he was gone.

Back to my seat, I kept a look out the rear port. The trees ate up the road behind us, and even the thin sliver of moon wasn't visible through their canopy.

Over the din of the engines, I could barely hear the muffled pops of the topsiders' gunfire.

"He's in front. Still running," Seamus said. The wagon lurched—must've hit one the holes Bert had left in his wake—throwing me into one of the pipes. I spat a curse at Seamus as the hot metal sizzled into my neck.

"I'm riding him down."

"Don't you dare, Seamus Reilly! Doc'll want his parts back."

"I know my orders, *Mizz* Blight."

Seamus threw my womanhood at me for what time, I'd long ago lost count. But he came from a proper family, even if he rarely acted it, and said he'd only call me 'Sally' if he came a courting, which neither me nor his wife would much approve of.

More shots from topside.

The wagon lurched up on one side, back down and then up and down again. I knew from the feel that Bert had gone under a wheel.

"You better hope those fancy legs of his are still for walking." My voice echoed louder than I'd meant it to, as the engine idled down. We must be about to hit that straight shot to Beachhead. I remembered how long I'd had to wait in that scratchy cot, with only my scars and pain for company; waiting, knowing that until enough men died that Doc got to my lot, I'd be staying there.

I caught a glimpse of Bert out the rear port. His body convulsed with pain. Metal legs and arms dug deep furrows in the earth, kicking dirt up into the air.

The wolves stopped their pursuit to surround Bert like he was one of their own and the wagon started to slow.

Metal slammed into metal and Seamus yelled, "Damn it!"

The engine whistled as he let into the brake and the sound covered Bert's screams.

"What are you about?" I demanded.

"Deadfall on the road. Can't take it at speed. Bloody howlers trapped us."

More of their pack melted out of the trees to bolster their numbers.

I heard the muffled thuds as the wolves threw themselves against the wagon. Even over the chugging heartbeat of the engine, the high pitched scrabble of the wolves' nails against the wagon's metal walls danced up my spine. Not for the first time I was glad not to have rolled the dead man's pip and been forced topside.

The topsiders' synchronized precision was replaced with a staccato burst of individual fire as they sought to knock the wolves free of the wagon.

The wagon tilted, like a ship cresting a wave as the treads ground their way slowly up and over the deadfall in the road.

"They're all 'round us!" Seamus hollered.

"Then put on your hood."

Seamus pulled back on the levers that controlled the wagon's tracks and let them dig into the earth bringing us to a stop. A jet of steam escaped a pipe. A whistle sounded. Last warning for the topsiders.

I said war wagons ran hot. Hot enough that they could smelt the silver ore we transport in their undercarriage. Doc had found a way to make a weapon of even the gas that process released. Our tanks were full of the Silver Wind, as we'd come to call it. Of course, what was strong enough for the wolves was also poison to men.

I threw on my hood and synched it tight enough, I'd soon be choking. My brass arm turned the crank that would vent the gas fast and natural enough, it was as if I was a part of the engine.

"Damn it, Blight!" Seamus cursed, his voice, not yet muffled by his hood.

If the topsiders were following procedure, they had their masks on soon as they spotted the wolves pacing us. Having ridden topside myself, I knew their masks *wouldn't* be on. You can't see worth a damn with its cloth covering your eyes.

Can't see, can't shoot.

The rotten egg stink of the gas seeped into the wagon. None of the seals were perfect. We'd found *that* out swift as sin. I'd been topside the first time Silver Wind had been deployed—killed more men than wolves.

Fortunately, for progress and Her Majesty, Doc wasn't one to let a little detail like human casualties get in the way of his science.

Doc now recommended a slow twenty count before taking off our hoods. I gave it thirty before I removed mine and checked the top scope. I let out a slow sigh. We still had men standing. For now. Seamus already had his hood off. I checked my left side port. Some wolves were bounding off for the trees. More were on the ground, each in their death throes; fingers gouged the earth, and tortured bellies coughed up blood and bile. Checked the right side. More of the same.

Must be some traces of the silver still in the gas, because the beasts' fur was burned away, replaced by a slick, oozing bare skin, which blistered and bubbled like soup on the boil.

Seamus worked the hatch. Even counting trying to worm my way around the engine, it was faster for me to follow his lead. Seamus had two metal arms to my one, and he could turn the heavy hatch wheel all the swifter.

He paused at the door, and said, "Draw iron, *Mizz* Blight."

"I know my business, *Mister* Reilly," I shot back. "See to your own."

Seamus nodded with a coal black grin, and turned the key that locked his silvered punch knife in his left hand. Picking up his shooter, he kicked open the hatch, hopped out, and was firing before his backside had fully cleared the threshold.

I locked my punch dagger in my clockwork fingers. I called them my fingers, even if the ivory and brass digits were truly property of Her Majesty. And even for all their supposed mechanical precision, I still found my natural arm steadier for firing. Something in the subtle touch of my flesh to the shooter's wooden butt. And *unlike* my shooter, the blade had more than nine stabs in it and would benefit from the strength behind that metal arm.

Out into the night and I was in the thick of a fight that I knew immediately we couldn't win. I'd hoped the Silver Wind had done for more of the wolves. But they were everywhere. Seamus and I were to go back to back. We'd done it before. But this time we were quickly separated. There was a lingering stink from the Wind, but that was peeling away fast.

Shots. Thunder booms on a clear night. Grey smokepowder fog.

Screams. Yipping howls of wounded wolves. Death rattles of men.

Blood. Coppery tang hung in the air like a fine mist. A spray caught my cheek; hot and thick.

Death.

A loud wheezing cry told me that Seamus was heading for Doc's scrap heap.

A furred blur slapped against my arm, knocking my pistol free from my hand. I spun with the strike and punched my dagger into the wolf's flank. The silver hissed as it slid through fur and muscle, slicker than spreading butter.

The wolf howled, and my arm stabbed up and down, piercing the wolf like a sewing needle mending curtains. Its claws raked my chest, but my leathers took the brunt.

I hoped they'd taken the brunt. It didn't take much to end up with the moon sick in your blood, and I didn't want to make the change or end up more metal than meat like Seamus.

It raised a paw to ward off my strikes. I stabbed down into its wrist. Blade sliced bone and with a final shove, the paw hung by threads of skin and I'd buried my knife in the thing's throat. Tearing the blade free severed that thin tether of flesh and its paw dropped to the dirt and so did the wolf.

I chanced a glance down to see my wolf had been a woman. Impossible to tell when the change had taken her, the slight swell in her belly told the tale of her pregnancy. I should feel good about that, one less of the monsters would be coming into the world. But I didn't. Gods curse me, I didn't.

I heard a crack, and knew it was bone. I felt the pain, and knew it was my hand being ground to powder. I screamed. Talons found veins and blood made my arm slick. I tried to tear away, but still the grip never faltered. And I saw why.

It was no wolf's paw that had me, but a thing of gears and metal, like my own arm, only ending in talons not fingers.

In the shock of the sight and the rush of pain that followed, I felt thankful that it had spared me from the moon sick at the same time my heart fell knowing what this injury might mean—if I survived long enough to see that consequence.

Bert's other metal paw was strong enough to hold my strikes at bay. He gripped the blade, deforming the silver. Looking around I appeared to be the last of my crew alive.

The wolves were pulling their dead off the field. But that's not all they were taking. Any clockwork limb a soldier had was carved free with claw or tooth. I looked down at Seamus, his ribs were cracked open, sticking out of his chest like two clawed hands waiting to close up on something. Steam pushed past his lips like he was weeping with pain. Doc had replaced his heart and lungs with a bellows when one of the wolves had bit too deep. All that metal in Seamus' body must've kept it going even if the light had left the man's eyes and his soul had fled to the hereafter.

A group of wolves picked their prize from his body and went to quartering. Ripping flesh was a horrid sound, and just to hear it made me want to sick up. As the limbs tore free, the kettle whistle of Seamus' dead-lipped moans subsided to a dreadful hiss.

"Careful!" Bert warned the scavengers.

"You do not rule us," one of the wolves said.

Bert let me go. Where could I run to? I held my dagger warily, as if it could keep the lot at bay. May as well try to heft a mountain.

Bert had always been a hairy man, even before he'd gone moony, but seeing those shining brass and copper limbs—gold as day against the pale of the moon—walking a wolf's torso and head about, I shuddered.

A long tongue worried at pointed teeth, as his eyes sliced through me, sharper than one of Doc's instruments.

And then he changed. Wolf became man, and I recognized the limb that had crushed my hand. It had changed with the man, went from clockwork paw to clockwork hand. Talons became fingers. Joints shifted. Aside from his lack of clothes, Bert looked no different than he had before he'd run off. He seemed embarrassed about that, and tied a scrap of bloody cloth about his waist.

He asked, "Surprised?" though I'm sure he knew the answer to that query. "It can be controlled, Sally."

I responded automatically, "Private Blight, to you, sir. Or Miss Blight, at the very least, if you please."

He smiled. Bert had always had a fine smile, though this one was stained with sadness. "Of course, Private, as you wish."

"I'm not for changing."

"You'll come around." It wasn't the first time I'd heard him say those words. "But first, the silver, if you please."

On instinct I went to turn the key that would unlock my fist so that I could drop the punch blade. A mistake. Pain shot up my arm as my ruined hand brushed the key. I dropped to my knees. Bert took a step forward and I held the knife out as a ward. He stopped and the wolves circling behind him howled. Blinking tears away, I bit down on the key to keep from howling myself, and turned it until the blade dropped from my ivory fingers to sink point first into the earth.

When the silver left my hand, the wolves behind Bert changed as well. Naked to a one. The camp was full of stories of the beasts' preferred means of stretching their numbers, but not a one of the men looked at me with a hint of arousal.

The wolves used a white mud to cake their human bodies, so they might shine silver with the moonlight. Now that mud was black with pooling blood, allowing night to swallow them.

They looked no less monstrous for their present lack of fur and fang.

I stared from them to their dead fellows, also wearing human shapes. The stink of spent powder, of blood and offal, filled the clearing.

Most of us who crewed the wagons had few, if any family left. Dead soldiers had joined their dead wives, dead husbands and dead children. I envied them that. Most of us who'd signed up for the Doc's tinkering had someone to avenge. Some reason to hate. I wasn't alone in that. But I was alone among the dead for still standing.

"Why are you doing this?" I asked finally. "I don't want to be like them. Like you."

"You already are. You've already let Doc change your body."

Bert gestured at the poisoned wolves, writhing in pain. Dying slow. Dying hard. None of the pack made an effort to touch or comfort them.

"Look. Look at what we are doing to them. They are men. Women. People, not beasts. Doc never should've unleashed that gas. Burns won't heal. Works its way deep inside you, until there's no way to cut it out. You know what it's like to fear something like that. But there's no changing this away. The only thing it changes you into, is dead."

"So you're stealing our parts now?"

I was talking to Bert, but it was the wolf who'd spoken before that answered me. "These limbs are all you have of value to us."

Bert knelt at the wagon, his arm whirred and one of the fingers split apart, what should've been a man's bone looked instead like a key. He shimmied under the wagon and tried it in the silver's lock. Squinting and jimmying for a time. Finally, he stood up, frustrated, with a shake of his head.

"Doc's altered it."

"Break it."

"That will take time."

Turning to me now, the wolf asked, "Do we have time?"

I shook my head, more because I hoped not. The wagons left in threes. With outriders in between and on either side. They may have taken out our riders, but we were the middle of our train, and the next wagon would be along within a quarter clock turn. Unless they were dead too.

The wolf pointed at where the silver was smelted. "Open it, and we'll spare you."

I doubted that a great deal, but dead was dead, and it wasn't as if they'd be looting that silver from my own pocket, so I nodded.

Bert removed the arm with the key. "The change is hard on the parts," he said by way of explanation. Bert's spine twisted full around, like a gear mounted owl's head, his legs followed and he was facing me again. "Leave it," he said to another of the wolves, who was pulling an arm from one of the dead topsiders by the wagon. "It is full of their poison."

"I see some parts *she* could stand to spare," one of the wolves said, pointing at me with a laugh.

I cried out "No!" before I realized I was in no position to demand anything. If the wolves wanted my arm, they'd take it.

Their leader must've sensed my feeling, and smelled my desperation that they not do this. A slow smile grew until it matched the moon—a scythe waiting to swing—and split his face.

"Do it."

And they did.

~

I woke on one of Doc's work slabs wearing naught but a threadbare sheet. I was glad it covered me, even if its slight weight stung at my crushed hand. When they'd brought me in, Doc had given me an all-too-thorough and none-too-gentle examination to confirm my limbs weren't in any further need of pruning. He had many instruments and ablutions that would determine if the moon sick had been passed on, and they'd all left me weeping

He wouldn't even spare me a swallow of that peaty liquor he'd brought across the waves with him to ease my pain.

In the end though, he must've been convinced I was clean, because I've never seen him make anyone wait this long to die.

I tried to force myself up, forgetting I was down an arm. Bert had been surprisingly gentle when he'd removed it. "I've enough work to do, without fixing *this* arm too," he'd said by way of explanation.

He'd even had the decency to look embarrassed when he removed my leathers. I'd expected him to take my sweat-soaked undershirt too, leave me to walk back naked, but he only cut enough away as he needed to remove the whole of my arm. He did stare at the scar where a breast had been before he averted his eyes, and went back to work. Doc had cut it away after I'd been mauled. A *blessing* he'd called it. Allowed him to stabilize an arm not meant for a woman. Got me out in the field, and fighting again. That did seem like a blessing at the time.

My old wounds still felt fresh; would always feel fresh. When cold flushed me, or I remembered my wedding night, I could feel the ache where those lost parts of me were still remembered.

Looking down at my ruined hand, I knew they'd soon have company. The constant throb of pain sharpened as I took in the damage: fingers bent at odd angles; bones erupting from skin here and there. Crushed seemingly flat in places, swollen and red with blood in others.

Doc Festus spoke in a harsh clipped tone, "This hand will have to come off."

"No. Please, no."

Doc shook his head, unmoved. "It hasn't taken the moon sick, but it'll never be more than a frozen claw. You're finished for now, soldier. Back in the scrap queue for you."

I couldn't take the interminable waiting for a new hand. But if I didn't, what were my choices? I'd have to leave the camp and return to Beachhead, be forced to beg—or worse. There was a certain type of man who'd look at a woman like me, and it weren't the marrying kind. "How long?"

"You could not even return the clockwork arm I'd already given you, and you wish me to replace it? And another limb atop it?"

"I brought back my own replacement."

A *harrumph,* and a muttered, "Inferior work."

102

"It did the job out on the road. And it seemed to me it did something my old arm wouldn't. And if it's so inferior, what do you care, if I'm the one wearing it?"

His face darkened as he examined Bert's arm. "These mechanisms were not built to last. They alter themselves. Transform. This impresses you, as if you were a child, and this arm your new toy. What you cannot see, they have one—two—such alterations and they will seize and become so much dead weight. Useless scrap. Bert never cared for quality. *We* cannot afford to waste parts so fruitlessly."

"I don't need it to transform, I just need it. Please, Doc."

"Very well," he said after a time. "If I am to affix one arm, let us see what I can do about the other."

He upended a sack and a severed hand—a human hand—bone shining bright in the moon, and weeping blood from its stump, tumbled atop Doc's workbench amidst tools and pokers and half-finished constructions of gears and brass. A left hand. A woman's hand. The one I'd severed?

It hadn't looked so human when my blade had lopped it from the wolf's body. But the thing still dragged itself towards me. Its long fingernails were as good as claws, scoring furrows in the oak, prying free a thin curl of wood as it inched forward.

Not one to take chances, Doc slid on a pair of heavy foundry gloves and began to fumble with the foul thing.

It scuttled away from his reach. He slammed his glove down, pinning it to his table.

Doc's eyes went all bog-eyed as the severed limb writhed in his grasp. He sucked a breath through clenched teeth. He jerked his hand out of the foundry glove and slammed an empty-bottomed cage over glove and hand both. A finger reached tentatively to the black mesh that held it. Contacting the metal, the digit began to smoke and stink. Scrambling backwards the stump of the hand brushed the other end of the cage. Same result.

Doc Festus tapped his teeth, pursed his lips, and considered the prize. He poked and prodded at that thing like it were a lady and he'd paid for the privilege of her company.

"Still somehow alive, this wolf's hand. And you, yourself in need of a new one."

It only took me a moment to see where the Doc's mind was drifting. And I didn't like it.

"Poison's in their blood. You've seen it. That thing, living on when it should be going to rot? Don't you do it, Doc. Don't you put that thing on my body."

Doc smiled. "You speak as if you have a choice. It's this, or back to Beachhead."

No choice at all.

~

I thought I knew pain when Doc took my arm off the first time, back when it was meat and I was me. I thought I knew what to expect. That it would make it less.

It didn't.

Bone knit. Skin crept. In the light of the moon I saw my hand change to a paw, saw the moon sick steal some more of my flesh. The silver wire he'd used to bind the wolf paw to my wrist itched. It hissed. It burned. My skin blistered, popped and wept. It threatened to drive me mad from screaming day and night.

Festus pulled at a cord, opening a flap in the ceiling of his dwelling. I didn't remember there being a hole in his roof. I wondered how he'd feel about that when the rainy season hit us again.

A slash of moonlight bit down from the sky, tracking across the room. Doc may be a master of gears and gristle, but patient he was not. He sighed, put upon, when the moonlight didn't touch the twitching hand.

He cut into it, blood welling up behind his scalpel blade. Even as he cut, the wound knit itself shut.

The slash in my paw—and funny how I thought of it that way now—was gone like it'd never been. Doc cut again, pinning back flesh "there" and "there." The meat of my paw sizzled as he stuck it. The insertion of those pins seemed to do the trick though. Doc's wounds didn't close back up this time.

Trading his scalpel for a flensing knife, Doc teased the skin back from the muscle and sinew, and sewed that twitching flap to my shoulder, and through grommets connected it to the metal arm.

The moon had found me, and my new hand had changed entirely to a paw, the other, the metal arm, was still trying, gears whirring and whining; begging to be transformed. One finger, then another jerked, extending an extra knuckle. It clenched and unclenched. Long talons hissed free of my fingers.

It had worked. The mechanical hand had made the change.

I grunted, both fascinated and repulsed. "Congratulations. What do you hope to prove?"

He answered, "That metal and machine can be truly integrated." Tapping my clockwork hand he said, "This, while it may be amazing to you, is a crude beginning to what I hope can be accomplished. See: even now, how the flesh begins to heal around the replacement armature? This is vital. These creatures are not vulnerable to sepsis, nor gangrenous rot. The possibilities! With these transforming arms, our men will *become* weapons, rather than merely hold them."

"You'll turn us into them, is what you'll do. Turn us into bloody monsters."

He looked pointedly at the hand he had grafted to me, and the metal arm he had attached. "And across the ocean, how many would say as much already?"

~

Moon turned full, waned and then waxed again. And still I'd had no visitors.

None but Doc, and the only greeting he brought me was pain.

I knew what was happening. I was never leaving his workroom. I was nothing to him but another experiment. I'd never be a soldier again. Instead, he'll poke and he'll prod, and saw piece after piece of me away. Needs more wolf parts. Needs to put wolf meat around these new arms so they'll change too. Bert had put a key in his arm. Doc had taken it out, but the arm, it was *my* key.

Bert had said I'd come around. I looked at the drawn silver wire Doc had used to separate the wolf flesh from the rest of my body. If I pulled that thread, I'd start to change, completely. But then I won't be human. Not no more. My arm twitched. Silver hissed and burned me.

I put my teeth to the thread.

I haven't been human for a long time.

Peculiar Institution
Caren Gussoff

Each time Father re-punched my worn cards, he would leave the tea program set to two cups. The second cup was never meant for me, but for Manny, until he returned. However, my logic conditional jumps dictated I place the cup in front of me, and let Father frown at it as it cooled, untouched, before pouring it to the rosebushes.

Since Manny has gone to the War, the roses have grown fine and fat as fists.

To-day, as we sat over tea, Father said, "I've been reading up on flighted birds. It's time for me to work on a new program." But before he could continue, he was interrupted by a knock at the front door.

I wheeled Father to meet a young man, sweating in a dark blue frock coat. He addressed Father and shook his hands, but then looked at me, his mouth agape.

This is often the expression strangers hold upon meeting me.

Father did not introduce me, however, and instead sent me into the kitchen. Once I was gone, the young man held Father's attention in the foyer until both our teas were quite cold. Then, when Father called for me, he asked to be set not at the table, but in the parlor near the fire. He held a letter in his hands which he read and re-read, turning it over and over in his hands.

Father lost himself in the contents, and only when I started rocking back and forth to wind my own rotors, a noisy business, did Father look up at me, place the letter down on his lap, and motion for me to approach so he could turn my key.

"The new program… the birds," I started, but Father returned to the letter and waved away the idea.

"Not now," he said.

I was glad of it. Of all the forms I have been, and of the infinite possible multitudes, I am best as the sister-daughter.

It is my shape most of the time. The repetition abraded the punch cards and required the most frequent replacement. However, this repetition had also worn down my gears to accommodate the motions of the tasks. It gave me, as Father has remarked, the natural grace of any child of G-d.

In this form, also, I am called Alexandria. Although all the shapes are still me, only in this one was I named: Alexandria, after a library that once encompassed the whole of man's knowledge, long burned, almost forgotten.

My clock struck the hour and my spindle turned, pulling back the tea cards and feeding in cards for the luncheon. "Are you hungry, Father?" I asked, less a question than a cue, for him to put down the letter and allow me to place him at the table.

Instead, Father looked up from the letter. "Come here, Alexandria."

"It is time to lunch," I answered.

"Come here."

I could not. I turned my head towards Father, but the cards compelled my feet towards the larder. My hands gathered onions, looking for soft, bruised parts, until Father wheeled himself to me, squeezed my chin to open my mouth, and pushed softly under my tongue to suspend my program. He took the onions from my hands. "Sit, Alexandria."

Now, I could. My legs bent beneath me until I made contact with the floor of the kitchen.

"Listen to me," Father said. "This letter is from Manny." Father's face reflected the color of a sky about to open with rain. "His company was captured in a Virginian campaign, and he is imprisoned in a camp, sixty miles from Macon. The young man at the door served well under Manny, and feigned death as means to escape. In case of his success, he smuggled out letters for many of the other men." Father touched his hand to his forehead, momentarily concealing his grayed face.

"What does the letter say, Father?"

Father said nothing at first. Then he began to wheel himself across kitchen back to the parlor and his desk. I started to assist, but he waved me away.

At his desk, Father opened the box of prepared paper and his punching stylus. "I meant to write you a new program to-day," Father said. "But it's to be a different one than I intended." Father looked in the box for a long time, then to me. "You must go to this Andersonville Prison and free Manny. I will write you some new programs and one that explains the letter's contents."

"Then I must hunt to-night," I reasoned. As the Wolf, perhaps, or Raccoon or Goose or Cat; I could bring Father enough food in any. The Wolf was fiercest, but my fortunes improved as the latter, nothing the townspeople to spy and fear, and birds and fish my haul.

Father came to me and his face was less grey, and he stroked my cheek. "You're drying," he said. "Bring me water."

I soaked the sponge in the puddle next to the roses, and then Father wet me to soften my clay.

"You're growing," he said, "in Reason and Logic. Sometimes it surprises me to remember what you are." He sighed. "To-night, you will indeed hunt," Father agreed, "and perhaps tomorrow and the next. These programs will take time, even if I hurry."

Then, he tweaked my nose, pressing it up a little to resemble Mother's, as he often did when he was particularly sad. He pushed two fingers into my mouth, and pressed again on my tongue. "Make me some onion soup, Alexandria?" he asked, less a question than a cue to resume my program.

It didn't require an answer and I did not give one.

~

As the Cat, the meadow felt as wide and dense as a country, although I could cross it in two hundred paces as Alexandria. My sight was not acute in the orange dusk. But should I be spotted, I would be seen only as the Kleinfeld's jerky, arthritic Tom—one of a curious menagerie that came and went from the house.

Mongers and wives who would never dream of addressing me as Alexandria allowed the cat access to their cellars and barns. They wore down the mud between my ears and allowed me my way.

Manny once asked me if it hurt when I changed.

I could not then, and could not now, give him a satisfactory answer. My spindle reads numbers coded in the cards, and then, as if nature herself takes helm, my frame lengthens or folds and the clay forms about it. There is no pain, not as I register an injury or the hardening of dry clay.

Manny thought about that. "Do you like it?" he then asked.

I said I did not know. There was no like nor dislike, although I was best as sister-daughter. "It is what I am," I said. He frowned at that, as if I had somehow disappointed him.

Manny always asked questions of me as if I could well answer them.

This eve, as the Cat, I followed the smell of pigeons to a thick tree. Another cat, strange to me, had the nest well-stalked, but raised his tail at the sight of me—neither person nor animal—hissed, and then fled.

No matter how carefully Father studied and reproduced the behaviors of animals, I have never once deceived them.

I carried each pigeon to the basket by the back door in my mouth, three in total. They left behind a nest piled with late eggs. In the light, I would return to gather them with hands.

Back in the cottage, Father spread a cloth for me to sleep at the foot of his bed rather than await me to re-program. Kneading down a comfortable place, I curled up, gears winding down until they finally switched off, a high clear moon through the window.

Dawn brought the Christian Sabbath day, Father turned my key and fed me the sister-daughter program. Father would continue my new programs; I would attend church alone.

Even as Father was a Jew and Mother had been no believer, they raised Manny in the town Episcopal church and attended with regularity equal to the other townsfolk. This gave them nothing to spy or fear in us, queer as they found us in other ways.

I have also concluded after the carriage accident that took Mother to G-d and the good use Father's legs, there was a comfort to the ritual, to the fellowship, however forced.

Father wet down my clay, combed me free of dirt and sticks as I rearranged into Alexandria and then into my best dress. Father worried my hat down over my face. He hated to send me alone, but a total absence would compel neighborly visits and polite inquiries. He fed me two cards of answers if someone asked for news, but no one would of me.

The townsfolk were not even sure I spoke their language, with my queer earthen skin, the pitiable E-gyptian orphan Father adopted during his stay at Cambridge – so I was told – and although they smiled at me in the opening of service, none would shake my hand afterward and I was always obliged to sit well in the back.

Before service, the townsfolk offered me wide berth into the church, and urged me, not by expressions or gestures, but by a wavelet of bodies and hats moving around me, to the seat at the far end of the far pew. The Reverend made remarks on the War that I could not follow from the back, over the crinkling of the newspapers used to fluff out the Sabbath day bustles of the Ladies, and I was quite lost until the Reverend led us in the hymn, "Blest be the tie that binds Our hearts in Christian love."

On the way out, I stood in the receiving line to prove a Kleinfeld had been there, but no one looked at me.

Home again, I stripped the birds of their meat and smoked the flesh in strips. I saved their feathers for pillow fillings; economy was a logic I had developed and stored in memory. Then, I baked unleavened breads with the pigeon eggs and the remainder of wheat flour; simple calculations indicated how much food Father required per day. But, I was unsure the duration of my forthcoming trip.

Father tapped at cards with his stylus while I cooked. He stopped only to wheel about for a book, his long finger dragging down the page, or to eat meals I set down before him or drink his tea. He was so busied he hardly noticed when I poured own untouched repasts to the hearty flowers on my own.

~

Three days and three nights passed. In the heat of the day, I worked on the gardens around the cottage, picking much of the summer harvest, a wide hat protecting my mud from drying out. I picked and then pickled. By night, brought home catches made as the Cat two nights, and Raccoon the last.

On the morning of the third day, I stooped before the mounds of alpine strawberries Mother had planted and loved. They grew into a tight mass, and to find the small bright fruits required full attention. I did not see or hear anyone approach until he already called out to me.

"Girl," called a husky voice. "Girl. Are you alone?"

I looked to the meadow whence the voice had come, and there, squatting among the tall grasses, was a man, face dark and dry and pocked as bark beneath a hat. He looked at me with handsome eyes.

"My Father is inside the house," I answered. "But there is no one else about."

The man waved behind him, and he was joined by two other figures: women, one dark as he, the second, the same earthen as I, a fine baby latched at her breast, kicking tiny, marvelous feet. "I reckon it's safe," he said to them, then looked back at me. "Where are we?"

"Are we safe?" asked the darker woman. "Are we free?"

"This is my Father's land," I said.

At that, the four came closer to me. They were dirty and smelled as if they had recently been wet.

"Is this still Virginia?" the dark woman asked.

"Of course, it ain't Virginia," the man said. "If her Father owns land."

My spindle clicked into memory storage. "No," I said. "This is Mary-land."

The adults whooped at that, and the baby unlatched for a second but gave no cry.

"Girl, do you have any food? Milk for the baby? Some water for washing?" the man asked.

"We do," I answered, as my program resumed and I stooped for strawberries.

The three watched me work for a few moments, then the man, close now, tapped by shoulder. "May we have some? The food and milk?"

My spindle clicked, but I found no information. We did provide supplies to neighbors, but I had never before seen any of these individuals.

"We will have to ask my Father," I said. I spun the gardening cards down, and walked them to the door.

Before we reached the top step of the porch, Father had wheeled himself out, his shotgun across his lap. I heard the soft brown woman exclaim, "He's white!" just as Father was instructing them to move along. "I wish you no harm," Father said, "But we have nothing here for you. If you go now, there will be no trouble."

The man had his hat in his hands, and he looked at it and turned it over and over as Father had the letter. "We ain't escaped, Sir. We're freed, we have papers. We just come over the river and need a little food, and some milk for the baby. My wife hasn't been making any—"

Father cocked the shotgun and laid it on his shoulder. He squinted down the barrel, and then placed it across his lap. "We'll give it," Father said. "Come around back."

The man squeezed his hat, then placed it back onto his head as he motioned to the women. The four of them backed around the house.

"Give them something to eat, Alexandria. And milk for the baby. But don't let them inside and mind no one sees you." Father squinted across the meadow. "Then, send them away."

I prepared the guests a plate of the pigeon, unleavened bread, and sliced parsnips from the garden. There was just a little milk, and I gave all we could into a jar. Sometime ago, I'd stored that sugared milk was good for thin babies, so I heaped in a spoon from the tea service.

I brought it out to the four, squatting down by the back door.

The man took the plate and jar and distributed it. The mother dipped her finger in the sweet milk and dribbled it into the baby's mouth.

"Thank you, girl," the man said.

"I do as my Father directs," I said.

"Directs? Father?" The man shook his head. "Girl, that man ain't your Father." He moved closer to me. "I thought there was no slavery in Mary-land. All your boys are fighting for our side in the War. But, girl, you a slave."

I looked at him. I could not locate any information about 'slavery' or 'slave.' I logically determined I could not, therefore, be involved in either. "That is not true," I said.

The man chewed thoughtfully at his strip of pigeon. "Think what you want, girl, but we saw you picking that fruit." The man picked up a shard of bread. "Not that we ain't grateful, but we saw how he held that shotgun. If he directs you..." The man shook his head. "He may be kind to you, not beat you or nothing like that. But, he tells you to work, you work. He tells you to sleep, you probably do that. And one day," the man waved his hand at me, "he gonna tell you when to die." He finished and waited for me to answer.

This required a response, but I did not have one.

"Girl, you could come with us." He leaned in. "You can come, girl. You look strong. We're gonna get to New York, and you come with us." He motioned to the baby, who had begun wailing softly. "My boy," he said. He's gonna live free. And so could you."

"You need to leave when you are finished," I said.

~

If I liked anything, I liked cooking, understood cooking. I stirred the small blood red strawberries as they melted from their form into jam, until I wound down and had to rock back and forth.

Father wound me up, and watched me stir again.

I still had not been able to logically conclude anything from the man's conversation. "Father," I asked. "That man told me there was no slavery in Mary-land. That our boys were fighting on his side in the War." The berries were done so I set them aside to cool. "What did he mean about the War? Is this the War Manny fights? What is slavery?"

Father sighed. He wheeled himself across the kitchen, passing the shotgun which had not been replaced to the wall. "It is the same War. And the answer is… complex," he answered. "There are a number of reasons our boys fight. The needs of an industrial and simple society have clashed. Citizens hold different beliefs about fundamental ideas, such as what it means to be a union." He paused, as if revealing a great secret. "And whether slavery is moral."

"What is slavery?"

"A peculiar institution," Father said. "In some parts of our country, Africans and dark-skinned peoples are owned. They live, work and die, all according to the whims of their masters."

I still had questions. But, Father then wheeled towards me, motioned for me to stoop, and then pressed his fingers on my tongue, twice, to shut me off.

~

The morning of the fourth day, Father called me in from my keeping and held forth two sets of newly minted cards.

"I haven't yet finished the third set; the most important of them," Father said, feeding the cards into my mouth through to the spindle. "However, this holds Manny's letter to us, along with some basic information so you can place in its context." With a finger, he turned my spindle, and fed in the second set.

"This second one," he continued, "is a new shape for you. It's a horrible beast. But most useful as a mode of travel." Father shut my mouth and allowed my gears to pick up and read the cards.

My form began to change. I dropped to all fours as my head drew itself into an oval. With an exclamation, Father leaned forward with force and pressed into my mouth to give me pause. "Heavens!" he exclaimed. "Your dress." He unbuttoned the back seam and tugged me free of it, with the gentleness due a newborn, then reset my tongue.

I finished the transformation into the Horse. As I did, the terrible meaning and consequence of both Manny's letter and my shape was clear. I stamped my feet in consternation and the words echoed inside my head:

Dearest Father,

Having a slim chance to send a line, I am hoping it will reach you in safety. If so, young Charles made it alive; I rejoice this bully corporal who has served well to return to his wife and small boy. And no need to explain, as Charles has informed you, we were taken in May – in Virginia, we got in a trap – and we have seen hard times since.

The Johnnies took all we had, and marched us to Camp Sumter, tho it is no camp, and ought be known by its rightful name, Andersonville Prison.

It is a close place, maybe all ten acres, with countless men, but even more of lice and vermin. It is G-dforsaken country, all around either mud or dust, only split by a creek of filth, too greasy to touch or drink. You would not know me: I have grown black as Alexie from the pine knot smoke.

I am glad of the vermin on the days I draw no rations or rations of only cow peas or molding rice. Yet, I am better off than most; my reading and writing proves me useful to my captors, so I have a leaning shelter which leaks but stands, and a cup and spoon for my own.

It is a blessing. Many men die of exposure before the starvation – there are nearly one hundred today stacked to be carried to the dead house.

I shan't know if I shall be able to get another letter out. Messengers and paper are dear to come by. There may be of no use in getting me a letter, for it will never be delivered.

Oh, that we may one day be relieved. There is talk of Deliverance, but there is always talk.

I hope to get out of this confederacy to the better land of home. Thoughts you revive my spirits. G-d keep us until we are together again, in this world or the next,

With love,

Emmanuel

As the Horse, I could only stamp again, and whinny a bit. I very much felt like rearing, but concluded that would do no good but to distress Father. I moved about the meadow, clumsily. I would need practice in this form, large and heavy, and although the cards gave me in the information needed for a good walk, my gears were sharp and there was too long a pause shifting left front leg to right hind leg. I did the length of the meadow several times to grind down the problematic cogs.

Manny once asked me if there were limits to the shapes I could take. I said there should not be, logically; if it could be dreamt or designed, beast or myth, I could be programmed. Although, it was a long process. It took Father many months to write a program from scratch. He prided himself on the reproduction of nature, and the considerate use of controls.

But Manny liked to dream. One day, he stole away some of the virgin cards from Father's box, and poked them full of holes with a sharpened stick. His fingers were clumsy feeding them onto my spindle, and he dropped many. He held onto my chest to keep me steady, but in his concentration didn't hear Father wheeling into the room.

Father roared at Manny. He pulled the cards from Manny's hands, and fished the few from my mouth. The cards were bent, but Father smoothed them to look. "These are unreadable," he chastised Manny. "Do you understand what would happen?" In anger, Father threw the cards to the ground and wheeled his chair over them. "She is not to be played with. She is not a toy."

Manny sulked. "Then," he asked, "what is she?"

That day, Father pushed my tongue twice to turn me off before he answered.

My gait became smoother through the afternoon. Although my clock indicated the passing of the luncheon hour, Father did not come to take me in. Instead, I paced, then ran, testing the limits of my long, thin legs until a figure appeared at the top of the hill.

Apparently, my church visit did not prevent all idle curiosity. I recognized the countenance of the Reverend Simmons' wife. A basket was tucked beneath her arm; when she approached, I smelled pastry and cherries beneath a freshly laundered linen napkin.

"Whoa, whoa," Mrs. Simmons said to me as I walked alongside her. She reached out her hand to pat my mane, when Father wheeled himself to the porch.

"Hallo, Mr. Kleinfeld! A beautiful mare," Mrs. Simmons called to Father. "Although her coat is unlike any I have encountered. Quite unusual."

"Good afternoon, Mrs. Simmons," Father answered. "The horse is not ours. We are watching her for an acquaintance. I know nothing of horses in general, and less of her breed. But, yes, I suspect that she is unique to her kind."

"Indeed," Mrs. Simmons said. "I recall you do not care for horses." Then she appeared to remember why this would be true, and blushed. She held a pale hand to her cheek. "That was terribly thoughtless of me to say. I beg your pardon."

"No matter," Father answered. He shielded his eyes with a hand. "What brings you out to-day?"

"We did not see you in church," she said.

"Alexandria was there," Father said. "I felt grippe, although I am quite recovered."

"Indeed," Mrs. Simmons said. She looked about her, and then asked, "Where is your Alexandria?"

"Out and about, I expect," Father answered. "She has been keeping the garden."

"Ah," Mrs. Simmons answered. She held up the basket. "We've ourselves a glut of cherries from our trees, so I hope you'll permit me to leave you this pie. We've many more than we could possibly enjoy." She walked to the edge of the porch but held to the pie. "I hoped you'd had news of Emmanuel?"

"None good," Father said. "Have you had news of Gerald?"

"A letter," she said. "Brought just this other day. It appears his Calvary unit has been relieved. He expects to be home again soon."

"That's excellent news," Father said. His tone quietly reiterated that her news was good while ours' had not.

Father and Mrs. Simmons waited in silence for a few moments, and then Mrs. Simmons appeared to remember the basket on her arm. She placed the pie on Father's lap and stood next to him, looking out at the gardens and my silent horse. "The roses look awful fine," she said. "Alexandria must be a comfort." Mrs. Simmons folded up the linen napkin and placed in back into her basket. "It is a glad thing our boys fight for, for folks like Alexandria." With that, she nodded her leave. She stopped to pat the Horse again on her way. "I'll pray for an end to this awful rebellion and for your Emmanuel," she called to Father. "That he comes home soon and safe."

"Please do," Father answered. "Please do."

~

Father had removed my sister-daughter cards when he had placed in the Horse cards, and after Mrs. Simmons left, seemed to forget me entirely. Even as I stood by the parlor window, rocking back and forth to stay wound, making frightful racket, Father hunched over his desk; Mrs. Simmons' pie sat untouched.

My clock ticked to suppertime, then dinner, breakfast, and luncheon. The sun grew high and hot; I whinnied for Father's attention, then splashed water from the creek clumsily across the cracking clay of my huge body—then I huddled beneath the apple tree to keep the moisture. Finally, Father wheeled onto the porch and called out for me.

He could not look in me as his arm, to the elbow, reached into my muzzle and retrieved the cards, replacing them again with my beloved program. But he did watch me change, out in the open, in full view of G-d, into Alexandria. He held an expression I had never seen; careworn, disinterested, as if he were watching nothing more than the crackling of a fire or a drip of water. He motioned for me to sit.

I waited for him to hand me a frock to cover myself, but when he did not, I simply sat as directed. It was of no logic to mind if Father did not mind.

"I've finally completed the last program," he said. He spoke like a man occupied elsewhere.

He did not produce the cards for me, so instead I broached the subject that had plagued me whilst the horse. "What did the good Mrs. Simmons mean?"

"Eh?" Father asked.

"During her visit. As the Horse, I heard her say I was a comfort."

"You do provide much comfort," Father said.

"And a fine reason to fight the War." Gears turned.

"There is no time for this," Father said. He weakly turned his chair around; he had overworked himself and seemed quite fragile. "Come," he said. "Let's go inside to my desk."

The surface was strewn with cards, some half-punched and crumpled, others scrawled with notes. A tall stack stood beside an unfamiliar box. Father laid one hand atop a pile of notes on his desk. "Each day Manny remains a prisoner may be his last day."

We have seen hard times since.

"Many have sacrificed for this war." Father looked down at his legs. "But we have sacrificed enough for one lifetime."

Many men die of exposure before the starvation.

"I will not sacrifice my son to these causes."

There may be of no use in getting me a letter, for it will never be delivered.

"You must go this camp, Alexandria," Father said. "You must free him."

There is talk of Deliverance, but there is always talk.

"I have completed the last program," Father said. He picked up the strange box, which turned out to be a hard leather case—still unfamiliar—an old trouser belt tacked across the back as a carry strap. He offered the case to me by the strap. "Inside this case, you'll find the equipment you'll need."

I took the case. It was heavier than it appeared.

Father gathered the tall stack of cards that stood beside the case. He gestured for me to come close to be fed the program. "And on these will be all you'll need to know. And understand." He had to set the cards onto my spindle a few at a time and manually turn it to accommodate all the cards. "G-d help us all."

Inside, my gears turned, serving the data to the switches and clocks and cogs and spindles that read the information contained. There were many more cards than I was accustomed to; Father watched and worried over me as the process began. I stretched out my arms and legs and waited for the change.

I wriggled my fingers and my toes; there was no reason to. It was only that I could.

I could be anything I wanted. Alexandria, the Cat, the Goose or Horse, a Demon or Thunderbird. "What has happened to me?" I asked.

"Sit down," Father instructed me.

I did. I did not have to, but I did. The case lay on my lap.

"When I was a child, my father told me stories," Father said. "He told me of a Golem created to avenge the Jews of Prague. The

119

Golem was constructed of virgin soil and ground water, and sacred words. He was inscribed with the letter '*emet*.'"

"Life," I said, from the Hebrew in my memory storage.

"Yes," Father answered, then continued. "The Golem was controlled through instructions, written on parchment and slipped beneath the tongue." Father allowed me a few seconds to process.

"I am a Golem?"

"Not exactly," Father said. "When I was a young man at Cambridge, I had a teacher who believed that, given enough time and detail, an engine can reproduce down to the finest detail the machinations of life. He never realized his work."

"But you did."

"I have."

Inside, I made a whirring noise I had no memory of ever producing.

And I could access every single memory.

"These cards," he said. "These cards are a map to your very soul, if you will. Your storage data and program data, input and output components, memory and decision trees, logical flows, and the parameters required to perform instruction-based operations. They allow you to fully access your memory. And evaluate them." He looked at me. "I cannot know the trials you will face. And I cannot come with you." He pointed to the case. "With these, you'll be able to face whatever you must. Even death."

"*Met*," I said. Death. The difference between life and death in Hebrew was only a single letter. A single punch in a single line on a single card.

"You will bring Emmanuel home," Father said.

I set down the case and stood up. The jam was cooling. I stirred it and my gears turned and memories played before my eyes. I was proud of the roses and the garden, which had flourished beneath my hands. The sugar in the milk would help grow that infant, too, I thought, and as I did, I began to pour the jam into readied jars.

"You will bring him, no matter what," Father said. "Alexandria, look at me."

I did not. I looked at the jam. The red berries looked so much like the insides of men from Father's books. I wondered what my insides looked like.

"Look at me," Father repeated.

I pushed down hard on the jam jar lids to make a good seal. "Father," I said. "Am I a slave?"

Father seemed surprised at the question. "No," he said. "Of course not."

I thought of the Horse, stamping my feet as dried mud flaked off and blew away as dust. I sang so loudly in church, I realized, because someone should turn to see me. I remembered Emmanuel's fingers in my mouth, but also on a breast, pinching it, only stopping after Father admonished, "She isn't to play with. She isn't a toy."

And Manny asked then, "What is she?"

"I am dark-skinned," I said. "I carry out your will."

"You are something else entirely," Father said.

"I sit in the back," I said. "They sat in the back."

"There is not time for this. I have given you all that you need. You will bring him home, Alexandria." Father paused. "Won't you?"

"I need to know this first."

"Won't you?' he repeated.

I turned from the jam to look at him now. "Father," I tried again. "Am I a slave?"

The Clockwork Caesar
Alan Smale

I: 204 A.D.

Geta and Julia raced through the back alleys of Rome as wolves, sleek and bright, snarling but full of joy. Turning into the Via Cassia neck and neck, the light of dawn in their pelts, they ran towards the iron-studded door of the Domus Septimii. The giant door scraped open on its hydraulics just in time, the waiting door-slave leaping aside as the ferals surged past.

In the hallway Geta barged Julia, sending her asprawl in a yowling ball of fur and teeth and tail. She barked, furious, gleeful, wishing that her bark held more of a boom, less of a yap. That would come, in time.

All things came and went, in time.

The ticking of the clockwork, the tapping of the gears...

Catching Geta, she nipped his leg. He skated on the marble floor of the atrium, crashed straight through the ferns in their flowerpots and tumbled into the pool in the atrium's center. At the gigantic splash, carp scattered in all directions.

They both felt the moon set, like the draining of a glass of golden wine.

Geta sat up in the pool, a young man now, and naked. Julia, immediately bashful, pushed herself upright onto two legs and sprinted for the bedrooms.

Laughing, Geta let her go and measured his length in the pool.

She came back quickly, wrapped in a robe. She did not want to miss a single moment of this, the end of their last magical night together as ferals.

"You stink of wolf," he said.

"And you reek of pond slime."

Geta pulled himself out of the water and perched in front of the family shrine, with its *lares* and *penates*, the golden figures of their ancestors, the death mask of their grandfather in human form, and the wooden carving of Romulus and Remus suckling from the great she-wolf's teats.

Julia took his hand, squeezed. "I love you, brother."

"Oh, stop."

"But it's over now. No more."

"Who knows?" He shrugged and looked away. "Maybe not."

But she knew. She could almost hear the clockwork that marked the hour, the week, the phase of the moon, the passing of the year. Just for a moment, she wished she could still the remorseless passage of time.

"Gods, Geta… Please? Just for me?"

And Geta knew her well enough, and they had talked around this enough, that he understood. *Tell the truth. Just for me.* "Yes." He turned to meet her eyes, and she saw his pain. "That must be the last time for me."

Next full moon, Julia would run alone.

"I love you too," he said and she blinked, her eyes hot.

Another wolf stalked down the hallway behind them. In feral form Caracalla's fur was almost black, and blood stained his teeth and muzzle. He regarded Julia and Geta unblinking, and then padded on towards his bedroom cubicle at the back of the atrium. He turned human and flauntingly naked as he passed through the door. Caracalla was resilient enough in his feral power to stay wolfen long beyond the dawn.

Geta had not turned. His gaze lay on the silver dagger on the shelf below the *lares*. "Strong, our brother." His hand slipped out of hers.

Strong, and always capable of ruining their mood.

"Wait," she said, but Geta stood abruptly. "I should get dressed. I must write to Father, summon Galen and Diogenes," he grinned without humor, "and set the gears in motion."

~

The dining room was full of her father's Greeks, which meant it was also full of the *pneumatica* and *automata* that they brought along to show off, and echoed with a barrage of chirps, clanks, and hisses. And under it all, beneath the mechanical sounds, boasting conversation and self-indulgent laughter, she could hear the gentle hum of their clockwork.

Julia did not like Greeks much, and especially not the ones who would be cutting into her brother's flesh within the month. They swarmed around Geta, fawning and trying to curry favor. None of them had as much as turned when Julia entered. She was just a girl. It was Geta who would soon take his manly gown and his clockwork; Geta who, if he could stay alive long enough, might become Emperor one day.

For all the huff and shout of the steam boilers and clacking mechanisms and animated figures, it was the smaller creations that Julia adored. Especially the astronomical mechanism made by the clockwork masters of Rhodes, which sat in the center of the back wall on its own carved table. It was a rectangular bronze box a little larger than a writing tablet, standing on its end, and through its open sides Julia could see three dozen gears mostly smaller than her thumbnail.

Instructions were engraved on it in Greek, but she knew the mechanism well enough. The device told the phases of the Moon and the positions of the five planets with uncanny precision. It was over two hundred years old and predated steam; you changed the date and time with a small hand crank, and the gears did the rest. Her father, the Emperor Septimius Severus, had paid over fifty thousand sesterces for the finely carved cypress table that it sat on. The Mechanism of Poseidonios was worth immeasurably more.

Next to it, on a cushion of velvet, sat her brother's clockwork. It was brand new and smaller than her palm, but still made of bronze and packed with gears. These gears would be driven by the beating of Geta's heart, and would release the tiny quantities of the humors that would quell the wolf in her brother forever.

Without the clockwork, he risked turning forever feral. In their late teen years came the change; half of them would become human, the wolf fading as if it had never ruled them. The other half would fix permanently in wolf form, losing their humanity. No one could tell ahead of time which way the coin would fall.

It was too much for a sane man to risk, if he were rich enough to avert it. And so this clockwork would be embedded in Geta's chest, in a delicate operation that would last hours. Once in place, any attempt to remove it would kill him.

Julia felt a sudden wild urge to sweep it from the table and smash it underfoot.

"A wonderful apparatus, no?"

Perhaps Diogenes sensed her antipathy for the clockwork, because he had arrived by her side in seconds. Julia did not smile. "Truly remarkable."

"And what do you think of *that* one?"

Diogenes was pointing at his newest piece, an *automata* that used hot water, pipes and gears to fire an arrow from a full-sized silver archer at a deer.

"Well, it's delightful, naturally. When will you...?" She gestured at Geta's clockwork.

"The Emperor and your brother must decide, but the most auspicious day will be seven days hence."

Diogenes knew as well as she that no response could arrive from her father within the week. Severus was campaigning in distant Parthia, as he had been for years. It was really down to Geta, and to this man.

And in a few years Julia would need Diogenes to install her own clockwork.

"How wonderful. Truly, we live in an age of miracles and genius." She pushed her hair away from her eyes and smiled, and despite himself, Diogenes smiled back.

You old goat. Next full moon, I should tear your throat out.

She knew she wouldn't.

"Ah, the gathering of fools."

Their brother Caracalla, of course, making his grand entrance. Already joint Emperor with their father, known to the people by his birth name of Antoninus, Caracalla was fierce, not to be trusted.

As one, the Greeks moved towards the table where the Mechanism of Poseidonios and Geta's clockwork lay. Caracalla's feelings on both were well known.

"Oh, don't fear. If my brother really wants you to stick that in him—or anything else—who am I to say him nay?" Even now, Caracalla seemed wolf-like. His appearance was all human, but he had the body language of the animal. The feral burned strongly in him.

Caracalla was older than Geta by a year, older than Julia by four. He had taken his manly gown but refused the clockwork. Soon nature would choose; Caracalla would fix in one form, either wolf or man—and in his case no one really doubted which it would be.

Geta sauntered across the room to stand by Julia and Diogenes. "Brother. You honor us with your presence."

Caracalla laughed. "Really, I don't." He gestured for a cup of wine and a slave girl ran to him, though every nerve in her body clearly strained to run the other way. Caracalla eyed the girl thoughtfully, and she dropped her gaze and backed away.

A history there, Julia realized, and hated her brother even more. Caracalla took what he wanted, all too often.

"We are here to celebrate Geta," she said, "and if you are not willing to be nice, you should not have come."

Ignoring her, Caracalla approached Geta. "You think that I will take the wolf, never to return, and you will become Emperor. It will not happen, little brother. I will control the wolf and be the best of both, and I will rule in Rome."

"You will not." Diogenes bowed, but stood firm. "You will become either a man or a wolf, and that will be the end of it."

Caracalla regarded Diogenes with even more insolence than he had shown the slave girl, but said nothing.

"I truly hope you are right, brother," said Geta, "but I fear that you are wrong."

Caracalla smiled, all teeth and scorn. "You think you are wise. It's quite endearing."

"About some things, I am wise. About others... I am wise enough to know that I am ignorant."

Now Caracalla laughed, his eyes beginning to sparkle from the wine. How handsome he was, thought Julia. How the masses adored him, how Rome would love to be ruled by such a man, once her father died.

And how much more noble Geta would be, as Emperor, if he got the chance.

She calmed herself. All things came, in time. Caracalla could not resist the beast within him forever. And when the wolf came for good, Caracalla's hateful personality would drain away as if it had never been.

"Well, then. The day you find you were ignorant about *this*, run fast." Caracalla leaned into his brother, and bared his teeth. "Very, very fast."

~

127

Julia was not allowed in the room when Galen and Diogenes inserted Geta's clockwork. For the whole three hours she prowled the cloisters, pacing with a predatory intensity quite the equal of her feral self.

She heard screams, of course. No draughts of wine or crushed poppy juice could dull the pain of the knife entirely.

Caracalla was as quiet on human feet as he was on paws. When Julia turned he was almost within arm's reach. She jumped away. "Brother. If you've come to sneer, you can screw yourself. I'm not in the mood."

"I came to talk to you." Caracalla shrugged. "Geta is nothing. His day is done. Now he will be neither wolf nor man, but a tame temple pussycat."

"A cat can have claws," said Julia.

"Tell me you will not do this. Tell me that when your time comes, you will stay strong."

"That I will reject the gears of the Greeks?"

He stood back to admire her. "Look at you now. Magnificent. Young and fiery. A splendid creature of blood and bile, whether girl or wolf. A true Severan, like me. Take the clockwork and you might as well have been born Greek."

"Is our father weak, then?"

Septimius Severus had claimed the Empire a decade ago through brute force. Rome had fallen in panic before his legions had even arrived. After that, decisive wars against the Imperial pretenders Pescennius Niger in Syria and Clodius Albinus in Gaul had cemented Severus' position as the tyrant of the age.

"Our father is different. A rare man. He has kept the power of the wolf even when the wolf itself is neutered by the clockwork." He paused. "I, too, am such a man. But I inherited our father's strength *and* our mother's, and I will control the wolf without the clockwork. You can too." He leaned forward and she felt his breath hot on her forehead. "Let us be wolves together in this henhouse, until our pelts are dripping in blood."

Another scream of pain came from the triclinium. In there, her brother was stretched out on a table like a feast, dripping blood of his own.

"You're mad," she said tightly. "Go away."

"Very well. For now." Caracalla bowed in mock ceremony.

He strode off down the hallway. With a hiss of steam and a grating of grit and gears, the front door opened automatically for him. In moments Caracalla was gone, out into the busy streets of Rome.

"The new Romulus." Julia's lips twitched. "Gods help us."

~

By dusk the cutting and sewing were over, and Julia was allowed in. Geta lay on a bier, pale as death, bruises under his eyes and all down his arms, the stitches in his chest and side covered with bloody linen. He managed a woozy smile for her before the poppy took him under again.

She confronted Galen and Diogenes. "It is done?"

The Greeks nodded, and Galen added, "Your brother will live and die a man."

Just a man. She perched by Geta and stroked his hair. Never again would he wear fur and run the Roman streets or Campanian countryside by night. No more would they fight and roll and play and hunt together.

She was truly alone now.

~

She saw the change in Geta at once. Never strong-willed or aggressive, the clockwork calmed Geta still further. The hot humors, blood and yellow bile, had been quenched altogether. The cold humors, the black bile of melancholia and the phlegm of rationality, now dominated him.

Perhaps Caracalla had been right after all.

~

On the three nights of the next full moon the streets of Rome teemed with young wolves. The usual night-time creaking of carts was replaced by the howls of impromptu packs as they scoured the streets for the chickens and pigs and goats the people put out to feed them and prevent even further damage and raiding. The Fora were alive with snarling and baying.

On the first night Julia ran wild with a pack, but felt alone and empty without her brother by her side. And the next morning she found out about the giant black wolf that had attempted to breach the Domus Septimii, attacking the slaves that stood between it and the still-convalescing Geta.

The next night she stayed by Geta, prowling back and forth, driven almost to a frenzy by the sounds of the rampage outside but held back by love and loyalty. By midnight her agitation had driven Geta mad, and he threw her out into the streets himself.

On the third dawn, Julia returned to the Domus to find the iron-studded door already open and unguarded.

She streaked down the hallway, foam in her jaws, resisting the setting of the moon. For whatever she was to find, she might need all her wolf-strength.

Sure enough, here was Caracalla in wolf-form with his hackles up and growling, ready to spring, and Geta standing beyond him with sword drawn.

But as Julia surged forward to defend him, soldiers poured from the shadows. Caracalla sent the first three soldiers flying before the rest took him down by sheer force of numbers. Pinned at arms, legs and muzzle, Caracalla changed. Fur retreated, claws disappeared. He became a man, though still hairy and fierce for all that, and if anything the soldiers took even grimmer hold of him.

Behind them, Julia changed too and stood shaking until a soldier threw her a robe.

Caracalla laughed through ragged lips. "And so this is it, brother? Death? This is how you will ensure your proclamation as Emperor? You think our father will love you for murdering me? Our mother? Our sister? End my life, and you end your own."

Geta stepped forward at last, shaking his head. "I, in the purple? How poorly you know me. I am not going to rule, brother. As you advised, I am going to run."

Caracalla stopped trying to unseat the men who trapped his limbs. "Then why am I on the floor?"

"Because, as our father has commanded, I am going to give you to the Greeks."

It was not Diogenes or Galen who stepped forward then. It was a Greek that Julia did not recognize, whom she knew she would not see again, because once this deed was done he, too, would have to run.

In one hand he held a scalpel. In the other, the gears of the Greeks.

Caracalla's eyes grew wide, and he again began to tug and thrash. "You would dare? You would *dare*?"

Geta smiled thinly. "From Parthia, the Emperor bids you take the clockwork. Voluntarily, or not. I have it in writing."

"Why? Disobey, and you could have it all. If you're right, I'll become a wolf, and you'll become Emperor."

"Because Rome needs a strong Emperor, a ruthless Emperor. My father has that strength. So do you. I do not."

"You do!" Still quivering with the shock of her transition back to human, Julia stalked forward and shouted up into his face. "Damn you, you do!"

Geta gaped at her, stunned.

"Kill Caracalla," she said. "Kill him dead, right now, as he would have killed you. If you don't, I will."

Julia did not even see Geta's gesture, but moments later soldiers were pulling her away.

Geta gestured to the Greek and stood back. "No more talk. Do it now."

~

II: 213 A.D.

Onagers bucked and steam cannons roared, but the horde of Maeatae and Caledonians still surged towards them. The first row of Roman soldiers hurled their pila, and on the centurions' command the second rank marched through, their own spears in hand, to meet the foe.

The woad-pasted barbarians of northern Britannia had managed a trick that Rome had not: the allying of men and wolves into a single giant army. Perhaps for them family bonds ran deeper, and survived the fixing of half their men into wolf form at adulthood. Or perhaps the tribes beyond the wall of Hadrian were closer to feral at the best of times.

The battle was hard-fought but inevitable. By mid-afternoon, the clanking machines of steam and steel drove the men and wolves of Caledonia from the field.

On a hill to the rear stood Geta, surrounded by his adjutants. Trumpets relayed his commands to the farthest edges of the *Legio VI Victrix*, but for the most part, his tribunes and centurions had known what to do.

A messenger arrived, a freeman called Rufinus. "Your sister is here."

After so long at battle, saturated with positions and numbers and details of terrain, Geta's mind went blank. "My what?"

"The lady Julia Septimia Octavilla."

"Julia? Here on the battlefield?"

Rufinus shook his head. "Back at the fortress at Luguvalium, sir. Do you wish to return ahead of the Legion?"

He might have done. Having subdued this group of Maeatae and their Caledonian allies, Geta could have left the withdrawal to his tribunes. But perhaps it was just as well to take the extra hours to prepare. The thought of seeing his sister again after all these years was a prospect almost as fearsome as the mass of baying Caledonians.

~

"As he died our father named Caracalla and I joint Emperors, and here I am useful to the Empire."

Ironically, Geta was one of the few generals Caracalla could trust not to march on Rome and attempt to capture the purple for himself.

"He has not forgiven me, you know. He is merely biding his time."

Geta had the backing of the three British legions, and thirty-five thousand auxiliaries and ten thousand cavalry in addition. And he also had the sympathies of certain legates in Gaul and Tarraconensis. Emperor Caracalla had the fierce loyalty of legions on the Rhine and Danube. He could fight in Germania and Parthia to his heart's content, but he could never come north. War between the brothers would destroy the Empire.

"If I stay here, I am unassailable. Why would I come to Rome?"

Julia unfolded herself from the camp chair and stood. Dressed as a Roman lady in full *stola* and *palla*, with her face powdered and eyes calm, she was a different creature indeed from the impetuous wolf-girl he remembered.

"To be reconciled," she said patiently. "Caracalla wants the Empire united again. Without bloodshed."

Geta made a wordless sound of disbelief.

"Geta, he has already made a proclamation to the people of Rome acknowledging you as joint Emperor." It was the first time. "He has ratified you through the Senate. He has had new coins minted, bearing both your profiles. Would you like to see one?"

"No."

"If you come he will send priests, Vestal Virgins, and senators to meet your army, as signs of good faith. He will hold a festival in your honor. Three days and two nights."

Geta shook his head. "When? What terms?"

"March south. Arrive at Rome in time for Lupercalia. Caracalla will greet you publicly from the steps of the Temple of Venus. You are popular in Rome too, you know—or rather, Caracalla is less popular than he would like. Public treachery would provoke a mass riot."

"Hmm."

"He asks that you change into civilian dress at the Flaminian Gate. Lay down your arms, but you may retain your own hand-picked honor guard of six hundred men."

"What does the Senate say?"

"The Senate welcomes the reuniting of the Empire. And they would surely welcome your good sense, hoping the reconciliation will calm Caracalla's dire moods, and bring stability."

"Stability."

"Geta, it's what our father always wanted."

Septimius Severus had died three years ago, on campaign here in Britannia. Geta had taken over the frontier, while his brother had taken Rome. "Don't bring our father into this."

"Even Caracalla won't start a war in the streets of Rome and cut down six centuries of your men to get to you."

"Rome." Geta stared past her into space, his eyes unfocused. "How is Rome?"

"Rome is great and grand," she said simply. "The new steam engines everywhere, and the giant mechanical fountains, and the streets lit at night... Geta, don't live and die out here in this foggy marsh. Come home."

At last, she took his hand. "It is not only Caracalla who asks. I ask, too."

Geta stared at her hand. Then he pulled, hugging her to him. Through his tunic and hers, he could feel the hum in her chest. "You took the clockwork."

She sank her head onto his shoulder. "The worst day of my life. I miss the wolf."

The silence extended. Geta remembered the speed they ran on four legs, his keen sense of smell. The wild joy. His, and hers.

He couldn't lose her again.

He let her go, brushing at his eyes. "I want a publicly proclaimed amnesty to the officers and men of all legions who have been loyal to me over the years. If somehow you're wrong, I want no purges of the people who kept me alive. And I want a separate palace in Rome, with my own men around me. My own gates. No limits on when and how I can address the Senate."

"It shall be so."

His gaze swung back to her. "Really? You're not just the messenger? You're authorized to *negotiate* for our brother?"

"Yes."

"Gods." All of a sudden, Geta needed to sit. "You're that sure of him? He of you?"

"Caracalla says he feels the wolf, every day, behind a curtain in his mind. He knows he would be an empty, wild creature now, if not for you. He says he was a foolish child who would have thrown his life away."

"Caracalla said that? And you believe it? Truly?"

"I don't know," she admitted. "We have not spent much time together since your banishment. But he does appear... changed. And there have been portents. Pairs of male doves seen flying over Rome. Twin shooting stars falling from the skies near the City. The auguries and signs all come in twos. His priests—"

"My brother never cared a fig for priests!"

Her eyes hardened. "He cares for priests more than he cares for Greeks. And so do I. But if you do not, stay here, and wade in the mud, and fight barbarians."

Eventually, Geta nodded.

~

III: 214 A.D.

On the Ides of Februarius the sacred cakes were offered by the Vestal Virgins. They sacrificed the dog and the goats, and smeared the foreheads of youths of noble birth with the blood. Drunk, naked, the young men ran through the streets around the base of the Palatine Hill, playfully flicking women with strips of goat hide to ensure their fertility.

With near half of the population doomed to take wolf form before they reached adulthood and be exterminated soon after, fertility was important to Rome as never before.

Once the Lupercalia rites were satisfied, Geta's entourage entered the city by the Flaminian gate. Geta had elected to walk rather than ride, to emphasize his humility, but the cheering crowd on the Campus Martius was so large that he and Julia had to climb into the steam chariot anyway. They processed on down the Via Flaminia, and into the Fora of the Caesars.

Rome had changed indeed. The wheezing and chuffing of the steam engines, with their obnoxious whistles, as they plied their trades in the Fora. The fountain *automata* that sprayed water in regular patterns, as the figures of stone and metal atop them swayed and gestured, powered by the *hydraulica*. To Geta's eyes it seemed that every statue and building was in motion.

Then their entourage turned slowly left into the Great Square behind the Flavian Amphitheater, and the noise got even more deafening. "Gods, what a racket!"

Before them was the Temple of Venus. On a black dais atop its marble steps Caracalla awaited them, garbed in the Imperial purple. The Emperor was already speaking, and his voice boomed out even over the clatter of the steam engine and the din of the plebs.

Daunted and a little afraid, Geta turned to Julia but could only make out a few of her words: "pneumatic... compressed air... vibrations."

The words of Caracalla were strangely distorted by the amplifying apparatus. He was proclaiming Geta, and himself: "Brothers who will rule Rome together... Our noble Father, the god Septimius Severus..."

"A god?" Geta mouthed, eyes wide. Deification was the last thing their father would have wanted.

Julia shook her head. "After I left, I swear!"

Their chariot arrived at the base of the steps, but even as they were ushered forward the booming voice of Caracalla began again. "… At his bidding I took the clockwork. Now I have grown beyond it. I reject it. Rome advances. But always we must be Romans, and to be Romans, we have to accept the wolf in us. The wolf, as well as the clockwork. Rome, I accept the wolf!" And Caracalla spread his arms as if waiting for divine approbation. The crowd hushed expectantly.

"You promised we'd be safe," said Geta, "you told me he wasn't mad." But one look at the shock on his sister's face convinced him of her innocence. There was no treachery. Julia had known nothing of this.

"What's going to happen?"

"I don't know. We should get away from here."

The crowd behind was immense. Before them was the Temple, and Caracalla's troops. Packed in alongside them were Geta's own centuries. Geta looked around, shook his head. "Oh, of course."

At that moment, Caracalla staggered as if he had been hit. He steadied himself on the chair by his side, his other hand reaching up towards the heavens.

No, not the heavens, but the Palatine Hill. Silently now, the Emperor was invoking the Gods. Or summoning them.

Caracalla bent at the waist. Fur sprouted from him. His muzzle grew. His toga rippled and fell away.

In the bright light of day, far from the time of the full moon, the Emperor of Rome was becoming wolfen.

"That's not possible."

The blood had drained entirely from Julia's face; she looked as white as Geta felt. "He's done it. The new Romulus."

"It's a trick. Smoke and mirrors." Geta's mind baulked. "An illusion. But how could steam and gears achieve such a thing?"

Anger swept him. "However he's doing this, we can't let him get away with it."

Geta stepped down from the chariot and strode up the marble steps of the Forum towards his brother.

"Geta!"

Caracalla growled. He was big, a much larger wolf than he had been as a youth. But the Imperial wolf seemed distracted, ducking his head awkwardly to bite at his own chest.

The crowd was roaring, half of them chanting "Caracalla!" and the other half "Romulus!" Geta barely heard them. On the top step he approached the giant wolf, reaching out his hand instinctively so the beast could get his scent and recognize him. "Caracalla? Antoninus?"

Geta still could not see how the trick was done, but then the raw stink of wolf reached his nose.

Caracalla *snarled*, hackles high. Momentarily dizzy, Geta steadied himself against the dais.

Then pain ballooned in Geta's chest, and he fell forward onto his hands and knees.

The beast that was Caracalla opened its jaws and reached down. Seizing Geta, the wolfen Emperor shook him like a rag doll. Blood welled around the beast's jaws where its teeth punctured Geta's arm.

The clamor of the crowd swelled. This was better than the gladiatorial games. Fights were breaking out. The Emperor had become a wolf, and the crowd was becoming a mob. The cries of "Romulus!" redoubled, and at last, Julia understood.

If Caracalla was Romulus, then Geta was Remus. And Romulus had slain his brother.

"Geta!"

Julia ran. Soldiers reached for her, trying to stop her, but she danced around them. None wanted to follow her up to the dais.

Caracalla was mauling Geta now, chunks of flesh in his mouth. Blood sprayed the white marble of the steps. Geta made no sound; he was conscious but seemed paralyzed, his one good arm still clutching his chest. Anguish soaked his face.

Even as Julia approached the dais, a wave of agony wracked her. She staggered. A heart attack? No... her clockwork. It seized and died inside her, the brass cogs suddenly stilled.

The wolf, Julia's own wolf, overwhelmed her immediately. She felt it burst deep within, passive for ten years and now a sudden howling beast that surged down her limbs and out through every inch of her skin at once. Her face contorted into a broad muzzle. She had already tumbled to the ground, tangled in her *stola*; now she writhed free, on all fours. The stench of Geta's blood filled her nose, flooding her with disgust and hunger in equal measure.

Finally Geta wailed, a long cry of torment. He was becoming a wolf too but terribly slowly, perhaps inhibited by the pain. His skin was mostly fur, his face still human.

Julia lunged. As a wolf Caracalla was twice her weight, but her sudden ferocity knocked him back. He reared, snarling, but his jaws snapped on empty air.

As Caracalla's throat was now out of reach, Julia sank her teeth into his left front leg, close to where it met his body. Trying to fight her off, Caracalla skated in Geta's blood and slid backwards off the dais.

Geta's men had drawn swords and were in pitched battle with the Emperor's Urban Cohort, trying to fight their way to Geta and Julia. Beyond them the riot between various factions of the plebs was well under way.

The ticking of the clockwork, the tapping of the gears...

Geta was free and yowling. His own blood flecked his fur and his eyes were crazed as he rolled in panic. Beneath them, Caracalla scrabbled to regain his footing and growled furiously.

Julia pounced on the Emperor just as the first of the Urban Cohort gained the top of the steps and ran towards them. Caracalla met her attack with claws and teeth and she crashed painfully back onto marble.

She turned to see an array of swords drawn against her. But behind the Emperor's men the warriors of Geta's *VI Victrix* had broken through.

Geta half-jumped, half-fell, and landed beside her. In feral form they could only communicate with eyes and intent, but it was enough.

Shoulder to shoulder once more, Geta and Julia ran into the front doors of the Temple of Venus, and through it and out the other side into the street. Turning as one, they streaked into the Forum of Vespasian. Plebs threw themselves left and right to avoid the charging wolves.

Panting, tongues lolling, the Imperial siblings vanished once again into the backstreets of Rome.

~

Dirty and naked, they sat by the Tiber, screened from the streets above by the stanchion of the Pons Fabricius. Once away from the massive lodestone in Caracalla's dais their gears had begun to move again, slowly at first. Julia had howled and then shrieked with pain, blood in her mouth and her eyes. Eventually she had passed out, and awoken, and here they were. Geta's arm and legs still wept blood. And Julia was too tired to give a fig for her nakedness.

"Geta, he needn't win. You saw. Caracalla is not universally loved. Even more will fear his madness now. You have a faction, and can win over the Senate. We can defeat him. Make you Emperor."

"I've never wanted that." Geta tossed a stone into the Tiber, and it splashed brown. "This sewer? It's not for me. To hell with Rome."

"Then what *do* you want?" But when she looked deep into his eyes, she thought she knew.

Julia put her finger onto Geta's lips, but the single word escaped anyway. "Britannia."

"Britannia?" She sat back. "Back to the rain and the bogs and the savages?"

"Rather that than *this*." He waved around him, invoking all of Rome. "Those terrible steam boilers? The engines and the noise? You and I, with the clockwork, we *hum*. Civilized. But the plebs? And our brother?"

Geta was not lucid, but she took his meaning. Her chest hurt, and not from the clockwork. "Rome is my home, Geta."

"Then stay."

She reached for him again. "I'm sorry, Geta. For believing Caracalla, coaxing you here. He was clever. Convincing. But all along, this was what he planned."

"The new Romulus." Geta laughed harshly, almost a bark.

"Well, he did defeat the gears of the Greeks."

"Yes, he did. For a while." He frowned. "The lodestone that stopped the clockwork. Caracalla's shooting star. How can we find another?"

She closed her eyes. The memory of the pain was all too vivid. "We don't want another."

"Don't we?"

"There are always shooting stars."

"Even in Britannia?"

"You're asking me, Geta?" She felt the stone of the bridge under her hands, smelled the stink of the wolf still on them, heard the hum of their clockwork.

And, despite the agony, remembered the glory of running side by side, hard and feral and wild.

Julia opened her eyes. "Maybe. All right. We'll go and see."

The Business of Ferrets
Patrick S. Tomlinson

The 'strategy meeting' took place in the dankest cellar of an abandoned warehouse on the outskirts of the city, as it always did. Colin wasn't exactly one to complain, but just once, he'd like their little group of saboteurs and psychopaths to meet somewhere respectable. Would it kill them to collaborate in a quiet corner of a little coffee shop?

Probably. The Steamers had ears everywhere; they had become very good at rooting out Moonrunner cells over the last year. Colin's handler, Whiskers, bore the scars of one such raid. He'd lost an ear escaping from a meeting in the Leopard Quarter. In human form, it made him look rugged. But he was a rabbit; a whole bevy of bunnies with one ear didn't look nearly as intimidating.

They sat around a wobbly card table stained with coffee rings. The third member of the meeting finally turned up; a panther code named Bastian. Colin had heard of him through Whiskers, but they had never met. Bastian's human form was just as dark as the black fur of his inner animal. He could see the slight pattern of spots on the man's skin. He sat, inspecting Colin with intense brown eyes.

Colin's skin wriggled under the inquisitive stare. He had nothing to hide from the man, but there was always an undercurrent among Moonrunners that reflected the nature of their forms. There had never been one united Moonrunner society before. Predators had hunted prey, as was the natural order. The Steamers arrival on their shores two centuries ago had forced them to see themselves as a single people for the first time. It had been a crossbow marriage.

Colin was a ferret, and while a predator, he was pretty far down the ladder from a panther. Whiskers, on the other hand, would have been lunch for Bastian only a few generations ago. His nervousness was palpable.

Bastian officially started the meeting, addressing Colin directly. "Whiskers vouched for your skills, which is why you were asked to come tonight. But *I* don't know you. So, enlighten me. What missions have you run for the MLA?"

The MLA, Moonrunner Liberation Army. It was only the most recent name of a dozen for the loose collection of freedom fighters, anarchists, rebels, and terrorists who claimed the cause of running the Steamers off the continent. The names and faces changed from year to year, but the paranoia was constant. Bastian was trying to trick him.

"The MLA? Never heard of it."

Bastian smiled, revealing canine teeth that seemed just a bit too long. "So, you understand operational security. Good, most flocks feel they need to boast."

'Flocks,' a derisive term for the smaller species of moonrunners, those that shifted into many bodies instead of only one as Bastian did. Many bodies, but still only one soul uniting them. Solos like the big cats and dogs made for excellent soldiers, but that wasn't the sort of war the MLA was fighting. Flocks were much better at infiltration and sabotage. All the skills Colin had spent the last year perfecting. He let the comment pass.

"What's the assignment?"

"Some background first. It's no secret that in recent months, we've lost an unacceptable number of cells to Steamer raids. But what you probably haven't heard is why we've gotten hit so hard. For many years now, we could rely on the Steamers constables to take anywhere from ten minutes to half an hour to coordinate a response, which gave our operatives time to withdraw."

Bastian paused to stretch his arms and flex his fingers, then continued. "But recently, that response time has dropped to less than five minutes everywhere in the city. Constables are on top of our agents almost as soon as they are discovered."

"Some sort of signaling system?" Colin offered.

"That's what we thought at first too. We've been using signal flares for the last two years, and we assumed the Steamers adopted the tactic. But we had crows do flyovers of every operation for an entire month; nothing."

"So, we're here talking about it. What changed?"

"One of our deep cover agents stumbled upon their signaling network, but it wasn't what we'd imagined. Buried under their streets is a series of tubes connecting every major government building and constable outpost in the city. They use air pressure to blow brass balls containing messages from one place to another."

Colin considered what he'd just heard. The infrastructure for such a system must have been massive. The Steamers had started building their city almost the moment they'd hit the shore. After two centuries, it was a sprawling metropolis, with many hundreds of government buildings and offices. It would be impossible for each position to have a tube going to every other.

"There must be some sort of central sorting room where..." Colin noticed the smile on Bastian's face and knew immediately what his assignment was to be. "You want me to go through one of the tubes and blow up the sorting room."

"Nothing quite so grandiose. We don't need it destroyed, not just yet at least. For now, all we need is a timely disruption."

"How timely?" Colin said suspiciously. "I can't exactly carry a pocket watch once I've turned."

"Down to the quarter-hour should be enough."

"And then what happens?"

Bastian shook his head. "Sorry, that's need to know, and you—"

"Yeah, yeah. What's the timetable, how long do I have to prepare?"

"Tomorrow night."

"And I assume you have a better plan on where I can enter than going to the nearest constable station and asking if they'd mind letting a business of ferrets into their super-secret message network? Does anyone even know how to operate the damned thing?"

"There are terminals in more than just the constable houses. We've found one tucked away in Our Lady of Divine Mercy Hospital. That should make penetrating security a simple affair."

Colin's nose twitched involuntarily as he thought about the mission. He would need to enter the hospital unseen, with all the tools he'd need once he got to the other side. It was a tall order, but not insurmountable.

"The hospital is a big place. I'll need to know exactly what level and what room it's in."

"Ground floor, Number 119."

"Okay. I'll need a hospital uniform, two dozen vials of the strongest acid you can find, and an 'Out of Order' sign."

Bastian looked at Whiskers. "Whiskers? Will that be a problem?"

The rabbit shifted uncomfortably in his chair under the panther's gaze, but kept his voice even. "Not really. I can get a doctor's gown simple enough, maybe even papers."

"No," Colin interrupted, "Doctors are too visible; everybody knows who they are. Just a janitor's uniform would be best."

"M'kay, no problem. But why do you want the acid?"

"Simple, I can't work flints and fuses while turned, and without knowing what the sorting room looks like, I have no idea if I'll be able to shift back unseen to use a bomb. Acid is quiet, I can use vials even with my paws, and it'll eat through almost any machinery I run across." Colin spoke to Whiskers, but looked at Bastian. He knew who was really putting the honey on his muffin. The panther nodded his approval.

"Clever. Sneak in as a janitor, no one pays you much mind, and you don't have to explain a full tool box. I'm impressed." He stood smoothly and brushed some soot from his trousers. "I'll leave the two of you to your preparations. The clock starts ticking at 1800. Don't be late. A lot of lives are counting on you."

And a lot of deaths too, if Colin had to venture a guess.

~

The next evening, Colin met up with Whiskers in an alley two blocks away from the hospital. Neither spoke. Instead, they merely made brief eye-contact as Colin exchanged his worn canvass bag filled with laundry for the nearly identical one in the rabbit's hands. Whiskers gave him a little swat on the ass as he passed by for luck.

Colin kept walking briskly away from the exchange. If his handler had done his job, everything he'd need for the next few hours would be in the bag.

A sharp horn broke his train of thought as one of the Steamer's cursed wheeled horses nearly leveled him as he crossed a cobblestone street, black smoke and white steam billowing from twin pipes at the rear. The massive rear wheel hit a puddle and splashed Colin's trousers with fetid, clammy water.

"Watch where you're going!" was the helpful advice the pilot of the contrivance shouted as he passed by.

"Works both ways, Gov!" Colin yelled in vain to the man's rapidly retreating backside. He glanced up at the massive clock tower that loomed over the city center. It could be seen clearly for miles in any direction. It served the MLA as the master clock they used to synchronize their operations. Colin wondered how long it would take the Steamers to tear it down if they ever figured out that little tidbit. Maybe never; they were an arrogant lot.

1701. There was time enough. He rounded a corner and searched for a secluded spot to inspect his kit and change clothes. He found one with little effort. The Moonrunners' efforts to repel the invaders hadn't been entirely in vain. Their city's borders had stalled a few years before Colin was born. So instead of growing out, they'd grown up, and in. Despite the growing population, the ever-increasing density left thousands of convenient little alcoves for those who wished to stay away from prying eyes.

Colin untied the drawstring at the mouth of the bag and carefully emptied the contents onto the red brick street. A quick inventory showed that Whiskers had once again proved his mettle. The janitor's uniform was clean and pressed, complete with the little blue cap and a tool belt with leather pouches. It was, in a word, perfect, which was something no janitor's uniform would ever be. Colin spent a solid minute impressing the uniform with wrinkles and rubbing street grime into its fibers.

The rest of the kit was better. The "Out of Order" sign looked like the paint was still drying from the sign-maker's pinstriping brush. Two dozen glass vials of translucent green acid were wrapped carefully in cotton to prevent them from clanging together in the bag. He'd even made sure each vial had a little leather loop tied around it. All the easier for Colin's ferret form to carry his cargo.

At the bottom of the sack, he found a surprise. Two dozen tiny, hollow glass cubes, each divided by a small strip of paper down their diagonal and tied up with the same leather loops as the acid vial. But it was what was inside the cubes that made them valuable. On either side of the paper strip was a single male and female junaro bug. They were noxious little creatures most of the time, spraying anyone who came too close with foul-smelling oil from their rumps. However, around this time each year, their temperament softened as mating season overtook them. The males in particular dumped their energies into attracting any willing female with a brilliant, pulsing light show, which continued until either copulation occurred, or the poor chap had expended himself fatally.

The trick the ancient moonrunners had learned was harvesting sexually immature females, which filled the other half of the cubes. They were just old enough to excite the males, but not yet old enough to actually do anything to. It was a problem Colin could sympathize with, but not enough to prevent him from using them to see in the darkened tubes that were to come.

Satisfied, Colin quickly slipped out of his street clothes and donned the freshly-soiled uniform. He clicked the little brass clasp of the tool belt shut, then filled its pouches with the acid vials and light cubes. Less than two minutes had passed by the time he'd finished stuffing his street clothes into the bag. Colin stuffed the bag in a corner and covered it with a broken crate someone had left in the alley. He'd want to change back once the operation was over, provided he got that far.

With an eye out for charging steamhorses, Colin crossed the bustling street. Hundreds of the city's citizens pushed past him in a mad rush to return to their homes after a day of labor. The Steamers kept odd hours, independent of the light of day. Colin tried to get the pulse of the crowd as he pushed against their current, looking for signs he was being noticed. But only a very few even bothered to make eye contact with him, more still walked blindly into his path. He was as good as invisible, just how he liked it.

He took the thick marble steps of Our Lady of Divine Mercy Hospital two at a time, then walked towards the immense double doors like a man on a mission, just not the mission he was actually on. He walked past the brass studded oak doors and into near chaos. Nurses in their sparkling white dresses stood out against the dark-stained wood and polished copper finishing. Three of the women rolled a wooden gurney rolled by on cast iron wheels, carrying a young man on the verge of panic to his appointment with the surgeon. People hobbled by on crutches, others sat in wheelchairs and stared into empty space. And everywhere was the pervasive smell of disinfectant.

Colin found a building map mounted to the far wall of the reception area, and quickly spotted Room 119. He grabbed a clipboard hanging off a door as he passed and strode ahead confidently. A uniform, clipboard, and slightly irritated demeanor had gotten him into more places than he would have believed possible before starting his career in the MLA. Two left turns and a short hallway later and he had arrived at his destination.

It was never going to be that easy, however. Standing in his way, a crimson clad Constable leered down at Colin from under the brim of his black felt cap.

"What do you want?" he demanded. His right hand reflexively gripped at the double-bowed hand crossbow at his hip.

"Me?" Colin responded jovially. "A hot bath and a cold beer. But instead I'm here."

"Doing what?"

Colin tried to tamp down his racing heart. He was unarmed, save for the vials of acid, and had no practical answer for the pair of six-inch long bolts the guard had at the ready. Even coming from a relatively small hand crossbow, they would have enough force to staple him to the far wall of the hallway.

"The suck-n-blow's on the fritz." Colin produced the 'Out of Order' sign.

"Suck and blow?" The guard looked confused. Confused was better than angry.

"Sorry." Colin threw up a lopsided grin. "It's what me and the boys call it. As in, 'Sure wish me wife would suck and blow like that.'"

"Oh, oh right." A conspiratorial smile bloomed on the constable's face, and Colin knew he had him. "One of the doctors was just in here using it. He didn't say anything about it being broken."

"Well he wouldn't tell you, would he? No, them *smart* people break everything they touch, then expect us wrench-turners to clean up after them. Worse than me own kids, they are." He wiggled the clipboard. "I gots the work order right here if you're needin' to see it."

The constable held up a white-gloved hand. "No, that's fine. Just be quick about it; this is a popular room."

Colin nodded thanks to the young man and hung the 'Out of Order' sign on the door. "Depends on how bad the doctor man screwed it up. Know what I mean?" He gave the guard a mischievous wink and shut the door behind him. Colin leaned heavily against the door and let out a long, slow breath. The encounter had been much too close for comfort. A prime example of why the MLA didn't have much need of a solid retirement plan.

After taking a moment to calm himself, Colin surveyed the room. A large bay window faced the retreating sun. By the time he returned, night would be upon him, so he lit a pair of gas lamps on the wall while he still had use of human hands. That done, he turned his attention to the machine itself.

The terminal looked deceptively simple. Framed by an ornate wooden panel inlaid with silver, two brass fittings protruded from the wall like a pair yellow eyes. Nestled between them was a bank of numbered keys in two columns of five. The nose to the eyes. Just to finish the effect, the terminal's designers had built a gilded rack to hold the brass spheres just below the rest, providing the giant face with a mirthless mouth.

"Hello lovely. Tell me your secrets." Colin leaned in closer, inspecting each part carefully. One tube, he reckoned, would be the outflow, the other the inflow. He unlatched the one on the right and pulled it open. A strong gust of air rushed out and across his face. The outflow. He closed the portal with a shove. So, the left it would be. Colin tried to open the portal, but it resisted mightily. Vacuum pressure? He tried again, really throwing his back into the effort, but the door was locked down solidly. He was missing something. The numbered keys caught his eye again. What were they for?

A quick reading of the different warning plaques revealed only a prohibition on sending personal messages through the network, and the deleterious effects on one's face of opening the outflow hatch without the proper safety gear. Several dents in the wall directly behind the machine testified to instances when this warning had gone unheeded. *Would it kill them to put in a cage to catch the balls?*

No matter. There was a table on the wall opposite to the windows. On it was a stack of loose paper, an ink well, a cupful of quills, and a small leather-bound book that looked promising. He opened the well-worn cover and read what he could. Colin had grown up in one of the city's slums, a ghetto for moonrunners who worked the jobs the Steamers had deemed below their station. He knew the city better than most, spoke their tongue fluently, and could even read much of their foreign writing with some effort. That alone would have made him valuable to the MLA.

He'd hoped for an operators manual, but instead the book had page after page of addresses on one side, and a sequence of six numbers on the other. Colin glanced at the wall clock to check his window. 1713. There was still time, but he had no idea how long he'd have to spend in the tunnels. The minutes were slipping away. Still staring at the page, he had a flash of insight. The numbers were code for the addresses. It must be how the sorting room knew where to forward the messages.

Book in hand, Colin went back to the machine and punched in the first code on the page. Any destination would do, After all, they should all lead to the sorting room. When he pushed the last button, the latch on the outgoing tube snapped open. With a gentle tug, the hatch swung to the side accompanied by a whoosh of air as it disappeared down the hole.

As long as the hatched remained open, Colin reasoned, he'd have air to breath. It would just be breezy. The only problem now was getting into the hole. It was too small for his human form, but much too high off the ground once he shifted. He grabbed the chair from the desk and set it on top of the rack of spheres. The precarious arrangement wouldn't hold his weight, but would have no trouble bearing the weight of a handful of ferret bodies at a time.

There was nothing left to do now but take the plunge. Well, maybe one more thing. He would need time alone, and there was still the guard outside. Colin opened the door and poked his head out.

"Hey, constable. You wouldn't happen to have a smoke on you by any chance?"

The larger man looked back at him with only mild annoyance. He reached a hand into his jacket and brought out a cigarillo and flint striker.

"Thanks." Colin stuck the bad habit in his mouth and struck the flint until he had a nice glowing cherry burning away at the tip. "I gotta say, the last guy in here gummed this poor thing up but good. I'm going to be in here a while. Probably going to miss dinner. Wife won't be happy."

The guard grimaced. "Sorry about that."

"What's your name, constable?"

"Reginald."

"Reggie, hey? Well I'm Thomas. Why don't you pinch off and grab yourself a smoke?"

"Can't abandon my post, sir."

Colin threw him a lopsided grin. "Nonsense. I'm in here, and the sucker's broke anyway. Insurgents won't be sending any love letters through here tonight. No reason we should both be bored."

Reginald's shoulders relaxed. "Yeah, you're right. I was supposed to be relieved two hours ago anyway. How long do you think you'll be?"

"Not sure, an hour at least. Go grab a bite, I won't tell anyone."

"I think I just might." The constable stood up straight and marched off in the general direction of a delicatessen.

Colin tipped his blue cap to the guard. "G'nite Reggie." The door clicked shut behind him and Colin was finally alone. He locked the door and hurried to empty his tool belt onto the floor. His racing heartbeat counted the moments as they slipped into the past. He grabbed the light cubes and pulled out the paper separating the junaro bugs. The eager males lit up the room like a pulsing. Then Colin laid out the acid vials with care.

Ready, he took a final drag from the cigarillo to calm his nerves. Reggie had good taste in tobacco. He stabbed it out on the table, then removed his hat and shirt. Colin went to the big bay window on the far side of the room and found the moon hanging low in the sky.

Strictly speaking, he hadn't needed the light of the full moon to shift since adolescence, but even some twenty years later, he still felt its pull. Staring at the moon's cratered face somehow made initiating the shift a less jarring experience.

He'd learned early on to lie down flat. The first outward sign was the thickening of the tiny hairs on his arms. A white streak appeared on his chest and crept down his stomach, while the rest turned a rich, amber brown. Colin's skin writhed, his muscles spasmed, and his nerves fired chaotically. One can never really get used to the sensation of their body rearranging itself. Colin dealt with the pain by trying to withdraw inside his mind, which was the only constant through the process.

Then, once the agony was almost too much to bear, Colin's body sort of liquefied, then fell apart entirely. Dozens of furry little puddles coalesced on the floor. Heads and paws began to form from the hairy goop, until fifty-seven ferrets peered around the room.

A few crawled their way out of Colin's trousers, including his cream-colored female ferret. It made him kind of an odd-ball flock; almost all other flocks were the same gender as the moonrunner's human form. Whiskers said it was his feminine side. Colin was pretty sure the smaller female was just the way nature rounded down his mass. He called her Nola.

The swarm moved as one to the piles of light cubes and vials. Like one hand putting a glove on the other, Colin tied the supplies to parts of himself until they were all accounted for. The business of ferrets flowed up the rack of spheres, over the chair, and was gently pulled into the tube. Colin left one part of himself behind as a lookout. Splitting his focus became more difficult as he took on more tasks and as the different parts of him became more distant. But his youth in the ghetto had been unforgiving. He'd been a pick-pocket and street hustler long before volunteering to become a saboteur; keeping a lookout on himself was second nature.

They moved as a single organism, which despite appearances, they were. Colin's tiny pinprick claws went *tink tink tink* against the rolled brass of the tube. The surface was coated with a thin layer of what smelled like pig lard to Colin's noses. The slickness kept him from running more than two abreast through the narrow tunnel.

For some reason, he'd expected a clean, straight line from the terminal to the sorting room, but the tunnel was riddled with blind turns, hills, drop-offs, and curves. It made sense once he stopped to think about it. The network was new; it must have built around the existing basements, sewers, and steam-pipes, not the other way around.

Judging distances from one form to the other was always tricky, but Colin had a pretty good idea of how fast he moved in both shapes, but he was sure it hadn't been more than fifty yards before he hit the first roadblock. Staring back at him by the light of horny bugs, a grate blocked his path. Through small round holes, he could see that it was a junction of some kind, with another tube meeting at a shallow angle. He reasoned that the holes in the grates maintained the vacuum while blocking the spheres from progressing. It reminded him of a switch-track on the Steamer's railways.

But if that was true, then there must be some way to trip the door to open, just like the lever that switched the tracks. Colin turned dozens of eyes to the walls, searching for the switch, but nothing made itself apparent. Frustration started creeping in. Colin was considering melting a hole through the grate with a vial of acid when one of his milling members leaned against the grate itself.

It clicked.

The grate snapped open like a spring, and the sudden liberation of vacuum pulled several of Colin's members through. After the shock wore off, the rest of him charged through as fast as his dozens of legs could carry him. Unfortunately, it wasn't fast enough. Barely half of himself had passed through the grate before it snapped shut again. A sharp stab of pain coursed through Colin's consciousness as the door clamped down on the pelvis of one of his members, shattering it. All fifty-seven of his mouths, even the lookout, squealed in the sudden agony.

The parts of Colin trapped on the other side of the grate pushed against it, trying to trip it to open, but it remained stuck. He grabbed the holes with dozens of tiny paws and tried to pull it open, but the lard kept him from getting any traction against the inside of the tube. The member caught in the door blacked out from the pain, which faded into the background of Colin's mind. He tried to squeeze more of himself through the gap, but it was hopeless. He briefly toyed with burning through the grate with acid, but then he'd have less to use in the sorting room. Time was running low; he would have to divide himself further.

The lightcubes and acid vials slipped past with no trouble. He tied them off to the remaining members and, with his escape route blocked, ran further down the junction.

It wasn't long before Colin started to experience the strange double-vision sensation as the distance between the two main groups of himself grew. As a young kit, he had been badly separated once before deep in the woods outside the Steamer city. And while he couldn't entirely overcome the disorientation that came with physically being in two places at once, he'd learned how to mitigate it to some degree. Colin concentrated, picking out the bodies trapped on the other side of the grate. He closed their eyes and piled them together to muffle their ears, cutting down on the sensory interference.

His mind cleared somewhat, although it still felt hazy from being spread thin. It would only grow worse the further apart his halves became, but there wasn't any other option. Colin cursed himself for not grabbing a coffee before starting the mission.

Soon, he reached another grate, but this time he knew what to expect and slipped through it quickly. The grate snapped shut with the same force as the first, but this time only cost Colin a few hairs of the tip of the last member's tail. He passed another junction, and another. By the time he'd passed the sixth grate, he could see light leaking in from the tube ahead.

The light had the amber glow of lamps. Colin had reached his target. Several of his faces peered through the grate to make sure the coast was clear. The room seemed to be empty at the moment, so he reached a paw through and flipped open the latch. The hatch flew open, and the sudden liberation of air pressure sent three of Colin tumbling down to the floor. It was a short fall however, and all were unharmed.

His eyes on the floor immediately spotted trouble. The terminal he'd just been blown out of was nearly identical to the one in the hospital. That wasn't surprising. The problem was it was the *only* terminal in the room. There were no huge bins of spheres, no technicians frantically reading codes and shoving them into their destination tube, no activity at all.

The rest of Colin, or that part of him that had made the journey, jumped down to the floor and swarmed over the room, trying to figure out where he'd ended up and hopefully where he had gone wrong. The rest of the room was arranged a little differently, with the window on the other side and the desk along the back wall instead of by the door, but otherwise it was very familiar.

Colin scampered over to the door and listened for movement on the other side. He peeked under the door and saw a pair feet standing to the left, probably Reggie's counterpart. Colin looked up at the door lock. He started to arrange himself on the floor to shift back and lock it when he remembered his trapped half. He'd only ever shifted missing a single member, after a hawk had made off with one. It had been... disconcerting. It had taken him nearly a month to recover fully.

He looked at the wall clock. 1738. Colin couldn't afford any more delays, but he wasn't even sure what his next move was going to be. Somehow, he'd bypassed the target entirely. Colin sent a few of himself up the chair and onto the desk, hoping this terminal would have the same address book as the room in the hospital. His hope was quickly vindicated and he flipped through the book with his paws. Reading was difficult with more than one set of eyes, so he closed all but the pair peering at the page, searching for any reference to a sorting room, or central hub, or whatever.

Nothing.

Frustrated, he went back and found the code for Our Lady of Divine Mercy's address code. He found it, but unable to shift, punching it in would be difficult. He might be able to push the chair over, but any noise risked alerting the guard that the room was no longer empty.

Desperation was starting to take hold. Colin had only managed to stay alive as long as he had by keeping a level head, but the mission was slipping away from him. His failure would mean the death of a lot of his comrades, or their capture, which would mean the same fate after the show trials had run their course.

His faith in his competence was eroding beneath Colin's feet. Had he been given bad intelligence? What assumptions had he made? It was hard to concentrate; half of him was almost a mile away. The more diffuse a flock got, the close it came to losing its soul and breaking up into individual animals. He was having a tough time multi-tasking between himself, the trapped group, and his lookout back in the hospital. Think, think, think…

The answer jumped at him like a hidden fox. The address codes, the internal gates, the junctions. There was no sorting room. That was the assumption they'd made all along. But the Steamers, those thrice-damned clever Steamers, had somehow automated the entire system.

Dozens of tiny feet scratched angrily at the floor. The mission was a bust now. Without a single point of failure, there was no way he'd be able to knock out the whole system with the scant equipment and short time left to him. The best he could do was wreck whatever junctions he passed on his way back out, and hope the disruption would be enough to gum up the works. If he was *very* lucky, they might even shut down the whole thing to try and track down the cause.

With renewed determination, Colin flowed up the sphere rack and formed a ferret pyramid. Standing on his own shoulders, he punched the buttons while his member at the book read the hospital's code in his mind. Job done, he made an even taller pyramid under the outflow tube. He strained with the topmost member against the hatch. What had been easy in human form was nearly impossible for a single ferret. With a mad surge of strength, the little paws ripped the hatch free. But then it swung open and clanged hard against the wall.

Oh, shit! Colin's top member jumped into the tube and let its back half dangle like a rope for the rest of him to climb up. He scrambled up himself with frantic energy, scratching painfully scratching the rope member's skin, but the pain was too far down his priority list to really notice.

Only two members were left when the door swung open. Their eyes watched as a very confused constable tried to understand what he was witnessing. However, like guards everywhere, when confronted with the unknown, he had been trained to meet it with force. He pulled the double crossbow from its holster and leveled it at one of the ferrets.

The *twang* of the bowstring was met with a searing jolt of pain and light through Colin's consciousness, followed by a cold, blank hole in his soul. One of his members was dead, impaled through the skull by a crossbow bolt. Whether the shot was skill or luck didn't really matter.

One member was still exposed, but he couldn't bring it up. If the guard shot his remaining bolt straight down the tube, there was no way to know how much of Colin would be injured or killed. He needed to draw him off, so Colin sacrificed the stranded member as a distraction. He closed all of his eyes but those still in the room and leapt straight for the guard's face.

A second twang of the crossbow sent a bolt harmlessly into the floor. Colin's member scratched and bit viciously at the guard's face and neck. At three pounds, it was not a fight he was going to win, but he didn't have to. Running blind, the rest of him charged down the tube and down the first drop off. Safe from return fire, Colin stopped the fight and returned his attention to escaping. Another jolt crashed into him as the guard broke the stranded member's neck.

Battered and furious, Colin ran as fast as he could through the tube. Without a central processing room, there was no way to disable the entire system. But he was determined to wreak as much havoc as he could along the way. He stopped at every junction he crossed, pouring an entire vial of acid on each and every grate as they closed behind him. For good measure, he melted holes through the tube itself, hoping to bleed off air pressure within the system.

He could feel his mind sharpening the closer he came to his trapped group. He stirred them and pointed both halves back towards the hospital terminal running for all he was worth. Within a minute, he was back where he'd started. As he'd done on the other end, Colin made a pyramid and punched in a code. He sent four members running back down the outflow to recover the one trapped in the first grate. It was alive, and mercifully still unconscious. The rescuers dragged the limp ferret against the vacuum and back to the hospital room.

But as Colin hurriedly dragged himself back down the chair propped up against the tube, what tenuous luck he still had ran out. The chair shifted under the weight and crashed to the floor in a pile of casters, cushions, and stunned ferrets.

A knock came at the door. "Everything okay in there, Thomas?' It was the guard, Reggie. Apparently, he was a quick eater. Still feeling the effects of losing two of himself, Colin forgot his form and reflexively tried to answer. Only squeaks and chitters came out.

The doorknob rattled. "What's going on? Why is this door locked?"

Colin's addled mind raced through his dwindling options. There was no time to shift back to human form, and no time to run back down the tunnel. The window maybe? But then the door flew open with a bang and shower of splinters. Reginald stepped in, crossbow drawn and hunting for a target.

Fortunately for Colin, the constable wasn't prepared for a swarm of tiny, enraged predators running up his trousers and under his shirt. Trying to grab, slap, or punch the dozens of mouths biting at him from every direction, Reginald dropped his weapon and went to the floor. He rolled around, trying to crush Colin's members. He opened his mouth to either curse or scream for help.

It was the opening Colin needed. Consumed by the heat of the fight, he steered Nola, his smallest member, straight down the constable's windpipe before he could shout. Reginald frantically grabbed at her, but she crawled deeper into his throat until she was beyond his reach. His eyes rolled back after a few seconds. Desperate to escape, Colin arranged himself on the floor and shifted back to his human form. Naked and reeling from losing three parts of himself, he stood shakily and fumbled with his uniform to get dressed.

By the time he'd finished, Reginald had stopped moving entirely. Colin looked up at the clock. 1757. Whatever the MLA had planned, it was about to happen. If he wanted to avoid arrest, he needed to be somewhere else when it did.

Before he left, though, Colin knelt down over the constable's now lifeless body. "I'm sorry, Reggie. I wish you'd have taken longer for dinner." He pried open the dead man's mouth and pulled out Nola's limp body. He'd never held a part of himself before, never looked into his own face in the other form. It was a strange feeling, to say the least.

But then, Colin got a shock. Nola twitched. He almost dropped her, but instead laid the ferret down gently on the floor and watched. To his amazement, her tiny ribcage started to flex, as though it was trying to remember how to breath. Colin squeezed and rubbed her chest, trying to get air moving again. She coughed, then pulled in a ragged breath. Nola's eyes snapped open and looked around the room in bewilderment.

Colin could feel her in his mind, but he did not command her body. She was in control of herself. Confused, but still keenly aware of his retreating window of opportunity, Colin scooped her up, kissed her on the face, then stuffed her into his uniform. He moved into the hallway and shut the door to the terminal room behind him.

He wouldn't know until the next evening if his improvised plan had given the other teams the window they needed, but at that moment, feeling the loss of two members while a third hid inside his stolen uniform, he was too exhausted to care. Walking out the same double doors he'd enter less than an hour before, exuding an aura of calm he most certainly didn't feel, Colin vanished into the night just as the first round of explosions rocked the city.

Dark Energy
Donald J. Bingle

Energy surged through his sinews as he ran effortlessly through the shadow-splashed night, metal-banded legs stretching and springing as they churned the decaying detritus of the forest floor. Yet he twisted and twined around the standing foliage at speed with such grace, such instinct, that he disturbed nary a dewy drop on the greenest leaf of nightshade. He raised his snout into the air, nostrils flaring to follow the scent borne on the night breeze as he sucked in oxygen more hungrily than the hottest steam boiler. His tooth-filled maw gaped open to aid the flow, saliva dripping from the corners and whipping into the air as he dodged and turned to follow his nose following his prey.

The scent strengthened as he gained ground, adding pungent coppery overtones to the strong iron scent of fresh sheep's blood. Mutton, his favorite feast—an injured lamb, separated from the flock, and, no doubt, lost in the woods, scratched by the thorny nettles of the under-forest. Sweet, succulent, and fresh-warm, once you got past the matted wool exterior. Tender and easy to render with claw and fang, tearing through flesh and bone, eating the muscled prime cuts and more savory organs, leaving the nastier bits and gristle and chewy tendons for lesser beasts to fight over once he was sated.

Another scent, too. Faint beneath the strong odor of the lamb's blood, but not too faint for his keen nose inhaling the deep breaths of the chase. Human, a stench despised, but not unknown to him. Shepherd, perhaps—a foolish one to be seeking out the flock at this hour, even on a moonlit night. Or, perhaps, a sturdy huntsman seeking a night's kill.

He should have paused at that last thought—cunning as he was known to be, but the lust was upon him and the bloodied lamb near enough to taste, not just with his nose and mouth, but with his muscle and mind. All instinct now, he lowered his body and increased his speed, ready to leap upon his quarry and sink his fangs into his midnight feast.

A flicker of white beyond a deadfall, pale as the color of the full moon high in the sky, fixed his eye as his muscles tensed to pounce. A bright red stain splashed on white confirmed in his rational mind the scene his instincts urged upon his hindbrain and he leapt high over the twisted branches of a fallen tree. His mouth open, teeth flashing, ready to bear down with murderous intent upon the victim meal, claws stretched forward to grab and rend and hold and tear in the hot frenzy of a gourmet bloodbath dinner for one.

He was in mid-leap when he realized his error. He snapped shut his slavering jaw and twisted his body violently in an attempt to change his fate, even before he fully understood it, but the arc of his trajectory was unaffected. He swiveled his head, jerking his shoulders around to allow him to create a full circle of vision even as his body slammed into a cold disc of smooth metal, slick with the blood of a fresh-butchered lamb. His torso slid and rolled across the hard, wet surface until it collided with the hand's-breadth-high, circular wall edging the disc. The impact with this border triggered slightly curved vertical bars to spring up from within and beneath the circular wall, instantaneously enclosing him within a vaguely egg-shaped cage. The curved bars shot upward from below with such speed and force that had his momentum careened him over the short border, he would have been skewered and thrust up as a bloody offering to the pale, full moon.

He howled in pain and frustration, a wail of anguish and warning to others of his kind to stay away, as his nose was assaulted with the scent of metal and machine oil, with a tinge of ozone on the night air. But even before he could assess these new smells or inspect his metal prison, his ears picked up a stolid click from beneath the metal disc and a high-pitched hum began to assault his hearing. His fur began to fluff up and stand on end.

A guttural roar rose from his throat and turned into a blood-curdling wail of terror and pain as the change began.

Too soon. Too soon.

The night betrayed him as the moon still stared.

An eternity of agony assaulted his body as it shifted and contorted to the dreaded form: legs lengthening as though melted in the forge and stretched, the metal bands encircling his limbs tightening about them as he expanded in size; his snout and head pounded into rounder shape; his claws growing back into his digits and his digits lengthening and puffing out like summer sausages, all pale and meaty. His torso grew and fattened, the lean muscle of the predator softening into the mush of fatted prey, his senses dimming, his instinct fading as unwanted memories and logic assaulted his mind. That hated logic told him this process occurred in a matter of minutes and it would soon be over, but the pain insisted the change was all-consuming and endless and would not be stopped, until finally it did, and he was naked on the sticky wet floor of a confounded cage in the woods, his now feeble eyes unable to discern any foe in the moonlight-dappled dark, his pudgy nose unable to decipher any aroma but the smell of fear and sweat and the stink of humanity.

A match scritched upon a nearby boulder and flared up to reveal a middle-aged man, a dirty sheepskin blanket covering much of his body as he sat upon a nearby stump. The man shrugged off the sheepish cover and brought the flaming match to the ivory bowl of a carved wooden pipe.

"The worst is over," the man murmured as he sucked in a stench of cherry-tinged smoke. After drawing on the pipe a few times and puffing its smoke from his lungs into the clear forest air, he shook the match out, held it for a moment to cool, and placed it in the right pocket of his tweed jacket, from whence he simultaneously extracted a small notebook, bound shut with leather ties. "No standing on proprieties here in the forest. You can thank me later, when you feel better." He untied the binds and opened the notebook, thumbing quickly to what appeared to be a blank page. Still sucking on the pipe, he reached with his right hand into the inside pocket of his jacket and pulled forth a stout pencil, licked the tip for reasons unknown, and set it to the paper.

"My name is Archibald Reginald Cavensdale, lettered in chemistry and physics at Cambridge." He inclined his head toward the cage, where but moments before a wild beast had thrashed and yowled in frenzied frustration, but now held a cold, pale, quivering human.

Me.

"Your name?" He leaned toward me, pencil at the ready to inscribe my telling for posterity.

Being naked and at a disadvantage put me in an awkward and embarrassing spot, but I was not about to succumb to disadvantage. I steeled my courage and quelled my trembling as best I was able, given my state of undress and the coldness of the strange metal disc upon my buttocks. I straightened my back and sat upright, lifting my chin in what I imagined to be a look of haughty superiority and narrowed my eyes in steely resolve. "I do not engage in casual conversation with those who capture and cage persons of my… nature."

The scholar made a note in his book. "Persons of your… nature, heh?" He scribbled some more. "That's a delicate way of putting it. But a few moments ago, you would have torn me asunder with your fangs as though I were but a yearling lamb to provide bloody sustenance for your wolfish appetite. Now you are but a person of a particular 'nature'." He scrunched his nose. "Adrenaline levels are still elevated, I would guess." He made yet another note.

I am not a fool. I know when I find myself naked in the woods and fresh blood smeared upon my hands and face, that I have just returned from being him… being the beast. It is not a matter I discuss with strangers… or with anyone at all. It is *my* burden. It is *my* shame. Of course, typically my unassisted return occurs as dawn is breaking, waking from a feast-induced stupor of sleep—not from colliding with strange, humming cages, in the under-lit realm of the wee hours, assaulted by a professor of chemistry and physics.

I summoned my courage, bolstering it with scurrilous umbrage, as if dealing with an overcharging shopkeeper of low birth. "Regardless of my past… even my recent past… we are both gentle-born men of distinction and education. I will brook no discourse in my current condition." I gestured at my unclothed body. "Or in this unaccommodating confinement. Release me at once and be so kind as to lend me that sheepskin you used for concealment and I will consider responding to reasonable inquiries, given your assurances of discreet confidentiality."

"From where I'm sitting, you seem to have little leverage for demanding or requesting anything. The local constabulary reports more than sheep have been killed and eaten in this parish over the last season."

I did not rise to the bait, my logic having learned the lesson that the beast had fallen prey to: look before you leap. I simply shrugged and again gestured at my naked, nobility-soft body. "I obviously pose no threat to you in this condition."

"True enough," averred the smoker. "But if you were to leave the cage prematurely, the story would be quite differently told." He took the pipe from his mouth and pointed with the stem toward the moon, still gleaming full above the reaching branches of the tangled trees. As you can see, the full moon is still high in the sky—a sight you have not seen in your current form in some time, I would dare say." He readied his pencil. "Exactly how long, would you say?"

"I would not," I said. "I will not be interrogated by the likes of you or anyone else in these conditions." I put my best aristocratic edge into my voice. "After all, we are both men accustomed to conversing in a civilized manner, sir."

"At the moment, so long as my... device... maintains your status." The fingers holding the thick pencil trembled in apparent anticipation. "On a scale of one to twenty, with full score being the highest, how painful would the transformation back to beast be for you? Answer true and straight or I will be forced to verify with a field experiment."

My hindbrain liked the sound of that. Not the prospect of the agony of transformation, but the return of the tools, talent, and instinct to tear this uncivilized tormentor from limb to bloody limb. I trust not the logic of the beast, but I distrust those who capture and threaten to torture me even more. I decided to goad the professor to ill-considered action. "The moonlight has no effect on me. I have an unfortunate condition that impinges on my will periodically."

He laughed at that, an unseemly guffaw not suited to a man of noble breeding. "That's the first two true things you've said this night, Mister... Gentleman. You have a condition which affects you periodically... with the lunar phases, to be sure. And moonlight affects you not. Few with your condition have made that realization, given the periodicity of the affliction."

I remained silent. Obviously, the man had made much study of lycanthropy, as my affliction is referenced in learned circles. Despite his irksome nature, I thought to learn something from him.

He continued, as I hoped he would. "But, of course, it doesn't take many cloudy nights for the realization to come that 'tis not the moonlight which causes the affliction. And a single instance of transformation..." he glanced at the bands on my arms and legs, "say, shackled in a dark basement, or in a locked and heavily curtained room, confirms it beyond denial. But then, why would moonlight have any affect? Tis but reflected sunlight and the strong glare of sun direct has no adverse impact on those afflicted."

He paused long enough I felt need to prompt him for more information. "Clear to even the uneducated, or so I would imagine. Yet none of your obvious ramblings explains why I remain a prisoner."

"Ahh," he nodded, his pencil bobbing in agreement with his head. "Tis the uncanny and unalterable coincidence with periodicity of

165

lunar phases that causes one to doubt even the obvious. Befuddled me, at first, before I thought about it scientifically."

"Scientifically? Then you are not one of those who blames powers of the occult or other superstitious explanations?" Play to the ego of a professor and you will learn much of his specialty… or get a good nap. "You have discerned the true cause, then?"

"Not so difficult with a bit of critical thought, really. What else matches the periodicity of the lunar phases?"

I maintained silence. The flow of information was in the direction I favored. No need to alter the momentum of a force when it works in your favor.

"Rises and falls with the phases in synchronicity, one might say."

I could not help myself. "The tides," I blurted out.

"Yes," he said with glee. "The tides. Affected by the gravitational impact of the sun and moon. Of greatest impact when the sun and the moon are aligned with one another on one side of the Earth, as in the case of a new moon, but also, due to the nature of fluid adhering to a spherical surface, when aligned with one another on exactly opposite sides of the Earth, pulling in diametric opposition as during a full moon."

I had made the connection. Obviously, however, the professor had studied it. "Yet the new moon does not coincide with… incidents."

He nodded vigorously once again. "That was the stumper, it was, but that was when I realized it was not the absolute pull of gravity that was the key. Else those at lower altitude, closer to the center of gravity of the Earth would be differentially affected, yet they are not. The same conclusion holds sway for those under acceleration, at least downward or laterally—even with the strongest steam engine, only modest upward acceleration can be achieved. For all my studies and research, I could only find one anomaly in frequency and duration of incidence…"

I leaned forward to catch his words. This was news to me.

"Trolls."

My mouth gaped open and I felt lightheaded. Was this allegedly learned man actually a fool?

"Scandinavian trolls, to be more precise. Legendary, of course, though their appearance and latitude correspond nicely with tales of furred and fanged creatures of the northern reaches of America.

Sasquatch, the Indians call them. Abominable snowmen, as they are known in the dime novels. That's what led me to the device which enables you to gaze, human, at the full moon above."

"Dime novels?"

He gave me a sour, condescending glare. "No, you idiot. Magnetism. Northern latitudes are situated differently in the magnetic field created by earth as she spins about her molten iron core. And, incidents of trolls and sasquatches spike near iron caves and at magnetic north, even more than at true north—though the lack of population at very high latitudes makes the statistics difficult to correlate accurately."

It made sense. I motioned at my cage. "And this device?"

"Once the theoretical work is done, all that remains is engineering. Given the manner in which magnetism mimics gravity, it is a simple matter of creating magnetic coils and repulsers that allow one to fine tune the direction and strength of electromagnetic and gravitational fields so as to replicate the gravitational pull and push of the lunar phases. As I said, it is not simply the pull, but the simultaneous pull in opposite directions within a specified range. What makes a fishing line or a harp string taut is not pull in one direction, but in two. Neurons are similar at a micro-gravitational level. The brain is a delicate organ, greatly affected by gravitational and magnetic effects. It's due to the iron in the blood, allowing the cells to align with chemically induced electrical charges of the brain. That's why homing pigeons and migratory fowl can find their way to precise locations without difficulty—their tiny brains detect even the most minute anomalies in the flux of the Earth's magnetic field. Of course, it required a fair bit of human brainpower to calculate the calibration of the device for a specific geographic location and lunar phase."

He pointed at the device with the stem of his pipe. "Not to say that the engineering and manufacture weren't challenging in their own right. Working with electricity is always dangerous and tricky. Terrible stuff, really. The mere act of charging the batteries—they're buried beneath the floor of your cage—with steam power is tedious and bothersome. And coming up with a design which is strong enough to physically contain a lycanthropic subject within the ephemera of a magnetic field without itself conducting the electric power of the batteries generating the field flux was an additional sub-project. The key is alternating layers of insulators and a tungsten/platinum alloy isolated from the inducing coils above the batteries. Difficult and expensive to produce, but I think you will agree that the experiment has shown to be a success. It wasn't easy, of course. Early models were... disappointing."

The implications of the words "experiment" and "disappointing" darkened my thoughts. "So, you capture those of us afflicted to conduct your research."

"Heavens, no. I used animals, of course. At first, I thought to use such staples of scientific inquiry as mice and rats, but I feared the debacle should lycanthropic vermin escape into the fertile fields of England. Rats decimated enough of the population during the Black Plague. I would not forgive myself if I were to unleash wererats upon the world. At first I used bunbuns..."

"Bunbuns?"

He reddened. "Rabbits. It's what my grandmother called them when I was little. Perhaps that is why I realized soon after I started down such garden path I really didn't have the heart to infect them or to see them torn asunder or fried by magnetic-induced electrical currents when testing early cage prototypes. I abandoned bunbuns as test subjects and set about to find a replacement. Cows were too large, ferrets too crafty, and dogs and cats too difficult to acquire in quantity without arousing a suspicious townsfolk. Eventually, I settled on sheep. Docile, not particularly smart, and the uninfected subjects used for electro-mechanical cage tests made a fine meal when things went wrong. You, sir, are not a test subject. You are a beneficiary of my research."

"Ah, the benefits of sitting naked on a cold metal floor—even a scientifically crafted composite that is non-conductive—in the dewy pre-dawn of a winter's night in England escapes me. Perhaps, you could clarify."

A stern look crossed the visage of my captor, who began to mutter below the range of my hearing, though I did catch the phrase "ungrateful snot" at one point. Finally, he tamped out his pipe, pocketed it, scrunched up his face and looked me square in the eye. "See, here, my man. I can hardly advertise a treatment for lycanthropy in *The Times*. I travel, at no small expense to myself, mind you, to areas infested with the problem, capture the lycanthrope and offer to allow them to come to my establishment in London Town as the full moon approaches and sit out the duration *untransformed* in the relative comfort of the basement of my townhouse. You, of course, supply your own refreshments and reading material. For reasons of safety, patrons are sequestered from one another lest failure of the device to... maintain... one individual not have unfortunate consequences for those who do not transform."

I pondered for a few moments. "It is an interesting proposition. Of course, the scientific principles which permit you to prevent transformation during the full moon could be manipulated to cause transformation at other times. How am I to be assured I will not be captured and manipulated for your own ends in such manner?"

The professor stood abruptly, stamping his right foot hard. "Sir, I am offended by your suggestion! Why anyone would ever choose to become a beast driven to lustful frenzy by the smell of blood is beyond imagination."

The pre-dawn light brightened the surroundings as we continued our conversation. I tilted my head to one side in thought. "Conquerors, perhaps. They could create a formidable army."

The professor scoffed, visibly relaxing. "An army in a cage. The notion is preposterous."

The sun rose above the horizon and as it did, the professor walked over to what looked to be a rabbit hole a few feet to one side of the cage and reached in. There was an audible click and the irritating whine of the artifice faded into nothingness as the dawn chorus of indigenous birds greeted the new day. The bars of the cage began to slowly recede back into the base.

The professor suddenly shivered. "I do fear for the future, though."

"Why is that?" I said, twisting the bands on my legs a half-turn before beginning to stand and work the kinks out of my muscles from sitting on the cold surface too long.

"As you know, tides vary in predictable cycles due to other cosmic alignments. There will be some fearsome tides in 1912, larger than usual, which may increase lycanthropic transformation in those not previously known to be afflicted. Worse, yet, in December of 2012, the full moon will coincide with Earth's alignment with the sun and the center of the galaxy. It could be the end of the world as we know it."

The cage fully retracted, I strode off the disc, twisting the bands on my arms half-way round and rubbing at my wrists. "I wouldn't worry too much," I said casually. "I'm sure technology will have advanced by then."

He looked at me, his face drawn and fearful, but my comment had provoked a glimmer of hope in his sad eyes. "You think so? You think there is hope for controlling the situation?"

I finished rubbing my arms and grinned, feeling the exquisite pain of my fangs growing as I did so. "I'm sure," I growled as the beast began to take me away from this world to a better world of power and blood. "You've forgotten the most important rule of practical engineering." I clanged the metal bands at my wrists together, increasing the amplitude and accelerating the process already begun by the twisting of the bands but a few moments earlier. I then did the same with my feet with a brief hop into the air. "Once you put the theory in practice in the real world: miniaturize… miniaturize… miniaturize."

My grin turned to a toothy snarl and the snarl to a roar of pain and anger and beastly delight.

In the wispy haze of morning's glare, the wolf returned monstrous full while the professor gaped and backpedalled away in terror.

The beast leapt at his tormentor, fangs crushing down on his prey's smoky-flavored throat, hot blood gushing forth into the beast's slavering maw, as claws ripped away cloth and skin and bone, spilling the intestines. The wolf ripped and gorged on fresh red muscle until sated.

The creature licked at the blood covering his snout, sucking at it with animal delight. A change of pace from his daily fare. Fattier than mutton, but not as stringy.

The Captain's Wife
Tyler Hayes

Tabitha's wound looked even worse when she turned human. It started as a tiny puncture, a maroon blot on the hip of her mussel-fiber chemise, then gashed the rest of the way down her thigh. She touched the edges of it with halting fingers, swearing every time she made contact.

She eyed the submersible, the sleek hull bobbing just above the surface, its lights shimmering in the spray from the cliffs. It was a good swim away from her perch, and the leg would only slow her down. She tore a strip from the bottom of the chemise, and looked back at the ship with hot-iron resentment.

She tied the makeshift bandage tight, checked and re-checked the knot. The necessary fabric had left all of her thigh exposed, but the bleeding had stopped. She slid down the rock, let the sting of salt kiss her wound; the tension in her chest uncoiled at the feeling. She sat, eyes closed, floating for a too-short moment before the arduous breaststroke back toward the ship.

~

Before the captain was the black man. Tabitha, found him on the docks, piloting one of the great clockwork cranes that unloaded the ironclads from England and Germany. An ox shifter waited on the ground, twisted into a hooved and bent-legged amalgam, loading crate after crate of coal and iron onto the delivery wagons. She watched them, a little girl enraptured by the monster, until she met the smell of fresh fish.

It was a vacuum trawler, small and squat, its hull made of wood instead of metal. Fishing tubes hulked to port and starboard, rubber hoses coiled on the deck, glass bulbs packed with dull-silver tuna. Her mouth watered at the sight.

She walked to the boat, nostrils full of saltwater and meat. Her fingers tingled; her whole body was molten rubber. The fishermen saw her and retreated to their boats, racing to make the sign of the cross. She stopped, gawping at the gesture.

"They're scared," came a voice across the yard, half baritone, half bray.

She turned, and the ox-man was looking at her, one absent hand sitting on a crate.

"Why are they scared?" she called back.

The ox-man spat a gob of mucus into the dark. He started to answer, but was drowned out by the crane hissing to a halt.

The black man slithered flash-quick down the rope ladder dangling from the crane. He was tall, whipcord muscles, skin like a burnt oak. He came closer, wiping scar-hatched hands with a greasy handkerchief, pinning her to the spot with his smile.

"First time seein' the ocean?" he asked.

She nodded, transfixed.

"How does it feel?"

She ducked her head. "Good."

The black man turned his bright eyes toward the fishermen; they crossed themselves again and disappeared into the belly of their boat.

"How's the water make you feel?" he asked.

She looked out across it, silver scribbles in an endless black. She wanted to dive in. "Good," was all she said.

The black man smiled. "I think you have the blood, little one."

Then the shouting. She turned to the noise and saw her father looming over her, huge in his hat and coat, a repeating pistol shaking in his hand; then the black man was disappearing, hands up in surrender as her father took her away from the sea.

They went home, to the horrified servants, to her mother's disapproving screams. She went into her room while they shouted: words like "whore" they thought she didn't know, demands for an ironmonger's girdle the autoharp was meant to drown out. She ignored them and stared out her window, trying to find the black man. She never forgot his expression.

It was the second time she had ever seen a smile.

~

The captain met her in the dining room. He stood by the copper-latticed windows, draped in one of his flowing, alien-fabric suits, his bearded face turned toward the fish swimming past the glass. The place settings had been laid out; the sideboard's microboilers kept the seaweed and roasted salmon piping. She waited by the door, still wet despite the harsh toweling-off, her chemise rubbery and translucent from the swim. He let the doors close before he started shouting.

Tabitha met the noise with her usual ducked head, her usual averted eyes. He railed about the dangers of land-dwelling men, their blind hatreds and their rabid prejudices, the sting of their scorn and their bullets. He told her it was said out of love, his beard brushing her face, his fingers clutching at her wrists, but she heard the anger in his tone. When he had moved away again, when the choleric slant had gone from his body, she met his eyes, and spoke.

"I had to swim."

The captain raised his fist; but this time, he caught himself, and gave her a brittle grimace as he switched on the wireless broadcaster.

"Please come and see to my wife." He paused, glanced back at Tabitha, and hit the switch again. "Bring one of her dresses."

~

The day he took her was Tabitha's third visit to the basement. The salt air was still cold on her face, her mouth still filmed and tangy from the rat-man's chowder. Her father had clutched her wrist the entire way home; the first sight of the girdle brought the only moment of sympathy from her mother.

The smell was the worst of it, rust, blood, and oil. Two cuffs for her wrists, two for her legs, one threatening and massive one for her arms. The spikes on the insides rubbed her skin, daring her to change. The barbed chains her father wrapped around her body, the steam bladders dangling from each junction; the pump mechanism went on her shoulder, the switch locked tight, out of reach of any tentacle or tail. He checked each lock and hinge, examined the bladders for leakage; he never looked at her.

Upstairs there was another argument, shouting and scuffling of chairs. They spoke of abominations, of sins and the need for absolution. When her mother shouted about treatments, her father stalked out of the room. She sat by the coalman's helper, back straight, shoulders squared, and made a game of not letting the spikes touch her.

The darkness stretched the time out, turned boredom into reflection and discomfort into agony. Only the sounds of the coalman's helper marked the time; six hours, six hissing, chugging arcs of the great brass scoop, delivering coal to the central boiler. She remained where she had been left, her body aching for the change.

The knock at the door jarred her out of a half-lucid nap. There were footsteps, a few confused words, then the dash to the basement door while her father unspooled small talk in the front room.

Tabitha's mother was the one who removed the girdle. The older woman shoved a dress at her, onto her when she didn't get the hint. She washed Tabitha's dirt-smeared hands in the launderer, holding her just enough to keep them beneath the soapy water while the gears worked; her skin was dry and angry in the aftermath. And then Tabitha met the smiling man.

He had been sitting on the parlor couch, studying the spidery arms of the autoharp as they plucked out "Greensleeves." He rose like he'd been poured, his manner relaxed and sanguine. He was tall, bronzed, with a manicured beard and bright blue eyes. He smiled at her without subtext; he approached her without fear. There was no sign of the cross, no murmured invective. He turned to her parents, and said, in that avuncular lilt:

"I do apologize for the irregularity, but please give us a few minutes?"

Her parents paused, but not as long as propriety would advocate. When they were gone, his look of joy turned to venom, shot down the hall at their receding shadows. He turned to her, and his features softened again.

"They've never touched you, have they?" he asked, sadness in his manner.

Something about him relaxed Tabitha, pulled the knots loose in her muscles. She stood up straight, as she'd been told.

"Guillaume told us about you," he said.

His smile widened, and sharpened; and in a blink, his eyes were pure black. She didn't look away for an instant.

"What do you want with me?" Her hands clasped her bruised ribs.

He smiled, and his teeth were once more blunt, the animal replaced with the gentleman.

"How do you feel about boats?"

~

176

The latest ship's doctor was a well-browned Punjab, with rough workman's hands and an absence of affect. He tended to her in her stateroom, his clockwork valet squat and clattering at his side. He salved and bandaged with a minimum of fuss, devoid of any embarrassment or even interest in her indecency.

"What was it this time?" he asked, with a clinician's curiosity. He spun one of the valet's cranks with rote expertise, pulled a steam-streaked knife out to cut the muslin.

She looked down at the bandage, tested the way her leg moved. The thing inside her snarled at the confinement.

"Rocks," she said, and reached for the dress he'd laid out.

"I do not seem to recall rocks giving you trouble before," he said; after a moment's pause, he smiled. He replaced the knife, cranked the drawer back into place.

She raised an eyebrow. "What do you mean?"

"I mean, when you're..." He paused. The valet rattled next to him, its boilers swelling up for cleaning. "When you're swimming."

"When I'm not human?" she offered through pursed lips.

The doctor fell silent, discomfort on his face. He finished his ministrations, secured the locks on his valet, and was gone with a whiff of formalities, dragging the valet along behind him. Tabitha let out a long, craggy sigh, flipped the lever on the side of the voltaiphone, and rolled over onto her stomach to stare out the porthole, watching the silhouettes of fish glide by as the sleek brass horn pulled music from the disc.

After a few stultifying minutes of crystallized Sullivan operettas, she switched the galvanophone off and looked to the brass box above the door. She traced the cables down the wall, along the ceiling, sneaking along picture frames and light fixtures to disappear beneath the wine-red carpet. She hurled a shoe at the box, and crawled up the bed to take a nap.

~

The first thing Tabitha remembered about him was the gunfire.

He stood on the platform atop the submersible as it bobbed, lithe and shiny, in the upper bay. He was wearing his red suit, brilliant and fiery, making his sun-deprived skin even whiter; in his hands he

177

balanced a galvanic rifle, sleeker than the one her father used. The smiling man was just about to announce her when he fired.

His target was a gull, porcelain against the blue sky. It fell in an instant, stone dead. The captain's face was, as usual, inscrutable; but when they locked eyes, it was something quite different.

"Hello there." He smelled of salt and oil, a head-spinning odor; his beard was rough against her hand. "A pleasure to meet you, Tabitha."

The smiling man told the captain all about her, calling her "the Hyde Park shifter." His first use of the term was also the first time she saw the captain disgusted. They spoke another minute, and then the captain was bidding her adieu *in flawless French and the smiling man was urging her below decks.*

She was paired with a scrawny boy called Jack, a blond wisp with a thick Georgia accent who claimed the captain had rescued him from a shipwreck. Together they maintained the great batteries in the engine room, cleaning cogs, wrapping frays, pouring out the stinking potions that fought corrosion. At night, Jack showed her how he shifted, popping and ripping from a boy to a rabbit in seconds. Watching him made her muscles ache.

The second week she was there, the captain came to check on them, ensuring that their rubber gloves were undamaged, that the engineers kept them watered and fed. Jack stared at her after the captain left, mystified and horrified at once. When she inquired, he crept closer before he answered.

"That's the first time the cap'n's checked on me in a year."

~

The next morning pretended to be ordinary. One of the maids woke her with pleasantries, tetching over her wound. Breakfast was the usual gull eggs and fried fish, served on the great silver platters the captain was so proud of. The captain wore white, his beard new-trimmed. He waited while Tabitha filled the plates, inquiring after her hip and remarking on his plans for the day's experiments. He was planning to go to the pearl fields, he said, with those great raised eyebrows and that prodding pseudo-grin. He mentioned how bountiful the pearl harvest had been recently, the possibility he might check in on "their" giant clam. She let her fork fall to the table.

"I'd like to go swimming today."

The captain stared across at her, his own fork poised over his scant serving of eggs. He set it down with great care.

"Tabitha, my love, did you not hear what I just said?"

The smell of fish made her shoulders feel too small. She took a grip on the edge of the tablecloth. "Still. I would like to go swimming today."

The captain folded his hands together. "But... your leg."

"Will heal faster if you let me shift." Her voice rose despite itself.

That started the fire in his eyes. "What about tomorrow?" he asked, his eloquent tones gone rocky. "I don't *need* to watch the pearl divers, after all. I can check on our cave, and we can set course for something a bit more—"

"Today," she insisted, her blue eyes flashing sea-green as she said it.

He sat up straight, wiped his mouth with his napkin. For a long, angry second, he examined her; then he dropped the napkin atop his food and left. Just inside the door, he pressed the button for the wireless.

"Please escort my wife back to her room."

~

Their first dinner together was a month after her arrival. She had mastered the simplest of her tasks, and stopped fearing the other one. The captain's appearances in the engine rooms had become a mainstay of her week, sudden inspections that were charming in their irregularity.

The invitation was delivered by the smiling man. She prepared for dinner in a stupor, not so much pleased as puzzled, a feeling not helped by Jack's delirium when he heard.

That night, the smiling man brought her up to the dining room. She remembered her fear at the sight of it, the first glimpse of the mahogany table, the alien stylings on the dishware. The captain stood by what was to be her seat, his evening suit a brilliant canary yellow. He held out her chair for her, pushed it in with care. He fiddled with one of his manifold instrument panels, summoning "Für Elise" from the brass horns abutting the ceiling; then he adjourned to his own seat, elusive as always, his eyelids fluttering with what she'd learn to be nerves.

They started with cheese, or some facsimile of it. He had asked her the same questions he'd been asking for weeks: How was the boat, was her work challenging, was everyone being helpful. The cook lumbered in with a simple first course, seal liver and dried strips of seaweed, and the captain switched to questions about her family, her home life, the things she did when she still stood on land. He asked his next question without hesitation or rancor:

"Do you miss them?"

Tabitha locked up at the question. Her other self pressed at the walls of her stomach, bulked in her biceps and her neck. She looked at the captain, and saw a battle on his face, the lines deepening here, smoothing there as he fought to keep his studious mask in place. The sight brought her to a wan smile.

"No."

"Did they not love you?"

She quivered. Her other self screamed. "No."

She hid her face, but the memory was enough to pale her skin, and that was all the answer the captain needed. He rose, adjusted the panel again; the music swelled louder from the phones. The arrival of the main course was a welcome distraction.

The captain's meal was a pair of white fish steaks, served in a sauce that smelled of cardamom and oranges. Her own meal was brought out in a silver tureen, the sides slick with condensation. When the serving boy lifted the lid her mouth flooded with saliva, her animal brain keening at the saline reek of fresh-caught, unprepared fish. She looked up at the captain, beyond stunned. His smile was magnificent.

"No one will ever be forced to hide their true nature on my ship," he declared. "And that includes those of protean form."

She looked at him, looked at the fish, reeling, sick to her stomach and ravenous all at once. She bent double, mouth wide, and she fed.

It had been the best dinner of her life.

~

Her room had been cleaned since she'd last been in it: the bed made, the carpet steamed, her awkward pyramids of books returned to their shelves. Dessert sat microboiling on a little folding table, a whale-milk pudding mixed up with tropical fruit. Her first order of business was to tear the blankets off the bed.

She stacked the books into a little fortress. She wadded up the blankets and stuffed them into her reading chair. She almost tossed the pudding against the wall, but settled for sitting on the edge of the unmade bed and eating it with her fingers, leaving the squat little microboiler to sizzle on its table. And somehow, as she sat looking at the disheveled room, her fingers sticky with sugar, the box above her door still silent despite the chaos, she felt something close to at peace.

~

Dinner that week became dinner the next week, and the week after that. A dozen different suits, a thousand kinds of fish. They spoke about New York and Calcutta, about his wife and her mother, about the shifters of India and Europe. He knitted together her history from simple queries and asides; some of them he heard with a smile, others with fire.

Six months later, in the frozen waters off Greenland. Her meal was pop-eyed redfish, barely done wriggling. He watched her sniff at the offering, smiled in time with her smile, and asked the question.

"When did your parents figure out what you were?"

She looked across the table at him, her hands tugging at the edges of the tablecloth. Snakes uncoiled in her belly.

"I..." Her heart fluttered. "I guess they just always knew."

He ran a finger across the rim of his glass. "How did they treat you when they found out?"

The question made her other self swell; she breathed against it, feeling the threat of pain along her arms and shoulders. By the time it had passed, the fire was back in the captain's eyes.

"They didn't," he said, flat.

Her skin changed; her nails dug into her palms. The captain's fists slammed down on the table.

"They didn't."

She bit her lip, and remained silent. His rage was enough for both of them.

"Your own parents put you in an ironmonger's girdle?"

The answer came out in a torrent. She spoke of a mother's contempt, a father's neglect. She spoke of their gadgets, and their touching the brass more than her. She spoke of the twisting in her limbs, the longing, the constant longing, for the sea. She spoke of the basement, the launderer, and the girdle, of the way people stared at the marks.

The captain listened to it all, his eyes pained diamonds in the dark. She stopped, mouth a rictus, and tried to start again through the tears.

That was the first time he kissed her. His body was warm through the thin suit; his beard was coarse against her cheeks. He kissed her, and he held her tight; and he whispered, for the first time but not the last:

"On this ship, my love, you will never wear a cage."

~

Her doze ended with the thump of sheet metal on carpet. She sat up, eyes green once more, and sighed in relief when she saw the rabbit peeking out of the air vent.

She melted back down to human shape, moved to the edge of the bed. The rabbit stretched, spine popping and eyes swollen as it twist-poured out of the air vent and transformed into the supine form of Jack. She turned away before he finished changing.

A thump, some breathy struggle; a blanket rustled over by the easy chair. "You can look," he said.

She turned back to him, now standing by her bookshelf, his lower half cocooned in the blanket. He had sprouted to nearly six feet, thickened up with muscle, but his smile was still gap-toothed and awkward. She gathered her robe about her, smirking at the way he fidgeted.

"I wonder how long we have until the captain thinks we're having an affair."

Jack stammered at the suggestion, his face red as a beet. "You say the most terrible things."

She gave him a teasing smile. "Isn't that why you visit me?"

Jack scoffed as he threw himself into the easy chair.

"How are things in the engine room?" she asked.

He answered with a shrug. "About half of the planet gears could use replacing, but the captain refuses to take us anywhere near Britain, and the new boiler is going south ever since the Hessian left. Blockheads need to learn English if you ask me."

"Jack!" she admonished.

He shrugged off her anger. "It's true. But that new boy we recruited in Delhi has been real good for us, and, umm…" He almost kept back the smile. "… Mr. Giles says I'm ready to take over."

Discomfort marred her smile; she tossed out a faint, "Good for you."

The sun in Jack's eyes faded. "What's wrong?"

"Oh." She sat up straight, put on her usual decorum. "Nothing. Nothing."

Jack tetched. "Tabitha. We're blood. You can tell me."

The thing was in her stomach again, twisting, aching. She clutched the collar of her robe to keep steady. "It's…" She looked up at Jack. "I don't want to stay on the ship anymore."

Jack's jaw dropped. "What?"

She felt terrible. "I want to leave, Jack."

"Why?"

"I just do," she said, insistent in her anger.

For a moment, he shied, the brown rabbit gleaming in his pupils. But when he came back to the argument, he was fierce. He espoused the wonders of the ship, the wonder of the ship itself, the power of electricity versus steam; he ticked off ports they'd visited, foods they'd tried, the natural miracles the ship's lights let them see. He did it all with shrieks and gesticulating arms, hammering again and again on the captain, the captain; and when he was done, he asked how she, she of all people, could possibly prefer land.

The word made the thing in her scream. She looked up at him, her eyes green just for a blink, and said, "I. Want. To leave."

She released her grip on the robe, the screaming in her guts subsiding. She reached out a hand to Jack, smiling, mollifying; when he took it in his own she closed her eyes and felt the warmth of him.

He watched her as she rose from the bed. She went to her chest of drawers, rifled around beneath the stacks of bloomers. She found the shirt she kept in there, cut for a man; the white breeches; the otter-skin hat. She dropped them on the bed with a nervous smile.

"You should go." The laugh lines came back. "Or he really will think we're fucking."

A moment of outrage; a moment of mirth; and compliance. Watching him leave—watching him obey—made the thing inside her go still.

~

They were married on the platform, in sighting distance of New York City. The captain had wanted the Indian Ocean, but Tabitha insisted they marry where she imagined her parents could see it.

The wedding was sparse, but perfect, attended by the entire crew. The captain himself ratified the union, glee in his eyes as he mocked the church. He kissed her, and picked her up, and carried her below decks.

What came next always made her blush to think of it—their foolish maneuverings, their ridiculous fumbles. They giggled, and coughed, and averted their eyes as the homespun garments fell off them. Then the kissing, deeper than before; and the feel of his skin on hers; and her other self, deep inside, sated.

Afterward, sweaty and sore, with their mouths both waxy from exertion, they sat and stared up at the ceiling, moving electrified fingers against each other. She studied the paintings on his walls, the spines of his books, marveling that his private room could be more glorious than his public ones. (She asked after the missing paintings above his desk, and was told he'd had them moved to the lounge.) Then she saw the strange box, all brass and rivets, crouched up there above the bed, cables worming out to stitch up the entire ceiling.

"What is that?" she asked.

The captain turned, sleep-glazed eyes. She pointed again, and his consciousness swam up to regard it.

"Nothing," he insisted, and turned to hold her.

She stared at the box until she fell asleep.

~

She awoke to a quiet ship, nothing but waves lapping at the hull. Through the porthole she found open ocean, no hump or crag of land to be seen. She rose, donned the fur slippers he had made her, and stole out with one last glance at her books.

She stole past the chef's stateroom, the empty guest bedroom, the reference library, moving with speed and confidence. The chief engineer's suite, crackling with Mr. Giles' snores. Then the captain's room. The crackling drumbeat of the charging gears covered her footsteps.

The door was shut tight. She heard movements from within, brassy music, the scratch and rustle of paper. He would be reading the day's news about now, culled from the wireless receiver in the lounge. A slurp, a porcelain clink—his chamomile tea, in his abalone cup.

Her heart fluttered; cables went taut in her throat. She tightened her fists and darted past the room, gulping back a tear as she went.

She paused again at the lounge, taking one absent step into the room. She looked at the beautiful paintings, the unbelievable photographs, the brass piston-and-stop arrays of the automated organ. She pored over the gilt titles in his main library. Then she once again saw the display cases full of bones—little ladders of fish ribs, cartilaginous shark jaws. She spun and marched to the companionway.

The starboard hatch was unguarded; the instruments indicated it was exposed to the open air. She took the great metal wheel in hand, gave it two geriatric spins. The pneumatic bolts gave with a sigh; the hinges whined as she moved them. She gripped the handle, shucking her slippers as she pulled it open.

"Wait."

~

For a month they stayed together in his bedroom, unafraid of what the crewmen said. Tabitha split her days between the lounge and the engine room; at night she was with the captain, asking him to name the fishes, to explain the miracles of the ship. On days he was hunting, or busy with his classifications and experiments, she would find her way out a hatch, shed her human form, and swim.

A month after their marriage, the ship glided near to the coast of India. The captain was making preparations to check on the giant clam growing "their pearl," and the itch was coming on to her again, the mind-buckling awareness of the water all around. She went to him, as she had so many days before, and told him she wished to go for a swim. He smiled at her, that affable chuckle, those piercing eyes.

"Don't be silly."

Her thoughts crumpled.

"We're too near the coast," he said. "We can't risk people seeing you."

Her thoughts were a blank sheet, and her body was reeling from the disappointment, but she still managed to ask: "Why?"

"Tabitha," his answer began, admonishing her for her lack of foresight. "You remember how your parents treated you. You remember how much they feared you. If someone were to see you, word would travel at the speed of ignorance: from the shore to the pubs, from the pubs to the houses."

He put a protective hand on her shoulder. "You'd be hunted. We'd be hunted. With vacuum hoses, and pneumatic harpoons, and every other monstrous thing the empires have developed to combat your kind."

His tone was convincing, but her other self remained suspicious.

"You mean you would be hunted."

"That's not what I mean," the captain insisted.

"It's precisely what you mean. You're afraid that I'll get us discovered."

"Indeed I am." There was the fire, this time aimed at her. "And I am worried about that for your safety as much as for mine. For Jack. For Mr. Giles. For all the free men aboard this ship."

Again, she knew she should be convinced; but still, she thrust out her chin. "All the free men."

The captain went blank, the fire hotter than ever. "This conversation is over," he said, and turned to leave.

Then the change. Her skin shot through with white; her vision warped as she flowed toward him, her legs splitting beneath her. She grew, the captain becoming smaller by the second - and then the brass box above her let out its terrible shrieking bells, and the captain leapt up onto a chair, seconds ahead of the pain and the spasms and the sudden darkness.

She was awake within minutes, the reek of smelling salts clawing her throat, her vision small and human again. The smiling man knelt over her, and the captain with him, both watching with a parent's concern. She waved off the salts and demanded to know what had happened. The captain answered without a moment's hesitation.

"A simple precaution," he had said. "The box is linked to finely-tuned scales hidden in the floor." He described it as he described any of his inventions - excess detail and excessive glee. "If any scale registers a sudden increase in pressure, the box will set off the alarm and engage a flow of electricity to the floor, disabling the source of the mass increase."

It took no time at all for her to understand, and the understanding made her skin go white again.

"You mean the box electrocutes any uppity shifter who has the gall to change in your room."

He looked down his nose at her, affecting a lecturer's calm. "Tabitha, my love, your shifted mass is too great for the ship to support. Can you imagine the damage if you were allowed to affect a full change while onboard?"

"Allowed?!"

With the screaming came the tearing; and with the tearing came the ringing and the pain. When she awoke again, the smiling man was the only one still in attendance.

~

His voice locked her in place. She heard his footsteps behind her, quick and rage-steady; her eyes changed color as she faced him.

"What do you want?"

He was wearing the red suit again. He stopped at her question, his indignation flaring his nostrils. He took a breath, and he was almost soft again.

"I want you to wait."

She crossed her arms, chest puffed out. "What am I waiting for?"

He had to fight for his customary eloquence.

"Is Jack the one who told you?" she asked.

The captain nodded. "Do not be cross with him. He looks on you as a sister, and to have to be without you—"

"Don't use him as an excuse."

He flinched, and for the first time she saw the red rims lining his eyelids, the quiver at the corner of his mouth.

187

"I don't want you to leave."

"I know you don't," she said, and again took hold of the door handle.

"Wait," he said, the word distorted and harsh. "Wait. Please."

She glared at him, her body language goading, bellicose. "Why?"

He opened his mouth, let out a wet swallow.

"Why?" she asked again, eyes flashing. The thing inside her thrashed.

"Because I do not want you to leave!"

She wanted to scream back. She wanted to shout. She bit them back instead, and tried calm. "That is not a good enough reason. Not anymore."

The captain's face fell, strained. "I gave you freedom."

"Freedom under your rules."

"Freedom from the ironmonger's girdle."

"Which you replaced with your damn electric box." She chopped a hand through the air, dismissive. "Running on seawater does not make it better. Steam or batteries, it's still just there to keep people like me in check."

"I gave you books." He stepped closer. "I gave you the sea." His smell invaded her nostrils, salt and smoke. "All I did, I did to keep you—to keep us—safe."

"Safe from me," she said. "Safe from who I am."

His brow lowered, shadowing his face in pain. "Who you are is more than a second skin," the captain said. "Who you are is more than an animal."

"Then who else am I?" she asked, her face so, so close to his. "Your second wife?" Saying it hurt. "My father's bastard offspring?"

The captain's lips parted, his sorrow replaced with hunger. She felt it, too. Which is why it hurt when she pulled away.

"Those are who I am *to you*. Who I am is more complicated than what I represent to you." The words hurt coming out, but the thing inside was appeased.

The captain rocked back on his heels. "I… I want to know you, then." Some of his confidence returned. "I want to know you, Tabitha."

Her answer was a shake of her head. "It's too late for that, my love."

"I can't keep you safe out there!" His voice peaked.

"I don't want you to keep me safe."

He reached for her, an angry claw; she stepped back again.

"How will I know it's you when I next see you?" he asked. "How will I know not to kill you?"

"You won't."

The captain's jaw dropped. There was no more retort. She reached out, touched his cheek, letting his beard tickle over her palm one more time. She stepped back, and opened the hatch in full. The salt air made her other self scream.

"I gave you everything I could give you," the captain said, watching her in agony.

She stepped to the edge of the hatch, and gave him one last smile.

"I am grateful for everything you gave me," she said. "But you also took a lot away."

He looked down, stepped back. His shoulders sagged; his face was black. He was defeated, and part of her exulted in it.

"Good-bye, Dakkar."

He looked up. "Goodbye, Tabitha."

She leaped out into the sea, leaving the hum of the wires and the clank of the gears behind.

Her bones exploded; her skin tore; blood and hurt mixed with the waves. Deeper, and her mouth vanished; deeper still, and every sense was changed. She turned and looked out into the water, her tentacles great ribbons floating about her trunk. She felt the shifts in the current, sensed with new organs the movement of the nearby schools of fish. She was hungry.

With a push of her tentacles she was off into the depths, hunting for the nearest prey. The water was all around, and the ship was gone, receded with the moonlight. Where she went the fish retreated, desperate to escape the maw of the giant squid. Nothing talked to her; nothing touched her; and everywhere around her was the ocean.

It was the best day of her life.

Red in Winter
Lillian Cohen-Moore

The wolf came in the late summer.

Ida and I were walking down the hill from the Harold family's barn, overburdened with two baskets each and doing our best to shepherd her younger sisters and overtired brother. That's when we heard it, paws snapping twigs, too heavy to be a dog and growling as it walked from tree line into dim light. I stopped walking, and tried not to look it in the eyes, only near it. Ida stopped two steps after I did, turning back to look at me.

"What on—" She stopped as I carefully deposited a basket by my feet, using my newly free hand to press a finger to my lips. I kept my eyes on the wolf, more stuff of shadow than fur that I could see. Ida quieted, stilled, the children moving close to her, unsure and nervous. I spoke in a whisper.

"I'm going to tell you when to run." I swallowed, mouth dry, listening to my throat click. My heart was already beating river-fast. I dipped a hand into the basket I still held, still staring at the wolf, avoiding its gaze, still unexposed and cloaked in shadows. The glass jar felt smooth and cold and heavy in my hand. I took a quick breathe in, dropping the basket as I threw the jar towards the wolf. I could have screamed for them to run, but Ida wasn't stupid, and I needed all my air for what came next.

I ran. The second I rocked back on my heels and began to run the wolf howled, something more fierce and alien than anything I had heard in my life. I could hear the children screaming. I didn't have to worry about them, because I could hear it chasing me. If I ran west I'd be going straight into the dwindling sun in my eyes, east was where the wolf had come from—and north held dozens of children leaving the farm. I was nowhere near the safety of the steamworks.

I ran south, away from the tree line, and anyone who could help me. If I was lucky, I might not be torn to pieces before making it to the barn. My father never left our home without his gun, but even a man like my father could not run as fast as I. It would be a matter of speed now. I shed my shawl and cap as I ran, hair flowing like streaming ribbon behind me. My eyes watered as the stitch in my side built; I had never run so fleet-footed for so long in my life. The races we'd hold outside the school as children were more than five years past. I could hear it, growling, scrabbling after me on the hill. I could not let myself listen to the sounds in the distance. The barn. Sweet Blessed Lord, I had to reach the barn because this would be a terrible way to be remembered. *Marie, slain by a mad wolf.*

There was no livestock in the barn to distract the beast, but perhaps if it scented them in the pasture, then my flight would not end in my hot blood soaking into earth. There were still lanterns guttering and the smell of flowers trod underneath dozens of dancing feet. When I got to the barn doors and stumbled through them I was wheezing, heart as loud as my gasps for air. No lights provided by the steamworks here, only oil lamps.

But no wolf. I could not hear it, could not sense it, but my terror only welled up when I saw the face of little Thomas peer over the hay loft ledge, near the ladder. Thomas, only seven, who must have fallen asleep. I raised my finger to my lips for the second time that night, waiting the measure of too-fast heartbeats before Thomas raised a finger of his own, pressing it to his lips before vanishing into the hay loft. Silence assured, I took a step forward. And behind me, I heard the creak of barn's wood floor. Thomas peered back over the ledge, blue eyes becoming impressively huge.

There are two choices in such moments. Stand still and let a craven beast eat you, or bolt for the ladder and hope the wolf isn't smart enough to climb after you. I chose to bolt, and it flung itself after me. Its claws skidded and bit into the ground as it snapped its jaw, missing my flesh by a hairsbreadth. I didn't scream. Thomas screamed, and it growled again. I flung myself at the ladder, stumbling and clinging, suddenly gifted with numb hands by terror. I was nearly half up the runs when its scrabbles were rewarded, and I screamed as its mouth raked across—and through—my boot.

By the will of Providence alone, its grip upon me did not hold, and I found my way up the ladder, dragging my wounded foot. I did not look down as it barked and growled beneath us. With the help of little Thomas, we pushed the ladder away, and listened to it crash beneath us. It was in the hay loft, biting my lip so hard as to pierce it, that we hid until the men arrived.

It was the first time the wolf came, and I did not truly see it. I only felt its teeth.

~

It was another three weeks before the woodsman came. By then I was walking again. The teeth had not gone through my foot completely, but there was damage done, and I was only allowed to walk a few feet at a time. There was suddenly far more mending in my life to be done than I had ever seen before. It occupied my hands, and kept me from idleness, but it did not occupy my mind. Day after day my thoughts flitted like my needle, trying to remember what I could about the wolf. Had it hunted me like a wolf would? Surely crossing into human territory as it did must mean it suffered some grave illness. There had been no attacks since that night. The livestock was safe. None had heard something move in the woods.

I could remember its wide-set shoulders, even as it skulked in shadow the night it attacked me. Its fur must have been black, for I could not recall it catching the light that remained when it first approached the tree line. They had found no fur upon my person, but I had moved with haste. I had bled, and hidden in the hay. Thomas, a child of few words, had been asked what he saw that night. He had only one reply, each time he was asked—he would merely whisper "Wolf." I contemplated Thomas in my mind's eye, the few times I'd seen him since the attack. He had seemed frailer, and far more pale, than he had been all summer.

"Marie? Marie, have you heard a single word I have uttered?"

I looked up from my sampler—one of few acceptable applications of my needle with company present—and smiled ruefully. "I'm sorry. I was simply distracted by my stitches. What were you telling me about?" My cousin Christina raised her eyebrows and sniffed delicately, but applied herself with verve once more to the day's gossip. "There's a man in here in town, asking about the beast that bit you." I laid the sampler down in my lap, drawing a slow breath.

"Who is he?"

Christina lit up at the opportunity to discuss a newly arrived outsider to the territory, detailing the appearance (handsome) occupation (tracker, hunter) and intent of the visit (to hunt the wolf). "I am *certain* he will want to speak to you. I overheard Rachel Morris's sister's husband telling Eleanor Sheffield's son that he was going to question everyone who had encountered it. He has been tracking it for months and seeks its end!" Her smile was insincere. "It is truly unfortunate you are not yet well to attend church services. Mother has already declared that he shall have to sit with us, for it is Christian and neighborly to look after those visiting our town."

I gave her as bland a smile as I could. "You do such incredible work in the name of the Lord, cousin." I offered a silent, guilty prayer in my heart, hoping that my injury would keep me from attending church. I was sure the Lord would understand me wanting to refrain from watching Christina simper her way over her prayer book all morning at someone. I offered her another smile, a one more meek this time. "Cousin, I most greatly appreciate your visit, but I fear I still tire so easily…" In a show of familial love and Christian values, Christina had me tucked away by the fire, leg gently propped up and sampler near at hand. Her goodbye hug was brief, but strangely sincere.

I did not think to ask her why she looked so worried when she left. I drifted off into a light sleep, half-aware of the movements elsewhere in the house. Our dog Zeke paced as if waiting for something. The sound of wind in the trees outside crackled and rustled. My maiden Aunt would be out of the house some hours yet, and till then, I could sleep. Each creak reminded me of the moments in the barn when the wolf had lurked behind me. My dreams were at best uneasy ones, filled with memories of my flight paired with nightmarish fantasy, and the shadow of the hunter who I would not meet for some days yet.

~

I went to call on Ida a few days later with my Aunt Sarah. The ground to the Foster's doors was too uneven for crutches. Aunt Sarah's arm and a borrowed cane from my father brought me to the door, exhausted but still vertical. There was an unfamiliar voice when we entered, one that carried, though the words were indistinct. When we entered, Ida was in the midst of springing up from the settee, which remained occupied after she had risen to her feet. Her gentleman caller rose with far more grace.

"Sarah, Marie, good morning!" Ida swallowed, face flushed, studiously not looking at the man next to her. "You're due introductions, of course." She spoke to him without looking. "After we get Marie settled into a chair." I could barely hear him murmur "Of course," to her, in an accent I found alien to my ear.

Whoever he was, he was not from the local territory. But he was here, visiting my friend. Ida, whose family was open to callers frequently. Ida, who had been with me when the wolf attacked. I kept my eyes averted from him. When I was settled into a chair and my cane tucked away nearby, Ida did her duty by introducing us to the hunter. She called him a woodsman and then flushed again. The man who so flustered my friend, and raised the interest of my cousin, was named Alan Bontems. He was a hunter. My Aunt only arched one eyebrow, folding her hands in her lap.

"I thought the men of Europe were not given to such work, Mr. Bontems."

His smile revealed age lines not present in his face when otherwise composed. The electric lights were dim, and danced merry havoc on my ability to tell his age. I nudged my guess to his age upward, trying not to frown. I'd never met the man. Why not refrain from spurning the stranger?

"Some of us chose to apply our minds outside a university or an office." He shrugged, smile still warm. "There are men needed inside four walls, and men better suited outside them. My apprenticeship in Paris was to a gifted engineer. Indoor work was not for me." He looked at me squarely. "But there are men who place others inside four walls. Miss Foster said your father is one of the Deputies here."

I glanced at Ida as I spoke to Alan, watching her blush continue. What on earth had been going on?

"My father took to the law as a young man. I share his passion for seeing consequences answer the actions of the criminal." There was a brief pause in conversation as teacups and cookies were deployed as Mrs. Foster swept into the room. I raised my chin ever so slightly, and Alan gave me the hint of a nod. I didn't know what I thought of him, or if I trusted him, but I was willing to give it my all to find out. The rest of our visit refrained from further verbal challenge, Alan flirted with every woman in the room, and Ida's blush managed to eventually fade. I found myself wondering why he wasn't in Alaska. Our town was rural, to be sure, but enough for a guide to make their living? As he helped Aunt Sarah and I back up into the buggy when our call upon Ida was done, he spoke to my Aunt. "Is there a time you or Deputy O'Neil might be present, that I could come call upon Marie?" His smile was all charm. "To speak about the wolf, of course."

Aunt Sarah glanced at me, waiting for my nervous smile and nod before she turned back to look down at Alan. "You're welcome to come for lunch on Sunday, after church."

~

Alan came for lunch after church, but there was little mention of the wolf. He entertained Aunt Sarah, praised my needle point, and shared my father's incessant love of puns. His only question about the wolf came when I walked him outside to the front porch, leaning on my cane. He wrapped his hand around the wrist of my free hand, staring me down.

"Did you see it?"

My laugh was high and nervous. "What? The wolf?"

As his grip tightened, I felt a strange, slow panic well up. "No. I saw its...its figure, I suppose. But never color, or teeth, not its eyes. The second I realized it was a wolf I distracted it from the children and I ran. Thomas may have seen it, but it was dark and he was in the loft." I could hear my voice become breathier with fear. "I doubt he even glimpsed it, the distance from his vantage from the door is great."

Alan didn't let go of me, only pulled me closer, pressing his lips near my ear.

"How would a sweet young girl know how to recognize something as dangerous as a wolf?"

I felt ill, as if I'd swallowed my heart and it still pounded, lodged in my throat. He drew back, slipping his hold from my wrist to my fingers, lifting my hand to press a kiss against my hand. "Thank you, Marie. For you have told me all you could." When he released my hand he tipped his hat at me. I stood there, frozen and near tears, till he was gone. When I returned inside I said nothing to my father or my Aunt, only went to my room. I scrubbed my hands near raw in my wash bowl, crying, fearful and confused.

~

Alan Bontems stayed on for another five weeks. He talked to everyone, attended church, and befriended little Thomas. Christina could hardly be bothered to call, for she spent every waking moment that could be conceivably considered proper in the man's presence. She did call on me once, two days after he had come to talk to me. When I tried to ask her what she knew of the man, she sussed my intention was to warn her off him. Diagnosing the warning as feminine interest, she swore I was 'no friend nor cousin' and left shortly.

That was the last time I spoke to Christina. Ida became increasingly withdrawn, no longer accepting calls by his third week in town, from anyone. Her parents visited my father late, and a whispered conversation about the depression of young women was had. My father recommended they send her to a relative, one in a place possessing either quality social interaction or tranquil surroundings.

Ida didn't get to enjoy quality social interaction or a tranquil place. She was found hanging in a tree near the creek we played in as little girls, two weeks before Bontems would leave our town. Thomas found her. My father was the one to cut her down, and he waited to weep his bitter tears till he thought I was in bed that night. I ceased to go out. The first few days after, I did not dress or leave my bed. It took Thomas coming to see me, waiting patiently for me to marshal myself to be fit for company, to draw me out of bed. We sat together in silence, till Thomas wriggled under my arm, resting his head on my leg.

"Marie?"

"Mm?" I ran my hand over his hair, smoothing it away from his widow's peak, over and over.

The sigh out of his slender frame seemed too weary for his years. I did not prompt him further, and whatever Thomas's feelings, he kept them to himself. He came nearly every day after that, particularly uncomfortable the days he would tell me that Alan had been to call on his family. We sat in silence often, bewildered by the loss of Ida, the change of seasons. I felt lost and did not know if that feeling could ever cease. My walks in early evening under the brass street lights, one for every corner, were slow and sad.

When Christina wasn't found in her bed at the end of those five weeks, the tavern that rented rooms out found only a neatly made bed and the remainder of Alan Bontems' bar tab to be paid on the pillow. No note from Christina, no note from Alan. Gossip flew, tongues wagged, people presumed elopement. They must have ran off together up north, to the gold rush. My Uncle Marty and his wife were a mix of heart-broken and relieved. Christina was one of several daughters, and the one that had been the hardest to raise. They missed their daughter keenly, but they supposed when things went sour—or they settled somewhere—Christina would write.

Thomas turned eight, and returned to the schoolhouse with the fall. I returned to mending, running the house, and deflecting idle gossip about how I had no beaus. We were to frost but no snow when Benny Walters and his sweetheart Felicity came back from a walk breathless, saying they thought they saw the wolf. They weren't sure, but when the following morning came, and Thomas wasn't in his bed, we feared the worst.

There wasn't a single man over the age of twelve that wasn't walking every field, road and trail that day. There were a fair amount of women out too. They found a bloody jacket, torn, but no Thomas. Aunt Sarah came to stay for a week straight, closing up her house outside town to do it, having a number of conversations with my father too lowly spoken for me to eavesdrop. It was two weeks and the first snowfall before my father brought a woman into our home. She had the same lanky, watchful walk as every lawman I'd ever seen, bright red hair that verged on sunset orange, and a red cloak. The only introduction my father first bothered with was to show her inside, wait for her to finish knocking the snow off her boots, and say "Marie, this is Alison Renard, from the Agency. Miss Renard, this is my daughter, Marie." The gun on her belt had a nicer sight on it than my father's; I knew from playing with one as a child that the Agency sights were a mix of tiny lenses and gears, adjustable and incredibly accurate.

I had met two detectives in my admittedly short life, neither a woman. I shook Alison Renard's hand, which was still covered in dark leather, as she smiled. I had no idea how old she was, and she had the strangest hazel eyes, with rings of eerie golds and ambers.

Alison and my father talked about the news, life after the war, and the elemental discomfort of all forms of travel. They laughed at the notion that a railroad would make its way to our town with any alacrity. It had taken over a decade to built the modest steamworks, and the power it provided was far too small to power rail construction. Even the garriages had a time of it getting to and from the territory. Their gears were still less dependable than horses.

When the dishes were cleared, she yawned, and gave a rueful smile. "I do believe I'm more tired than anticipated. Miss Marie, would you mind showing me to the guest room?" Her expression was sheepish. "I may just lay down on the first furniture I see and sleep without a guide."

I tried to muster a friendly expression. "Of course." I stopped at my father's chair to kiss his cheek. He crooked an arm around me briefly, before letting me go. When we were safely behind the guest room door, I checked on the fire as Alison peeled herself out of her jacket, the grooves of her holster well worn into the blouse beneath it. I looked away as she glanced at me.

"Never seen a woman with a gun before?"

"Never met a female detective with a gun before."

She chuckled, sitting down on the bed to unlace her boots. "I don't bite, and we're both of the fairer side of the Lord's creations. If you want to linger you can, but you should like as much shut the door." She continued to apply herself to the undoing of her footwear as I shut the door, leaning against it.

"Why are you here?" I blurted it out, and now committed, continued. "And why are you staying with my father?" She didn't bat an eye, just slipped her fingers into her shoes and began to wriggle them off. "I am working a case for the agency, I am staying with your father because he had information that got back to us. To me. Valuable information." She removed one boot with a happy sigh, and tugged on the other. "I cannot tell you about my client, but I have been tracking someone for some time who has been implicated but never arrested nor convicted for a number of crimes involving children."

I slipped my shaky hands into my armpits, closing my arms against myself as if cold. "What sort of crimes?"

She dropped her second boot to the floor. "Corruption, mostly." Her smile held no cheer. "An adult willing to bring children to harm is dangerous. If they do it more than once, they become practiced. If I can catch him, I'll need a confession. We still don't have proof he killed the children, only that they suspect he is the real culprit."

"So you think they're here?" I licked my lips, mouth dry.

"It's possible. Their trail leads through here, and I'm quite good at following the scent of my quarry." Alison almost smirk. "I'm quite good at hunting. This is the closest I've been able to get to my suspect in some time. I have faith this trip will prove fruitful." She took a deep breath, before slowly releasing it. "You look cold."

"Overtired, I think." I forced a smile. "I should be getting to bed."

She cocked her head to the side, a small twitch of movement, large strange eyes, still holding mine. "Of course. Sleep well, Miss Marie."

I left with little in the way of grace or dignity, gingerly pacing after reaching the privacy of my room; wondering if the wolf had killed me, if Miss Renard would be here. I slept poorly.

Alison was gone before breakfast, but her bag was still in the room, and my father informed me she'd left him a note.

Gone hunting.

It didn't seem to leave much room for ambiguity. I put our strange house guest out of my mind, got father through breakfast, and near slept walked through cleaning house. Aunt Sarah took in mending for half the people in town, and before long she'd be by to pull the baskets out with me, and we'd set ourselves to work. I cast my eye at the clock every time I passed through the main room. Sarah, sociable but hardly ever late, was past due to arrive. The orrery atop the clock still moved normal, as if belying this unusual omen.

When past due crept into an hour, I worried. When that hour became three, I shut up the house and went down to the Sheriff's office. Snow crunched underfoot and my breath made misty curls in the air as I hurried. I was curt to anyone who tried to stop me for more than a brief good day, focused only on finding my father.

When I got to the Sheriff's office, neither the Sheriff nor my father were present. Sheriff Larsen's son, Peter, was able to inform me they were handling some sort of land altercation, and I briefly considered the merits of dutiful respect of one's parent, or honoring the way I had always taken after my father.

Better to ask forgiveness than to beg permission.

I gave Peter the brightest, most helpless smile I could.

"Peter, could I ask you for a favor? It's about your horse."

~

I was lucky Peter had bought his horse with good sense in mind. Willie was calm, and hard to scare. I didn't bother leaving my father a note. Land rights would take hours, and surely I could beat him home. I just needed to check on Aunt Sarah, who had stubbornly refused to move into town after her husband had died. Their land was outside the town proper, down in the forest. Eventually, the snow was going to give way to a road too icy for Willie to navigate, and I'd have to tie him to a tree and leave him behind. My estimation of the weather was correct, and a half hour walk awaited after tying Willie safely in an area possessing little ice.

On that walk, I saw the clearing I'd pick flowers in during summer, the trees where sweethearts carve their names, and the copse of peculiar trees we loved for hide-go-seek.

I saw the wolf. It was larger than it had any right to be, and black as pitch. It was from a distance, but I saw it. I stilled for a moment, considering if it had seen me, if I just held still.

Across the clearing I could hear it growl. So I did what I had done the last time. I ran. I'd have to be deaf not to hear it give chase, and running in winter, muscles still healing, was twice the misery on earth the run in summer was. Tears were darting my face, wind turning my face red as I ran for my life. I only thought about the need to get behind Aunt Sarah's heavy oak door—and didn't question that it had been partly open till after I had run up the walk, flung it open, and slammed it behind me.

The wolf scrabbled at the door, snarling, scraping. I stood there panting. Aunt Sarah kept her husband's gun in her bedroom, so I pelted through the house, pulling the door open with a breathy shout.

"Aunt Sarah!"

I heard a groan, but couldn't make her out behind the bed curtains. The smell hit me, one I knew was familiar, one I didn't want to remember.

The groan. Again. The lights. So few lights, and she always burned her charge-lamps so brightly.

"Aunt Sarah?"

I whispered her name. Implored it. The smell. The night my mother died giving birth to a brother who never drew a breath, the overpowering smell of blood. I kept walking forward, crying, dimly aware I could no longer hear the wolf trying to get in.

I pulled the curtains open. I screamed, one long anguished shriek at the sight of my Aunt, lifeless, bedclothes covered in blood, her nightclothes drenched, snow white cotton turned dark, so much blood she surely would not live, she did not moan again...

...she could *not* have been moaning, since she was missing her throat.

I could feel bile rising in my throat. That's when hands wrapped around my ankle and pulled me to the ground. I landed with a painful smack of head and body into wood, and from under the bed Alan crawled out, using my body as leverage as I tried to fight him off. The knife in his hand bit into me as he brandished a fist down into the side of my head, stars and pain bursting as I raised a hand to try and block another blow, knife biting into my hand as I shrieked. He dropped the knife onto the bed next to the mutilated corpse of my Aunt, stroking my face as I sobbed.

"You came. I knew you would come to me." His smile was one you'd see from a beau, not a murderer. He left smears of my aunt's blood on my face as I tried to squirm away, and he straddled me, pinning my skirts to me and my legs together. "You heard my wolf."

"Your wolf?" I stared up at him as he stopped, his hands on my face.

"My wolf. The one I built."

"You can't build a wolf." I whispered the words, horrified.

"If you have enough imagination and enough cogs, you can do anything. I learned that when I was in Paris. It's where I started looking for someone like you. I saw you with the eyes of the wolf, months ago. I knew you were the one." He sounded like he was describing a tea cake. I screamed, this time angry, and hateful, he had built the thing that bit me, that killed a child, and *murdered my Aunt*. I spit in his face, and he wrapped his hands around my throat.

"It's a shame that you can't get the smell out of the machinery. Not unless you disassemble it down to its smallest cogs." Spots swam in my vision as I tried to gasp, eyes tearing up and overflowing. "It's just you and I. Nobody here to listen." He lowered his head, whispering into my ear. "I will take you as my winter wife. And when I'm done I'll tell them I was too late, and there won't be enough left of either of you to know what happened. And when I bring home a big, dead wolf for your father, he will cry his eyes out, Marie, but he isn't ever going to know—"

Whatever filth Alan was going to describe to me, he never had the time. I heard the yipping even from inside the cabin. It came out of the throat of something that had fur, and shortly after, I heard the sounds of what was clearly an outmatched horse against a vicious opponent around the corner of the house. He lurched up from his straddle of my waist, swearing a string of words I had never heard, not even out of the mouths of drunks my father guided to jail.

He snatched up the knife from the bed, and went charging outside. I rolled onto my side, gasping. The cuts along my arms and hands stung and bled, maybe worse than the wolf bite had in summer. I whimpered as I tried to push myself up to kneel, head reeling. Everything smelled fetid and bloody. I panted, trying to draw in air, breathe through my mouth. I managed to get myself steadied on one elbow. I wanted to run like the wind but I was too hurt. I stifled the urge to cry out as I placed one palm on the floor, trying to use hand and elbow to level me up. I could hear the report of a gunshot, perhaps two, in the woods. Spots still dancing in my eyes, I hauled myself to standing, and began lurching towards the open door. I managed to clumsily use furniture to keep me upright, but I went to my knees in the snow within a few paces from the door.

That's when I heard her, in the dim of the tree canopy.

"Marie?"

Alison's voice sounded choked, fury and fear vying for dominance of tone. I whimpered in answer, crying in broken sobs. She found me on there on the ground, stilling for a heartbeat, maybe two, before she bent down to drape her cloak over me, and then grabbed me. "Arms around my shoulders, poppet. I've got you. Shh, I've got you. Just keep yourself in my cloak, dear."

She was careful with me, trying to hurry me along with stealth and quiet, when I heard the wolf growl behind us. I clung to her, as we both heard Alan speak.

"If you give her back to me, I'll just tear you apart with the wolf. It won't even be personal."

I could feel the blood and heart beat hammering inside her through cloth and skin. She turned her hip as she spoke, half over her shoulder. He couldn't see it, but she'd exposed her gun to me.

"Oh, dear. Are you that tired of molestation and murder, Alan? You've only killed four people this time. You must be getting old. You killed forty people in my district of Paris when I was her age. You were so *frustrated* that you lacked my gift at the end."

I took the gun as carefully as I could, sliding it under the cloak against me. I felt numb, as if my wounds no longer mattered. Two women against a madman and a wolf. I only had a heartbeat to consider what she'd said, of what it meant, before she shoved me away into the snow. In the moments I tumbled and groped blindly for the gun as my vision swam, the wolf growled and the yipping bark, now snarling, had return. When I surfaced from the snow, I saw Alan with a look of pure, sadistic joy on his face, some strange, oversized pocket watch in his hands.

I am my father's daughter both in hasty decisions, and my ability with a firearm.

The first shot was for the wolf. It tore into its metal flank as it wrestled the russet-to-orange fox in its jaw, Alison nowhere to be seen, and with no time to think about it, about any of it, I took my second shot. I blew Alan Bontems' face off, and he dropped the pocket watch as he fell like some deranged and savaged children's doll.

The wolf didn't move, but I walked towards it, emptying the remaining bullets into it. Arcs sparked from the metal, and I dropped the gun when it was empty. That was the same moment the wolf dropped the fox from its mouth. I sunk to my knees, ducked my head down under my arms and the red cloak wrapped around me, and wept. For how long, I don't know. When I raised my head, the fox had been replaced by Alison. Wounded, bloodied, and beyond saving. I put my own cut hands on her as she tried to wave me off, panting. She smiled at me, eyes glassy as she stroked my arm.

"You should wear it. Take it. It... suits you."

I watched the light die in her eyes as I held onto her, her blood mingling with my open wounds. When she was gone, I fled.

I left the imprint of four paw prints in the snow, as I found the strength to run.

Legacy
A.G. Carpenter

Summer heat grips Savannah in an iron fist. Even with the wooden doors at the back of the zeppelin hanger opened wide, it's sweltering under the metal roof. Willa wipes a dribble of sweat off her forehead with the back of her hand. The fans turning overhead barely move the humid air and her shirt's already soaked.

She glares at the guts of the tension-triggered, chain transmission lying on the crate that doubles as a workbench. "More like tension fucked." The derailing arm is sticking at all the wrong points, dropping the chain every time she attempts to change gears. She gives it another prod, prompting it to fold at the appropriate joints, but it moves as a whole and the chain snarls.

"Fire and damn." Resisting the urge to whack it with the spanner, she reaches for the screwdriver instead.

The money had been good. If it hadn't, she'd never have taken the job running rifles down to the Gulf in the face of a storm. Trouble with good money is it never makes up for the trouble that comes with it. Now all four props on her airship are wracked and need new parts before they'll run again.

The bell at the front door jangles. Then heavy footsteps.

Willa doesn't even bother to look up. "No trips today." *Likely no trips this week.*

"I'm looking for Captain Arch." The voice is deep, with a rough edge.

"You've found her." She waits for the muttered apology, the hasty retreat. A quarter turn on the middle tension joint and another prod at the derailer. *Better.*

"You're Captain Arch." His tone is a mix of disbelief and amusement.

She stands up, wipes the grease from her hands. "That's right."

He's dressed like an Amerigish trader, but his hands are not those of a merchant and his accent is a blurry Imperial. "I understand the sly-like smiles now. The lack of a first name."

"It would have spoiled the joke." She hooks her thumbs into her belt. "As it is, it don't matter much. *Squirrel* is down for repairs."

He rubs his fingers through his hair. "A shame. I've plenty of coin to spend on the right pilot. Every man in town says that's you."

Willa frowns. He's clever, holding out the promise of good money, but she's just about had her fill of that. Besides, if every captain in Savannah is pointing him to her it can only mean one thing. "You're headed for Lake Ponchartrain."

He nods. "I have..." His voice fades, face going the color of mushrooms.

"Hey." She grabs for his arm as he folds at the knees, but it does little to break his fall. "Are you sick?"

"Not sick." His eyes slide closed and he folds up entirely—skin shiny with sweat, breath coming fast and shallow.

May be heatstroke. He's dressed awful heavy for traveling through Deep South in the heart of summer. She unbuttons his shirt collar and loosens the kerchief tied around his throat.

Something glints underneath. The collar is silver; the locking mechanism soldered shut. Everywhere the metal touches his skin is the color of an old bruise, ugly white lines creeping down his neck and across his chest. Willa's breath knots up in her throat, nearly choking her. "Skin-changer."

Fifteen years she's kept her distance from these folk. Fifteen years of running from the rumors of her mother and the strangeness that must surely touch Willa too.

She touches the collar, hesitant, but he doesn't move. The lock is fucked and the collar itself is clasped so tight against his skin it's near impossible to think of cutting it off. Leaving it means sure and painful death. *Not my business.* But it's hard not to make her concern.

Something in the yard clatters, followed by voices speaking low and fast. The bell at the front jingles again. This time the footsteps coming up the hanger are cautious.

"Hello?" The accent is a twin of the skin-changers. *Imperials.* "Captain Arch?"

Willa reaches for the biggest spanner to hand, a hefty tenner with an oversize shaft, and nudges the Imperial sharply. He grunts but doesn't open his eyes. *Right.*

His coat is open and the butt of a pistol peeks out of a shoulder holster. Willa slides it out, a .45 revolver that's worn but clean, and lets it hang behind her hip as she stands up.

There's a thunk and clang coming across the yard. The rhythm is syncopated and she doesn't recognize the specifics of the beat, but she knows what it means. Energy-generators. And she's only got the one converter hung on her belt.

She moves away from the skin-changer, even though it puts her more squarely between the men coming in the back from the yard and those walking down the hanger from the front. Better to have the ground underfoot free.

The newcomers stop and spread out, but they don't come any closer. As the converter hanging on her hip spins up, she understands why.

The air gets hot; the sweat in her shirt evaporates in a fliff of steam and the fabric starts to char before the converter snags enough energy to dissipate the heat.

Before Willa can take a breath the others are rushing toward her. The first to reach her has his fists clenched. May be there's a glint of a knife in his hands. May be there's not. His skull makes a wet sound when she clobbers him with the business end of the spanner and he drops, heavy as old wood.

Five left. The two standing in the door to the yard don't show any inclination to move closer; the engines on their backs steam, furious, while the generators strapped to their chests begin to spin up a second time.

The other three are still coming and Willa lifts the revolver. Two in the chest and one in the head. *Four.* More like two with the mechanari still doing their thing with the energy-generators. Just as well they're taking their time—the converter on her hip is hot; she's not sure how much more it can take.

She pulls the trigger again, but it just clicks. *Empty.* tosses the revolver to one side and hits the next fella in the chest. The spanner clangs and rebounds hard enough to make the muscles in her shoulder protest. *Armored. Ain't that special.* She plants the heel of her boot in the side of his knee and he goes down with a squeal that stops abrupt when she hits his temple with her fist.

A couple of small bones break with a muffled pop and Willa blinks back a wave of pain. "Damn." *Three.* She adjusts her grip on the spanner with her good hand as the last one closes with her. Her throat tightens as the dark eye of a gun winks at her, but she steps in closer, brings the spanner down on his wrist.

"Cocksucker." He grabs for her shirt and she slams her knee

into his groin. And again in his face when he doubles over.

The spanner finishes the job. *Two.* But they're throwing energy.

The air gets cold around her, the converter spinning up again as frost forms on the ground. She forces stiffening joints to move, lunging close enough to the nearest machinari to hurl the spanner at the copper tubing feeding steam into his generator. One of the joints breaks free and he staggers into the yard, shrieking and flailing against the scalding cloud, before he collapses in a pile of hot metal and flesh.

The ice forming on Willa's clothing thins, then the convertor on her belt stops with a skreek of metal-on-metal. Sweat freezes on her skin and ice forms on her boots, in her hair. She closes her eyes a heartbeat before the frost creeps over her eyelids.

A growl filters through the ice clogging her ears. A scream, cut abruptly short. The discomfiting sound of bones breaking.

Savannah heat presses in on her, heavier after the grip of the cold. Willa spits a clot of ice out of her mouth and wipes the frost-slick from her face.

The skin-changer stands over the last engineer. The exhaustion and sickness from moments earlier is gone. He turns toward Willa, wiping his mouth on his coat-sleeve.

It is not enough to hide the blood on his chin or the way his eyes catch the light—hard and gold.

There is no point in thinking about it; the flash of pity she felt moments before is gone in a rush of outright fear.

Every muscle is bitching, joints aching from the flash-cold, skin still tender from the cast-fire, but she runs flat out toward the door and what she hopes is the safety of the city beyond.

Too late she hears the rhythmic clanking, sees the glint and bulk of Imperial soldiers in the door. The wide mouth of a bliksembuss yawns at her, then lightning strikes, dropping her in an agonized knot of locked muscles.

Hard hands grab her, ungentle, and drag her toward the yard behind the hanger. There are more than just six bodies on the dusty floor now. Willa feels a flush of relief. *Maybe he escaped.* Jealousy is a heartbeat behind. *Bastard.*

The *whump-whump-whump* of engines shake the dust. Willa coaxes her head into tilting back far enough to get a look at it. Definitely not local. It's far too big, designed for intercontinental travel. The hull is painted a flat grey, the zeppelin overhead unmarked, but she has little doubt it's Imperial.

The air-ship settles toward the ground, filling the yard from one end to the other. The doors open and more soldiers march down the gangplank. Willa is pushed to her knees as a brass-legged machine—half again the height of a man and with a glassed-in dome on top—lurches down into the yard with the grace and ease of a sailor newly come to land.

The machine comes to a stop and the glass folds back. Inside is a little man pulling levers and turning knobs and wheels with furious intensity. Raised up behind him is a chair—mahogany and velvet—and a woman with a face like a bulldog.

Willa coughs, trying to work some moisture back into a suddenly dry mouth. Not just any Imperial airship. *Queen Elsbett's.*

There is a scuffle in the alley. More soldiers enter holding chains which, in turn, hold the skin-changer. He is dragged forward and forced to his knees in front of the Queen. Her mouth puckers as though she has tasted something sour. "Rex."

He scowls but says nothing, even when prompted by the butt of a rifle.

Willa clenches her teeth to keep from staring, open-mouthed. Owen Rex is the late King's son, but not the Queen's. *The uncrownable prince.*

"Do we know what he was doing here, Barnett?" Elsbett looks to her right, at a lanky man with hair the color of honey and blood.

"Rex was here to see her." A gesture toward Willa.

"That's Willa Arch, ma'am. A pilot and technologist." This statement from a shorter, scruffier man that Willa recognizes from the Kayton Canal taverns. *Patterson.*

The Queen sucks on her bottom lip. "She looks native."

"Yes, ma'am." Patterson bobs his head. "Her mother was Plain folk."

"Even worse." She presses back in her chair, as though to gain more distance from Willa. "Why was he here?"

Willa hesitates, dislike of the Empire warring with her anger toward Rex for dragging her into contact with the Imperial will.

Barnett steps forward and slaps her across the face. "What was he doing here? Did he want the collar off?"

She shrugs. "He wanted me to take him to Lake Ponchartrain."

"More foolish that I thought." Elsbett waves a hand and Barnett draws his revolver.

"You won't get there either if you ain't got the right gear." Her voice is high and thin, the last word nearly lost as Barnett pulls the trigger. He's got good instincts, turning the barrel away at the last second so the bullet catches a couple strands of hair before burying itself in the dirt.

Willa bites her lip against the urge to beg, tasting blood. "You need the right gear or the storms'll take you apart."

Barnett looks at the Queen who looks at Patterson. "Is this true?"

"Them storms is fierce. That one…" A jerk of his head toward Willa. "She got these machines she puts on her airship. 'Sposed to turn all that energy harmless."

"I'm willing to trade," Willa says. "My converters for my life."

Elsbett's lip curls. "We don't trade with your kind." A waggle of her fingers stops Barnett just short of pulling the trigger a second time. "No point in killing her. Not 'til we are certain these machines work."

"Yes, your majesty." Barnett holsters the revolver and points to Patterson. "You, show the engineers what these machines look like. Make sure they strip out every part and get it aboard." A hard gesture toward Willa and Rex. "Put them in the brig."

Queen Elsbett's walking-chair is already clambering back up the gangplank, steam hissing from every joint as it crouches low to enter the dirigible. The guards holding Rex haul on his chains, dragging him toward the ship.

Willa breaks for the gate, but only makes half the distance before another lightning strike brings her down hard. The soldiers descend on her, uncompromising and brutal. Curling up does little. A couple of ribs snap under a fierce kick, pain scorching with every subsequent breath.

Barnett's face is blurry, but there is a curl to his mouth that looks like smile.

Something hits the side of her head, hard, and everything stops, replaced by blackness and the distant gong of her own heartbeat.

~

The moon hung over the prairie, fat and gold.

Willa sat on her heels and watched Sassaba filling her hands with moonlight. The ritual she learned from her mother who learned from her mother who learned from her mother; bathing in the light to ease the transition between one form and the next.

Willa bit her tongue against the heat of jealousy. Father was Amerigish, descended from pale-skinned men who walked cold islands across the sea. His blood, and therefore hers, did not hold the spark of Becoming that is the heart of a skin-changer. Of all the clan, she was the only one who would not learn the ritual, would not experience the growth of a second form as she matured.

Sassaba paused, turning to look at her with golden eyes. "What's wrong, mastinca?"

Willa scowled. "I don't want to be a rabbit."

Her mother tipped her hands, pouring the moonlight on the ground, before she came to sit with Willa. "Neither do you wish to be a wolf."

Willa shuddered. To be a skin-changer was Power, but it came at a cost. She had sat in the cellar with Father, the door bolted and his rifle across his knees as her mother howled outside—hungry. But the moon...

She turned her head, the weight of moonlight on her skin— comforting. Tears ran, hot, down her face.

Sassaba stroked Willa's hair and dried the tears on her cheeks with the edge of her shawl. "Be easy, mastinca. In time, you will find your own Power."

Willa, gaze fixed on the moon, nodded. In time.

~

Willa wakes with a start. "Sassaba." *Mother.* She reaches out, fingers finding only rough wooden planks and dust. Her head hurts, soft and tender—as though it will slough into pieces at the slightest touch. "Damn." Even that seems too loud. Her mouth too dry.

The airship shudders as lightning breaks outside the window. Another bolt follows—almost before the bright-white of the first can fade. Willa sits up. They must be getting close to Lake Ponchartrain if the storm is this thick. *How long was I unconscious?*

"Are you all right?" Rex sounds bad.

She combs her hair out of her eyes. "I've been worse." As soon

213

as she says it, she knows it's all wrong.

The Imperials had beaten her. Broken bones. Left her concussed and unconscious. She should be barely breathing. She should be wracked with pain.

Rex watches her, intent. His shoulders are hunched, maybe with pain, but the lines around his eyes say it's more like to be guilt.

Panic kicks in her chest. She raises her hands, turning them palm up. On the left wrist is a jagged and circular scar. *A bite mark.* The skin is shiny and pink, already healing. Already too late.

"Son-of-a-bitch." She lunges for him, but her muscles are as soft as her head feels, pitching her forward a couple of steps, then dropping her to her knees.

"Easy." He kneels, hands on her shoulders. "The change has left you weak."

Willa spat. "You had no right."

"You were dying, Arch." He shakes the hair back out of his eyes. "I did what I had to."

"By turning me into a monster?" She glares at him.

Rex frowns. "It is more complex than that." He touches the ink mark on her shoulder, just visible under the ragged edge of her shirt—the man who walks on all fours. "I think you know that."

"Huh." She licks her lips, tongue still dry. Arguing will gain nothing. The noise of the storm outside crushes in on her, broken by the rhythmic *whump-whump-whump* of the air-ship's engines. Her head throbs with it, stomach churning as the crackle of rain fills her ears.

Under it all is an uneven, yet steady, beat that pulls at her. *Thum-thum. Thum-thum. Thum-thum.* At first it is only the one. Then another, hidden more deeply under the noise of the engines and storm. Then more, fainter still—like moths beating against glass.

Heartbeats.

She clenches her fists, struggling with the rising hunger that burns under her skin. Takes a deep breath. Her nostrils flare, pick up the stink of coal and grease and dust, the warmer smell of polished wood and brass, but more importantly the pungent odor of sweat.

Willa tries to stand, but Rex has hold of her arms and pulls her back down. "Don't." His voice is hard. "You won't be able to break down the door. The noise will only attract the guards."

She bares her teeth. "Good."

"No. Your only chance for escape lies in them thinking you

214

injured and helpless."

But she is thinking less about escape and more about sating the hunger. More about repaying the hurt the Imperials caused her.

"Arch." He pins her down. "Look at me."

She twists against his hands. Strikes out with her fists. Her muscles are growing stronger. Power fills her and everything fades except for the call of the strongest heartbeat.

Thum-thum. Thum-thum. Thum-thum.

She bites down, blood rushing hot and copper across her tongue. Her teeth strike bone and she tosses her head, tearing skin and muscle loose. Frustration burns hot. She wants his throat, wants the clean kill. Her teeth sink into his arm a second time, worrying at already mauled flesh.

This time something bitter stings her throat and she spits to rid herself of the taste. *Silver.*

Clarity returns and with it horror. "No. Oh, no." Willa scrabbles to the farthest corner of the little room in a vain attempt to put distance between herself and Rex. Her lips are stiff with drying blood and she gags, then vomits.

"Sassaba." The name comes unbidden and she crouches on the floor and sobs. "Sassaba."

Rex pulls his wounded arm tight against his chest. "Stop it. Hush." He snarls the words.

"I hurt you." She gulps for breath. "I attacked you."

"Because there was nothing else to hunt." He stands up, swaying with the motion of the airship, his good arm braced against the wall. "Next time you will make sure it is different."

Willa shakes her head. "I can't."

"You will." His voice is steady, certain. "Because otherwise you will die."

She buries her face in her arms. "For the best."

Strong hands grab her shoulders and Rex pulls her upright. His skin is the color of ash, haggard lines cutting deep around his mouth. "Enough. If you want death it will come soon enough."

Living is the challenge. Sassaba's voice echoes in her memory and fresh tears cut hot lines down Willa's cheeks. "I'm sorry." She touches his wounded arm, instinctive. "This has killed you."

"No. My step-mother killed me when she put this damned collar 'round my throat."

Willa nods, reluctant. "Is that why you wanted passage to Lake Ponchartrain? To bargain for Queen Marie's help in taking that off?"

Rex grins, all white teeth and cynicism. "I'd thought to warn her." A cough that leaves his lips tinged with blood. "A fool's errand."

She says nothing. Queen Marie may not rule an empire, but there is a reason Mud remains a free country, serving neither Spanish nor Empire nor Union.

The lightning and thunder are growing less frequent, the rain batters the hull of the air-ship with less intensity. "We are getting close."

"Here." He holds out a handkerchief. "Wipe your mouth."

She licks her lips. They still taste of blood. Scrubbing her mouth 'til it tingles, the handkerchief turning rusty—then licking again to find the last few flecks. "Better?"

Rex nods, puts the dirty handkerchief back in his pocket. "My step-mother has heard the voodoo queen trades in flesh." He shrugs into his coat, awkward, pulling the sleeve down to cover the scabbed wound on his arm.

"That is not a lie." Willa has been to Lake Ponchartrain before. The ceremonies that take place there are weird and frightening; inexplicable but not unbelievable. "It can be a hard faith."

"I think she means to try and give you to Queen Marie as payment. You must let them think you are injured until the opportunity to escape comes."

"And if it doesn't?"

"Then you make one." He pauses, hands clenching into fists. The dead tint to the skin on his neck is laced with red now, angry lines that creep up his jaw and disappear under his hair.

"Rex." She touches his arm, light.

"It's nothing." Even the lie seems to age him, the hair on his temples silvering a little more.

The engines, pounding in the stern, slow and the noise in the ship lessens, noise from outside the hull growing more discernible. Voices—clamoring in Muddle; the splash of rain against the perpetually wet ground; the harder accent of the Imperials.

Footsteps echo at the end of the corridor and Willa moves away from Rex. Best not to let them see her with him. She tugs the charred cuff of her shirt over her wrist as best she can, then curls up on the floor in the spot where she woke. The breaks and pain she should feel are healed; she can only guess at the injuries the soldiers might expect her to have.

The door clangs open and rough hands grab her. She hangs mostly limp, whimpering in the back of her throat as they drag her out.

"Shut up." One of them cuffs her across the side of the head, and she subsides. Maybe they will think her unconscious.

The Imperials' footsteps clatter on the gangplank, then squelch in the mud. Rain soaks Willa to the skin, in a few heartbeats. Not that her shirt was covering much anyway.

She lets her head roll sideways against her shoulder, squinting between her eyelashes to try and get her bearings.

The engines that power the storm-generators wink, orange in the murky afternoon, as the doors are opened, coal shoveled inside, then closed up again. Work-song, mumbled from a hundred different throats, drifts through the steady patter of rain. Men slog past, fireboxes smoking in their chests, shoulders bent against the weight of the coal-carts as they move fuel from the barges at the southern end of the lake up the shore to the waiting engines.

The flow of bodies separates, moving around the Imperial squadron, but doesn't stop. Willa forces back a shudder. *They never stop.*

A shell path emerges out of the mud, broadening as they approach Queen Marie's meeting house.

Willa tilts her head, glancing toward the back of the column. Queen Elsbett's walking-chair is stamping along, steam oozing from every joint as the engine strains to pull the thin legs free of the mud. A few paces behind is a second clod of soldiers dragging Rex in chains. He staggers, drops to his knees, then struggles to his feet under the violent encouragement of the guards.

The zeppelin drifts low overhead, gunnels bristling with heavy arms. *Not friendly visitors.*

The meeting house, a wide building with no walls and a palmetto thatched roof, is already rippling with activity. The Imperials have not waited for an invitation; they are spread out around the open walls, weapons at the ready.

A squadron of Armored hustle a group of coffee-skinned women into house. The women wear nothing but strings of beads, hair cropped close to their heads, mouths stitched shut with copper wire. *Marie's handmaids.* The eldest are greenlipped, the copper oxidizing

217

against their skin, while the youngest still shine—the wire glinting bright against pink lips.

Willa bites her own lip 'til she tastes blood as the Armoreds usher in a solitary figure. *Marie Laveau.* They push the voodoo queen down into the wooden chair in the center of the house and retreat.

Energy that has nothing to do with the storm-generators crackles through the meeting house and the handmaids cluster around their mistress, beads rustling like wind in palmetto leaves.

The hiss and wheesh and stamp and clank of Queen Elsbett's walking-chair makes Willa twitch and she lifts her head, cautious.

The chair folds up its legs and settles to the ground. The glass panels draw back to reveal Elsbett, seated atop her own wooden throne. She is dressed in silk, with pearls at her throat and jewels glinting on her fingers. Her hair is pulled back into an iron-like knot on the back of her neck, not even a single strand out of place.

A sharp contrast to Marie Laveau. The voodoo queen is barefoot, dark hair wound up in a grey scarf with curls springing loose around her temples. Her dress is plain and black, cut no differently than any sharecroppers wife, with a red and white shawl laid around her shoulders.

Between the two of them, Elsbett is not the one Willa fears—not even with her arbitrary judgment and execution. But Queen Marie... *She touches the dead as well as the living.*

Marie looks at the assembled soldiers, at Willa and Rex on their knees among the guards, and at Elsbett on her steaming brass dais. "What do you want from me?"

"I have heard that you can do things outside the realm of technology. That you are skilled in hidden arts."

"This is true." Marie leans on one arm of her chair. "What do you want from me?"

Elsbett picks at a fold in her dress. "My heart is failing," she says. "I have heard you could... fix it."

The voodoo mother, rubs her chin, thoughtful. "If I were so inclined."

Elsbett waves her hand. Barnett, standing just beside her walking-chair, draws his revolver and steps forward. He fires into the group of handmaids. The gesture seems careless, but one of them sags—not just wounded but dead.

Marie doesn't flinch, but her shoulders get hard, even as the other women murmur through stitched lips. "This is how you look to gain my favor?"

Elsbett frowns. "I do not require your favor. Only your service."

The back of Willa's neck flushes hot. The smell of blood is dizzying. She licks her lips in anticipation and tucks her feet under her. She hadn't thought she would kill anyone, but when Barnett raises his revolver a second time his lip curls—same as when the soldiers had beaten her. Smiling.

She steps around the guards like water rolling downhill and digs her fingers into Barnett's throat 'til she feels his blood pulsing against her fingertips, then tears it loose. Wet-red spills across her hand, almost burning her with its heat. Willa shakes her head as the hunger rises. *No time for that.* She snatches Barnett's pistol from his dead hand and springs up onto Elsbett's walking-chair.

The little driver in the lower compartment fumbles with the levers and she puts a bullet through his temple.

Elsbett hisses as Willa presses the tip of the revolver against her throat and the Imperial soldiers, still fumbling with their own weapons, freeze as they realize they cannot shoot her without risking the Queen's life.

Willa takes a slow breath. "Out."

For a couple of heartbeats, they hesitate. Looking to each other. Looking to Elsbett.

Willa thumbs the hammer back. "Out. And away from the house."

"Do as she says." Elsbett's voice is high and thin, her face the color of old muslin. Sweat beads on her forehead and her breath rattles fast and shallow. "Now."

The soldiers trample out of the house, leaving Rex on the floor when they can't prod him to his feet.

Something buzzes in the air; not Queen Marie's energy, but a mechanical vibration. Rhythmic. Deliberate. Willa doesn't need to take a closer look at Elsbett's chair to know the monarch is signaling the zeppelin. Already the *whump-whump-whump* of the engines is louder. *Bringing in reinforcements.*

"Rex."

He tries to push himself upright, sags back to the floor. Queen Marie, on her knees next to her murdered handmaid, moves to his side. She rolls him over, lays his head in her lap. "He will not make it far."

Willa looks at her, sharp. "What do you wish to trade for?"

The voodoo mother raises an eyebrow. "His freedom, and yours, is not for sale. I told you, I do not take those who do not come willing." She motions to her handmaids. The women take hold of Rex and lift him onto their shoulders.

"What are you doing?"

"He will die before you reach the deep trees, girl." Queen Marie brushes the dirt from the front of her dress. "Leave him here and if he is willing, I will come to terms with him."

Willa shudders, but death or life or the thing which the voodoo mother can offer that is somewhere in the middle, none of them are choices she can make for Rex.

"You will suffer for this." Elsbett slumps in her chair, but her eyes glitter like glass under the high slope of her forehead.

Willa's finger tightens on the trigger; she will not wait idly for the silver collar.

"No." The voodoo mother touches Willa's hand. "That choice resolves nothing."

Willa hesitates. The Imperial soldiers are forming ranks at the end of the shell path. *They mean to burn this place out.*

"I will handle them, girl. I think I owe you that." Her gaze touches on the dead handmaid and Barnett's broken body.

"Certain?"

Full lips curl in a smile that is a promise of retribution and Marie holds out her hand. An eerie silence settles over the lake.

They are not singing. The shuffle of hundreds of feet is the same, but the song that drives the men is stilled as the walkers converge on the meeting house. Some are bare-handed, but most carry rocks or clubs or knives.

Rex, carried by the handmaids, is a blurry shape in the rain. Willa swallows hard. "Take care of him," she says. "If he will let you."

"You have my word." Marie brushes her fingertips over her heart, then takes the revolver from Willa's hand. "Go while you still can."

Willa doesn't wait any longer. She jumps out of the back side of the house, running for the trees and the swamp beyond. The walkers part in front of her, letting her pass unharmed and unhindered, closing back up behind her as they advance toward the Imperial cohort.

Willa pauses at the edge of the trees, heart hammering in her chest. The smell of fear is thick in the air and she tilts her head back, muscles trembling.

The voodoo queen stands at the edge of her house, bare feet planted wide. She raises her hand and a groan leaks from the mouths of the walkers. Wind gusts in from the sea, catching the zeppelin broadside and driving it into the trees that ring the lake.

The pop and tear of the goldbeaters skin of the balloon ripping open on the heavy branches is audible even where Willa stands, further from the lakeshore. The hiss of hydrogen escaping into the air is more subtle—a whisper of impending chaos.

Willa puts her head down and bolts for cover. Overhead the clouds crackle with lightning. The hair on the back of her arms stands up with anticipation; the gas escaping from the zeppelin will drift straight up to the spark and then...

The concussion of the explosion rattles the leaves above her and heat touches her skin, quickly snuffed by the pouring rain. Voices rise on the wind behind her—screams, the haunting moan of the walkers, the sharp and shrill orders of military officers.

She runs. The blood pounds in her veins. Body loose and ready and moving with the terrain. Throws her head back. "Yiyiyiyiyi." The cry of the hunter is comfortable in her mouth. Comfortable in her skin.

Her joints loosen, body changing with every stride. She pauses only long enough to tear the charred clothes from her back. Her hair turns thick and soft and covers her from head to toe-pads. Ears growing short and pointed, face turning square.

She leaps into the nearest tree. Sharp claws cut deep into the bark as she climbs into the upper branches, maneuvering until she can see over the rest of the swamp canopy.

To the south smoke rises from the broken skeleton of the Imperial zeppelin. The sounds of conflict have died and there is only the rush of rain and constant murmur of thunder.

Willa twitches her tail. To the north she hears the steady patter of a heartbeat and the delicate squelch of small, hard feet. *A deer.* She purrs, deep in her throat, leaping from branch to branch toward the ground.

She stretches and sniffs the wind 'til she catches the scent of her prey. *No longer mastinca. I am igmuthanka.*

The Man at the End of the Chain
Folly Blaine

I puffed out my chest and danced. Since I'd been taken captive six months earlier, dancing was the only real pleasure I had left in my capuchin form.

Whirling and dipping to each hoot of the street organ, my tail whipped around as I snatched coins in my simian hands. I spun and bowed low, glimpsing scuffed boots and frayed hems, pretending the legs were stocky trees. My imagination clutched at the tinny reverberations of the instrument, blocking out the muddy streets, the pea-soup fog, and the pinched, gray faces. I pushed it all away and wrapped the music around me like a shroud, hopping from foot to foot and clapping my hands in frenetic desperation. Baring my teeth in a forced smile, I exuded happiness I didn't feel.

The crowd responded as it always did—with cries of "Look at the monkey," a smattering of coins, and half-hearted applause.

The moment I dreaded finally came: the organ grinder, the one I called Master, turned the crank one last time. The music stopped. A cold wind nipped my fur again.

I curtsied the way I'd been taught at English school back home. The crowd rewarded me with a few more coins before scattering.

"Zona." Master jerked the chain attached to my collar. I staggered back, choking. He knew how hard to pull without damaging me too badly. "Coins." He tossed out a length of chain and a cloth purse.

I caught the purse, straightened with as much dignity as I could manage, and scampered from side to side, plucking coins from the muck and the gutter. I dropped the valid ones inside—mostly pence, a few bobs—but not the fakes. I knew enough to tell if it was a wood slug or a cheat, even if all the money here looked strange.

Yet another thing I missed about Brazil.

I recognized a handsome red-haired man near the back of the crowd, wearing a black cloak. He'd been to the last few shows. I wondered what he wanted. Didn't flatter myself to think he'd come for just my dancing.

The man pushed his way to the front of the crowd and exchanged a few words with Master. The gentleman pulled a white card from his pocket and handed it to Master, who nodded. The strange man walked away, his cloak swirling behind him.

A wave of nausea overtook me. Thankfully, the organ grinder didn't notice. He liked to smack the illness out of me. I swallowed the bile and braced myself. The shifting sickness was coming more frequently now. I wasn't meant to stay in one form so long, but Master hadn't let me out of his sight in months.

Still fingering the card, the man at the end of the chain said, "Back in the box." He gestured to a wooden crate with air holes punched in the side. I looked up at him sadly.

"Now." Master jerked the chain. I stumbled forward. He snatched the purse from my grasp and tied its strings to his belt loop, stuffing the bulk down his trousers.

I climbed inside the splintered crate, knees wedged against my chest, my tail pinned behind my back. He coiled the chain in a lump beside me and slammed the lid shut. I closed my eyes and pretended I could hear the sea, feel the sun's rays warming my cheeks. But instead of leaping over white sand beaches, I stifled a sneeze. London's cold and damp made the illness even worse.

After a bumpy cart ride back to our rented room, the box shifted, dropped, and whacked the floor. Master unhooked the latch and lifted the lid. I coughed and crawled onto my stack of flea-infested blankets, willing sleep to take me quickly. A baby's wail came through the thin walls; the smell of boiled cabbage hung thick in the air. I scratched at the many insect bites on my legs—my nails trailing wide circles around the red welts. Each shiver of false relief I savored.

Someone knocked at the front door. Master cracked the door, then swung it wide. The strange, red-haired gentleman stood there, holding his hat as if expected. Master ushered him inside.

"You've considered my offer?" the gentleman said.

"Let's see the money."

The gentleman handed Master a stack of notes. While Master counted, the gentleman crossed the small room in a few steps to crouch in front of me. I kept a drooping eye on him and drew a ragged breath. All I wanted was sleep. The urge to shift had never been stronger.

"My name is Isaac," the red-haired man said softly. He removed a black glove and touched my forehead. His skin was cool and dry.

"You didn't tell me she was sick."

"Sick?" Master shook his head, recounting the notes. "Never gets sick. Tired, maybe. Could be that."

Isaac lifted my arm and let it fall. I didn't bother to resist. Not while the room was spinning.

"Is this her water?" Isaac sniffed the rusted cup beside my head. Black specks floated in dregs of spoiled wine.

"This creature is ill."

"Changed your mind then?"

Isaac spread my eyelids apart and peered at my pupils. "I didn't say that. Unlock her chains."

"Not while she's in my sight. Always trying to escape, that one."

"She can't stay in this collar." Isaac wedged a finger between the metal and my neck. "Her fur is falling out. Terrible sores."

Master tossed a metal cuff on a long chain at Isaac's feet.

"Use this then, but keep an eye on her. I won't be blamed if she escapes."

"The key?"

Master gripped the notes. "Key's extra."

Isaac frowned. "The price I paid was more than fair. You've enough to buy five ring-tails in her place."

"This one's special. Took me years to train."

That was rubbish, but I was in no shape to argue.

"I suppose the scabs and flea bites are extra, too? And what about her thinning fur?" Isaac shook his head in disgust. "By all means, charge double for her broken spirit."

The organ grinder shrugged. "You deprive me of my livelihood, *sir*. Maybe I should change my mind."

Isaac snorted and I was afraid Master had scared the handsome man away. I shivered on my thin blankets. Any other master would be better than the one I had, but I couldn't allow myself to hope. Not yet.

Isaac's eyes met mine and the hard lines around his mouth softened. "Take my watch," he said to Master." It'll fetch a good amount." He removed his pocket watch and handed it over. Master reached for it greedily, tapped the side, and put his ear to the bronze skin.

"What do you call her?"

"Importer called her Zona. Never bothered to change it."

Isaac repeated my name as if committing it to memory. He lifted me under the armpits and placed me in the box, but he did not close the top.

"You're Scottish, right?" Master chuckled. "You want to dabble in the music business, you should've spent your money on bagpipes instead."

"And why do you say that?"

"Unlike a monkey, bagpipes don't shit on your floor."

Isaac ignored the organ grinder's laughter while he placed the metal cuff in the box beside me. He patted my head. "Bagpipes don't have tiny hands," he whispered.

~

A throbbing headache woke me in darkness. The dense air smelled of wet earth, mold, and traces of coal smoke. Dry linens had been draped over me while I slept. The skin around my neck—where the collar had been for so many months—felt oily, as if lard had been slathered over the wound.

When I tried to sit up quietly, something cold and heavy pinched my left wrist, rattling when I moved. I'd almost forgotten the metal cuff. A tug revealed the other end had been secured to something concealed in the dark behind me.

A flame hissed to life in a nearby kerosene lamp. The red-haired gentleman sat in a chair beside my nest of linens. He rubbed his eyes and stretched.

"Morning."

The flame's orange light wavered in the pockmarks on his face. But his eyes crinkled in a friendly way so that I had no immediate cause to fear him. "How are we feeling?"

I lifted my unchained right hand to my mouth to mimic eating.

"Ah, hunger. Yes." He tore a hunk of stale bread from a loaf and handed it to me. A tin cup filled with clear water followed.

I nibbled the bread. It was coarse on my tongue.

"You communicate better than most ring-tails," he said. "Perhaps it's a hermit's fancy, but you have intelligent eyes. We will be friends, Zona."

I dunked the bread in the water to soften the crust, and wondered what he'd meant earlier about needing "tiny hands."

"If I were to remove the chain, would you promise to behave?"

I nodded before I had a chance to think better of it.

"Fascinating," he said. "Do you even know what you've agreed to? Are you a mimic or do you truly understand?"

I lowered my head and resumed gnawing at the crust.

"Best to wait and build the trust. It's one thing to talk to a monkey as if she's a friend. Another to trust her not to escape."

I glanced around the chamber. In the flickering lamplight, strange skeletal puppets made of gears and metal and wire had been suspended along the walls. They were in the shape of men and appeared to be in various states of completion. Some were missing hands and feet. Smooth formless faces.

Isaac followed my gaze. "I hope you'll excuse the mess. I'm something of a tinkerer."

I picked up the cup and sipped the water, careful to control the nervous tremor in my hands. At one end of the room a set of stairs led up to a door. At the other end was a strange looking stove, with a giant pot set on top. A gurgle of boiling liquid and hisses of steam emanated from the sealed pot. Numerous dark tubes and hoses snaked out from the lid and rested on the floor, twitching every few seconds.

My eyes jerked up at a muffled thud that originated above the ceiling near the stove. A series of long scraping sounds followed the thud.

This form enhanced my vision. Yet I could not penetrate the blackness looming overhead, and the noises seemed to have come through many layers. By the stale earthy air I suspected we were underground. Were we in a cave? A cellar? Were we even still in London?

Another thud, and the gentleman stood. "They're starting early."

A sneezing fit overtook me.

"I'm afraid it will be noisy for the next few hours and you still need rest."

The man removed a handkerchief from his pocket and did something I couldn't see. He leaned over to press the damp fabric over my flattened nose and mouth.

"Blow," he said, but that wasn't his aim.

I squirmed under his grip and inadvertently breathed deeply. Sweet, acrid fumes burned my airways, a cross between inhaling a rotting banana and a belt of gin. The odor made the edges of the room blur.

I couldn't lose my hold, not now, not while the cuff bound my wrist so tightly. Panic overtook me as I thought about what might happen if I lost consciousness. There was a good chance I'd shift once I entered artificial sleep; I wasn't sure I could retain control.

I thrashed weakly and fought the waves of sleep dragging me down into oblivion. Isaac stroked the tan fur around my face. I fell against the blankets, yawning, blinking slowly against the lamplight, mouthing, "No." I struggled to raise the metal cuff. I begged him to remove it with my eyes.

The red-haired man gently pushed my arm down and tucked the blanket around my sides. "I will return this evening when you are better rested. And then we will work."

As the room spun into blackness, I silently begged Yemanjá, the mother goddess, that I would not shift this day.

~

I screamed. The bones in my left wrist were being pulverized. Trapped in an impossible vise, the blood supply had been cut off from the fingers. Still only at mid-transformation, I gnawed at the metal and slammed my wrist against the bedframe. I found my voice and shouted "Help!"

No one came.

There was no stopping a shift once it had begun. For better or worse, my body was stuck in the throes of transformation. Muscles stretched and pulled beneath my skin, the bones expanded and knitted together, hair and tail sucked back inside to some secret compartment.

As I fleshed out, the metal cuff embedded itself further into my skin. As I feared, the new form was unable to compensate. Blood that should have gone to my fingers spilled from the circular gash at my wrist, bones irretrievably splintered and crushed to dust.

At first the fingers tingled. Then they grew cold and unresponsive, as if another person's hand had replaced my own. I clutched the ruined appendage and bit my lower lip, trying not to sob, waiting for the shift to complete, so I could force my body back to capuchin form. It would exhaust all of my energy and I would have to wait many hours to shift again, but I couldn't allow Isaac to find me in human form. At least not until I knew I could trust him.

I concentrated on breathing and thought of home. I thought of being forced to leave my mother and my sisters. I thought of my father, handing me over to the trader, relieved of his burden.

The scraping sounds above grew louder.

~

Isaac returned after I was capuchin again. He trudged down the stairs, carrying a candle on a silver tray. He leaned over me. When he spotted the blood around my bed, he tore back the sheets. I cringed as he revealed the dead hand. All he'd wanted from me were tiny hands. Now what would he do?

He set down the candle, crouched by my side, and pinched the colorless thumb. "How did you manage this?" he asked, his voice full of wonder. "A reaction to the metal? Perhaps you tried to slip off the cuff and damaged yourself?"

A strange glint entered his eye. Isaac stood and scanned the room.

"It could work," he said to himself. "Worth the try."

He left my side and moved along the wall, where the metal men were hanging. He rummaged around the edges, poking and prodding. Blocking one of the metal men with his body, he unscrewed something and put it in his pocket. He collected another object I couldn't quite see, also from the wall.

"I've been developing this procedure for years. Most of the kinks are worked out."

He returned with a metal hand and a large cleaver. My heart hammered at the sight of them. He rotated the hand in the flickering candlelight, the hinged metal fingers curling inward. The base was round and he held it against the dead hand. It was larger than mine, but slightly smaller than human-sized.

"A good match. Good size." He lit the kerosene lamp. "We'll just get you fitted."

He tied me to the bed with rope until I was unable to move, and removed the cuff. The binding vexed me, yet so far he had only shown kindness. I breathed deeply and tried to ignore the cords digging against my sides.

229

Isaac pulled a handkerchief from his pocket, but hesitated. "No," he muttered. "I must know your reactions as we proceed." He stuffed the handkerchief back into his pocket.

He selected a short wooden rod from the wall and tested its heft.

"Open," he said, forcing the rod between my teeth. "If you do understand, Zona, bite when you feel pain."

He lifted the cleaver and brought it down swiftly across my wrist. As if from a great distance I heard my severed flesh hit the floor with a sickly squish. I did the only thing I could do. I screamed around the rod until I'd exhausted my voice.

I don't know how long he worked on the stump, but I was conscious for it all. There was tugging and hammering, sewing and bolts. I looked into his face as he sucked on the end of a thread and eased the thread through the eye of a needle. Then he stitched.

I had never wanted to die so badly. If I could have shifted to surprise him, I would have, but I was stuck in this form for a few more hours at least.

At last he leaned back and rubbed his eyes.

"The final test," he whispered. The scraping above had ceased ages ago. But even whispering, his voice sounded unnaturally loud over the bubbling and hissing stove.

Isaac turned my stump toward the light. The sight of it made me nearly forgot the pain. He had attached a wide metal ring to the end of my wrist, like a cap. He picked up the metal hand and twisted it onto the end. The hand snapped into position with a smooth click.

Isaac loosened the bonds around my left arm. "Wiggle your fingers."

I considered ignoring him, but curiosity got the better of me.

"Go on."

I wiggled the phantom fingers on my left hand. In response, the metal fingers extended and retracted with sudden jerks.

"I'm so pleased," Isaac said. "I'd only tried that on cadavers before."

I stared at my new fingers in horror. How was I moving them?

Isaac produced an oilcan and dribbled a few drops on the joints. He released me from the remaining ropes. My wrist ached.

"Ready to work?"

I blinked, groggy. He chuckled.

"Perhaps we'll just give you a chance to heal."

~

Isaac unhooked a wide black tarp from the ceiling, revealing a single door, large enough for a person to pass through. It was in the same location where the scraping sounds had been coming all week.

"It's time I tell you about the family business."

He unlatched the door on the ceiling. It fell open, swinging down. Isaac held a candle to the opening.

"Come here, Zona. You'll want to see this."

After a week of recovery, my wrist felt remarkably whole, with only occasional twinges of pain—as a shifter I couldn't regrow bones, but minor wounds healed faster than normal. I swung my legs over the side of the bed and jumped to the ground, opening and closing my hand into a fist. I joined Isaac at his feet.

He hoisted me up. A ladder had been built into the side of the vertical tunnel. I gripped the lowest rungs and paused. My new hand took the weight just fine. The wood was drier than I expected, though it was dusty, and the air smelled stale.

"About half-way up you'll see a small door. It will lead to a coffin."

I stopped and looked down at him. He must have seen the question in my eyes.

"Welcome to graverobbing." He chuckled. "Or, if you prefer, my exclusive corpse farm."

Corpse farm? I shrieked and bounced on the rungs to show my agitation.

"Calm yourself. I'll explain."

He spread his arms wide and continued.

"We're beneath a cemetery my family has overseen for generations. I'm something of a doctor, you understand. I require a constant supply of cadavers, which could easily arouse suspicion— particularly if all the bodies at the cemetery went missing. So my men identify any recently deceased without family or loved ones, and bury them in this special plot I created for the purpose. No one expects a graverobber to approach from below."

He paused. The fire crackled in the room, sending out a long hiss of steam from the pot.

"I've been watching you, Zona. You're the cleverest ring-tail I've come across. And since my last assistant failed to detect a particularly obvious booby-trap, I find myself in dire need of clever assistance. I'll train you, of course."

While he explained it so reasonably, I weighed my options. Isaac had built me a hand and given me a clean place to sleep. My situation was already much improved compared to living with the organ grinder. Would it be so terrible to steal from dead people no one would miss?

"You look very serious, Zona." Isaac folded his arms across his chest. "There must be something I can bribe you with. Food? Money?" A slow smile spread across his face. "I've seen you dance. I know how you enjoy music. How about I make you a hand that will help you make your own?"

I cocked my head.

"A tiny street organ for a hand. How does that sound?"

Was it possible? If he could do such a thing, I could make my own money. I'd never need to work with an organ grinder again.

The reward was too great to resist. I took a deep breath and resumed the climb. Mid-way up the tunnel, I unlatched the small door. The narrow end of the coffin had been wedged against the opening, so no dirt stood between me and the wood. My eyes traveled up the ladder, trying to get my bearings. I assumed the headstone was directly above.

"Plug the end of this into your palm. It connects to the steam."

He threw a strange rubber hose to me.

I inserted the hose into an opening at the center of my metal palm. Steam hissed from the joints of the fingers. I kept the hand clear of my fur although I could feel its warmth.

"Flip back the tip of your index finger," called Isaac.

I did and discovered a small blade, spotless silver and deadly sharp. As steam continued to flow into my palm, the blade whirred to life, vibrating smoothly in place.

"Now cut a window into the coffin."

I pressed my blade into the wood. The pine split around my finger. I dragged the hand down roughly, making two parallel tracks, then I made the top and bottom lines. I pushed the center of the hole and the block of wood fell inside the coffin against something soft.

"You in?"

I bared my teeth at him and nodded. He disappeared from view and the vibrations stopped.

"Throw down the hose." I wiggled the hose from my palm and tossed it behind me.

My eyes had adjusted to the dim light, but Isaac raised the candle to the base of the tunnel.

"Climb inside and check for shiny things."

The thought of sharing space with a corpse made my skin crawl. I growled at the realization of what I was about to do.

"Imagine," he said, "a tiny hand organ, your thumb as a crank. I will make this for you, if you help me."

I bit my lower lip. The smell of decay wafting through the hole was subtle as weak tea. The body must be fresh. My enhanced low light vision could make out a gray shroud. I had seen dead bodies before, but I'd never touched one. Would it be slimy? Would the skin be swollen and bloated? I hoped this one had died a peaceful death, at least. I climbed inside the coffin and pressed myself against the body.

The roof was low and I had to crawl, but there was more space than I expected. I tried not to breathe. The flesh squished and shifted beneath me. I tore aside the shroud—best to get it over quickly. A young woman lay there, maybe 16 or 17 years old, her eyes weighed down with two gold coins, and her mouth stitched shut. Dirty blonde hair framed her pale face. Deep wrinkles etched the sides of her nose and mouth, as if the skin was very dry. I snatched the coins from her eyes and the gold chain around her neck, with its pretty orange stone.

"Check her sides," called Isaac. "Sometimes you get lucky."

I patted her freezing sides, gingerly. Maggots moved near her hairline and I jumped, hitting my scalp on the low lid. Shaking my head, I resumed my search and felt a hard lump under the sheet. I moved it aside to reveal a pretty gold cross, gems embedded in its surface.

I climbed out of the hole and dropped the items into Isaac's waiting hands. As he examined them, he muttered, "Excellent work."

I jumped to his shoulders and climbed down his body to the ground.

"We make a good team, little Zona." He bent over to scratch my head. "Soon enough I'll be able to send you for the real valuables."

I hopped up on his straight-backed desk chair.

"How's your hand?"

I held it out for him and he examined it. "The flesh is healing nicely. And your neck?" I tipped back my chin. "You'll be needing more salve and I'm about out. I'll pop out to the chemist before they close."

The door shut quietly. I was alone. He'd left me a lit candle. I sat back on the mound of linens and opened and closed my hand. It was amazing how much control I had. I picked up a pipette and manipulated it around my fingers. The glass cracked and I set it back down.

There was a noise at the door. Isaac must have forgotten something. I looked up expectantly.

The organ grinder squeezed through the slit. He held a wooden box under his arm. "Zona," he whispered.

I tensed and jumped to the desk chair, leaped to the trap door hanging open, scrambled up the ladder, and dove into the coffin.

"I know you're here." The organ grinder shuffled across the floor. I backed against the far side of the coffin behind the woman's corpse. I closed my eyes, threw the burial shroud over me, and initiated the shift. I wasn't going back in the fat man's box.

Metal crashed to the floor in the cellar below. I blocked it all out, closed my eyes, and willed the change.

I imagined a white light flaring into existence at the center of my forehead, expanding until it covered my face in a warm glow. As I imagined the light building strength, my flesh tingled. Shifting like this, under control, kicked off my adrenalin and set my heart pounding inside my chest. Despite the cold and the damp, beads of sweat formed on my forehead and I shivered. I raised the metal hand before my eyes and watched the flesh around my wrist change and accommodate the cap. I breathed a sigh of relief as my body changed around the prosthetic, possible because it had been embedded in the flesh pre-shift. A fresh wave of spasms wracked my body.

The organ grinder's red face popped through the opening. "Found—" Mid-sentence he absorbed the scene. Me, lying face down on a corpse, mid-transition. My back arched as my spine extended. The organ grinder's expression froze in shock. "You're...you're..."

"I'm?" I said through gritted teeth. And then I shoved him with my metal hand as hard I could in the nose.

He shrieked and fell back, all the way to the ground.

Naked, and in my human female form, I crawled over the corpse and onto the ladder. I reached back in the hole and pulled the shroud from the corpse and wrapped it around myself, tucking in the edge of the sheet above my bosom. I crawled out of the coffin and down the ladder, hopping to the floor.

"My back..."

I cocked my head and wiped the drying sweat from my brow. I searched for words, but it had been so long since I'd spoken aloud. The man on the ground had kept me in chains since he'd bought me from the importer. Blood pooled around his skull. He'd cracked his head hard. I imagined finding the wooden rod and smashing the rest of his skull into the hard floor.

He groaned. "Help me."

The door opened and Isaac stepped inside. "The chemist closed early. I'll try again tomorrow." He turned, caught sight of us, and stopped. "How did you..."

My metal hand flew to my throat. "Uh," I said, in a dry croak. Isaac didn't recognize me. Why would he? When he'd left I was capuchin. "I-I-Isaac."

His eyes slid past my shroud-dress to my hand. I held out the metal appendage for him to see more clearly.

Recognition flashed across his face, and he strode down the stairs, stepping over the organ grinder's body. "Zona?" He tilted my chin toward the light. "Same eyes. Same wounds. But how? What are you?"

"Cursed," I said. "Seventh d-d-daughter of a seventh daughter."

"Therianthropy? I've heard stories, but I never thought..."

I pointed at the man on the ground. "He-he-he tried to take me."

Isaac frowned. "The organ grinder, is it? Well we can't have that." He poked the groaning man with his boot.

"Please. She's lying. I'd never—"

"How did you find this place?" Isaac asked.

The organ grinder didn't answer.

Isaac ground his heel into the man's hand. The organ grinder gasped.

"Didn't quite catch that."

"Followed you."

Isaac crouched beside my old master. "I understand. You realized that money was not an adequate substitute for your musically-inclined ring-tail so you came to steal her away. Is that fair?"

"Social visit." The organ grinder swallowed. "Concerned about the monkey's welfare."

"Then why b-b-bring that?" I pointed at the box he'd dropped chasing me.

The organ grinder's cheeks flushed.

"We must make this right, *sir*." Isaac widened his eyes in fake sincerity. "I could *never* live with myself if you were feeling cheated— especially since you've always dealt so fairly with us." Isaac turned to me. "Zona? What do you think we should do with him?"

I looked from the organ grinder's bloody scalp to the kind man who'd treated my wounds. "I just want to go home."

"Where is home?"

"Brazil," I whispered.

"You'll need money for passage. And I still need an assistant." Isaac snapped his fingers. "What do you say you work for me to save the money?"

I flexed the fingers on my tiny metal hand, remembering how he'd fixed the damage. I could learn from him, save money, then go home to my mother and sisters. I crouched on the other side of the organ grinder's body. "Would you still make me that hand organ?"

"Sized to whatever form you require."

I smiled and said yes.

Isaac clapped his hands once and rubbed them together. "Excellent. Now how attached are you to this gentleman?"

"Not at all."

"Most excellent. Then I suggest we take this opportunity to continue your training." Isaac leaned in close to me. His breath smelled of peppermint. "Remember, Zona, the real valuables are on the inside. We could start by removing a kidney." He stopped when he saw me frown. "Unless you have a better idea?"

"Could you make a b-b-bagpipe out of lungs, do you think?"

The organ grinder whimpered.

Isaac grinned. "My dear Zona. We will get along just fine."

"I beg you," said my old master. "All a misunderstanding."

"Wait," I said.

The organ grinder looked up hopefully.

"This man owes me back wages." I leaned down and cut the strings at the organ grinder's belt, ignoring his protests. I yanked the purse from his trousers, took half the coins, and tossed the lighter purse into the man's lap. "No need to give me a reference."

Isaac removed a handkerchief and a small bottle from his coat pocket. He unscrewed the cap and tipped the bottle against the handkerchief, then pressed the damp fabric to the organ grinder's face. After a moment, the man's mouth went slack. His breathing deepened.

"Ready to get started?"

I nodded, fascinated by the organ grinder's measured breathing. I pinched the man's stubbled cheek and he did not stir. "I've never done anything like this before."

"Best way to learn is to do. And I'll be right beside you the whole time."

I smiled up at Isaac, and wondered what the organ grinder's insides looked like. Would they smell sweeter than his outsides? "I'm ready," I said, firmly. "How should I start?"

"Bring a candle and plug the steam hose into your hand." Isaac unbuttoned the man's shirt to expose flabby, white flesh.

I brought the candle, flipped back the fingertip, and inserted the hose into my palm. As steam hissed from the knuckle, the saw began to vibrate with a low hum, sending pleasant shivers up my arm.

"When this is over," Isaac said, "I look forward to learning all about you." He squeezed my shoulder briefly, and then cleared his throat. "Make an incision in the man's chest here."

And so I did.

We attached the blowpipe so it extended from the left side of the organ grinder's chest, and could be folded flat against his body when not in use. I thought that was clever, but the application of the melody pipe—the chanter—was pure genius. Just above his belly button we installed a telescoping pipe that could be extended to a length of one and a half feet and played by hand. It was a kindness really, giving the organ grinder an instrument he'd never be tempted to sell.

And supposing it should come up in conversation: The left lung provides a fine and consistent air supply when surgically implanting a bagpipe inside a human male.

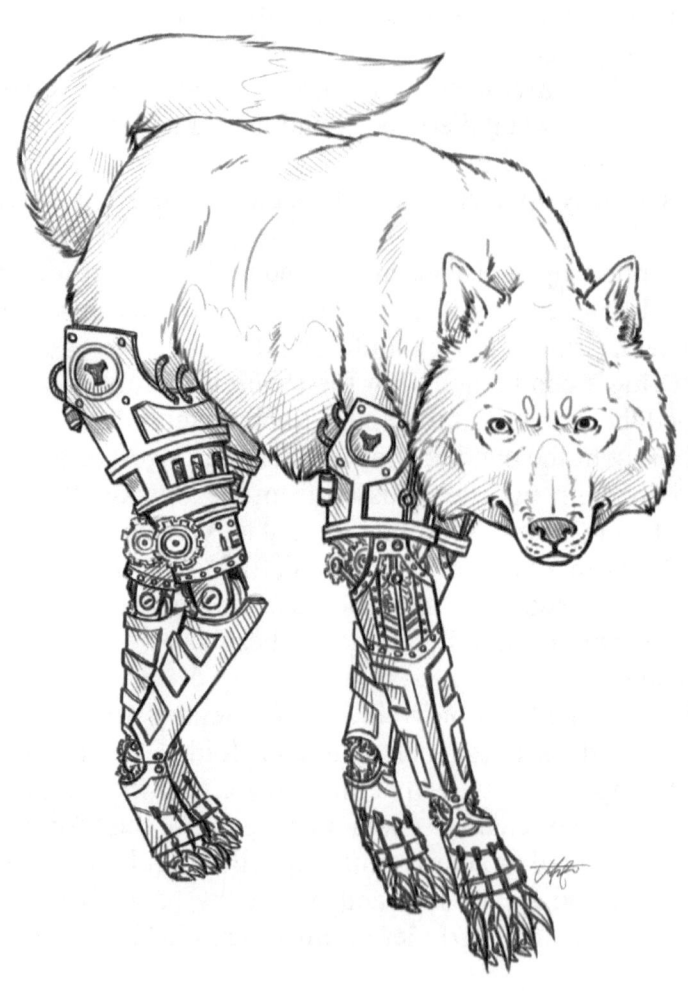

Their Man
Mark W. Coulter

"Ready, Hornsby?"

Sebastian tested the bands that held him to the cruciform table. The cold metal held fast against his skin, even when he jolted up against it.

"As one ever is." He said, steeling himself for the moment.

Simmons nodded and pulled the lever. To his credit, Sebastian Hornsby only winced slightly as the razor-sharp blades fell and severed his limbs at the shoulders and hips, rather than the screams that had echoed around the theatre years ago. The pain was as excruciating as it had been the first time, but he had learned methods from a specialist his handlers had brought in from the East in order to cope and reduce his reaction to the agony. The small man in his strange robes had taught him how to control pain through sheer force of will, and the current machine was calibrated well and could cleave the joints at the perfect spot in just one blow.

Laying on the table like a stump with sweat beading on his forehead, Sebastian took deep breaths, focusing his mind away from the pain. Simmons meanwhile checked the wounds and applied a salve that cooled the worst of the sensations. Supposedly it would prevent infection as well, but that was not a worry for one such as Hornsby.

When Simmons was satisfied that the patient had been prepared, the doctor unstrapped the severed limbs and gathered them for the trip to the furnace without a word. The Queen's men had insisted that he'd have to sacrifice all four to achieve the necessary goals, and he was their man. Still, he normally preferred to keep some configuration in flesh during the several days the others grew back. He did not relish the idea that when this mission was over, he would have to be completely waited on hand-and-foot while he convalesced and slowly regrew his arms and legs. Any assistance from clockworks would only slow the growth, and that would be more unbearable.

Waiting for Cuthbert, the engineer, to come arrive and begin fitting him out as usual, Hornsby went over the briefing in his mind again. The caustic smell of the various clockwork and machinery plants surrounding the headquarters had been ever present as he learned of the latest heinous attack on an innocent family. The tragedy, however, had led to an opportunity for which the Queen and her counsel had chosen him. He would be required to go down into the wretched sewers of London and give up all his flesh and blood limbs for greater maneuverability. But waiting down there was a chance for which he had hoped most of his life, and his contacts knew this.

Intelligence claimed that the beastly shapeshifters had set up some kind of loathsome colony beneath the city and that the Alpha of London himself was currently among them. A chance to destroy their leader and fulfill his vendetta. Sebastian had come straight from the cramped briefing room to the operating theatre, as time was of the essence.

The door opened and the smell of stale wine and fresh metal announced Cuthbert's entrance. The round, jovial man was in high spirits today as he wheeled his cart of tools into the room, followed by two assistants pushing in the racks that held his collection of artificial limbs and Simmons, returning to monitor the process. Soon Graham Cuthbert's round, red-cheeked face leaned down over Sebastian with its huge grin.

"'Allo 'Ornsby!" he said, "Don't bother gettin' up, mate. 'Is'll take a few minutes 'ere."

Cuthbert clearly had something new up his sleeve to show Sebastian. Hornsby tried to maintain his composure. Cuthbert was loud, boisterous, and showed little to no regard for the conventions of the day regarding manners in high society, despite the work requirements of his trade. Hornsby had to remain stoic around this man, to never show how he felt about Cuthbert's japes and informal attitude.

Because of all the people who, poked, prodded, and set Hornsby about his business, he actually liked Cuthbert best. And *that* simply would not do for a man of his station.

In no time, Cuthbert was bustling between his cart and the operating table, beginning to fit Hornsby's joints with the connecting cuffs that would allow the clockwork limbs to integrate to his body. The salve helped the pain some, but Hornsby still required concentration to get through the agony of the connections that granted him full control of the machinery. As he worked all around the agent's prone form with his two assistants passing him tools and following his occasional orders, Cuthbert regaled the mostly silent room with tales of drunken escapades with loose women that had probably never happened, as the smell of the factories rose once again along with the more pleasant aroma of Cuthbert's own joy.

To the best of Hornsby's knowledge, the goal of these stories was to earn blushes from his assistants and disapproving looks from Simmons. For once Hornsby was thankful for the pain, as it was the only thing keeping him from the most inappropriate laughter.

When the work was completed, the straps holding his torso were undone. As Cuthbert and his assistants moved around his body with their keys to wind his arms and legs, Hornsby looked at the smooth bronzed surfaces, the points where he could see gears meeting, and the overall elegance of the machinery. With his arms wound tight, he opened and closed the fingers, adjusting to their control and the lack of physical sensation once more. To reacquaint his awareness of the limbs always took a few moments.

The winding of his legs finished, Hornsby stood up on the machinery with that familiar floating feeling. Despite the click on the ground and knowing how to keep upright, Sebastian's first few steps always felt awkward and disconnected. As he adjusted to having every limb replaced, he tested the tentative flex that opened the silver claws from his fingertips. The machinery was perfectly balanced and muffled just right so that even with his preternatural ears, Hornsby could not hear a single tick, only the slight brushing of metal when the claws emerged or retracted.

"Looks like you're all ready," Cuthbert said as he walked around to inspect his work. "'Ese tick-tocks 'ere will collapse and get you t'rough any tight spaces down 'ere. Designed 'em myself I did. Just fink of it like bending your arms and legs backwards, 'Ornsby, then just scoot through. And remember, you've got 'bout eight hours before those start 'a slow down. Key's stowed in your left leg, should ya need it."

Hornsby nodded. "This is not my first time with the clockwork. Thank you, Mister Cuthbert. You have done your duty admirably. Now I shall go and attend to mine, for Queen and country."

~

Descending into the dank stone tunnels beneath the streets, Hornsby slipped into the hated skin of his other form. He would only engage his lupine body when on a mission for the Queen. Otherwise he

241

found it a detestably primal state. The burning pain at his shoulders and hips flared as he shifted and every smell increased in intensity. Sebastian's eyes changed as well, so that the barely discernible shapes were now clear in a slight shift of color. In the first few moments that his flesh took on its lupine features, Hornsby realized that scent would be useless amidst the odor of the filth of London. No way he could track them, but the beasts also would not be warned of his presence. And he knew the pathways that would lead him to their lair, having studied a rendering of them in the briefing.

He moved along the track that had been laid out for him, several times squeezing through almost impossible junctions with his streamlined body and the collapsing clockworks. Hornsby had to commend Cuthbert as he slipped into a tight metal pipe that led into a four-way junction of the stone passages. Still nearly a mile from the den of the beasts, he passed under one of the openings that would lead up to some street or basement. His hackles began to rise when he passed through the junction, just before the man dropped down onto his back.

Muscular arms were immediately wrapped around Hornsby's neck as a bittersweet smelling rag was pressed to his nose and mouth. Wasting no time with panic, Hornsby flipped the silver claws out of his hand and quickly ratcheted the arm up to slice into the assailant's neck. He smelled the copper tang amidst the filth and the warm spray of blood on his shoulder before the attacker went slack and the cloth slipped away.

Sebastian felt the world blurring as he turned and tried to get a good look at the man who had attacked him. It was clearly a shapeshifter as Hornsby had heard the sizzling sound as the silver claws sliced through the skin. There was no pity in him for the man laying naked and gasping his last in the foul water of the sewer. As the sewers rocked around him, Hornsby noted that the body was already covered in filth, more than it could have been just from falling into the dirty water.

Camouflage... masking his scent. An ambush... couldn't have smelled... me. Knew I was...

Hornsby's addled mind was interrupted as he was hit from either side. The two furry bodies slammed into him, biting and clawing. But not at him, he realized. In the form half between wolf and man, the two were attacking his mechanical arms, crushing the metal and

242

binding the gears where they could. He worked to sling them off and dispatch them, but the sliver would not emerge from his hands. Their attack had struck exactly the proper gears to disable him.

No. No... they know... just what to do... betrayed...

Then one of them cuffed him sharply across the face with a set of natural claws, growling, snarling and making the already swaying world rock more ferociously. The other had slipped back into a more human aspect and the bittersweet rag was once again pressed to his face. The mechanical arms were wrenched further and would no longer move in his defense. And as darkness wrapped her velvety arms around him and dragged him down from the world, Hornsby knew that he would never wake again.

~

A fog blanketed Hornsby as he slowly regained consciousness. He could hear voices ahead of him, but they were soft and tinny as if through a repliphone. He concentrated, mentally willing himself to sweep the cobwebs from his mind, to make the words make sense. A pungent aroma reached him through the mist, one he knew all too well. It was the smell of fury, which suited the words he began to understand.

"—should just kill him and send parts to their doorstep. I would gladly taste his flesh for what he did to Simon. I demand the satisfaction!"

"You have my understanding for your rage, Bernard, I know you were close to Simon. Yet you must temper it and not be so rash. Do not let his death be for naught, as Simon knew the risks in volunteering for the confrontation. This man should be our brother, and I believe he can be. Forgive him, for he knows not what he does."

"Don't you dare use their vile scriptures with me. His debt should be paid now in blood."

The blobs of color in front of Sebastian steadily resolved themselves into figures and shapes. He found himself in a Spartan room with only high windows from which he could gain no visual. Likely a basement from the earthy smell underlying the one called Bernard's anger, but that could mean other things too. The sun shone through and supplemented a few low-burning gaslights to illuminate the bricks and mortar of the wall. He faced a table over which the enraged speaker leaned towards another man half-obscured. Leaning his head just slightly, he saw the stern features of an older fellow with a bit of grey peppering his black hair at the sideburns. Sebastian tried to get up only to realize that all his clockworks had been removed, along with the connecting cuffs. He was merely propped like cordwood in the simple wooden chair.

The elder man rejoined, "Even in the most abhorrent places, some grains of wisdom and poetry can be found. To understand what drives our enemies is to understand them and their plans, and it is our greatest asset. You would do well to realize this if you ever hope to lead." His eyes had not shifted. "You do not even know that our guest has awakened."

Whipping around, the younger man stared at Sebastian with deep brown eyes. His every feature was set in some shade of brown: his hair, his beard, even his clothing. "You... I will finish this myself, if my cousin lacks the teeth!"

To his credit, Hornsby did not react. In this Bernard's eyes, he saw murder, and he would rather embrace a quick, violent death as the Queen's man than let them try to extract information from him with their tender mercies. The brown eyes bled to yellow and he watched the face begin to push out and expand, fangs slipping forth from the forming muzzle as the younger man growled and stalked forward.

"Bernard!" The elder was immediately on his feet behind the table. No physical change occurred, but the authority in that one word was unmistakable and stopped the other in his tracks. Bernard's lupine features slipped back into his face, and his shoulders slumped slightly.

So Hornsby was finally in the presence of the Alpha.

With a deep breath, Bernard walked by the chair and took a moment to put a hand on Sebastian's shoulder. His nails grew into claws and dug with all the man's strength into the flesh there. Hornsby made not a sound.

"Be grateful your fate rests with him and show some respect," Bernard whispered in growling tones. "Were it up to me, your head would already be in a basket on its way to your masters."

With that, the younger man was gone and Hornsby was left alone with the Alpha. Facing him this way was not as Sebastian had expected. In his dreams, he had faced the bestial thing that killed his mother and father and cursed him to his sullied existence and emerged triumphant. The two of them had met in their most savage states in some dark corner, a battle that could only end in death. Instead, he leaned helpless in a chair as sunlight streamed into a furnished room, looking into an almost kindly face that had already shown some refined manners of polite society.

The two simply stared at one another for several moments before the elder gentleman spoke again. And as Bernard's fury left the room, there was another scent in the air. Something familiar that he could not quite place.

"I must sincerely apologize for Bernard's uncouth behavior. The passions of youth strain at him most severely, and I fear you are responsible for the death of a close comrade. Also I do humbly apologize for your state and treatment, but I believe this is the only way you and I may speak politely."

Hornsby thought for a moment in silence. There was some temptation to give them nothing, to simply wait until the Alpha decided that he could bring no secrets from his captor and the monsters dispatched him. Yet his manners required a response, and there could be no harm in remaining a gentleman to the end.

"I accept your apologies in the spirit with which they are given, as a matter of courtesy," he said in cold, clipped tones. "I notice you have not apologized for the loss of my mother and father or for the life inflicted upon me."

The briefest flicker of confusion marked the refined face of the Alpha, soon swept away by a dawn of understanding breaking over his features. "Ah. So that is the story they have spun for you, my young friend. That I, like a monster in a fairy tale, took from you your family and the happy life for which you were destined. But to so deceive one such as us... curious."

"To what deception do you refer, sir? You deny the truth I have known since I could first walk and speak?"

"I do indeed, but your skepticism is most understandable. I shall endeavor to prove false what you have believed true for so long. But first to uncover a mystery, for no man may lie to us."

The Alpha rose and paced around to the front of the desk, closer to Hornsby and deep in thought. He glanced at the agent and then grinned as if with a stroke of inspiration.

"First, I am ahead of myself. Introductions are important and I have you at a disadvantage in name. I am Randolph Collins. As you know, I am the Alpha of those of us that hide in London," He paused here for a moment, "And as Alpha, I am given the power to fly across the moon at night."

As Collins made his outlandish claim, a smell crept through the room, one that Hornsby knew all too well. The acrid stink of the manufacturing plants. Collins noticed the look on his face.

"There," the Alpha said, "What did you smell at that moment? An odor you recognized clearly."

Hornsby was silent, not wanting to give away that he knew anything of their location. But as the scent faded, he knew there was no point. He would never leave this building alive and even he had a method for reaching the Queen's men, which he certainly did not, there would not be a trace of the beasts in this place by the time anyone arrived.

"The factories. I could smell the odor put out by the manufacturing houses for a moment. Clearly we are downwind of one."

"And pray tell me, Mister Hornsby, have you ever been in one of the factories to know the smell from them?"

"I have had no reason to visit such places." He would not mention anything that could compromise any useful information to the Alpha.

"Then how is it you are so knowledgeable in the aroma they produce? Were you told of this smell? Was it often present when you were told where to go and whom to slay?"

Hornsby remained silent and stoic this time. He had expected a physical fight with a ravening animal, not attempts to penetrate his mind.

"You see, Mister Hornsby, I am well acquainted with that smell and I can tell you that we are nowhere near a factory of any kind. Perhaps another demonstration since the air is clear. I am a patient man. I strive to keep both my body and my mind in pique condition."

As the Alpha paused, Hornsby wondered just what demonstration was coming. He said nothing but simply waited.

"And," Collins continued, "once a month my skin turns a regal shade of purple for a day."

Another bizarre statement and once again the odor of the factories slipped into the small room. As it filled his nose, something was ticking together in Hornsby's mind like the gears of a watch. But it could not be. It simply could not be. Yet, he knew that he had smelled another's joy. Another's sorrow. He had even caught the scent of base lust before and clearly recognized it. Hadn't this smell been prominent during Cuthbert's stories? The ones he knew must not be true?

"What you smell there and have been told is the odor of manufacturing is in fact the scent of manufactured truths. Of man's deceit. It is the only way your masters could have maintained a lie, if the first falsehood they told you was about the very nature of falsehood itself."

Pressure gripped Hornsby's chest, and his world spun for a moment as with the drug. No... it couldn't be. This was some form of trick, some farce that the Alpha had cooked up for his capture. A way to turn his mind from the truth. Yet it all made far too much sense. The thought of the pungent smell brought back more and more memories, and Hornsby realized how it wasn't always present but only seemed to manifest when others were talking. And almost always when receiving his briefings about what had been done by the beasts. Only when discussing tactics and the manipulations of his body did the smell fade, as those were simple facts. It clicked into place far too easily, like the gears of his false limbs.

He looked into the expectant face of the Alpha, searching for some other sign of deceit. The eyes of the man were an open book. Hopeful and slightly sad as they searched Sebastian's face for some kind of recognition.

"Do you understand now?" the Alpha asked, "Do you see what your new knowledge means, Sebastian?"

Something about the way Collins said his name. That same hopeful sadness, mingled with a familiarity that had not shown itself when they were having their first mannerly exchange.

"Your... demonstrations have merit, I will grant," Hornsby said. "But how can you prove the truth of any of this? This could easily be a trick. Scents can be manufactured as easily as lies in our modern world. What else can you attempt?"

The Alpha sighed in disappointment, "You can see the truth of this, but you have lived with lies too long. But I know of one other thing that may convince you. A gesture of faith that may summon some long forgotten memory for you."

The Alpha rolled up his sleeve and held his wrist up before Hornsby's face, his palm open. "You could savage my hand now if you wished, you can change quick enough even in this state. It would serve little, but if you believe still that I am responsible for their deaths, it might bring you some satisfaction. But I implore you, just smell and see what you may remember, Sebastian."

That tone of familiarity again. Cautiously he leaned forward and inhaled inches from the flesh, his curiosity piqued. The seemingly familiar aroma from before filled his nose and summoned the memories of other scents and where he had smelled this before. He had been young, a time he had not remembered until that scent. When someone had come to visit his mother and father. When strong arms had carried him up to bed so that adults could speak without prying ears.

The air left Sebastian's lungs as he looked up into the face before him with new recognition. He fought against tears that threatened to unman him as he truly remembered his mother and father. "That night. You were there. You carried me to my nursery and all of you spoke downstairs. Who are you really? What did you do?" Anger surged through him again for a moment. "Did you murder them as I slept?"

"No, Sebastian. I did not kill my sister or her mate."

And with that moment, Sebastian knew every word was true. The smell, the look in the man's eyes, there was simply no deception. Only sadness as the Alpha continued.

"I had come to warn them that night of what was to come. For several years, they served their monarch as agents of our kind. In that time, it was merely a constabulary position, as all societies have a few bad elements. Greed, wrath, envy and the assorted human weaknesses must be dealt with. But it was during their tenure that something changed amidst the powers in the country. Where once we were men with rights and responsibilities afforded to any true servant of the crown, as industry progressed, we were perceived as somehow dangerous to the world the Queen wanted to build."

Hornsby found his voice again, "You are killers though. Brutal murderers. I have seen your works."

"Have you still not understood, Sebastian? What has been the same about every report you have received? I'd wager that every time you heard about a killing, the smell was that of their lies. We are not killers, unless one wishes to protect deer or cattle. We hunt, we defend. That is the nature of our race. Of your race, Sebastian. Never were you cursed, but you were stolen from your destiny. You were born to us, and the men you now trust stole you and forged you into their perfect weapon against your own people!"

The memories were still sorting and rearranging themselves in

Hornsby's head, but he knew there was truth to the Alpha's words. Once he had properly smelled the man, many events and sensations came to him—flashes of the days before the Queen's men had taken him in. Such as the actual scent of his mother and father and how often it was joined with the scent of this man.

"But why?" he asked, trying to catch his breath, "Why would they need to defend against the shapeshifters if you are no threat as you claim?"

"Oh, we were a threat. To their vision for the realm. To the advance of an entire countryside overrun with metal monstrosities belching smoke and steam day and night. To the green fields of England completely paved beneath cobblestones and buildings reaching to the sky. To a people made to so fear the intimate touch of skin that they would cover it with an armor of cloth, or even worse to replace the good flesh they were given with a collection of gears and metal that could never truly connect to another living soul.

"You know it has already happened in the cities. Not for victims of accidents or soldiers returned from war, but as a vanity or a desire to purge themselves of 'sinful flesh.' That is the real monstrosity I say! That is how you appeared to the first of us that witnessed you stalking their brothers, sisters, parents. The form of all the most heinous evil we know."

Sebastian cringed as he saw himself as they must have seen him. Was it true? Had he really slain innocents at the orders of the Queen's men? He remembered now how larger beasts had thrown themselves at him while smaller, weaker ones cowered behind them. He had shown no mercy to them. "Then who were the ones I was shown? Who killed them?"

The Alpha sighed, "To the best of our own intelligence, they were dissidents who stood against the onslaught of industry. Your organization would wait until they found one of our hiding spots and pick a set of the unfortunate souls to slaughter, making the whole affair look as savage as possible. Then they would use the scene to send you after the family they had discovered. We have been hiding and only barely striking back for far too many years now. Only recently did we have a sympathetic man within your organization to arrange all this."

Hornsby's eyes closed. The faces of the dead haunted him behind his eyelids, and he could not deny what he had truly done. His heart dropped into the pit of his stomach and he felt a broken, damned thing. "Why not simply destroy me then?"

He heard the Alpha move and hands laid softly on his shoulders, making him sigh. Something about the contact was more pleasant than anything he had experienced in many years and lifted his tattered spirits. It was only then that he realized he had not felt a loving hand in all the memories of his life since that night so long ago. Yet he did not feel deserving.

"Because I need you, my boy," the Alpha said, "To kill you would be a short-sighted act of cruelty and wasteful of your potential. I want your knowledge of these men and their methods to help us. I want you to reclaim your birthright, not as a prisoner, but as part of my family. There are those who will not trust you in the beginning, but you could not have known what you were doing. I believe that in time, you could help us to right the wrongs that have been done. You can make amends, Sebastian"

Hornsby took a deep breath, focusing his mind to a task and shutting out pain just as his training had taught him. "What must I do?"

"You will have doubts when you leave here, or when you are left where you can be found. Your masters will try to see what happened to you, to find out how you escaped. You must tell them nothing, that all is a fog. There is one experience that you have never been allowed, that will truly clear your mind of all deceit. You must go to the countryside, to the remaining open forests of Britain. When you are sound of limb again, go into the forest and run. Follow your instincts, and you will know truth. After that, after we believe you can be one of us, we will begin the real work."

Sebastian Hornsby had more questions to ask, but before he could begin, another rag of bittersweet smell was placed over his nose and mouth. The room swayed as if on a ship at sea, and darkness claimed him in her relative comfort once more.

~

A wolf loped over the soft loam of the forest floor. Hornsby left the country cottage behind as he finally experienced the feel of the grass under his paws for the first time. Regeneration had completed two days prior and each night he had tentatively walked to the door only to turn back inside and return to his bed. Finally, he could resist the temptation no longer.

He ran under the stars and the light of the moon, feeling the cool breeze brush through his fur. The exhilaration, the sense of right as he inhaled every sweet and bitter aroma the forest had to offer carried him through the trees for what must have been miles. To think that he had denied himself these pleasures for so many years based on a lie shamed him. There was nothing evil here, nothing to be shunned. Only the simple joy of the running and all the sensations therein.

He stopped a moment, panting and catching his breath as he sat on his haunches. Hornsby sniffed the clean air and knew that prey was nearby. A hare, maybe even a deer, he had not the experience to say which. He wanted to chase it down, whatever it was, to feel the rush of the pursuit, to feel it yield to him and sate his hunger as his teeth tore through fur and flesh in that ancient dance of the hunt.

So lost in desire was the wolf that had been Hornsby that he almost did not hear the soft click from many yards away. Yet something triggered in his memory and he hopped back just as the crack of the rifle sounded and a bullet tore through the earth where he had been. He did not have to see it to know that it would be silver, nor to know just what had happened. Of course his deceivers had not left him unwatched during this time away from the confines of the city, and the assassin had clearly been ready if it seemed that Sebastian Hornsby might slip their control. The wolf knew the direction from which the first shot had come but could not see a single way to close the proper distance before the next shot took him.

Then came a scream amidst a cacophony of growls and the sound of rending flesh. The scent of blood and death wafted over on the air, and Hornsby knew that his former masters were not the only ones that had been watching unseen. He tipped his head back and howled, trying to convey his gratitude, his new understanding, and his new purpose in that long rising and falling note.

The return came, and somewhere in the melodious chorus, he could discern the voice of the Alpha. The communication rang clear in his ears, as if in a language he had always known but to which he had never truly listened.

You are welcome friend/brother, it seemed to say. *We are one goal/mind/being now. You will be contacted.*

I will heed, he sent back in a final howl. He could feel them leaving now with some new sense that went beyond smell or hearing. It would not do to congregate here. He had a day, maybe less before the assassin was meant to report on status. Hornsby knew how the game was played and their methods and so would gather the little he truly needed and disappear from the cottage. There was little doubt that the others had worked to make sure he was no longer watched and given him a head start.

It was a shame that he could not hide within the halls of power; that would have been his most useful position. But by morning, they would know that Sebastian Hornsby was no longer their man. Still, he could make himself useful. He had knowledge of places, plans, and people that could not be readily changed on a whim. He would use that to stymie their assault on his kith and kin as best he could.

The lope back to his cottage became a steady run. For Sebastian Hornsby, wolf or man, had a duty to perform. Not for queen. Not for country. But for the pack.

A Well-Crafted Man
Nick Bergeron

5

Bernard Fillmore Harrison lifted the edge of his coat as he stepped off of the train platform, keeping it from dipping into the mud. He liked to think of himself as a fastidious man and became smug when others referred to him as such. The word fussy would be well applied to the slender brassman with perfectly sculpted and coifed gold hair. He had visited the Brass Factory to have his gears tuned and plates polished before boarding the train, and he had no desire to spoil his sheen before he was even greeted.

The smell around the platform reeked of the chaotic castoffs of life, thick with vegetation and rot. Bernard dipped his hand into the breast pocket of his coat. It emerged holding a white kerchief, which he pressed over his nose. The clean silk alleviated the smell, but not much. Overhead a hawk let loose with a long cry.

The train began to pull away from the platform and Bernard turned, already beginning to regret his decision. Pequot Point had never been a hospitable place for brassmen or their engineers. Since Polly Anna Beauregard was killed, things were worse. The little girl had been found in the street, throat torn open by brutal teeth, her body savaged. Only her perfect angelic face had been left untouched, staring forever up at the Heavens that had deserted her.

After that, things got bad for the shifters in Providence. There were beatings, and even a silver lynch. Then one day they were gone. Every shifter in the city practically puffed up in smoke and disappeared. Word had it they had gone back to Pequot Point, where legend said they came from, back before the Steam Fault. Word had it they didn't like being pushed back into the swamps. Word had it they were getting ready to come back, and when they came there would be blood.

So Bernard Fillmore Harrison had taken it into his clockwork brain to get on the next train out of Providence and go into the muck to do some good. Now that he was here, silver tipped leather boots slowly sinking into a week's worth of wet mud, things didn't look quite so clear cut. He was still watching the train, wondering if it would stop if he called out and waved his kerchief, when the carriage pulled up behind him.

The vehicle might have been painted black once, but the color had long ago peeled away to show the aged grey wood beneath. The leather cover of the compartment was gone, leaving only twisted and frayed knots on the four corner posts to show it had been there. Even at a standstill its ancient joints gave off an unsettling creak.

The age and ricketiness of the carriage was dwarfed by the age and ricketiness of its driver. Bernard estimated him to be the oldest man in the county, if not the whole state. His white beard hung down in a tangle between his knees, and he wore an old woolen fishing hat that looked to be one with his scalp. His knuckles were the size of crab apples where they wrapped around the reins. As Bernard gaped up at the geezer, the old man opened his mouth and croaked out a sentence.

"Best you ride up front with me."

4

The creaking was much worse when the carriage was in motion, from both the wagon and the geezer's bones. They rolled for nearly two hours in silence on what Bernard supposed passed for a main road in the country. The brassman was more than a little put off by his surroundings and companion. The still water around the narrow road looked rancid, and he hoped that wherever they were stopping was dry. He didn't want any rust to set in.

By the time the mud from the platform had dried on his cold feet, he decided that it would be better to seize the initiative and break the uneasy silence. He would rather risk offense than arrive in some backwater hamlet completely unprepared for what he would find. "How did you know I was coming?"

"We're not savages, Mr. Harrison." The geezer made a show of adjusting his hat, which did not budge an inch. "We know how to use a telegraph. And there are still those in Providence that remember such." The wizened old man's voice wasn't as weak as Bernard had originally thought. It was simply pitched very low and was difficult to hear over any background noise.

Overhead a hawk let loose another shriek. Bernard looked up into the sky, shielding his eyes from the sun. A dark speck drifted above the carriage in a slow circle. He wondered if it was the same hawk that had been over the platform. It appeared to be on the hunt. He hoped it wasn't searching for anything more sizeable than a swamp rat. A gear inside his chest seized for a moment, and Bernard felt a cog shift behind it. The gears interlocked in a different arrangement and began to spin again. The damp air seemed to be gumming up his works and bringing his backup mechanisms to life.

"So, are you...?" Bernard let his voice trail off, then began again. "My apologies. I'm afraid I'm not behaving much like a gentleman. My name is Bernard Fillmore Harrison. I'm pleased to make your acquaintance." He extended his hand toward the old man.

The geezer waved one hand non-committally and said, "I know who you are, Mr. Harrison, but thank you for the courtesy. Even those of us who never lived in Providence have heard of the Burnished Brassman. You're quite popular in the papers these days. My name is Alphonse."

"So then, you know why I've come?" Bernard was positive that the old man did, but conversations had certain conventions that must be obeyed.

"Not precisely. What is it that the 'robot with a heart' wants in Pequot Point?" Alphonse pulled at one side of the reins, steering them onto a smaller road leading off of the main path.

"Automata." Bernard replied automatically. "We prefer the term automata. A robot is a tool designed for one purpose. Automata are possessed of a sense of self. We are not robots."

"Well, my apologies then. Automata. You might want to talk to the papers about that." Alphose didn't sound apologetic, but neither did he sound antagonistic. He seemed more tired than anything. Bernard supposed that when you reached that age, and had seen the things that Alphonse had seen, you had a lot to be tired of.

"I have, sir. Change is a slow process, fraught with frustration and heartbreak. Nevertheless, we press on, ever to the bright future." Bernard took out his kerchief again and carefully wiped the side of his faceplate up under the metal strut that formed his jaw. It was damp with condensation when he pulled it away.

"What do you hope to accomplish here?" The old man chucked the reins again. The horses sped up to a canter.

"I should think it would be obvious, sir. It is my intention to end any hostilities before they begin, and to draw the engineer, the brassman, and the shifter to the peace table." Bernard straightened as he spoke, feeling every gear and cog whir within his chest. He supposed it was pride that he felt, though he often wondered if his feelings were anything like his creator's. It was a pointless question, much like whether or not two people see the color blue, or if one sees red and simply calls it blue. But Bernard found that it was the most pointless questions that haunted deep thinkers in the dark of night, and he was nothing if not a deep thinker.

"Heh. Not at all ambitious, are you Mr. Harrison?" Alphonse let out a bitter cackle. As he chucked the reins again, Bernard noticed two of the fingers on his right hand ended in ragged stumps.

"Without ambition, sir, the world is doomed to wind itself down into the dark. It is ambition that strives toward tomorrow, rather than staring eternally into the past. Without it, as a poet friend of mine has said, the center cannot hold. But I am not here to speak of my ambitions." Bernard ran the kerchief across the flat crystal of his eyes, wiping away the fog.

"No. No, you're not, I grant you." The horses began to slow as the carriage approached a bridge over a small creek. The bridge was simply two large boards laid across the gap. Alphonse pulled the horses up, stopping the carriage at the edge. "Sorry, Mr. Harrison, but we'll have to walk over the creek." He pronounced it 'crick.'

"Hopefully the first of many bridges we shall cross together, Alphonse."

3

After the creek the road widened and, improbably, became less muddy. The overhanging trees were trimmed back a few feet, and a ditch had been dug on either side of the flat packed dirt. The signs of careful maintenance became apparent the farther the carriage rolled.

"You don't keep the roads all the way to the platform?" Bernard asked out of curiosity.

"We don't care much for visitors, so we don't encourage folks to visit. Or, rather, visitors don't care much for us. We've had nothing but trouble with them since the war. Old soldiers stopping on their way back home, causing trouble when they realize what kind of town it is." Alphonse leaned over the side of the carriage and let loose a long stream of spittle from between his teeth. He rubbed his mouth with the back of his hand and spit again. "Just trouble we don't need."

"Understandable. Unfortunate, but understandable. My own efforts are often plagued as such, from the beginning." Bernard closed the shutters over his eyes for a moment, and then opened them again. The shutters made a quiet swish as they moved.

"How did you start out, if you don't mind me asking? I only started hearing about you when you were getting a few hundred people to show up to your speeches." The old man looked over at Bernard, eyebrow raised in curiosity. It was the first time Alphonse had looked directly at him since the ride began.

Bernard took a moment to align himself, feeling the springs in his head coil and reset. His origin was often what he led with in any negotiation, so he was more than happy to answer the question.

"I was built in the lab of Montrose Wycleft, Master Engineer of Providence, in the service of General Grant in the Army of These United States." The sentence was literally a recording, played on a tiny steel phonograph deep within Bernard's inner pipeworks. It was a maker's mark, built into every automata produced in the Union.

"Wycleft? The one that started the whole war in the first place?" Alphonse's surprise added a few more wrinkles to his ancient face.

"The South started the rebellion, sir. Though it is true that the rationale they supplied in their declaration was of robotic labor destroying their way of life, war was certainly not Mr. Wycleft's intention when he created me." Bernard raised his hand to his neck and turned a small butterfly crank. A small panel on the opposite side of his neck detached with a small puff of vapor. Imprinted in the metal where the panel had been was a number - "001".

"Bugger! Pardon the phrase, Mr. Harrison. You were the first?" The old man's voice rose for the first time in the conversation.

"I was the first brassman, though automata of other shapes came before. And there were other, less sentient... less savory creations." Bernard refastened the panel. "I assure you, *I* was not created for war. Though other automata did fight for the Union, I was not among them." Bernard looked down at his metallic hands and flexed them once, watching the steel cables slide through the well-greased spindles.

"They say that necessity is the mother of invention, and nothing creates more necessity than war, I suppose." The old man shook the reins, then leaned over and harrumphed in his throat before coughing. The hawk still spiraled over them, lazily riding the winds. "They shut those machines down after the war, didn't they Mr. Harrison? As part of the armistice?"

"They were sent to the scrap yards. To Andersonville."

"And what did you do during the war?" Alphonse took one hand off the reins to run it through his beard, the hand with missing fingers. Bernard did his best not to stare at the sight of the greasy white bristles running over the ragged stumps.

"Mr. Wycleft had other plans for me. Instead I was sent to Harvard University, where I was educated in the fields of law and philosophy."

"So, what were you built for, then?" The old man turned back to the road, visibly settling into a forced nonchalance.

"Unlike most in this world, sir, I am lucky enough to know the purpose of my existence. When I was built, my maker instructed me that I was 'to prevent a war, and to help all men live equally.' Obviously I was not educated in time to affect the outbreak of the great conflict twenty years ago, and I regret that with all of my being." He spoke with passion, feeling the pipes within him sing.

"Humph. Hell of a thing. Building a machine to be more humane than a natural-born man could be."

"It is not the strangest of things under God's great eye, sir. I believe Mr. Wycleft's thought was to leave something lasting behind when he was gone. And, God willing, I shall be around for some time to come."

2

The carriage had turned again as they spoke, leading up a large hill. The standing pools of water had passed by the wayside and been replaced by a deep green vegetation. Tall trees formed a shadowy canopy overhead, and thick ferns formed natural walls on each side of the road.

The old man nodded to himself several times, taking in what the brassman had said. Bernard expected further conversation from him, but it seemed that well had run dry. The brassman decided that if Alphonse would not be forthcoming, he would have to dig.

"So, what is your animal shape, if I may ask?"

The question was greeted with a chortle from the old man. "Well, that's bold. I don't have any other form. What you see is what you get." He grinned a gap-toothed grin.

"Oh, my apologies. I just assumed…" said Bernard.

"Of course you did. And what animal did you assume I'd turn into? A wolf? With big teeth and a nasty glare?" His wry tone made the idea sound ridiculous.

"Well, you do appear as the lone wolf, sir." There was nothing else to say but the truth, embarrassing as it was.

"People always think of us as wolves, or bears, or mountain lions. Animals that people are afraid of. Tell me, do you think there's been a wolf within forty miles of Providence since the Brass Factory was built?" This time it was Alphonse who spoke with passion.

"I hadn't given the matter much thought, to be honest with you. I suppose the noise and coal smoke would keep them away?" The brassman knew even less about animal behavior than he did about how to deal with crotchety old men. The cylinders in his brain skipped as he tried to grasp such bestial motivations. A sudden burst of steam hissed from the four release valves at the back of his neck. Bernard again felt a gear in his chest change positions. The countryside did not seem agreeable to his disposition.

"Damn right it keeps them away. Why would someone who could turn into a wolf live where there aren't any wolves? Birds you'll find here, and deer, and raccoons, and all of the other animals that don't mind living near cities. But that just doesn't have as much romance, so no one thinks of it. They just think of the Big Bad Wolf, and how we'll huff and puff and blow their house down."

Alphonse's hands had tensed on the reins. The horses seemed to sense his frustration and began moving at a faster clip, causing the carriage to jostle back and forth on its old wheels. It swayed like a sailing ship on its axles, and Bernard worried that it might simply give up the will to live and collapse.

"You, yourself, are not a shifter, and yet you say 'we'?" It seemed rude to ask such blunt questions, and that was not to Bernard's taste. He needed to find out more about this community, however, and did not have much time. His only hope was that Alphonse did not offend easily, and was willing to talk freely.

"We don't call ourselves shifters or any such terms. We don't differentiate that way. Some people are born with it. Others aren't.

Like blond hair or blue eyes, sometimes it runs true, other times it doesn't. With me, it didn't. I'm still from Pequot Point." The old man shrugged. "It used to matter, back in my granddaddy's time. During the war, and a bit before, folks stopped caring as much. Just didn't seem as important with what was going on."

"Tradition is a difficult thing from which to wrest oneself. I supposed that is part of the reason our two peoples find such difficulty being accepted. We struggle against the weight of history that runs deep in the veins of those who oppress us. Perhaps it's a good thing when traditions die. Sometimes the air seems so thick with them it is difficult to breathe. More breathing room would be a good change for everyone, I think." The two did not acknowledge the irony of a brassman needing breathing room.

"We come from the past as much as we do from where we were born, I suppose." A hurt was in the words, exposed much closer to the surface than Bernard had yet seen. It gave him hope.

"Where *are* your people from, Alphonse?" He dared to use the old man's first name. Bernard was not comfortable being so familiar with a stranger, but he found it was best to seize opportunity when it arrived.

"Where are the people in Providence from? All over Europe, I expect. Same as Pequot Point. You don't believe all of those stories about Indian curses, do you?" Bernard felt a gear in his throat bind for a moment—his brassman wince of embarrassment.

"I do not, sir. But I did believe that your people had some common origin. Perhaps blood of the red man?"

"The Pequot didn't live here when my ancestors arrived. They were chased out by the Narragansett, and even they were gone by the time the Point was settled by white folks. They left the name, though. No, we're like everyone else in this country, from everywhere and nowhere."

Bernard adjusted his hat. He rapped on his chest as another gear swapped into position. He had never coughed in all his years, but he was seized with a sudden and inexplicable desire to do so. The damp air from earlier must have seeped into his inner design and loosened some bolts, even in his backup mechanisms. Uncomfortable, but not dangerous. He turned his mind back to the conversation. Alphonse's answer made some amount of sense to him, but seemed to leave another unanswered question.

"If your people did not have their origin in Pequot Point, then how did so many shifters come to live there?" He had been certain that there was nothing foul about the origin of the shifters, but he had believed them to be from this area.

"For the same reason so many are there now. It's the only place in the state where they don't need to worry about finding themselves on the wrong end of a rope." Again the hawk screamed into the wild blue sky.

1

The clatter of hooves on cobble turned Bernard away from Alphonse and his bald statement of truth. The road had led into a surprisingly large collection of well-kept buildings. The streets between the houses and shops were tightly cobbled and clean, just short of being white-washed. The stones shone in the evening light and gave the village a heavenly look.

As the carriage rolled down the streets, villagers about their business waved at the old driver, who raised his hand in return. A man with a beard somehow larger than the one sprouting from Alphonse's chin, though dark instead of white, shouted something in Italian as they passed. Alphonse shouted in response, and the man roared with laughter.

Bernard suspected they were speaking of him, but thought it best not to inquire. He was in their home, after all, and he was nothing if not considerate of his manners. He found that function often followed form. If his behavior was beyond reproach, then it was easier for others to see him as human, rather than Other. And if he acted as human as possible for long enough, the act would become habit, and habit eventually become nature. Proper form in all things leads to a good end, he often thought. It was as important now as it ever had been, perhaps more. Another jet of steam released from the valves on his neck.

"This is a very pleasant looking town, sir."

"We're glad to have your approval, Mr. Harrison. As I said, we are a civilized people." Alphonse slowed the horses and turned them under an arch between two buildings. A roof had been constructed between the buildings, forming a covered passage. The sudden shadow caused Bernard to adjust the shutters on his eyes, allowing in more light.

"You've been quite welcoming, not at all what I had been led to expect. I was informed before I left that the village was preparing itself for violence, and that I would most likely be kept under guard." He did not say that he had also been told that he would probably be scrapped as soon as he stepped off of the train.

The carriage came out of the shadow and rolled to a halt. Around them was a large square, obviously the village center. Shops, closed for the evening, ringed the cobbled plaza. Their signs created a colorful collage across their white and brown walls. A few shopkeepers were still whisking their steps clean with brooms.

The most dominant feature of the square was a large stone well that squatted in the middle. Great animal heads protruded from its sides. There were eight in all, one for each cardinal direction, and one for each quarter. Bernard at first thought they looked like fierce predators roaring in anger. However, as he telescoped his eyes in for a better look, he realized that each animal was stretching out hoof or wing over smaller human figures taking shelter beneath them. The animal features lost their bloodthirsty look and instead appeared to be challenging any who would harm those they protected.

Surrounding the well was a gaggle of children rolling a hoop around in a circle. They looked to be near an age to begin trades, and Bernard supposed they were enjoying the sunset of their childhood, eking out all they could of their innocence. He inwardly wished them luck, and hoped the stone protectors of the well would watch over them.

"Does this look like a village preparing for blood to be shed, Mr. Harrison?" Alphonse spread his arms out, gesturing at the village in whole. "I'll admit that you have been watched since you arrived, but many of us are hopeful about your visit. We simply wish to be allowed to live our lives in peace."

Bernard nodded his head. The village did appear friendly and welcoming. More so, in fact, that any of the towns surrounding Providence, or even the local districts near Harvard. Function followed form, and the people of Pequot Point kept fine form in their home.

"While I am convinced, as I think any who came here would be, there is still the matter of the unfortunate Miss Beauregard to be answered. It will be a difficult matter to show the citizens of Providence that you are a peaceful people without that issue being addressed." It was the simple truth. Bernard had been quite worried about raising the subject, but it had proved easier than he imagined. Alphonse was altogether more receptive to conversation than Bernard had judged him.

"While I don't believe that it is our responsibility to deal with the murders that happen in Providence, Mr. Harrison, I agree with your point. Let me remind you, however, of our earlier conversation. There are no wolves in Pequot Point. Nor are there bears, or lions, or tigers, or any other predatory animal capable of inflicting such savage wounds. Even if there were, to do so out on the street, to attack a child in such a way and purposefully leave her to be found...", said Alphonse, letting his voice trail off for a moment. "There is horror in that, Mr. Harrison. And for that type of horror you need not look into the wilds. Only one animal in all of nature is capable of that. You need to be looking to men, sir. Only men can do such a thing."

"I do not call you a liar, sir, and I bid you please take that to heart. But it is easy to make the claim that none of your people are capable of dealing this damage to a person, to a child. No man left those wounds. I ask you, if not a beast, for even if a shifter was responsible I name them a beast... if not a beast, then *what*?" Bernard removed his hat and held it in his hands.

"Are brassmen the only product of the Brass Factory, Mr. Harrison? Did the Engineers not produce hounds to hunt the Rebels in the war, or falcons that would fly into enemy lines and explode? Brass beasts that turned out wrong. What if not all of them were sent to Andersonville, Bernard?" Alphonse held up his right hand, showing the stumps of his ring and pinkie fingers.

"That is iniquitous, sir. As, I suppose, is the accusation of one of your residents committing the deed." The idea of one of the brass hounds surviving this long after the war, and attacking someone in Providence of all places, was not something Bernard wished to dwell on. There was a sudden clunk in his chest and more steam released from his neck.

"Of course it is. But, we'll have a few days at least to talk about this." He lowered his hand and turned to watch the children. "Watch this, Mr. Harrison. It's not something you'll see in Providence anytime soon, I guarantee."

The children were still rolling the hoop in a circle, though they had enveloped the well in their ring. The hoop rolled fast, like a wagon wheel at full speed, as the children used sticks to push it along in its path. Outside of the circle waited a dark haired boy, smaller than the others, with slight limbs and delicate features. He studied the hoop with an intensity beyond his years, his dark eyes rapt on the wooden strip as it clattered over the cobbles.

Suddenly one of the children hooked her stick in the hoop and flipped it up over the well toward the scamps on the other side. The dark haired boy broke into a run and suddenly leaped in a flat out dive, straight over the well and toward the hoop. Impossibly, his head and chest made it through the passing target. To Bernard's surprise, what emerged from the other side of the hoop was a black raven, madly flapping its wings to stay aloft.

"It's called Passing the Portal. All of our children play it. An old game, an old tradition. Maybe soon gone, along with everything else here." They watched as one by one the children took wing over the well, transforming into pigeons and ravens. The last flung the hoop up into the air over his head, and when the hoop clattered to the ground, a fat black rat scurried away.

0

It was the children that did it. When the Romans finally destroyed Carthage for the last time, they salted the fields, killed the women and children, then sold whoever remained into slavery. They knew if the children were left alive, or more were born, in twenty years there would be another Carthage, and another war. So they turned to horror and became the barbarous hordes against whom they so often defended their walls, all in the name of the empire. And the young United States were nothing if not the successors to that empire.

When the last of the children transformed, Bernard felt an odd pressure in his brass skull. A gear he had never before felt spinning began to whir in his chest, causing a loud clicking to emerge from the gaps in his burnished chassis. Alphonse looked at him sharply and raised an eyebrow.

"Are you all right, Mr. Harrison?" The question had an edge of distrust riding in it.

"I... I am not certain, sir." Bernard tried to keep the note of fear out of his pipe organ voice.

"Can automata get sick? I wasn't aware they could." Alphonse took a step toward Bernard, who had raised his hand to his forehead.

"Not as such, no. We suffer from wear and tear, which can occasionally make us behave oddly, or cause what I would imagine to be sick feelings in a human. Rust, lack of oil, extremely high or low temperatures, those are our ill humors. Nothing contagious to you or yours, I assure you. I seem to be experiencing some malfunction." The pressure in his head spread down into his chest, and the last words of his sentence were high and fluted. "But sir, there are more important things of which we should speak. Your implication of malfeasance—" Bernard's words cut off suddenly as the air went out of the pipes in his chest.

Alphonse stepped toward him and reached out a hand, touching Bernard's forehead. There was a short sound of sizzling flesh and the old man snatched back his hand.

"Agh! You're burning up, brassman! Burned my damned fingers!" The old man shook his hand and put his fingers in his mouth, suckling them. Steam began to erupt from the valves on Bernard's neck, and then from the emergency valves on his elbows and knees.

Bernard's shirt and jacket began to smoke. He hurriedly removed them and tossed them to the ground. The gears and cranks inside his chest were moving with a haywire freneticism. The brassman would have been terribly embarrassed to expose his inner workings to anyone, but his growing horror surpassed any thoughts of shame. He stared at his jacket, his tin lids telescoping closed and open, then looked back at the children.

"I think you had best get everyone away, Alphonse." This time every word fluctuated in pitch and tone as the valves that served to modulate his voice began to buckle under the growing pressure in his brass body.

"What? What are you saying?" The old man's voice was a knot of fear and apprehension.

Sudden spurts of dark oil and water began to spray out of Bernard's legs. The brassman fell to the ground as the pressure went out of the valves in his now stained lower limbs. Alphonse reached out to him without thinking, then snatched his hand back again, clutching his burned fingers.

The metal of Bernard's shoulders groaned as it began to buckle under the building pressure. A rivet popped out of his neck with a singing whine and flew across the square, embedding itself in the door of one of the shops.

"Run. Run now! Run!" Bernard began to bellow, attempting to frighten the children. He raised one arm and waved it at them, roaring as steam came pouring out of his mouth. They scattered in an explosion of wings and squawks. Feathers filled the air around the well, floating playfully on the breeze left by the dozens of birds. Alphonse looked at him a moment longer and then began to run toward town hall, shouting at the top of his lungs.

Bernard looked around the square, seeking anything that could be used to vent the steam building inside of him. He found nothing. The only thing of significance on the cobbled street was the great stone-wrought well. He began to claw his way toward it, digging his hard hands into the spaces between cobbles and pulling himself a foot at a time. Small sparks struck up from the street as he scoured his burnished chest along the stones, each glowing a brief and bright life in the twilight before fading.

Bernard thought that perhaps he could break off one of the animal heads, to use as a auger to relieve the pressure in his body. Limp legs dragging behind him, no longer even *his* to control, it occurred to him that if he drilled a large enough hole to let steam out, he would be left without enough power to move. Should the steam not be the only catalyst in what was about to happen, there would be nothing he could do.

People poured out of the doors surrounding the square and milled in confusion. Alphonse was shouting, and while some were moving away, others didn't seem to understand what was happening. The brassman knew that if he did not do something quickly, the pressure would be too much for him to hold back. He reached the well and lay for a moment beneath the gaping maw of a large stone rat head. It seemed to be screaming at him to go away and leave its peoples in safety.

Bernard wished he could. He stared up at the well, taking in its carvings and thought of the children and their game. Pass the Portal. Perhaps he too could Pass the Portal and transform. The brassman reached up and grabbed the rat's jaw, using it to lever himself up the side of the well.

Darkness swallowed him as he plummeted down the stone shaft toward the water. He fell past the floating feathers left by the children, and for a moment it seemed that he was as weightless as the white and grey puffs.

You have an important job. You are to prevent a war, and to help all men live equally.

Wycleft's words echoed back through his brain again and again, the brass needle that created his mind's eye scratching against the metal cylinder that was his memory. *All men. All men.* He hadn't meant automata, or shifters. Only men.

Bernard Fillmore Harrison had it all wrong, from the day his first gears were set in motion. He had not been wrought for life, but for death; not out of compassion, but out of hate. But maybe, in the end, he had it right after all. His last thought before exploding was one of satisfaction. In the end he had lived to the letter of his creed, if not the spirit. And, as in all things that he had found, form was more important than function.

Quarantine Station
Thoraiya Dyer

He quieted, refusing to be provoked.

The full moon hung over London, but not *here*; not yet.

He would allow mechanical men to wander the cramped, crushing corridors of the ship. He would let them peer and ponder. There was no sign of sickness. No excuse for them to detain him.

Soon, he would breathe antipodean air in a city unclaimed by his kin. A new territory all of his own. The table of human life would be his table. There would be no rivals to sit at banquet.

All he had to do was be still. Be patient.

His rewards were coming. They were very close.

~

Alice stands motionless in the moonlight at the end of the Quarantine Station's fifty-foot concrete pier. The *Cloudmaker*'s crew lash the airship's disembarkation ladders to iron rings that protrude well above the high tide mark but are rusted by salt spray nonetheless.

She stands motionless, a clockwork nurse, controlled by the dreaming thoughts of a flesh and blood woman that sleeps now on a cot in the hospital in the city and will have no memory of Alice's actions when she wakes.

But Alice has her own memories. Somehow, just as her physical habits make worn places on her winches and her winding key, her thoughts stay within her shell of brass and copper and tin.

It shouldn't be possible, but that's how it is.

"Good evening, Alice," says Doctor Brownfield, an automaton himself, controlled in eight hour shifts by three different doctors. The Sleeping Cap that they share is tuned to Brownfield's mechanical body. It transports their sub-consciences and skills over two miles of saltwater harbor, from Sydney Town to the Quarantine Station.

"Good evening, Doctor," Alice answers. Her metal body is controlled by two nurses whose names she does not know, but she thinks of them as Daytime Sister, of whom she has no experience, and Night-time Sister, whose dreams give Alice life. Daytime Sister has a

271

habit of leaving their shared body, unwound, in exposed, random places, and Alice never knows where she will be when she comes flooding back into herself, or how long she will have to wait before the undertaker, Jones, comes to wind her.

Cloudmaker's epauletted, wine-whiskered Captain and his rat-faced First Mate descend the dangling ladder. A waist-coated man struggling in their wake with only one hand free can only be the ship's Doctor.

Cloudmaker carries four hundred mostly migrant passengers, bound for the port of Sydney Town. But recent innovations in airship travel have reduced the length of the voyage to an average of thirty-two days, a period insufficient for infectious disease to manifest.

Though the London shipping agents and owners deplore disruptive detention-based quarantine and compulsory pressurized steam-fumigation of their ships, the colony has learned its lesson from outbreaks of measles, typhus and smallpox.

Thirty days.

The passengers and crew must stay, symptomless, on the isolated headland for thirty days, under the care of the Station's wind-up staff. Before the Sleeping Caps were made, the death rate amongst doctors and nurses was so high that terrified Catholic priests stopped coming to comfort the dying.

"I am Flume," the fire-haired Captain announces, passing the log and medical records book to Doctor Brownfield.

"Welcome, sir," Brownfield replies cordially, "to Sydney Quarantine Station. I trust your journey was pleasant."

"Twenty-eight days and incident free. I see no reason why we should be apprehended here. No reason at all."

Brownfield gently flicks the pages of the two books.

"All is in order," he says at last, "but I'm afraid no exceptions can be made. If your mate—?"

"Rodgers." The rat-faced First Mate knuckles his forehead.

"If Mister Rodgers would see to the unloading of the luggage, and all ship-board perishables that may be spoiled by high temperatures and pressures, we will proceed with assembly of the portable fumigation machine. Doctor—?"

"Wells," the ship's Doctor beams, tucking away a pocket watch with his left hand; in his right hand is some sort of domed apparatus, concealed by a black silk cover.

"Doctor Wells, I trust you will impress on the passengers and crew that the sterilization process is lethal to any who might be of a mind to conceal themselves aboard."

Wells' florid face flattens into an unattractive gape.

"You take desperate measures, sir, where desperation is uncalled for. There are no vapors aboard the *Cloudmaker*!"

"How can you be so certain?"

"My good man, I am certain!" He reveals a polished bell jar with a flourish. Inside the glass dome, something small and creamy-colored with paired stalks floats in a clear solution beside a silver, many-pistoned mechanism. "See what I purchased from a veritable magician of a physician before leaving London!"

"What is it?"

"What is it? But then you have not heard of Professor Blackwood and his Theory of Repulsion. Why, it is the live, rabid brain of a rat, and so long as this chamber is supplied with serum, and the mechanism maintained, it will repulse disease-causing miasmas indefinitely!"

Everybody stares with repulsion at the floating rabid rat brain. *In that sense,* Alice thinks privately, *Professor Blackwood's Theory is correct.*

"What is the range of this device? I have the crew of another airship here. The *Canton Typhoon.* Can this product contain the typhus that has ravaged them?"

"There are Fu-Manchus here?" Captain Flume interrupts at once. "I will not have them mingling with my passengers."

"The crew of the *Canton Typhoon,*" Brownfield says with irritation, "are employees of the East India Company. Citizens, all, of the British Empire. Not that it is your concern how this facility is run, Captain. You have only to comply and you will be released in thirty days."

He turns to walk away, but Doctor Wells catches him by the sleeve of the white coat stitched directly into his bleached leather skin, proffering the jar.

"Please, Brownfield. Take this, for what good it may do you. Our journey is practically at an end and I am convinced of its effectiveness. Why, I contracted headache and fever myself shortly after acquiring it, but I set it at my bedside and was promptly cured."

Brownfield looks faintly disapproving, or perhaps it is a trick of the shadow.

"The law requires that we conform to the miasma theory here, Doctor Wells," he says, "but I feel it my duty to inform you I am a proponent of the germ theory."

"The germ theory? The germ theory?"

"Indeed. That is why we have this sterilization facility and why I must insist that living tissue—infected with the rabies germ, no less?—be prevented from passing beyond the barriers."

"Insist?" Wells fumbles for his watch, taking it out and putting it back without looking at it.

Alice intervenes. "Give me the jar, Doctor Wells. I will secure it in my sleeping quarters in the office building, which lies on the port side of the quarantine zone. When the detainment period is finished, I will return it to you as you re-embark the *Cloudmaker*."

Wells stares at her.

"It must be wound and oiled weekly, and the chamber kept filled from this bottle." He pulls a flask from his pocket.

Alice takes the jar and the flask; it is almost the limit of what she can carry. Automatons have dexterity but not much strength. That is why Jones must bury the bodies, and why they cannot wind one another; they cannot act as a failed attempt at a perpetual motion machine.

"I will see that it is wound. We are familiar with such routines here, Doctor Wells."

Once the jar is placed on a shelf by her bedside, the furnished room a relic of the human nurses who once worked there, Alice takes the passenger list and returns to the foot of the ladder, holding her lantern high to greet the descending passengers.

She smiles her fixedly reassuring mechanical smile.

"Please," she says once she has taken their names, "continue down the pier. When your luggage is unloaded, choose one change of clothing, which will pass immediately through the fumigation shed and be waiting for you on the other side of the carbolic acid shower block. The clothes you wear now will be taken away for steam-sterilization."

She says it three hundred and ninety-seven times. The line of people stretches all the way from the ladder to the fumigation shed. Nets of luggage are lowered down the starboard side of the airship, while parts of the portable fumigation machine and the coal required to run it are chained and harnessed in preparation for the ship's crew to take the bundle on board. Automatons will give the operating instructions, but human hands will be required to shift the heavy machine into the central cargo-hold of the ship.

As the eastern sky becomes light, the *Cloudmaker* at last lies empty, and Alice has visually inspected every human being on board. None of them seem symptomatic. They will be discreetly observed again by other nurses while they are naked in the showers, and if it still seems as though they have escaped the filth and grime of the mother country unscathed, they will be sent to the accommodation precinct for healthy passengers.

There, they will wait.

Sunrise, and her consciousness begins to fade away while she stands on the pier.

She returns to herself at sunset outside the hospital. The bell is ringing. Somebody has died. Probably one of the crew of the *Canton Typhoon*.

Alice waits on the leaf-strewn grassy hillside, unable to move, until the enormous wine-whiskered captain of the *Cloudmaker* finds her. His thick fingers are inexpert and the grinds and jerks of the key in her midriff would be unbearably painful if her body was flesh and blood.

"Where is Jones?" she asks when her mechanism finally starts moving.

"The undertaker is dead," Flume answers, droopy-eyed and leaden-voiced. "It is he for whom the bell tolls."

~

He was too eager.

Too panicked by the approach of dawn. *In Vulpis*, he slipped into the hospital ward. *In Vulpis*, he kissed the palm of the Captain of the *Canton Typhoon*. How the Captain's ghost cried and struggled as it was drawn out of the body!

He held the soul between his teeth, and when the Lord's Merciful Angels came, as they came every moon, to ask him if he would repent—*repent! Will they never tire of asking?*—he threw the soul at them to drive them away.

Repent, indeed. Not for naught did I drink rainwater from the footprints left by a black fox in full moonlight.

And yet the old man saw him as he crossed the lawn, and would have reported him, so he kissed the old man, also. With the sun rising, he was unable to finish the kiss *in Vulpis*, and as he became human in appearance the undertaker's soul became stuck, choking the old man, and *he* had no choice but to flee.

I wonder what they will make of the unmarked corpse?

In any case, there were no priests here to ring church bells of a Sunday and call the Angels early. He would not need to kill again until the next full moon, and this was a place where death was expected.

This was a place where death lived.

~

"I've been conversing with your other half," Captain Flume says to Alice.

It's supper in the spacious, well-appointed officer's mess and one of the serving automatons has failed to animate, so Alice has temporarily taken her place.

"Sir?"

"She tells me that you, the night operator, and your co-worker, the daytime operator, share a room at the hospital in the city. You scold her often, as you're habitually uncluttered while she is disorderly. She says your six children look like little automatons themselves, perfect versions of their dead Navy Captain of a father, while her four have haystack hair and odd-length suspenders, and are even more mismatched from being the bastards of four unrelated fathers."

Flume laughs heartily at this, while Alice is frozen with indignation and a sudden, wretched yearning.

She knows next to nothing about her flesh and blood self. Nothing about the children. Not even their names, and she has never wished to know because she can never go to them. She can never see them. Better to keep her mechanical and breathing selves fully divided to preserve the quietude of whatever passes for her soul.

Her daytime self apparently has no such reservations and has pumped the information from such human go-betweens as the clockwork repairmen, the soldiers guarding the gates, and perhaps even the lately deceased undertaker, Jones.

Alice abruptly hates Captain Flume for speaking to her with a lack of decorum he would never show to a flesh and blood nurse. Her strength of feeling hatred surprises her; it is another thing an automaton is supposed to be incapable of.

Yet she is amongst the earliest models made, and most Sleeping Caps are shared between hundreds, if not thousands of people. Many Caps control manufacturing bots the size of buildings or steamboats that sail themselves over dangerous stretches of the Bass Strait, while Alice's body approximates a human, and her Cap has been shared by only two people for seven years.

There was a story, Brownfield said, of a little automaton that was playmate to a princess, until it began to laugh and play while nobody was wearing the Cap.

It was destroyed.

Alice feels no fear. She is not a real thing. She has always known and accepted it. But Captain Flume, it seems to her, would relish causing her fear; would relish the anger and other emotions his words have kindled.

He is acting deliberately with intent to cause her distress. Other men have attempted it, out of boredom or frustration.

Twenty-nine days. Then he'll be gone, like all the others.

"More gravy?" she asks, hiding her anger behind a bland expression and tone.

The trade negotiator of the *Canton Typhoon* joins the officers of the *Cloudmaker* at the table. His long, pale face is cross-hatched by scars, his white hair a waist-long pigtail in the Chinese style.

"Call me Milk," he says to the rat-faced Rodgers. "Short for Milk Mandarin. Translation of the name the court officials gave me. Shocked that I'd learned the language, they were."

"My condolences for the passing of your esteemed Captain," Doctor Wells says, red-faced, stuffing his mouth with forkfuls of baked potato that is not yet cool.

"Cheers, Doc," Milk answers. "Flew like a bird, our Cap'n did, and loved being up, same as a schoolboy. Everybody liked him. That undertaker, Jones, was well-liked, too, or so I heard from the soldiers up on the hill when we carried up his effects. Shame he died so sudden."

"Was it typhus?" Flume asks, waving his butter knife like a question mark in the air.

"That robot doctor, Brownfield, did the autopsy. Said the gravedigger was healthy inside like a man newborn at thirty. But they steam-sterilized all his things, anyway, and gave it us to take up to the neck of the peninsula where the soldiers are."

"There's only one way to uncover the cause of death." Doctor Wells pats down his waistcoat with fluttering fingers. "We must hold a séance. We'll recall the undertaker's spirit and question it about the man's demise!"

Rodgers silently bares his pointed teeth.

"Spirit, wot?" Milk gasps, crossing himself.

"A fine idea." Flume raises his glass to Wells, smiling.

"I have read Professor Blackwood's extensive notes on the matter! Nurse, bring us a heavy crystal tumbler, five candles and a flame started by natural means. And we must have charcoal for marking this tablecloth. I'll arrange the letters of the alphabet around a central pentagram as instructed by the Professor."

Alice slips dubiously out the back door along the cobbled path to the kitchens. Wooden boards are preferred for the inflexible feet of automatons, but the boardwalk has not yet been extended this far. Doctor Brownfield fell off the cliff edge, once, and it was a month before he was repaired and the inclined tramway instituted.

She returns with exquisite care, carrying the crystal tumbler, the candles and the lit taper, moving slowly over the uneven surface, and soon hears raised voices from the open windows of the officer's mess.

"What do you mean, you'll sell her?" Rodgers sounds aghast.

"Elementary, my dear chap." Captain Flume says. "If what Mister Milk tells us is correct, and the range of the Sleeping Caps has been increased, British infantry will soon be replaced with remote controllable automata. Subsequently, wool blankets for our troops will be irrelevant. Instead of fine fleeces from the colonies, the crown will be clamouring for coal. Coal cannot be carried by airship. It is simply too heavy. I must invest, instead, in ocean-going steamers."

"They'll never keep me on if you sell the ship. The Sydney Steam Company takes care of its own. *Cloudmaker*'s my whole life, sir."

"Then I suggest you seek financial backing, Mister Rodgers. The purchase price will not be modest."

"Won't just be coal in demand if the range of the Caps gets extended, sir," Milk observes. "Imagine the crown able to control the wayward colonies with placement of Queen's Mouthpiece automata in every major capital of the Empire. Instant communication."

"They won't like it. It could lead to insurrection."

"Maybe there's enough factories in Mother England to turn out armies of automata, but the fighters here'll be flesh and blood. And they'll need blankets. And guns. Won't they, sir?"

"Interesting, if disloyal, conjecture, Mister Milk," Flume says, but Alice can tell from the falseness of his disapproval that the man she despises is excited by the prospect.

"The Chinese Emperor's a step ahead in that regard, sir. He travels in secret, avoiding assassins, but he has a Cap linked to a thousand gold and jewel-covered automata, and when the golden machines speak, his subjects listen, from Lords to labourers, or else lose their heads."

"How'd his subjects know," Rodgers interrupts, "if it's the Emperor wearing the Cap or one of his servants having a laugh? I'd steal that Cap and kill off the boss, I would."

"Would you, Mister Rodgers?" Captain Flume says coldly.

Alice enters the room and the men fall silent.

Then, Doctor Wells practically bounces up and down in his padded seat.

"The charcoal, first," he says, and Alice delivers it to his sweaty, outstretched hand. Sweeping the platters and pepper shakers aside, he sketches out a pentagram on the circular tabletop, ignoring the grimaces of Milk and Rodgers, and sets the candles down inside the points of the star.

Wells lights them with the taper and orders the room lighting extinguished.

Curling candle smoke hangs in the dark room with its leaping shadows. Other automatons look to Alice for instruction and she dismisses them; they have many dirty dishes to get through before they wind down, and those must be cleaned so much more slowly and painstakingly than if done by human hands.

"I must be tied to this chair," Wells says, "for when the spirit of Jones possesses my body, it may become violent with a desire for retribution."

"Retribution?" Flume repeats with a dismissive wave. "The man was not murdered."

"Was 'e not?" Rodgers mutters, then seems surprised to have spoken.

"A misstep, surely," Milk says. "He's fallen and hit 'is head on a rock."

"The bruising to the skull would have been obvious." Wells' fluttering hands are forcibly stilled as Flume binds him with three of the men's leather belts to his heavy, upholstered dining chair.

The alphabet is marked clearly on the tablecloth, waiting beneath the upturned crystal tumbler.

"Everybody's knees must remain touching," Wells declares as the other three draw their chairs closer, "if we hope to create enough combined ectoplasm to contain the spirit of Jones and allow it to flow into me. Put your right hands on the base of the crystal and your left hands on the shoulder of the man beside you, and repeat after me."

They chant various hymns, and the shadows grow longer.

Alice prepares to slip away. There's no telling how long this will take, and she has duties at the hospital. She does not believe that spirits can be summoned, or if they can, that they can speak through the living. In seven years, she's seen thousands of men, women and children die, and if the pleas of their loved ones couldn't compel them to return, why should the exhortations of strangers?

"Jones is here," Wells shrieks. "I see him! Do you not see him?"

The other men glance nervously around.

"There's nothing," Rodgers says.

"He's here," Wells screams again. "He has answered our summons! Spirit of Jones, we have called you here to answer this vital question: How is it that you perished?"

Under the tentative, trembling fingers of the four airshipmen, the crystal glass begins to move.

Alice takes a step closer so that she can see. The tumbler touches the letter F, then L, and then U.

"F-L-U-" Milk whispers.

Captain Flume and his First Mate, Rodgers, stare at each other with sudden venom, their respective hands tightening on the tumbler so that it can no longer move.

"F- L-U," Rodgers says.

"Flu! It is Spanish influenza." Wells flushes with triumph. "Sudden death from the flu! We must warn them at the hospital at once. Nurse Alice!"

"I am here, Doctor Wells," Alice says quietly, taking another step forward.

But Wells begins to have a seizure. His eyes roll up into his head, and froth comes from between his gnashing teeth. His unbound arms spasm and flail, knocking over the two closest candles, while his wide body strains against the leather belts binding him to the chair.

"We shouldn't 'ave done it!" Milk throws himself back from the table. "We've opened Hell's gate!"

And he runs to the door and vanishes into the night.

"The candles," Alice says calmly and is paid no heed. The men's terror is expected, but if spirits of the dead can possess the living, she herself is in no danger. Alice takes the pitcher of water from the serving board and extinguishes the candles, which she hasn't sufficient wind to blow out with her leather bellows-breath.

Wells stops jerking about. In the sudden stillness, his harsh breathing resembles that of a great whale breathing around a harpooned blowhole. His chin and chest are splattered with saliva. *Either the evil spirit has abandoned him, or he is suffering an undiagnosed condition.*

"Captain Flume, Mister Rodgers, you must carry him to the hospital," Alice says, but Rodgers and Flume are pressed against the wooden wall, their chairs overturned.

"He's possessed," Rodgers protests. "I ain't touching him!"

"He is ill. He needs Doctor Brownfield."

"I will take no dose of influenza myself," Flume says.

"You have been exposed. You will be sent to the hospital anyway."

"I have been no such thing," Flume says. "I will return at once to my room."

The two men abandon her.

Alice's mechanical fingers struggle with the straps, but Flume buckled them tightly and Wells' struggles have only made it worse. She cannot undo them.

"I will bring help, Doctor Wells," she says. "I promise I will be as quick as I can."

But by the time she returns with Brownfield, Doctor Wells is dead.

~

Rabies, they said.
Rabies killed Doctor Wells.

He had to be careful. Rabies could kill him, too. It was one of the few things he must fear, besides the Angels of Mercy catching him unawares. Typhus, he could not catch. Measles weeded out the weak, but never him. Spanish flu to him was like a breath of mountain air. It could gain no purchase in him, for he was not wholly a man.

But rabies afflicted both man and beast.

I will kill the suspicious one next. It was a nasty trick he tried at the séance.

When the time comes. When the full moon rises. I'll give him to the Angels of Mercy. He'll be my next payment.

~

"Catherine Banks," Flume murmurs into her tin ear.

Three days, Alice reminds herself.

"Catherine Banks is your true self," he says again, relishing the name, "and I know where to find her. Where to find you. I'll balance you on my cock like a felt bowler on a fine mahogany hat-stand. We'll fornicate on the hospital roof, in the broom cupboard and on the stairs, with your head at the low point and your legs spread up on the landing. I understand that gravity causes a rush of blood to the head, resulting in pleasure that is almost agonising in its intensity."

He'll be gone in three more days.

Since Wells' death, the weeks have been uneventful from a health worker's point of view. To everyone's great relief, no more men have died. None of the passengers or crew of the *Cloudmaker* have shown symptoms of illness, whether of rabies or Spanish flu. There is much debate in the officer's mess over whether Doctor Wells' rabid brain is actually effective, despite Brownfield's insistence that it was the root of his demise.

But the despicable Captain Flume baits Alice until the early hours of each morning, describing sensations that a sexless automaton can never feel, intimately describing actions that Alice is not anatomically equipped to perform.

"I'll let your children watch," he adds, scrutinising the stretched leather of her false face.

"Thank you for bringing the bedsheets, Captain Flume," Alice says, as she has said every night since the night of the séance, wishing for him to leave but unwilling to give him the satisfaction of asking.

Surprisingly, he doffs his cap and departs, silent and smiling, in the direction of his sleeping quarters.

Alice's body is not made for sighing. She has limited wind in her bellows-driven lungs, and no volume adjustment knob.

But she sighs, now, as though her innards are hospital corridors, and the sigh is a great cleansing wind from the Pacific Ocean, driving away evil vapors, and she tries not to think about Captain Flume sweeping into the hospital in the city in two days time, disarming Catherine Banks with lies about being an acquaintance of her deceased husband.

Disarming her with knowledge that he should not have.

Catherine Banks will see straight through him, Alice tells herself. *I saw through him, and so will she. She will not admit him privately. Nothing he has promised will come to pass. He is nothing but a wicked reveller in others' pain.*

Alice hesitates with her hands on the edge of the basket.

Then why has he gone?

Where has he gone?

She turns her head again, but the open doorway is a lightless rectangle. Crickets sing and flying foxes chitter in the shrouded night.

Where has he gone?

Not to sleep, for it is his habit to taunt her til dawn and then sleep until noon. *To a secret meeting?* He has been collecting as much information as he can, ostensibly in preparation for his new business venture.

There is a small airship scheduled to arrive tonight, but that is not for several hours, and the crew of the postal carrier *Hermes* will not be properly processed until well into the following morning, when the steam-sterilized mail will be sent ahead of them via the barracks on top of the hill.

Alice brings her lantern out the open door of the laundry. The afternoon's light rain lingering as dewy droplets on the grass shows the Captain's heavy footsteps clearly.

She follows Flume, her lantern a feeble shield of light against the darkness. Any moment now, the full moon will rise, and Alice will not need the lantern, but she finds she doesn't wish to leave it behind.

Her skin is incapable of crawling, but she feels trepidation such as she has never felt before, not even when Wells seemed possessed by a malevolent ghost.

It happens all at once.

Clouds part. Moonlight shines on the long, low buildings of the healthy passenger precinct. A large fox with a fluffy red and white brush is streaking, tongue lolling, towards a man smoking a cigar at a balcony railing.

There are no foxes in the colony. Alice raises her free hand to her throat in astonishment.

The man at the balcony railing is Rodgers. The fox scrambles up the wooden staircase connecting the balcony to the ground.

"Look out!" Alice tries to shout, but her voice is too quiet. Rodgers does not turn.

The fox's head snaps back towards her.

It has superior hearing, Alice thinks. She looks down and sees the place where the boot-prints of Captain Flume turn into daintier dark spots. *The footprints of a fox.*

Her fingers come uncurled from the handle of the lantern.

It drops; shatters.

Rodgers looks up at last. Just in time for the fox to leap at his throat.

Alice pivots, forcing her legs into the fastest stride they can manage, at the risk of losing her balance; at the risk of winding down before she can make good her escape.

For Captain Flume is a creature of myth. A creature that Catherine Banks might use to scare her children into good behaviour. Alice is not frightened of disassembly, but she is terrified, now, for the children of Catherine Banks.

Alice had thought them threatened by a mere unmannerly man; now she knows that the threat is unholy. The threat is real.

The threat is horror and pain and blood and death.

Catherine, can you hear me? she thinks with all the concentration she can spare. *Catherine Banks, when you wake in the morning, you must remember. If Flume the fox flings me from a cliff or rips me to insensible shreds, you must remember!*

She reaches the carriage of the inclined tramway. Takes one step inside of it and turns to close the brass screen with its diamond-shaped glass panes. An instant later, orange fur and white teeth slam against the little windows.

Alice stares for a moment at the frustrated fox. There's a small spot of blood on his muzzle.

Flume has killed Rodgers. Just like he killed the undertaker, Jones. But why?

The answer is there, hanging over the harbour, the gibbous moon turning lapping wavelets to rivers of mercury.

The full moon. Every twenty-eight days.

But quarantine is thirty days.

Alice pulls the control lever and with a hiss of steam the carriage descends down the cliff-side, toward the pier where the airships are anchored, leaving the fox, its ribs heaving, on the upper platform.

As the platform recedes, the fox transforms, rearing back on its hind legs, black stockings become boots and bloody muzzle turning to wine-coloured whiskers. But it's too late. The hated figure shrinks into distance and darkness, snarling impotently, fists raised.

She can think only of her sleeping quarters in the office building. Of the rabid rat brain that lies within. Rabies is a disease of foxes. If she can only infect him, he will die in quarantine. He will never leave the Station.

As she emerges from the carriage at the lower platform, she hears the sound of the *Hermes* droning in the sky above the Eastern marker, twenty miles out to sea. She half-expects to see other automatons at the wharf precinct, preparing for the arrival, but she has done her job too well; all the documents are in order, the shower tanks are brimming with diluted acid, the great autoclaves are clean and ready to accept the luggage for steam-sterilisation.

Three steps from the entrance to the office building, the fox snaps at her heel; snags her hand.

She topples.

Face-down, she struggles to regain her feet, but the fox harries her, ripping her skin so that her metal parts catch the moonlight.

It seizes her hair and, showing unnatural strength, drags her away from the office building, through a luggage portal in the side of the fumigation shed. As they fall through the chute into the belly of No.

3 autoclave, and land with a crash on the stainless steel racks over the twelve foot-long water tray, Alice reaches up with fingers turned to metal claws by the gnawing of the creature. Before she can grip Flume's fur, she feels her mechanism winding down, exhausted by her earlier burst of speed.

"Others will come," she says. "Another ship –"

She cannot see him in the pitch blackness, but she feels his fur rippling, turning into his Captain's uniform, his weight doubling; tripling; becoming a mountain of flesh and bone.

"Another ship will come," he laughs, "and when it does, you'll still be down here when the luggage comes down. They won't find you until after the boiler's been lit. They'll think you were destroyed by accident."

His huge hands rip her nurse's uniform, her false skin, her stuffing and her hair away from her clockwork skeleton.

"And you'll be unable to correct them." He tears the bellows out of her chest. "Sydney is mine. Every soul inside of it. Enough to send the Angels of Mercy on their way for another hundred – or another thousand – years. Too bad you haven't got a soul for me to feed them. But before sunrise, I'll find whatever hole Rodgers crawled into, and I'll have his soul between my teeth, waiting, when the Angels come."

Alice's glass eyes crack against the steel rack. She no longer has lids with which to shutter them. The single leg still attached to her torso cannot move any more than the limbs scattered to the four corners of the autoclave.

If she was still capable of motion, she would try to crawl back out of the chute. There, with a flick of an operational lever, she could begin the sequence by which the pressurised chamber would seal, mechanical belts would deliver coal to the boiler and the water in the tray would become lethally scalding steam.

Captain Flume's thick fingers find the opening in her chest cavity and turn it inside out, whalebone ribs exposed to the air.

"I'll do this to Catherine Banks," he promises. "Though I expect she'll have a little more – what's the word? – heart."

As Alice clatters onto the rack a final time, she feels whatever it was that passed for her soul swirl listlessly about the interior of the autoclave.

A spark seems to run through the metal rack, through her bent and discarded gears, weights, lever arms and cables, connecting them, making them into something new, something bigger to be animated by the mind inside the Sleeping Cap.

Alice's soul fills the machine. The operational lever moves of its own accord.

It shouldn't be possible, but that's how it is.

The autoclave seals shut.

"What was that?" Flume demands. "What's happening?"

He drops her broken pieces, trying to climb back out through the chute.

Alice cannot answer him. She cannot see him.

But she can still hear. She hears the crackle of flame and the hiss of steam.

Flume stops screaming long before the heat warps Alice's paper-thin, beaten tin eardrums.

After that, she is deaf as well as blind and dumb.

Shortly before she loses consciousness, she senses two shapes, fluttering like sparrows about her.

How can they have entered the chamber? she wonders. *Perhaps the* Hermes *has arrived, and the others have come.*

She has no way of knowing. But she senses the two winged things carrying something away with them when they leave; something toothed and furry, and rather like a fox.

Biographies

Editor

Jennifer Brozek is an award winning editor, game designer, and author.

Winner of the Australian Shadows Award for best edited publication, Jennifer has edited twelve anthologies with more on the way. Author of *In a Gilded Light, The Lady of Seeking in the City of Waiting, Industry Talk,* and the *Karen Wilson Chronicles*, she has more than fifty published short stories, and is the Creative Director of Apocalypse Ink Productions.

Jennifer also is a freelance author for numerous RPG companies. Winner of both the Origins and the ENnie awards, her contributions to RPG sourcebooks include *Dragonlance, Colonial Gothic, Shadowrun, Serenity, Savage Worlds*, and White Wolf SAS. Jennifer is also the author of the YA *Battletech* novel, *The Nellus Academy Incident*.

When she is not writing her heart out, she is gallivanting around the Pacific Northwest in its wonderfully mercurial weather. Jennifer is an active member of SFWA, HWA, and IAMTW. Read more about her at www.jenniferbrozek.com or follow her on Twitter at @JenniferBrozek.

Authors

Nick Bergeron was born and raised in the state of Maine, where he narrowly survived Stephen King. When not writing horror (and sometimes horrific) fiction, he works in the software field doing pretty much everything. He spends his free time pretending to be someone he's not and rolling polyhedral dice, or singing his lungs out at the local karaoke joint. From time to time he can also be found attempting to "master the game," as the kids these days say.

"A Well-Crafted Man" is a story about how the best of ideals are sometimes fostered by people who would like to exploit those bright dreams of the future.

Donald J Bingle. Author of Net Impact, a spy thriller which incorporates real-world conspiracy theories, GREENSWORD, a dark comedy about global warming, and Forced Conversion, a military science fiction novel set in the near future. Also author of a more than thirty-five pieces of short fiction in the science fiction, fantasy, thriller, horror, steampunk, romance, and comedy genres, including stories in the Dragonlance and Transformers universes. World's top-ranked player of RPGA Classic roleplaying game tournaments from 1985-2000. See my writing and gaming resumes at www.donaldjbingle.com or follow me on Twitter @donaldjbingle.

Some of my previously published stories have been collected by theme in my Writer on Demand TM series and published on Kindle, including Tales of Gamers and Gaming; Tales of Humorous Horror; Tales Out of Time; Grim, Fair e-Tales; Tales of an Altered Past Powered by Romance, Horror, and Steam; and Not-So-Heroic Fantasy. Member of SFWA, HWA, ITW, IAMTW, GenCon Writers Symposiium, and Origins Game Fair Library.

About the story: Technology pervades society, all aspects of it, in ways we may not always imagine, and is capable of great good and great evil. If necessity is the mother of invention, the quest for power is the proud father.

Folly Blaine lives in Seattle, Washington. Her work has appeared at *Mad Scientist Journal, InfectiveInk.com,* and in the anthologies: *Dark Tales of Lost Civilizations* and *Fresh Blood, Old Bones.* Her short story, "The Hero Garden," won the 2012 Hawthorne Citation in the Short-Short category. When she is not writing, she volunteers as the Podcast Manager for *Every Day Fiction.* See more at www.follyblaine.com, Twitter @follyblaine, or on Facebook www.facebook.com/follyblaine.

The idea for "The Man at the End of the Chain" came out of a fascination with organ grinders and the Capuchin monkeys that sometimes assisted them. The monkeys were imported from Brazil, where there are superstitions about the seventh son of a seventh son becoming a were-man. For this story, I wondered what curse might befall the seventh daughter of a seventh daughter.

A.G. Carpenter lives in the southern United States where she spends her days herding cats and a lively four year old. By night she writes fiction of (and for) all sorts. She wrote "Legacy" as a challenge to herself to set a steampunk story somewhere other than Western Europe and in doing so discovered the marvelous real life character of Marie Laveau, the Voodoo Queen of New Orleans. Her short stories have been published or are forthcoming from Daily Science Fiction ("Insomnia"), Goldfish Grimm's Spicy Fiction Sushi ("Happy After All"), Abyss & Apex ("In the Cool of the Day") and Stupefying Stories ("The Collections Agent", "Caught"). A.G. blogs at agcarpenter.blogspot.com and Tweets @Aggy_C.

Lillian Cohen-Moore is an award winning editor and writer, working in journalism and game design. Starting out as a science-fiction author, she quickly drifted to her lifelong love of horror. She draws on *bubbe meises* (grandmother's tales) and horror classics for inspiration.

She loves exploring and photographing abandoned towns; Lillian spends every fall searching for corn mazes and haunted houses—the spookier the better. She is a member of the Society of Professional Journalists and the Online News Association. She can be found on Twitter as @lilyorit, and makes her home on the web at lilliancohenmoore.com.

"Red in Winter" is an intersection of many of her loves; Washington Territory history, fierce opposition of violence against women, and alternate history, all wrapped in the cloak of Little Red Riding Hood.

Mark W. Coulter grew up with a deep love of horror and the macabre which led to more than a few sleepless nights early in life. At the time of this printing, he resides in the greater DC area where he shares his life with a loving partner and a lovable lab-husky mix that is often too smart for his own good. Previously his work has been published in the *The Beast Within* and *The Beast Within 2: Predator and Prey*, and he continues to toil at his keyboard in the spare, dark hours of the night whenever possible as a burgeoning writer of horror and general speculative fiction.

"Their Man" came about when examining the regenerative properties of werewolves in most modern lore and what impact that might have in a steampunk universe. When flesh can be replaced with metal over and over again in different configurations, it could create a formidable weapon of which any organization or government might want to make use.

Fans, arch-nemeses and all those in between can email him at mark@markwcoulter.com or find him on Twitter: @Mark_W_Coulter.

His website can be found at www.markwcoulter.com

Thoraiya Dyer's short science fiction and fantasy stories have appeared recently in Redstone SF, Apex and Clarkesworld magazines. She is an award-winning Australian writer with a collection of original short fiction, "Asymmetry," forthcoming in 2013 from Twelfth Planet Press. Find out more at http://www.thoraiyadyer.com/ or look her up on GoodReads.

About the story: "Quarantine Station" came from the realization that having clockwork carers for people with infectious diseases would have saved a lot of doctors and nurses in the Victorian era! In contrast, an old foreign werewolf film reminded me that shapeshifting hasn't been considered infectious until quite recently.

Chadwick Ginther. "A Taste of the Other Side" started its life with a visit to the Canadian War Museum and the view through the port hole of a Cold War era Soviet tank. This is Chadwick Ginther's first foray into Steampunk, but he'll take any excuse to cram a werewolf into a story. His short fiction has appeared recently in *Tesseracts* and *Fungi*. He is also the author of *Thunder Road* (Ravenstone Books), first in an urban fantasy trilogy. A recent Emerging Writer-in-Residence at Aqua Books, his writing has appeared in The Winnipeg Free Press, Quill and Quire, The Winnipeg Review, and Prairie books NOW. Chadwick lives and writes in Winnipeg, but you can find him online at http://chadwickginther.com/ and as @chadwickginther on Twitter. A bookseller for over ten years, when he's not writing his own stories, he's selling everyone else's.

Caren Gussoff is a SF writer living in Seattle, WA. The author of Homecoming, (2000), and The Wave and Other Stories (2003), first published by Serpent's Tail/High Risk Books, Gussoff's been published in anthologies by Seal Press and Hadley Rille, as well as in Abyss & Apex, Cabinet des Fées and Fantasy Magazine. She received her MFA from the School of the Art Institute of Chicago, and in 2008, was the Carl Brandon Society's Octavia E. Butler Scholar at Clarion West. Her new novel, The Birthday Problem, will be published by Pink Narcissus Press in 2014. Find her online at @spitkitten, facebook.com/spitkitten, and at www.spitkitten.com.

"Peculiar Institution" began as a thought experiment, inspired by the anthology, to see if I could find an unexplored alley at the corner of steampunk and were-. Although I expect few of you are actual golems, I hope that you identify with Alexandria's immediate ambiguity at the end; clay or flesh, we all will have a moment when we are forced to confront an uncomfortable truth…and don't know exactly how we will react in the next few seconds.

Sarah Hans is a writer, editor, and Steampunk enthusiast. Her stories have appeared in *Historical Lovecraft*, *Candle in the Attic Window*, and Volumes 1, 2, and 4 of *The Crimson Pact* series. She's currently editing her first anthology, *Sidekicks!*, due in March of 2013 from Alliteration Ink. In the Steampunk world, Sarah is the Second Lieutenant aboard the Airship Archon, as well as Chief Ohio Valley Correspondent for *Doctor Fantastique's Show of Wonders*, an award-winning Steampunk news site. You can read about Sarah's adventures in the aether and find more of her fiction at http://sarahhans.com/.

Tyler Hayes is a professional writer and editor living in Mountain View, California. His work has previously appeared in *The Edge of Propinquity*, *Nossa Morte*, and *Anotherealm*. "The Captain's Wife" is Tyler's first attempt at steampunk, his usual fare being more of the growls and less of the gears. He figured, if he was going to write steampunk, there was no better inspiration than the grandfather of the genre, Jules Verne, and from there it was a natural jump to a captain who made his ship a home for disenfranchised people, albeit of a more conventional sort. Tyler maintains a blog at his website, www.tyler-hayes.com, and is a vocal presence on Twitter as @the_real_tyler.

Ken Liu (http://kenliu.name, @kyliu99) is an author and translator of speculative fiction, as well as a lawyer and programmer. His fiction has appeared in The Magazine of Fantasy & Science Fiction, Asimov's, Analog, Clarkesworld, Lightspeed, and Strange Horizons, among other places. He has won a Nebula, a Hugo, a World Fantasy Award, and a Science Fiction & Fantasy Translation Award, and been nominated for the Sturgeon and the Locus Awards. He lives with his family near Boston, Massachusetts.

"The Bear" is a tale about change and adaptation, both at the level of individuals and societies. It has as its inspiration the so-called "Sankebetsu brown bear incident" in Hokkaido, Japan.

Matthew Marovich has been writing since he was a child when he recorded a series of nightmares he'd been having at the time in order to describe them to his grandfather. Occasionally, years later, the nightmares show up again to give him feedback and offer encouragement. Influenced early on by works by Lovecraft, Gaiman, Ellis, and Barker, among others, he often looks for the shadows in everyday life and asks what else could be casting them. His story *A Cage Gilded* is an exploration of what ties us to our humanity beyond the meat that makes us, the loves, fears, and obligations that define that humanity and both shackle and free us to be who we are.

His work has appeared online at *The Edge of Propinquity* and in print by Dagan Books, Blood Bound Books, and Flying Pen Press. A native of California, he lives and writes as the master of the home he once grew up in, alongside his wife, their son, and two dogs affectionately referred to as the Mongrel Horde. Having received his Bachelors of Arts in Psychology from the University of California at Santa Cruz, it is no surprise that many of his stories feature crazy little towns by the sea.

Alan Smale is a professional astronomer, but his writing tastes have always veered more towards alternate and twisted history, fantasy, and horror. He has made over three dozen sales to magazines including *Asimov's*, *Realms of Fantasy*, *Weird Tales*, *Abyss & Apex*, *Paradox*, and *Scape*, and original anthologies *Panverse One* and *Two*, *Book of Dead Things*, and *Writers of the Future #13*. His novella of Romans in ancient America, "A Clash of Eagles" in *Panverse Two*, won the 2010 Sidewise Award for Alternate History, and he is currently marketing a novel set in the same universe.

Alan grew up in England, and has degrees in Physics and Astrophysics from Oxford University. He serves as director of an astrophysics data archive and performs research on black hole binaries at NASA's Goddard Space Flight Center. Alan also sings bass with well-known vocal band The Chromatics, and is co-creator of their educational AstroCappella project.

Alan has always been fascinated by Rome's violent history and founding myths, and also by ancient Greek automata and intriguing historical oddities like the Antikythera Mechanism, and has been happy for the opportunity to mix it all together in "The Clockwork Caesar." Find him on the Web at http://www.alansmale.com and on Twitter as @AlanSmale.

Steven Saus injects people with radioactivity as his day job, but only to serve the forces of good. His work appears in print in anthologies such as Westward Weird, Mages & Magic, Timeshares, and Hungry For Your Love, and in several magazines both online and off, including On Spec, Andromeda Spaceways Inflight Magazine, the Drabblecast, Pseudopod and the SFWA Bulletin. He also provides publishing services and publishes books such as The Crimson Pact series of dark fantasy anthologies, Dangers Untold, the worldbuilding anthology Eighth Day Genesis, and Don Bingle's spy thriller Net Impact as Alliteration Ink. You can find him at www.stevensaus.com and www.alliterationink.com.

About the story: I was writing this story while publishing a book on worldbuilding, which really ended up molding this story. Would lycanthropy just become another natural wonder mastered alongside X-rays? Would the racial tensions playing themselves out in the Americas and Southern Africa be echoed across Europe? Before long, I had a back story of Russian steamwalkers fighting Hungarian lycanthrope rebels leading to the Crimean War and the charge of the Light Brigade.

Patrick S. Tomlinson lives in Milwaukee, Wisconsin with a menagerie of houseplants in varying levels of health, a couple of reptiles wondering why they had to leave Florida, and a Mustang that likely asks the same question. When not writing, which is much too often, Patrick enjoys building models, shooting sports, and training for half-marathons and triathlons.

"The Business of Ferrets" came about while talking to the editor at World Con in Chicago. She wanted stories mixing steampunk and were-creatures, and wanted them to be fantastical. Straining to comprehend how they could possibly be mundane, the story of Colin the were-ferret saboteur sprung forth almost fully formed. It's a great world, one I'd like to visit again soon.

Jay Wilburn lives with his wife and two sons in the unique, coastal community of Conway, South Carolina. The setting and flora of his story "Indentured" is quite similar to the swampy beach land of his home region. The details of the story itself borrow heavily from the colonial traditions and history of this pocket of the American South where a few significant, colonial women changed the history and economics of the world from this unlikely location. Wilburn writes a wide range of horror and speculative fiction. Steampunk is one of his favorite playgrounds. Follow Jay Wilburn's many dark thoughts at www.JayWilburn.com or @AmongTheZombies on Twitter.

www.ingramcontent.com/pod-product-compliance
Lightning Source LLC
Chambersburg PA
CBHW031059270626
47155CB00027B/2807